DRAGONFLY

TRISHA HUGHES

Copyright

The characters and events in this book are fictitious.
Any similarity to real persons, living or dead, is coincidental and not intended by the author.

All rights reserved. No part of this publication may be reproduced, distributed or transmitted in any form or by any means without the prior written permission of the author.

Copyright © 2019 Trisha Hughes

ISBN 9781707968619

The right of Trisha Hughes to be identified as the author of this work has been asserted by her in accordance with
The Copyright, Designs and Patents Act 1988

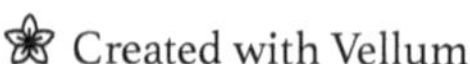 Created with Vellum

ACKNOWLEDGMENTS

My biggest thanks goes to my husband David for his support and encouragement. He has patiently read every draft of every book I've written and has talked through ideas with me over a glass or two of wine when I landed at a dead end. Sometimes his ideas came out of left field and these are the ones I love the most. Maybe it was the wine but I'll take the help wherever I can get it. I also have to thank him for his tactful editing because if truth be told, I punctuate like William Shatner, pausing dramatically, and putting a, comma often where, it shouldn't, really, go.

I also want to thank Stephanie Waegemans for editing and giving me the encouragement I needed to finally push the publish button. Her enthusiasm and praise was overwhelming and greatly appreciated and I'll be forever grateful for her help.

Another big thank you goes to my friend Jordan Rivet of the Fire and Steel series and The Fire Queen's Apprentice series for her endless patience during sessions of coffee and blueberry muffins at Starbucks. Her knowledge in the process of publishing was invaluable and it made every thing run smoothly. Thank you for not snickering, not even once, at my basic questions.

I can't forget Anita Rodgers, the author of the Dead Dog trilogy, for making me laugh when I was very close to hitting the trash button. And for just being a true friend.

Most important are my readers who have faithfully read my historical series and have supported me through the years. You know who you are. Thank you. I hope you enjoy this book.

Lastly, I should thank my beautiful red setter, Scarlet. Without her insistence for regular walks, I would probably have turned into a question mark, hunched over the keyboard. My best ideas came during those walks so she should be included in my heartfelt thanks.

CONTACT THE AUTHOR

Contact the author at
trisha.hughes.books@gmail.com

For updates and discounts on new releases,
join Trisha Hughes mailing list at
https://www.trishahughesauthor.com/contact

Cover Illustration by Deranged Doctor Design

1

———

There are four types of murder. Accidental: where your car inadvertently slams into another resulting in a death. Justifiable: as in self-defence. Second degree: where recklessness has a big part to play. And of course, first degree: which requires premeditation, wilfulness and malice aforethought.

I've always prided myself on having an inbuilt instinct when it comes to sleuthing. After all, uncovering the truth was what I used to do. But if you'd asked me which category Joe belonged in before the events following that fateful night, I'd have said none of the above.

So much for instinct.

I was sitting on my back deck in a mild state of melancholy when the first shrill peel of the phone sounded. My head snapped towards the sound penetrating the silence and a phrase my mother used floated across my consciousness. *"There is no such thing as good news in the middle of the night."*

The first heavy drops of rain had begun to fall and I was fully expecting to be sitting in the darkness for another hour or so, a beer in my hand, listening to the mozzie zapper crackling and the gutters overflow as lightning illuminated the steel-grey night sky above the mountains. Even the crickets were chirping wildly in anticipation of a deluge.

I could make out a few trees and a couple of straggly looking dogs sniffing a rubbish bin amongst some philodendrons and bromeliads in the neighbour's yard behind mine. Occasionally, I could hear a car slosh past and somewhere in the distance, a baby was crying. The scattered lights of a few houses and a streetlight shone like a halo through the moist air as I sat absently staring into the darkness.

That's when the phone rang.

I pushed through the screen door, dodging the cat as he fought to be the first inside the house, and paused to switch on the kitchen lights. Squinting at the sudden brightness, my eyes glanced at the clock on the wall above the fridge just as the shrillness sounded for the second time. 11pm. With my heart beating hard in my chest, I reached over to grab the mobile phone resting in the charger on the bench.

Joe stuttered four desperate words to me. "Please help me, Jack."

The words jarred me because Joe didn't need anybody's help. Especially not mine. But the desolate tone of his voice was enough to send me rushing from my home through the quiet streets of Coomera Waters, pushing every speed limit, despite having downed three beers in the past hour. The frantic tone of his voice and his despairing words had sobered me instantly.

Twenty minutes later, I found him naked and slumped over on the front steps of his house with his head buried in his hands as rain fell softly on his shoulders.

This was not the way I was used to seeing Joe. He was a confident, poised solicitor I'd known for years, sure of himself, sure of his place in society and sure of his promising future. Everyone looked at Joe and wished their life was like his. I liked Joe and he is one of the few friends I have.

Looking at him now, I suspected the worst.

"What the hell are you doing out here in the rain, Joe?" I managed to say as I looked around.

A curtain twitched in a house across the road, but the interior remained in darkness. Luminescent eyes peered timidly out at me from beneath a parked car, tense and ready to run if even the slightest danger was suspected. The street was quiet except for rain gurgling down drainpipes, the soft patter of rain on the paved driveway and Joe's trembling voice.

"I didn't do it. I swear I didn't."

Joe was shaking his head and sobbing the words repeatedly over and over in a voice wracked with emotion. As his body trembled, his voice rose like the whimpering of a broken dog.

"I loved her, Jack. I wouldn't...I would *never*," he wept.

I stood staring down at him, silently watching his shoulders rise jerkily up and down as rain dripped off his forehead. He looked up at me, desolation written all over his face.

"You know that, Jack," he pleaded. "I really loved her."

That's when I noticed a gun by his feet.

I raised my eyes to the house and saw the door was open and I had this terrible, sinking feeling in my gut. I knew something bad lay inside that door and all I could do was stare at it. I was almost too scared to go inside to see what lay in there, because in a world full of uncertainty, there is nothing more certain than death.

I found I'd been holding my breath as I stared at the open door and to get the blood flowing through my heart again, I took a deep breath. There was a whooshing sound in my ears now like wind blowing in seashells. My palms felt clammy, opening and closing at my sides, and I could feel a balloon of heat rising from my stomach into my throat. The rush of blood to my temples pounded and a chill ran down my back.

I leaned over and picked up the gun by the trigger guard, not willing to leave it within Joe's reach. God only knew what more damage he could do with it. I placed it in my raincoat pocket and looked up at the house again, the rain bouncing off my face. After one more glance at Joe, I slipped past his heaving body and stepped towards the house.

Later on, the press would describe the house as a lover's nest but that raises images of red silk sheets, velvet wallpaper and a mirrored ceiling. Nothing could be further from the truth. It was just a modest stucco house in a quiet suburb on the Gold Coast with no pictures on the walls and sparse furnishings. There was a cheap pseudo-suede lounge suite sitting in the lounge room and a smallish television resting quietly on a wooden unit. In the bedroom, I knew there would be some build-it-yourself chest of drawers bought from either A-mart or Ikea, a desk in the corner with papers and bills lying on the surface, a chair and a double mattress on the floor. In the ensuite, I knew there was a spa. The furnishings made you believe you were biding time or making do until real life began and the real furniture arrived. Either just moving in or just moving out.

With a double mattress on the floor, maybe the press would get it right after all. Maybe it *was* a lover's nest and maybe the mattress on the floor was the dead giveaway, excuse the pun. What would true lovers need with fancy furnishings and fussy wallpaper and what would true lovers need with a hand-carved mahogany bed supporting a canopy of silk hanging over it? Such luxuries are for those who need more in their lives than love. True lovers need only a mattress on the floor to make the world slip away.

Rain dripped off my coat as I inched my way along the quiet hallway. There was no need for caution, I knew that, but I still had to fight the urge to tip-toe. As I neared the bedroom, I slowed down even more because a complex scent pressed itself upon me like a smothering pillow. I could smell the sharpness of cordite and something sweet beneath it, something coppery and sour. As an ex-cop, it was a smell I knew well. In a few more steps, I'd be in the master bedroom.

A dim light from inside the silent bedroom allowed me a glimpse of the corner of the mattress on the floor. My heart skipped a few more beats because I knew that's where I'd find her.

As I turned the corner, shallow breaths shuddering in my chest, there she was. Her frail, pale body was twisted strangely among the bloodied sheets, her hair fanning the pillow, now askew. A quilt covered her legs but it was pulled down far enough to reveal her body in a silk, black teddy. Crimson spotted the luminous white of her skin and the teddy was stained around the heart. Her dragonfly pendant had fallen to the side and the diamond that was the eye glinted through the cascade of her tousled black hair.

There would be no need to check for a pulse.

I stood there for longer than I can remember, just staring at the sight of her still body, my breath still trembling in my chest. As I stared silently at her body, a suffocating sense of futility suddenly enveloped me. Her posture, the colliding scents of gunpowder, pot, blood, her perfume and the brutal mark on her chest was almost overwhelming. I can't tell you exactly what was whirling through my mind because I was lost to the moment but when I recovered enough to function, I'd made a fateful decision.

I'm not sure *how*, but I know *why*. I certainly know why. I made the decision and I have never regretted making it, except for the part that made me look like a hypocrite. Just two short months ago, I had been a police officer, sworn to uphold the law, and what I was about to do was nothing short of tampering with evidence. Pure and simple. But I knew for my own survival it was necessary and for the rest of my involvement in her death and the aftermath of it, that decision has guided me every step of the way.

I took a deep breath and entered the bedroom. Squatting down shakily, I leaned over the mattress as I touched her jaw with the back of my fingers, still slightly warm, but perfectly slack. I noticed the skin at the bottom of her arm had turned a purplish red and as I pressed a finger into the skin, I watched it whiten for an instant before the colour returned. She had been dead about an hour, I calculated. Still squatting, I leaned further forward and let my eyes roam over her beautiful face one last time. Someone was making a low moaning noise and it took me several seconds to realise it was me.

Her name was Shannon Connor. Black hair, blue eyes, long-necked and pale-skinned. Even in death her mouth was set in that expression of hurt and abandonment I knew so well. She had been thirty-one years old and stunning, and while she was alive her beautiful eyes had peered out at the world with a sort of indifference. She had seen too much of life to expect anything other than blows and her mouth curved so achingly, you couldn't look at it without wanting to kiss it. And her stare, her mesmerizing stare, daring you to hold her gaze, could weaken knees. To gaze at Shannon was to experience your throat tighten with wanting. And not just sexual wanting, though of course that was part of it, but something else more powerful. Believe me, I know.

Some people spend their lives hoping for something to happen that will change their lives. They look for power or love or the answers to their biggest questions. What they're looking for is another chance. Some way to lead another life where all the mistakes they've made will be erased and all their possibilities are still in front of them. Before the phone call that night from Joe, I thought I'd found my chance. At least I was hoping I had.

There is a gap, I suppose, between all we ever wanted and all we will ever have, and that gap can sometimes be a source of bitter regret. But sometimes, just sometimes, there is a glimpse of hope that the gap might narrow and might even be eliminated in one brilliant magical moment. In Shannon's beauty, and the silent dare to break through her barriers, I had experienced that glimpse of hope. A desperate yearning that her detachment and her barriers would not prove absolute. To hold her, to kiss her, to *win* her and make her mine seemed like a chance to conquer life itself.

Yes, she was achingly beautiful, and she had drawn Joe Banner away from his wife Sarah, from his mini-mansion on the water at Sanctuary Cove, from his fine furnishings onto a mattress on the floor of her small stucco house in the suburbs. And now, I suppose, as was inevitable from the very beginning, Joe had crashed upon the rocks.

On the floor by the mattress, along with her black-rimmed glasses, an alarm clock, a lamp and a couple of books, sat two phones - a small red mobile phone and a walk-around landline.

If anyone had seen me arrive at the house, I didn't want too much of a time discrepancy between when I entered and when ooo logged my call. I picked up the handset of the landline, dialled ooo and reported the murder. Then I went to work.

The first thing I did was grab the red mobile phone lying on the floor and drop it in my pocket with the gun. Finding it on the floor like that had been a lucky break for me because it had been absolutely crucial that I find it. Then I took a quick look around.

In the bathroom, soapy water still filled the spa. A set of earphones and an ancient portable CD player sat on the floor along with a small plastic bag of weed with a pack of papers inside. I left the CD player and the earphones but stuffed the weed inside my pocket as well. Joe didn't need anyone finding that. I didn't need the cops taking Joe in on a drug misdemeanour because there were things he and I needed to talk about first.

I picked up a sock from a pile of clothes on the floor in a corner and placed my hand inside before I opened up the medicine cabinet. I ignored the cosmetics and over-the-counter medicines and went right to the plastic bottles one by one. Valium prescribed for Shannon. Prozac prescribed for Shannon. Nembutal prescribed for Shannon. The whole Marilyn Monroe adjustment kit. And then sitting to the side sat the Viagra for Joe.

Back in the bedroom, I worked quickly, opening the drawers of a dresser looking for something but not knowing exactly what I needed to find. Not much other than clothes, loose change and condoms. Under the clothes was an envelope filled with money. One, two, maybe three thousand dollars. I eyed it for a second then put it back.

The top drawer of the desk held a coffee mug full of pens, post-it-notes, golf tees, loose batteries, rubber bands, paper clips, an old driver's license and knick-knacks. I picked up the license and examined it. It was Shannon's license, but the picture didn't really look like her. Her hair was flat and dull looking and the glasses she wore were less than flattering. Shannon was glamorous, but this picture made her look anything but. Still, I took it and put it in the pocket with the rest of the contraband. You just never know.

Then I spotted a little wooden box filled with more change, paper clips and keys. Car keys, a house key, filing cabinet keys and I used my sock hand to rummage around. I was tempted to take them all, willy-nilly, because you never know what lies behind a lock. But I had to leave something for the cops to find so I only took one key, the one I wasn't sure about, and slipped it into my pocket before closing the lid.

As I hurriedly searched, I tried not to think of the body on the mattress behind me. When I think back, I am amazed that I could still function and make such snap decisions no matter how wrong I knew them to be. I know I wasn't thinking clearly otherwise I would have taken the money too. Even so, what I took proved to be invaluable and I am stunned at my level of functioning, given the circumstances.

It all sounds deliberate and cold-blooded, but then this account is only the voice of remembrance. I can assure you my knees were trembling uncontrollably as I moved around the room. Tears were running down my face and my stomach was turning over from the scent of her perfume, blood and the sickly-sweet smell of marihuana. Grief, I've learned, is just another expression of love. It's all the love you want to give but can't. It's that unspent love gathering in your eyes, the lump in your throat and in that hollow part of your chest. Grief is just love with nowhere to go.

I wiped my face with the back of my hand and mentally shook myself. I had made a decision and that calmed me a little, but I was still only seconds away from vomiting all over the crime scene. The Forensic Team would have been pleased about that.

Then it was time to go back outside to Joe. Standing at the door, I turned and took one last look at Shannon.

We all want to go back in time for some reason or other. It has to do with the illusion of control that we all want to use against helplessness in a world that we can't really control. But there are no guarantees in life and rubbish gets thrown at all of us at some time in our lives. How we deal with it is who we are. All it takes to change a life in a split second is a single phone call in the middle of the night and there you are.

I wiped the tears away from my eyes and took a deep shuddering breath. In movies, you see people walk away nonchalantly from crime scenes but it's not like that at all. Everyone who leaves is in shock of some sort. It can feel as violent as a physical blow that weakens a person and it can result in a physical collapse or depression. Hell isn't a place. It's a state of mind.

In the hallway, I opened a closet door and took out a raincoat.

Joe was still collapsed on the steps, naked and drenched. I gently placed the raincoat over his shoulders and squatted beside him like I had squatted beside Shannon. It was strangely quiet and peaceful in the street at this time of night except for the stutter of rain and Joe's crying. The world smelled fresh and clean.

I stayed silent for a moment and let the rain cleanse the tears from my own eyes.

"Why Joe?" I said finally in a voice barely loud enough above the rain.

There was no answer. He just sat there sobbing.

"Joe. Why did you kill her?" A little louder this time.

Still no answer.

I smacked his head with my open palm and said harshly, "BLOODY ANSWER ME!"

"I didn't," he said through the wracking sobs. "I loved her. I...gave...up...everything...for her...and...and...now....now..." His voice trailed off with a fresh wave of sobs.

I stayed silent and let my own emotions settle.

"I gave up everything for her," he repeated quietly.

I reached down and put my hand on his shoulder. "I know you did Joe. I know."

"I swear... I didn't ... I didn't."

"Okay. I believe you for now." Of course I didn't, but it wasn't the time to go down that track right now.

"Oh God. What am I going to do? What? You have to help me, Jack."

"I'll do what I can, Joe," I lied. "The police will be here any second. They're already on the way. Do NOT talk to them. Do you hear me? Don't say a word until I find you a lawyer. I'll do what I can."

"I loved her."

"I know."

"Jack. God. I loved her so much."

"I know, Joe. I know. That was the problem."

Joe was always one step ahead of me, even with shitty luck.

I was still squatting beside him when the police cars arrived with their sirens and their flashing lights and the three of us, Joe, me and Shannon were no longer alone.

2

———

There's something disturbing about recalling a warm memory and feeling utterly cold.

I remember the night Joe first introduced Shannon to me. It was the day before Valentine's Day and almost a month after my resignation from the police force. My big plans for the next night was a table for one at my sofa, Godzilla versus Predator on Netflix, one of my favourites by the way, a Thai curry that would burn my mouth and a six-pack of Boags Beer to quench my thirst. Who said romance is dead?

It was dusk and I was standing by the ocean on a patch of white sand watching a string of boats bob softly in the harbour in the growing darkness while the temperature dropped five degrees in as many minutes. The water had turned a dark iron grey and the white tips gleamed in the growing moonlight. Palm trees swayed, a smattering of pelicans and gulls squawked, children laughed and the nutty smell of coconut oil wafted in the gentle breeze along with the mingled scents of salt water and fish entrails. The compelling scents of salt, seaweed and the aroma of French fries blended together making me remember my childhood home in Hobart and the long, easy days moving to long, easy nights. Male and female joggers, bodybuilders with great tans and tourists moved through the endless streams of people and everyone was smiling as the setting sun glistened off the ocean like it was jam-packed with diamonds. You've got the picture? Yep, idyllic. Surfers Paradise is beautiful. Ask anyone.

At times on the Gold Coast, it's easy to believe that you're living on a movie set. It looks real but somehow you can't quite believe that so much beauty exists in one place. What never ceases to amaze me is whether it's winter or summer, you can always expect magnificent blue skies and endless starry nights. Then, without forewarning, the heavens seem to have a fit, exploding with thunder and lightning, washing away the smoke from the bush fires and leaving behind crystal blue skies the magnificent colour of topaz. That's the way it is in this city. Heat then rain. Rain then heat again.

I was gazing south towards a forest of palm trees that almost obscured the restaurants, skyscrapers and fast food outlets stretching into infinity when my mobile phone rang. As I dug in my pocket to find it, waves crashed on the shore, spray drifted upwards above the rocks and heavy foam droplets arched lazily through the air.

"Jack, my man!" Joe's voice boomed over the phone line. The background noise of glasses tinkling and laughter was recognisable as any pub in the world.

I held the phone a little away from my ear to lessen the echoing noise through the speaker. "Joseph Banner, I do believe," I replied.

"Now that the introductions are over, what are you doing?"

The first bank of yellow streetlights of the evening had just clicked on. Kids were throwing a blue Frisbee back and forth in the park and a speedboat full of laughing teenagers roared past, splintering the air with a deafening roar, drowning out the sound of the ocean.

"Right now?" I asked.

"Yep. Right now."

I heard a gulp and knew that he'd just downed his drink and by the sound of his voice, it hadn't been his first. Joe is not a disciplined drunk. He goes at it full-pelt, knocking back Jack Daniels on ice three to everyone else's one.

"I'm sitting in Anzac Park watching the street lights come on along Marine Parade," I replied.

Joe snorted. "As enthralling as that sounds, how about you meet me in Gilhooleys Bar and have a couple of drinks with me? My shout."

His voice was already lazy with booze and I had a feeling I'd probably be driving him home afterwards.

"Gilhooleys at Surfers Paradise?"

Of all the bars that front the Gold Coast Highway, the Irish bars are the best. This section of Gold Coast Highway running through the centre of Surfers Paradise boasts three but Gilhooleys beats them all. I'd never heard of booze induced fights breaking out there involving fists or maybe a beer bottle over someone's head.

"That's the one." In the background, someone roared with laughter.

What else did I have to do? I asked myself. All I had to look forward to tonight was a visit to a liquor shop on the way home, which I knew would be dotted with yellow-tinged faces and florid noses caused by broken capillaries. Maybe a few drinks with a friend was what the doctor would have ordered.

"Sure", I shrugged unnecessarily. "Why not?" I hesitated for a second before adding. "Is everything okay, Joe?"

As silent seconds ticked away, I heard a seagull craw and a foghorn sound from the Stradbroke Island Ferry.

Eventually Joe replied, "Talk to you when you get here."

The phone clicked as he hung up his end of the line.

There was nothing but wind in my ears for a minute. *Curious*, I remember thinking as I ambled to my car. I clicked on my indicator and looked over my shoulder, then pulled out into the steady flow of traffic making its way to Surfers Paradise. I gauged it would take me ten, maybe fifteen minutes to get to Gilhooleys at this time of night. Finding a park would probably take me just as long. I hoped Joe was sitting upright when I got there.

As I drove, Surfers practically sparkled in my headlights.

Gilhooleys is smack in the middle of what I call the Ho Chi Minh Trail due to the amount of Vietnamese, Chinese and Japanese restaurants that have popped up over the past ten years. You can drive through Surfers at any time of the day and see buses overflowing with Asian tourists complete with cameras around their necks being dropped off at the shops that target them – souvenir shops, t-shirt shops, jewellery shops that specialise in pearls, and shops that sell nothing but boomerangs, stuffed koalas and leather kangaroos.

When I was a cop, I'd heard about the alleged gangs working down there, but I never encountered them. I saw Asian kids with spiked, gel-saturated hair and bright reflective sunglasses, standing around trying to look cool, trying to look hard, and I found them no different than I was at their age.

On any given night, this area is normally buzzing with activity, but I was lucky enough to find a two-hour parking spot a block away from the pub and as I stepped out of the car, a police car roared past, sirens wailing and lights flashing, bathing the streets in a wash of blue and red. People paused in conversations and heads swivelled as they watched the speeding car disappear as if they were watching a strange species vanish into the night.

Over the span of my career, I was one of those strange species. What the general public called *'you people'*. As if they belonged to an exclusive club and we were only allowed into it from time to time to view the horrors of their world. All of a sudden, I was a part of that club and it scared the shit out of me. I was spending my time watching people go about their daily lives while my heart lies like a rock inside my chest and I seem to hover on the fringe of reality.

I mentally shook myself and walked into the brightly lit bar, scanning the clientele as I entered. Diners occupied tables to the left, positioned so they could overlook the bustling street, and four guys were huddled around the corner of the bar closest to the door. Small groups of two or three people sat at wine barrels that served as tables, making the place look cosy and inviting. A bartender glanced up at me as he drew a beer and looked me up and down before nodding a welcome and turning his attention back to the beer and his customer.

It looked like a normal Monday night crowd – professional drinkers and people congratulating themselves on having managed to get through the first day of another long week without a public holiday to break it up. Joe was sitting on a bar stool with his drink resting on the bar and a lit cigarette hanging from his lips. He must have seen my reflection in the mirror behind the bar because he turned around and waved me over with a slow smile of recognition on his lips. Cigarette ash dropped down the front of his Armani suit that I knew had cost him well over $3000.

Joe could be categorised as a blue-collar street kid who made average grades in school but made it good in the corporate world despite his poor beginnings. But from what I'd heard, Joe's poor childhood hadn't been his big problem. His parents were.

In Surfers, Joe's father was thought of as a decent but weak man whose rundown hardware store was an extension of its owner's personality. Many a time, a sympathetic policeman would take Joe's father out the back door of a hotel and drive him home. Joe's mother tried to compensate for her husband's failure by smothering Joe with affection and treating him as a vulnerable child, thus making him known as a 'mummy's boy'. Kids used him as a punching bag until he stood up to one at the end of his ninth year at school and put him in hospital for a week. No one touched Joe after that and he struggled through high school, then university and eventually, he married a woman who reminded me vaguely of his mother.

Then almost four years ago, Joe divorced his wife and married Sarah, a beautiful woman who was twenty-five years his junior with a taste for diamonds, the good life, and re-decorating. Stupid was a word that came to my mind at the time, but I would never say that to Joe's face.

But maybe stupid wasn't the correct word to use because Sarah wasn't just any woman. Sarah was stunning, no doubt about it, but it was her family connections that would have been the deciding factor with Joe. Her father owned a prominent law firm in Surfers Paradise and within weeks, Joe went to work for him. But instead of advancing in criminal law as Joe had imagined, even hoped, his father-in-law buried him in a corporate office and as far as Joe was concerned, he would never leave it. Joe's job was to pull so-called respectable businessmen out of the cracks they fall into when dealing with other so-called respectable businessmen.

This wasn't where Joe saw his career going and his health began to worsen as his drinking increased and weight increased. In that time, his weight ballooned up to 90 kilos mainly due to the amount of alcohol he consumed.

As I walked towards him, I noticed his eyes almost bulged at me due to his blood pressure that see-sawed between dangerously high and Vesuvius. Right now, both his hands were wrapped around a glass as if he was scared someone would take it away from him when he wasn't looking.

I realised that there are two close points in any friendship: one when you don't know enough about the things you need to know and another when you wish you didn't know what you did know. The sliver of time between those two states is almost negligible as the human brain reads the slightest tick of an eye or the smallest twitch of an eyebrow and computes the data like a machine. In that instant, lives lay open like books.

Joe saw the intenseness of my gaze and his eyes dropped to his glass as he swirled the ice through the remains of golden liquid on the bar top.

I pulled out the bar stool just as the bartender came over to me, wiping the bar with a cloth at the same time. His name badge said *I'm Sean. I hope you have a good night.* Looking at Joe, I was hoping the same thing.

"What's your poison," Sean smiled.

"Jack Daniels on ice," I answered.

Joe downed the last of his drink and said, "Make that two."

The only noticeable movement from Sean was the eyes that travelled from Joe, to me, and back to Joe again. His face remained impassive, but I could read the uncertainty there as clearly as if the words were written on his forehead.

Silence can sound as loud as a gunshot in a shooting range. It's as if the absence of sound creates a vortex and all other sounds are muted. I could still hear distant laughter from other tables and the sound of the Coors singing a song about running away on the TV screen above the dance floor. But the total emptiness around *us* was enough for Joe to turn his head and stare belligerently at Sean before saying loudly, "And make them doubles," almost as a dare.

He tapped the cigarette on the edge of an ashtray then stuck it back in his mouth as he watched Sean walk away.

I watched Joe for a second before commenting, "Looks like you've been here a while."

Joe carried his weight well, perhaps because of the expensive suit, and most women still regarded him as handsome. His salt and pepper hair was still thick and well cut, giving him a Sean Connery look, but when you studied his face, you saw his health fading. The alcohol was taking its toll and there was a dark haunted light in his eyes that hadn't been there three years ago. Only infectious optimism had shone from those eyes and an irresistible force that persuaded level-headed men to take risks they would never have dreamed of in the sober light of rational thought.

Something had happened to change all that.

He gave a series of guttural grunts that could have been chuckles or could have been a series of coughs. "Hello to you too, Jack," he said.

I nodded at the drink in his hand. "How many have you had, Joe?"

His head spun around to face me and ash flew onto the floor. In hindsight, I wish I'd thought first before saying the words because it was obvious I'd touched a nerve. But the words were out and they couldn't be taken back.

"What? You're my mother now?"

In the short space of time it had taken for me to drive from Anzac Park to Gilhooleys, he gone from affable to belligerent. He almost spat the words at me and the intensity of his gaze had a magnet's pull which made you want to look into his eyes even when you knew you should look away.

Shrugging, I said, "I'm your friend." I closed my eyes as though to shield myself from what was coming, then opened them again.

Bitterness crackled off him. "Christ! If I want a lecture, I'll go home."

There was a hardness about him, an implacability that seemed a hundred years old and seemed to judge you and your entire life in a glance.

"And if we're getting personal here, Jack, why don't you use all this energy you're expending on perception and lectures to generate some work instead of sitting around watching reruns of CSI and feeling sorry for yourself?"

The words were like poison and as his statement hung suspended in the crystalline silence, I felt my stomach clench. Even though I knew it was the drink talking, my chest tightened so suddenly that I found it hard to breathe. I tried not to let him see my pain or anger, but it was hard to do that when I knew my face was red.

Unwanted visions of Mount Tamborine jumped into my head and my stomach turned a bit more followed closely by an unpleasant taste in my mouth. The horror that was in my recent past was something I did not need to be reminded of and I couldn't believe how casually he was talking about the charred wasteland of my life.

In the emotional trough left by the remark, myriads of images bubbled up from my sub-conscious. Images shot through with violence and I steeled myself against them. In a flash, the events of a month ago played through my mind like a surrealistic film filled with horrifying images.

If you've read the brochures, you'll know that Mount Tamborine is the showcase of the Gold Coast and *oozes* charm. The flat-topped mountain rises 580 metres above the surrounding countryside and is home to 6,000 residents who share it with tourists on weekends. There wasn't much charm on the day I was called to a crime scene. The air buzzed with a nervousness it gets when the wind begins to blow, dry as a bone, cooking the hillsides into kindling that can snap into flames hot enough to melt car chassis. The air smelt of smoke from 'controlled burning' to halve the devastation that happens around that time every year but as I drove through the dappled light filtering through the trees and listening to the cacophony of birds, I remember being pretty impressed. When a fire does start, it's big news. Despite the flames and the heat, news choppers dive close enough to ignite because next to terrorist activity and whatever Nicole Kidman was currently doing, fires are our largest spectator sport.

We discovered one body that day but by the next day, we'd uncovered five more tiny graves surrounding the first one in the low foliage that glowed a luscious deep green with thick coarse vines. In my mind, I can still smell the sweet, cloying odour of eucalyptus along with musky animal smells. After the forensic anthropologist viewed the bones, the report stated that each child had died a year apart from each other starting with the first one buried approximately six years ago. The anthropologist also discovered that the first child, a boy, had suffered tremendous physical abuse and a great deal of pain in the short ten years of his life. And then there was Stephen.

Stephen was the killer's last victim, taken while we were investigating the other deaths. To cut a long, painful story short, I bungled it. I was so confident of where the killer was taking Stephen, I missed the obvious signs along the way and went to the wrong location. By the time I realised my mistake, Stephen was dead, buried alive like the others.

I had been the lead on the case, so I took full responsibility. Not that anyone blamed me for the outcome. In fact, it was the opposite. But it hit me hard and I lost all faith in my ability as a policeman. I left the force that very day. Everyone said I needed time to heal but in fact, I was scared. Scared that the same thing could happen again, and my mind would not be able to cope the next time. If it happened again, I would be sitting with Nurse Ratchet instead of nursing a drink with Joe.

Once I realised what I done, I panicked. I spent much of the first two weeks with my head in my hands as I sat on the edge of my bed. I didn't shower for days. I rarely ate until I realised I was ravenous. I was in shock and reeling.

Slowly it all sank in and the reality of my situation took over. I was furious at myself for being weak. Furious at my inability to competently do the job I'd been trained for, yet furious at myself for giving it all up. I screamed at myself. I pulled my hair. And like all fires, after it ate itself up inside me, the anger subsided leaving an empty shell.

I still feel fear - cold, nauseating and sphincter-clenching fear – when the truth of what happened hits me. Fear may be the subject of endless jokes but it's a serious condition. The terrible thing about fear is it doesn't leave room for anything else like peace or happiness. I'm in that dark space where you know you've screwed up big time but you have no way of knowing how to fix it, even if there was a way to fix it at all.

I'd become too involved in the case and I should have remembered that once my fire is stoked, I have to be careful not to let the following sea, a huge wave that comes up from behind you, hit me in my blind spot and tip me over the edge. During that last case, I was struggling to keep my emotions separate from my work. And that's when it happened. My mind had had enough and it simply shut down.

Viewing the horrors of life is one of the many things that a policeman endures. This is not to say that it has no effect on us and that we become immune to these horrors. Our minds just have to find a way to cope with it. I still don't sleep without wondering what I was going to do with my life, but I am sure in time something will surface. The extra invigorating air I am getting can't hurt.

Sean deposited our drinks in front of us without a word and Joe snatched his glass and took a gulp while the cigarette still hung from the corner of his mouth.

I closed my eyes for a few seconds and tried to clear my mind while I listened to a hundred thoughts milling like elusive fish at the edge of my subconscious. Anger was still bubbling just below the surface, so I drew a few even breaths to try and calm myself. My therapist says anger is a good sign. It means I'm undefeated or something of that sort.

When I spoke, I tried to keep my voice even.

"The world isn't always how we'd like it to be, Joe."

My voice emerged almost as a whisper. I felt vulnerable and as I searched his face for a sign of regret, I thought I saw a look somewhere deep in his eyes.

I took a deep breath and watched Joe staring down at his drink in silence. I downed mine in one gulp, savouring the burn in my throat, and swallowed loudly. I got to my feet, brushing the seat of my pants. In the silence between us, I felt the need to justify myself.

"Recently, I've had time to realise that terrible things happen in life. Things like the Holocaust happened while the sun was shining and not so long ago, while little children were being butchered twenty kilometres from here, people were having picnics and lying on the beaches, soaking up the sun with a margarita in their hands."

His eyes were still staring into his drink as I spoke.

"It's been good seeing you again, Joe," I muttered. "Thanks for the drink."

I was about to execute my dramatic exit when he looked up from his drink in surprise.

"Are you getting sensitive on me too, Jack?" He patted the barstool. "Sit the hell down. I'm sorry. I'm a stupid man with no sensitivity."

I hesitated for a second, thinking he sounded genuine. My irrational mind told me that the yawning silence that seems to bounce around the empty rooms of my house is all I deserve. I was tested and found wanting and I must endure the pain as all pain must be endured – alone. But my heart said otherwise. My heart says that in some dusty journal of cosmic debits and credits, I have suffered and survived and now I am here with Joe in this noisy pub because Fate has willed it. Sadly, I didn't feel any relief in this knowledge. I felt like a man who has just lost both legs being told he is lucky to be alive. I dropped my eyes, wondering at the price I was willing to pay in order not to be alone.

Joe smiled a crooked smile that exposed teeth with the first evidence of nicotine discolouration. "It doesn't do to live in the past and forget to live, you know."

Anger flared in me as I raised my eyes to meet his. "I'll come right back at you with a saying I read somewhere. The past is never dead: it's not even past."

"I suppose we all see the world differently," Joe said as he stubbed his cigarette out and reached for the crumbled pack sitting on the bar to his right and he continued talking. "Knowing you as I do, you're probably thinking this new life you've inflicted on yourself is a payback for something you did. Karma or fate. Maybe even God's will. But you know what, Jack? You'd be wrong. There's no universal tally board of good and evil, balancing out the rights and wrongs. What happened was bad, for everyone including you. But it's life, not fate, that we struggle through. All I'm saying is we all deal with things in our own way."

He looked up at me, surprised to see me still standing behind the stool.

"Sit down Jack, for Christ's sake."

I sat down and waited, letting him get around to the reason he called me in his own good time. Joe always did better when he set the stage for himself. He dried his lips with one knuckle before he put the cigarette back between his teeth. He took out a pack of matches and lit up, extinguishing the match flame with a mouthful of smoke. He crossed his legs and ash dropped into his pants cuff, leaving me to worry he'd set his socks ablaze.

"I want you to come and do some work for me. Investigating."

I took a deep breath and started to lie. *Too busy* touched my tongue but didn't quite make it out.

"Whatever you need, I can't help you anymore, Joe."

"The world doesn't stop because you resign from the force, you know." He was tapping his cigarette nervously in the ashtray again and I knew he had something serious on his mind. "I'm surprised you haven't thought about doing some private investigation work."

I harrumphed. "Doing what? Snapping bare arses in hotel rooms?

Kicking down doors? Follow cheating husbands and wives and cultivate a hard look like some B-grade Hollywood hero? As tempting as it all sounds, the answer's simple. I don't have a licence."

He sighed like a man trying to hold an intelligent conversation with a two-year-old. "Well," he wiggled his head from side to side, "While you're applying for one, I've got a job for you."

I squinted at him. "What sort of a job?"

I tried to make the words sound casual, but they came out sounding tentative and hesitant and I instantly regretted saying anything at all. It doesn't do to give Joe the upper hand. He's the kind of person who instinctively senses a weakness and jumps on it.

"Have you heard of Jessica Harding?" he asked.

I remembered reading about the missing three-year-old. She'd disappeared from Surfers Paradise three weeks ago and the city had become obsessed with her whereabouts. The police had put more men on the search than any other case in the past twenty years and the mayor had pledged that no stone would remain unturned until she was returned safely to her mother. The press coverage was saturated with nightly television telecasts and morning updates between the soaps and talk shows.

And in that time, they'd turned up nothing. Jessica Harding had simply vanished. Her mother had put her to bed on a Wednesday night then checked in on her before she herself went to bed and found only dented sheets with the wrinkled impression of her daughter. She'd heard no noise and the room showed no sign of a struggle.

Each day in this country, dozens of children are reported missing and of those, a large portion are abducted by one parent estranged from the other. Another portion of missing children are runaways who don't usually stay missing for long because their whereabouts is easily ascertained: a friend's house being the most common.

Another category is the throwaways: the ones some parents don't bother looking for. They are often the children who fill shelters, bus terminals, laneways, street corners and jails where they disappear and never return. No one - not parents, police, friends or care centres - knows where these children go. Most of us presume they have gone into the homes of paedophiles or perhaps black holes in the universe where they will never be heard from again.

But Jessica Harding had been different. She lived with both her parents who apparently loved each other and adored her. And being only three years old, she hadn't climbed out of the window and run away in the dead of night.

I felt an invisible punch to my chest and I knew that no matter how much I tried or how much I wanted it, I could not take evil out of the world. This is the one true thing I know in my life and it's not something you want to consider. This truth did not allow me to rise above it. It held me down like chains and it weighed heavy in my heart. Just one month ago, my life's mission was to go to places where this evil existed and all I could hope for was that it didn't drag me down into its depths as I fought the ugliness. Twelve years and countless cases and still the horror etched deep grooves in my heart.

"What do you need with me, Joe? She's been gone a while now and the cops have it all covered."

Some might say that it is unfortunate that I still have the detective's perspective because I know that once you rule out runaways or abduction by a parent, a child's disappearance is similar to a murder case. If it's not solved within seventy-two hours, it's unlikely it ever will be. That doesn't mean the child is dead, but the probability is high. If the child is alive, she's definitely worse off than when she went missing because there are two types of people: those who help and those who exploit. While the methods of exploitation vary – ransoming for money, abusing them sexually for profit or pleasure, murdering them – none of them stems from kindness. And if the child doesn't die and is eventually found, the scars run deep and the pain is never erased.

Most people who live and work in Surfers Paradise every day take life for granted. When they first arrive, they see the bright lights and tourist traps and even if they close their eyes, the images are still there, imbedded in their mind. But like sunspots, the images eventually begin to fade. They begin to see the flaws. They see the homeless kids sitting on pieces of cardboard in the shade of buildings. They see drunks lying in the parks with empty bottles of cheap booze lying by their side. They see the ten-year olds on pushbikes, one hand on the handlebars to steer and a can of beer in the other hand. And then one day, like me, they see monsters lurking around the corner waiting, and waiting.

Joe was silent for a few moments before he spoke.

"I need your expertise, Jack." His voice was low and deep.

Something in Joe's voice set an alarm off inside my head. It wasn't just the words. It was Joe himself because he never worries about things that don't concern him. That may make Joe sound like a callous bastard but that's just Joe. He would give you the shirt off his back if he considered you his friend but he wouldn't give a stranger the time of day if you asked him in the street.

The undercurrent in his voice gave me pause and I felt a trickle of electric current run down the back of my neck. He stared down at the drink in his hand. Finally, he blinked, a series of rapid-fire clicks like someone coming out of a trance.

"I'm working for the parents of Jessica Harding. They have had no satisfaction from the police so now they want me to look into it for them."

I shook my head and shrugged. "I'm sorry, Joe. I still don't know what it is you want."

His lips disappeared into a fine line. "I need you to help find that little girl. That's what I need."

My eyes narrowed suspiciously. "Is this a pity thing?"

He made a sideways movement on his stool and turned to face me, a look of shock on his face. "Are you telling me you won't help me, Jack?"

"I'm asking you why *me*, Joe."

"Because you were the best damn detective I've ever known. Because you walked away from a great career for something that wasn't your fault. Because I can think of no one better to help me find a little child than you. Does that answer your question?"

"I don't know if I can handle this right now, Joe."

Emotions are by nature erratic. When put into words, our

passions often come out sounding melodramatic, even pathetic. I closed my eyes and breathed through my nose, making a horsy noise while my mind played over images of tiny skeletons in tiny graves and I tried to calm myself.

"This?" he asked.

"Oh, for Christ's sake, Joe! This! THIS!! You know what happened. Do I really need to spell it out to you?" I took a deep breath, trying to calm myself, as I sloshed the fast disappearing liquid around the glass in my hand. "Seriously. Do I need to do that?"

In my career, I thought I'd seen everything, but it turned out I was wrong. The scene at Tamborine Mountain reminded me of photos I'd seen of Germany at the end of the Second World War. *Defeat* was not a big enough word. Perhaps *Armageddon* was more like it. I'd read somewhere that every time the phone company dug a trench for a cable, they found skulls and bones and bits of china. Every time ground was broken to lay foundations, a priest stood by before the bulldozers took their first bite. *They started it,* our parents used to say about the Germans, but those children on that idyllic mountain hadn't started anything. I felt like the wretched senator in Godfather 2 who went to bed with a beautiful girl and woke up with the head of a horse in the bed. It was like existing outside time or on the very edge of the eye of a cyclone.

In Hollywood, the hero would dust himself off and walk sagely into the sunset. In the real world, you're left alone with the horror, desperately needing to talk to someone but scared to do just that in case they strapped you into a padded cell while white-coated nurses popped needles into you. Despite all these anxieties, some part of my brain had continued to operate in survival mode the way a soldier with a blown-off arm remains rational enough to search for his bloody limb and carry it back, eyes like blank doll's eyes, to the aid station. Instinct drives you long after the brain functions have shut down. But only for a short time.

"I think you're up shit creek without a paddle and don't know a good thing when it's handed to you on a silver platter," Joe taunted. "That's what I think. Or have you just lost your nerve?"

I looked at him with my mouth open, afraid to put it into words, to hear them hit the air, and knew that I was refusing to help someone find a child. I tried to keep my face impassive, willing it not to burn. I said nothing for a moment while I collected my thoughts, not willing to be drawn into his game.

"Okay, Joe. Here's a question for *you*. What if she's dead?"

In the mirror behind the bar, the redness had gone from my face and had been replaced by a shade of grey.

"That would be bad," he admitted.

I stared at him in disbelief. "Bad?" I blinked a couple of times. "*Bad,* Joe? It might be bad for *you,* but that word doesn't even begin to cover it for *me.*"

I shook my head in incredulity and managed to say, "I can't give you an answer just now, Joe. This is something I need to think seriously about first."

In my peripheral vision, I could see people were beginning to move inside from the beer garden. The wind had picked up and lightning stroked, burning eerie images onto my retina. Then a colossal peal of thunder shook the building. Before long, rain would be lashing the windows in silver sheets turned golden by the streetlights.

Something else was stirring in his eyes and I knew something was working its way to the surface. I felt a strange heat in the back of my neck as I took a deep breath. The hairs on my arms were standing erect but I couldn't interpret my emotions. Fear? Excitement?

Then it hit me. Joe was in corporate law. What was he doing investigating the disappearance of a child?

"There's something else here besides the Jessica Harding case, isn't there Joe?"

The statement hung in the air like a volatile gas and I felt a wave of heat rush from my face to my toes at the realisation. There was a low-grade buzz in my brain as I tried to sort everything into some semblance of order.

In the uncomfortable silence, Joe glanced over my shoulder and up towards the entrance then hurriedly picked up his drink and climbed down from the bar stool faster than I would have given him credit for. He pointed to my half empty glass and grabbed my arm, indicating with a jerk of his head to follow him to a table vacated only minutes before. As I snatched my drink off the bar, I watched him wave to someone behind me.

And that's when I turned to see a vision in black walking towards us. Not so much walked but flowed. She was so stunning that a couple of men talking at a nearby table stopped mid-sentence and watched. Joe held out a chair for her and I sat down on the opposite side as she glided into the offered seat and crossed her legs in one fluid motion.

Dark lustrous hair swept her shoulders and as I looked at her long, graceful neck, her full lips painted a vibrant red and her impossibly blue eyes framed dramatically by long dark eyelashes, I tried not to gape. Around her neck, on a thin gold chain, nestled between the gentle rise of her breasts, sat a dragonfly pendant with a tiny diamond for an eye that caught the light and flashed. As I looked at her, I almost forgot to breathe.

As she swept her hair behind her shoulders, her gaze travelled over my face, down my throat and back again to my eyes where it lingered unashamedly. I felt the heat rise in my face and my heart clenched so tightly it felt as if she had reached into my chest and squeezed it.

"Jack," Joe said. I dragged my eyes back to him. "I'd like you to meet Shannon Connor."

My heart lurched. "Pleased to meet you," I said. And believe me, I was. I felt a great love for my friend Joe because he thought enough of me to set up this meeting. Was there ever a dearer friend?

Instantly, I sat a little taller in my seat, conscious of my hair that is beginning to thin a little and the down-curving lines at the corners of my mouth that seem a little judgemental and stern. Sometimes, I catch sight of myself in a mirror and I've noticed that when my face is in repose, I look tired, even a little pissed off. On the whole, I've never sent a woman running from me because before that happens, I try to be charming. Then I try to be even more charming to make up for the false charm, and then I'm basically turning into Barry

Manilow: begging her to love me. It's a basic flaw, I know, but I'm working on it.

At this stage, I hadn't begun to realise that a whirlwind romance of two apparently mismatched people who'd met each other at the right time was just the stuff of tacky sit-coms. We recognise the truly significant events in our life, the ones fate has a hand in, purely in retrospect. And it's probably just as well. If you were told you were about to meet the love of your life, the pressure would be so enormous that most of us would blow the opportunity. The state you're in during that fateful encounter could be crucial to the outcome and to think that your chances of finding that one true love hinged upon you being exhausted, stressed and an overwrought mess is enough to make a well-adjusted male cringe. And yet I realise now that she slipped through the barriers because my guard was down and finding a life partner was the furthest thing from my mind.

They were sitting close, side by side, and that should have been my first clue.

As Joe ordered another round of drinks, Shannon shook out a cigarette from a gold case that flashed in the light and I smiled charmingly. While we waited for our drinks, he told me that Shannon was also a lawyer and I asked her what kind of lawyer she was.

"Mostly criminal defence, but I also pursue the intentional crimes that flow out of crime. Fraud, assault, wrongful death, that sort of thing."

"Lucrative?" I asked, trying not to stare at her mouth.

"Sometimes, sometimes not," she replied with a shrug as she tapped the cigarette absently on a tinfoil ashtray on the table. "It keeps me busy."

"Shannon and I are going to be partners," Joe said almost nonchalantly, looking down at the glass in his hand.

I stared at him. Was I going mad because I could have sworn only five minutes ago Joe had asked me to help him with a case? I had assumed it was with his firm, Simmons, Ryan & Holtzman. But now I wasn't so sure.

As if reading my mind, he looked up and said, "I'm taking a page out of your book and I'm going to try it on my own. My New Year's resolution." He raised his glass in a salute.

My eyebrows rose high on my forehead and I glanced quickly at Shannon. I wasn't sure if I should voice my opinion, but the words were out before I could stop them.

"But you're six months away from getting a promotion in corporate law. You said so yourself," I stated.

"I've always hated corporate law. I want to start off fresh somewhere else and I already have this case with Shannon." He glanced over to Shannon and smiled briefly at her. "It's a great start for me. Us."

I blinked a few times. "What does Sarah have to say about this?"

"Sarah doesn't have a say in this at all," he said certainly as he put his arm around Shannon's shoulders. "I'm leaving Sarah too."

And there it was. My charming smile froze on my face and the love I had felt for my friend withered instantly. It wasn't a setup for me at all. It was an announcement.

I turned my head and stared at Shannon in shock. She mashed out her cigarette and excused herself and Joe scrambled to stand as she stood and walked away towards the restrooms.

I watched her sway all the way before turning back to Joe.

"I'm pleased for you, Joe," I lied. "Really. You look happy." Even though he suddenly looked positively miserable.

"I am happy. Like I've never been happy before."

Seconds ticked away before I asked, "Where are you going to live?"

"Shannon has a small house. Nothing fancy. A lounge suite, a television, a mattress on the floor."

"A mattress on the floor?"

He gave me a boyish grin that made me want to smash him in the face. He read my look and his grin disappeared. "You don't approve?"

"It's not up to me to approve or disapprove. I'm only trying to understand what you're doing."

"I'm changing my life."

"Just like that?" I asked sceptically.

"I really don't have a choice. I love her and I want to be with her." He swirled the alcohol absently around in his glass. "I'm sure you remember the happiness and peace that comes from being in love with the right woman." He glanced up at me briefly, probably realising what he'd just said, then he dropped his eyes again.

I closed my eyes and thoughts of my ex-wife, Sally, jumped into my head. She left me after thirteen years of marriage and took our twelve-year-old daughter, Jasmine, with her. 6th March. Wednesday afternoon. 4 o'clock. I had always been able to read Sally's moods, but I missed them in the months leading up to her departure. In the beginning when things were good, it made me happy to be able to read her thoughts but towards the end, the open reflections of pain only made me withdraw more from her.

Joe's voice broke through my reverie. "What else is there to understand?"

I took a sip of my drink and I was suffused with the bitter aftertaste of disappointment.

"Well, that's great, Joe," I said with an edge to my voice I couldn't hide. "Just great. I'm happy for you. Really, I am," I repeated, somewhat unconvincingly. I was trying to play by the rules. Maybe *rule* is the wrong word. Protocol? Nicety? But there was an irritable testiness in my words I couldn't hide.

Sometimes I can see myself as though from the outside, looking down, like I'm someone else. And a lot of those times I don't like what I see. Sometimes that person is cruel and I don't have any control over him. Unfortunately, I can't say it's someone I don't recognise because I've been seeing that person quite a bit of late.

What was happening to me? What was I turning into? Then I reminded myself that everyone has their limits, when their composure cracks.

I was in this moment of self-flagellation when Shannon returned and the conversation turned awkward. There was no longer flirtation in the air. Joe talked, I listened, Shannon smoked. Once again, I was like the Wile E. Coyote of romance. I kept chasing, chasing, only to end up always standing in mid-air, the edge of a cliff behind me, the bomb in my hand, the fuse burning low.

At the end, we parted and said our goodbyes, and in the minute when Joe walked away to pay the bill, Shannon pushed a business card across the table towards me and silently mouthed, "Call me."

And of course, I did.

3

I could barely look at Joe as he sat at the dining table with his head in his hands. A policeman had brought him out some clothes to wear and rain no longer dripped off his body, although his head was still in his hands. His lower jaw was trembling as my hand gripped his shoulder, making sure he kept quiet until I'd worked out what to do. It was a good plan, but it hinged on him following the script.

Joe sat quietly, not talking, maybe not even thinking either. Love can do that to you. It can send you higher than a bird, it can rip your heart out and it can make you sit at the dining table with your head in your hands and your jaw trembling.

It had grown crowded in the little house. Someone was in the bedroom taking pictures. Someone was dusting for fingerprints and swabbing the blood. Someone was outside examining windows for signs of forced entry. Someone was going door-to-door, asking questions. Television vans were parked on the street waiting for news of any sort or a glimpse of the victim or the guilty party. The noose around Joe's neck was tightening and there was precious little I could do, or even wanted to do. I felt restless, nearly itchy with the overdose of caffeine running through my system. I could feel the stimulants dancing around in my head and I wasn't sure if the emotion I was feeling was due to anxiety or caffeine. Sometimes they both have the same effect.

The medical examiner's van turned into the driveway by the front entrance, lights flashing. From experience, I knew the attendants would wait for the medical examiner to finish the work and while they waited, they would sit in the front seat drinking coffee.

Tonight's medical examiner was Mary O'Brien and I knew her well. She was a petite blonde who is way too attractive for such a ghoulish job. She looked surprised to see me and came over to me with a frown on her face.

"What are you doing here Jack? Are you back on the job again?"

I shook my head. "I wish that was the case, Mary."

She eyed me up and down. "You've lost weight and you're a little toned and buffed. That can only mean you're tired of the bachelor life and are seeking out the fairer sex." She wiggled her eyebrows up and down a few times. "Jokes aside, how are you doing Jack?"

I looked over at the door as her team began to filter in.

"Living the dream," I quipped. The half-hearted smile I gave her must have resembled a rictus smile. "Although sex and drugs gets a bit tiresome after a while. Pretty soon you want something more meaningful and fulfilling in your life."

"Apparently you picked the wrong day then," she said as she patted me on the arm before walking down the corridor to the bedroom to join her crew. From where Joe and I sat in the dining room, I heard her mutter, "Sweet Jesus."

Mary's reaction did not surprise me. She could never manage being a cold observer. Most people think an M.E. stays clinical and detached and the bulk their job is to examine bodies and fill in the appropriate forms. Not Mary. She looks at the body, then looks at the crime scene and then looks at the pieces leftover from their lives before she makes a decision. It involves far more detective work than people give her credit for. People are not tissue and messy chemicals to her. I've seen her almost cry over bodies plenty of times and she handled John and Jane Does with incredible respect. I'd even seen her perform autopsies as though she was trying to make the person recover. Perhaps those much-flaunted tricks of divorcing one's mind from the victim's humanity works for some, but not for Mary and as I glanced at the faces of her team who have seen this sort of thing so often before, I saw that there wasn't coldness there either. There was only quiet compassion.

Joe looked up at me, his eyes dull with shock, not saying anything. I had packed a small gym bag for him with a change of clothes and I'd optimistically tried to exit the house but had been told politely to remain until the detectives arrived. What they didn't know was Joe wasn't going to talk to any detectives tonight, on my instruction.

More footsteps sounded behind me and I turned to see who the duty detectives would be. That's when Sam entered the room and dormant moths in my chest did a frenzied dance.

Detective Samantha Neil was beautiful, five feet four inches tall, curvy and when I'd worked with her a month ago, she clearly preferred to wear lightweight skirt suits. Tonight, she wore grey tailored trousers and a pink lightweight blouse that couldn't hide the gentle curves beneath the fabric. Her dark hair was pulled back into a ponytail and her chocolate brown eyes stared silently at me. This Sam Neil certainly did not look like the Sam Neil from Hollywood. This one was dark haired and swarthy with a little Italian somewhere in the background and apart from being nice on the eye, what I remember most about Sam was that she was the best partner I'd ever had.

Tonight, the teasing that could usually be heard in her voice was missing. Also missing was the lop-sided smile and the little lines that crinkled at the corners of her eyes.

"Hello, Jack," she said then glanced over to Joe. "Hello, Joe."

Joe raised his head and looked at Sam but said nothing. His eyes were impressively red-rimmed and had the look of the seriously bereaved.

"As you can understand, Sam, it's been a very difficult evening for us all," I began.

I missed working with Sam. I guess that's another thing I'll always miss about the job. I even miss Inspector Grayson. Grayson is a veteran of 25 years standing at six feet tall, a little over fifty years old and solid looking – well, fat really. The last time I'd seen him his head was devoid of any hair and his eyebrows hovered over his eyes like giant grey caterpillars. Despite the bags under his eyes, there was a sharp perceptiveness about him and I felt an ornery kind of kinship to him. He was tough, emotionless and harsh but he knew his business.

Sam nodded at me but her eyes were taking in the chaos around us. "This is Detective John Cavanaugh, Jack," she said absently, jerking her head in the direction of a detective leaning on the door-jamb behind her, watching us both. "My new partner."

I moved my head slightly to the side to see around her and nodded to him. He nodded back, doing that thing where you look the person in one eye, then the other, then back to the first. I just stood there and let him size me up.

At a glance, I put him at around thirty-five but on closer inspection, there was a Tom Cruise innocence about him. There were grey streaks in his blondish hair, crow's feet around the blue eyes and lines on either side of his nose leading to his mouth, adding ten years to my original estimation. Under the double-breasted suit, the subtle blue pinstriped shirt and the loosened Calvin Klein tie, he had the build of a man who worked out three or four times a week. Not big but muscular. A clotheshorse, I decided. The kind of man who never passes a mirror without glancing into it. But as he looked at me, arms crossed over his chest, I sensed a piercing calculation. He might stop at mirrors, but I doubt he ever missed anything going on behind him when he did.

A lot of cops like John Cavanaugh share the same look. All I can call it is the 'cop look' and it's probably just the way they carry themselves, loose and wary at the same time, with hard caution in their eyes even when they're laughing. A wolf in sheep's clothing. The sense you get from all of them is that you could go from being their friend to their enemy in a split second. It didn't matter either way to them, it was your choice, but once that decision was made, they would act accordingly and immediately.

"I'm sorry for your loss, Mr Banner," Cavanaugh said to Joe as he pushed himself away from the door and straightened up. "I've been doing this for ten years," he said, "and it is still a tough thing to see."

In three confident strides, he was standing beside Sam, eyes skimming the room and I knew my previous assumption of his general awareness had been correct.

Joe tried a thank-you with his quivering jaw but failed.

"Ms Connor was what to you, Joe? A friend?" Sam asked.

"His fiancée," I spoke up instead. I wanted Joe to know that I wanted him to stay quiet.

Both heads turned to me and Sam frowned. "Fiancée? But I thought..."

Sam knew full well Joe's marital status. She'd shared many drinks with Joe and me over the year that I'd spent with her on the force, although she'd never gone so far as to call Joe a friend.

"They were getting married as soon as Joe's divorce from Sarah came through."

Sam shot me a look that I tried hard to avoid.

Cavanaugh turned to look at me, raising an eyebrow. "And you are who, Mr Curtis? A friend? An associate?"

"A friend. He called me when he found Ms Connor on the bed. I'm also a friend that knows that a man in shock over the death of a loved one is not at his best when talking to the police."

"It is if we want to catch the person who did this before the trail grows cold." His response was quick, and the hard look directed my way reminded me that he was someone to watch out for.

"I don't think you'll get much in his present condition," I said quietly, my eyes intent on holding his gaze.

Sam stood silently by and listened, hands in her pockets, chin almost resting on her chest and her eyes intently watching the floor. Knowing Sam, a lot was going on inside her head.

"Who's going to answer our questions?" Cavanaugh asked.

"I'll answer what I can." My mouth had gone dry and I resisted the urge to swallow. It wouldn't do to show nervousness at this stage of the investigation.

Cavanaugh looked at Sam and raised the eyebrow again. This is when the cops usually get angry and indignant and it's when everything turns adversarial. This would be when Cavanaugh would start to get threatening and Sam would hold him back and the whole bad-cop, good-cop routine would play itself out. I knew it was coming and I was anxious to get Joe out of the house, so I steeled myself for the onslaught of police craft. But instead of a snarl, Cavanaugh smiled.

"We appreciate your help here, Mr Curtis. Having you here to assist us will make things easier. But at some point, we will have to ask Mr Banner some questions."

"Could those questions wait till tomorrow?" I asked with a plastic smile molding my face.

"Why should we wait until tomorrow?" he asked politely.

"Shock," I replied, trying to match his civil tone.

He nodded slowly, eyes intent on mine. It was my guilty conscience nudging me, I know that, but I could swear he could sense the bulge in my raincoat. I needed to get home and hide the gun.

I could feel a trickle of sweat run down the middle of my back as he replied, "If that's what you think best."

"I do."

"Of course you do." He even managed to sound sympathetic. "We know Mr Banner is going through an ordeal. His fiancée is dead with a bullet wound to her chest. Anyone would be in shock. You just want him to pull himself together before we question him. Am I right?"

The snarl wasn't quite evident but I knew it was inferred. My good angel and bad angel were having a battle at the moment and it wasn't looking promising for the good guys. I said nothing for a moment, letting the silence hang as I thought of a witty retort. It was on the tip of my tongue when Sam interjected.

"What about tomorrow morning, Jack?"

"I think that would be best. I'll let you know if his condition worsens. I'm going to take Joe home with me for the night."

"Good idea," Cavanaugh muttered as he stepped over to the windowsill and examined it. "Mr Banner looks like he could use a stiff drink."

"And make sure he knows not to leave the area, Jack," Sam said.

"I'll make sure of it. I'll bring him in myself in the morning."

"Along with his attorney," Cavanaugh added. He smiled at me and I smiled back. They were playing good-cop, good-cop and I supposed this was a new tactic devised since I'd left the force.

"If you don't mind, I'd like to take Joe home now and let him get some sleep."

"If it is any consolation, Mr Banner," Cavanaugh said looking straight at Joe, "we are definitely going to catch the bastard who did this. We will put all resources into digging out the truth and believe me, dig it out we will. We will not rest until the killer is found, tried and convicted. We want you to know that, Mr Banner and I hope that gives you some sort of comfort."

"Yes, well, thank you Detective Cavanaugh," I mumbled. All I wanted was to get out and head home. "Now, if you will excuse us."

"Before you leave, Mr Curtis. Can you just give us a few more moments of your time?" Cavanaugh asked politely. "Alone?"

Cavanaugh and Sam both turned and walked out of the dining room and I patted Joe on the shoulder to tell him I'd be back soon and followed them.

Sam seemed absorbed in some paperwork as Cavanaugh asked me, "Can you tell us what you know?"

I shrugged. "I was at home when Joe called."

"What did he say?"

"He didn't say much. It was all pretty incoherent. He sounded confused. He didn't know what to do so I told him to stay put and I'd be right over."

"What number did he call?"

"My mobile number." I gave Cavanaugh the number and he wrote it down in a small notebook he produced from the inside of his jacket. "When I arrived, he was sitting on the steps waiting for me."

"In the rain?"

"Yes."

"Was he still confused?"

"He was crying and he was naked, so I guess the answer is yes, he was still confused. I ran inside and found her on the mattress in the bedroom. I used the phone to call 000 and then I took a raincoat out of the hallway closet and went back out to Joe and covered him. We waited out there together until the police arrived."

"When you were in the bedroom, did you see a gun?"

I looked him straight in the eye and lied. "No."

I tried to stare him down, but he stared right back. People believe maintaining eye contact is a sure sign of honesty but like most things, too much indicates an issue. Besides that, I knew for certain that eye contact is the first thing cops learn. Module 101.

He nodded slightly as we stared at each other a little longer. My paranoia told me he knew I was hiding something.

"Did you smell anything odd?" he asked.

"Just gunpowder and blood." I said nothing about the reefer.

His eyes never left my face as he spoke and he stood silently for a moment, chewing his bottom lip with his teeth. "It must have been a shock for him."

"I'd say that's an understatement."

His eyes were staring hard into mine. "So why call you first? Why not a doctor or an ambulance? Why not 000? I don't know if I'd call a friend first who happened to be an ex-policeman."

I shrugged. "He burned a lot of bridges and lost a lot of friends when he left his wife and moved in with Shannon. I was about the only one who stayed in contact with him. He had already introduced Shannon to me a few months ago so maybe there was no one else to call."

"You say he left his wife for her? What's the wife's name?"

"Sarah Banner. They're not divorced yet."

"Do you have an address?"

I gave him Joe's old address at Sanctuary Cove where Sarah still lived.

"Nice place, Sanctuary Cove. Any idea who else might have wanted to kill Ms Connor besides this Sarah Banner?"

"I never said Sarah wanted to kill her and I don't know anyone else."

"What was she like? The victim, I mean?"

"Sweet in her own way. Intelligent. Beautiful. A nice girl."

"Were the couple having any problems at the moment?"

"They were in love," I said a little too forcefully. "Anything else?'

"You want to get him out of here?"

"Yes, I do."

"Okay. We'll see you and Mr Banner tomorrow. Is nine too early?"

"It's going to be a tough night. And it's late. Let's make it ten."

Cavanaugh and Sam shot each other a look. "Okay. Ten it is," he said. "Oh. I forgot to ask. You don't by any chance have an umbrella?"

He was pulling the bumbling Columbo routine. I knew it well. It had been my favourite when I suspected a witness was holding something back from me.

"No. Why?'

"Thank you for your help." He reached over and took the file from Sam. "See you tomorrow at ten."

I left the two of them huddled together and headed back to the dining room. I heard Sam say, "I want to speak to Jack for a minute before he leaves."

I could hear her shoes clopping like hooves behind me and slowed down.

"What was all that crap about, Jack?" she whispered bluntly.

I smiled at Sam. "Oscar Wilde was firmly convinced that men are the more sentimental sex." I winked. "I think he was right. Don't feel bad."

She looked at me like a doctor about to give a terminal diagnosis. "If you could just be serious for a few minutes," she held up her hand to ward off anything I might say, "and I know that's an unpleasant thought, but you're in a spot of bother right now."

The dark look on Sam's face silenced any retort that came to my mind. Instead I smiled tightly at her.

"I'm beginning to feel a little sorry for your new partner Arnie over there."

She ignored my question. "What are you doing, Jack?"

"I'm going to take Joe home to my place and look after him."

"What you've got is rocks in your head."

I smiled at her. "That's what I hear too."

After a megawatt of eye contact, she said, "You don't seem very perturbed by any of this."

I shrugged but inside something was uncurling in my chest, something I haven't felt in over a month. It was like a hunter's tension, charged with a current and aching for resolution.

"And *you* seem a little *too* wired about this, Sam. What's going on here? Isn't this," I did a little thing with my hands that included her and me, "a little unethical?"

I've known a lot of cops. I've hung out with them, drunk with them and considered a few such as Sam as my friends. But even when one is your friend, it's a different kind of friendship than you have with civilians. I've never felt totally at ease with another cop because part of their nature is to be secretive. Cops always hold something back.

Sam didn't reply. There was no reason in the world for her to answer me at all except that we had once been partners and she knew she could trust me.

When she spoke, her voice came out in a murmur and she glanced over her shoulder to where her partner stood reading her notes. "You know I'll help as much as I can, Jack, but there are a few guidelines here that you have to understand. *A.* You don't get in the way and you report anything you find to me. *B.* We did NOT have this conversation and *C.* You or Joe do NOT talk to the press about *anything.*"

A dark thrill rippled through my chest and I felt a burst of adrenaline. "What was *B* again?" I asked.

There was no smile in return so I continued, "We can help each other here."

She shook her head. "I know you, Jack. When you sound like this, you'll pull down the church to find the truth."

"Isn't that what you want? The truth? I remember *you* sounding like this once, too. Don't make me sound like a crusading liberal. Nothing could be further from the truth."

Her eyes flicked back at Cavanaugh. He was down on his knees looking intently at the carpet at the front door. "I've got to go."

She raised her eyebrows at me and sent a telepathic message: *Watch your back*, and then she walked back to her partner and they began talking softly in a huddle. I left them to it and walked back to Joe in the dining room. I helped him stand and put on his raincoat then picked up the gym bag. Gripping his arm, I helped him towards the door just as Cavanaugh moved towards us with more confidence than a real estate agent guiding you around a property he knows you're going to like.

He dropped his hand on Joe's shoulder and smiled.

"One last thing before you go, Mr Banner. I know you must be tired, but would you mind performing one small test, just for our peace of mind?"

There you have it. He had his spiel ready and he looked like a salesman who was happy with the product.

"I'm not sure that's a good idea," I countered.

"Just one small test. It won't take a moment. Just a precaution really." He turned to a technician hovering by the door dressed in white coveralls over his clothes. "Carl, come over here please." He turned back to Joe and me. "Carl is one of our Forensic Unit technicians. Carl, could you do what you have to do with Mr Banner's hands?"

What Carl was going to do was test Joe for gunpowder residue. Anyone who has watched programmes like CSI and Criminal Minds knows that any gun that has been fired leaves a residue on the hands of the person holding the gun and the result will be used as evidence when the case came to court. Firstly, they'd take wide strips of clear adhesive and press them on the back of Joe's hands, concentrating on the webbing of flesh between the thumb and the forefinger. Then one at a time, they would rip them off and carefully place them on a fresh backing. Then they would do the same for each palm. Knowing what I knew, I felt nervous of what they would find. What I needed was time to process what I knew and formulate a plan. After that, they could do what they wanted with him. I'd even help them. But until then, I needed to talk to Joe and hear the story from him. And I needed to do that first before he talked to anyone else. If Carl found residue on Joe's hands, he'd be in a holding cell tonight. I couldn't let that happen.

"I really should get him home." I put my hand on Joe's back, urging him forward. "Can't this wait for tomorrow?"

"As you know, Mr Curtis, this won't take a moment. The strips have already been prepared which makes the process very quick. You'll be out of here in no time. It will also help move the investigation along. Hold out your hands, Mr Banner."

Cavanaugh's voice had taken on a commanding note that left no possibility of refusal and like a hypnotist's dupe, Joe did as he was told.

Carl did his work quickly and ripped the strips off with a flourish.

"What do you think?" Cavanaugh was leaning over, looking down at the strip in Carl's hand.

"His hands seem a bit too clean." Carl turned to me. "How long was he out in the rain?"

I shrugged. "Could have been half an hour, could have been more."

Carl shook his head. "Doubt there'd been anything left, but you never know."

Cavanaugh turned to me and said, "Thanks for your co-operation, Mr Curtis. We'll see you tomorrow."

Nice as you please. Butter wouldn't melt in his mouth. But two could play at that game.

"Thank you," I smiled, nodding my thanks. Deep in the pocket of my raincoat, I felt the weight of the gun and the phone dragging it downwards.

As I guided Joe towards the front door, I couldn't help thinking that something was wrong here. If this had happened in Brisbane, it wouldn't have gone down with such sweet understanding. The city cops would have taken Joe into custody right then and there. They would have seen him as the obvious suspect, well the *only* one really, and have him call a lawyer at the station. The fact that he called me before he called an ambulance, or the police, would have been absolute proof of guilt for them. I know that for a fact because I would have thought the same thing. The next day, I'd be standing behind Joe in a crummy little courtroom as he was being arraigned for murder. No doubt about it. The crime would have been noted as a capital one and the judge would have denied bail and Joe would spend the next year in jail growing thin as he waited for his trial.

But things seemed to be going Joe's way. And since I'd assigned myself as his protector, they were going my way. I'd made a decision and I needed Joe out of jail to carry it out. It was why I scoured the crime scene like I did against all instincts, why I took the reefer and didn't tell them about the gun or the mobile phone. Even so, I didn't think it was going to be enough. Even the greenest cop would have taken him in. But you see, we weren't in the city. We were on the Gold Coast where the cops are forever helpful and polite. Despite the incident with the gunpowder residue, the cops had sent us on our way.

4

———————

Shannon and I met for a drink one night not long after our first meeting. Nothing secretive or furtive. We were out in the open. We were just friends having a drink in a public place where Joe could walk in at any time and join us. But even though Joe wasn't with us, his presence was very real. Shannon drank a Martini and I drank a Jack Daniels on ice and her eyes were bluer than I remembered, her lips redder and her lacquered nails in constant flighty motion. And I couldn't take my eyes off her.

Finding someone to replace Sally has been difficult considering the challenging hours of my past occupation and even more so now, given my current state of unemployment. But I've been moving closer to the notion. That's not to say I've made my peace with it either, more a matter of managing my expectations. But I was a long way from thinking straight that day.

"Have you considered Joe's proposal?" Shannon asked, interrupting my thoughts.

"Is this a business meeting?"

"What did you think it was going to be, Jack?" Her tone was accusatory, but her smile said something else. It felt like seduction but I was so out of practice, I wasn't sure who was supposed to be seducing who.

"Are you going to destroy him?" I asked bluntly.

"Would that concern you?"

"He's my friend."

"And that's why you're here, having a drink with me? Because you're his friend?" Her lips twisted into the semblance of a smile as she tapped her cigarette on the edge of an ashtray.

I remember hesitating before I answered. "No."

"Good. That's settled then."

"Is it that easy?"

"Yes, it is."

And she was right.

We courted like Victorians, slowly and chastely but Joe's presence was always there making us pretend that we wanted only to be friends. Just friends.

There were more drinks in pubs. She crossed her legs and we bumped knees under the table. Just the thought of her sent heat through my body. But she wouldn't let me kiss her. She said nothing could ever happen, that she was devoted to Joe. Her rebuke allowed me to tone down any guilt that our meetings were anything but innocent. But then she'd cross her legs, and our knees would bump again.

On nights when Joe was busy, we had dinner. She ordered but never ate anything. She drank more than she should have and she smoked when she drank. Mostly we talked about incidental things, like movies. She had no time for chick flicks, preferring action adventures with car chases and explosions. She liked Arnie. And Jean Claude Van Damme. She said she had a serious thing for Mel Gibson after watching *Braveheart*.

One night I asked, "Has Joe moved in with you?"

"Oh, yes. Yes, he has."

"How is it, living with Joe?"

"Great," she smiled through the cigarette smoke.

Not exactly the answer I was hoping to hear.

I told her stories about my childhood and I told her how my

younger brother had died in Afghanistan and my father had died of a broken heart not long after. I told her about my mother's losing battle with cancer four years ago and my ex-wife and daughter living here on the Gold Coast. I told her about Tamborine Mountain and the low foliage that glowed a deep green with thick coarse vines and the hidden horrors beneath. As I talked, I could still smell the sweet, cloying odour of eucalyptus along with musky animal smells and the unmistakeable smell of decaying bodies.

She was a great listener. I made inane jokes about my sensitivity to cover up my pain and she laughed, pretending they were funnier than they really were. I was so insulated when I was with her, she made me feel like we were the only two people on the planet and I had no need to play-act with her.

I had come to believe that there was nothing new in the world for me to discover. We stare at the wonders of the world. The pyramids. Avalanches. Icebergs collapsing. Volcanoes erupting. And I couldn't remember seeing a single amazing thing firsthand that I didn't immediately reference to a TV show or a news flash. Or a commercial. I had gotten to the point where it didn't even matter anymore and I would do *anything* to feel real again. Enter Shannon.

She told me of her own childhood in Bundaberg in central Queensland, how her parents had died in a car accident when she was eight and how she'd been sent to live with her only relative, an uncle on her mother's side. Her father had been a lawyer, which is why she had always wanted to be one as well, like walking in the shoes of her father she laughed. But it hadn't been easy with an uncle like Uncle Bob. He'd been a gambler and a drinker and he had a thing for little girls. She'd winked at me when she'd said that, like it was a joke, but deep in her eyes I saw the truth, the pain and the wretchedness.

As she talked, she twirled the familiar dragonfly pendant hanging around her neck, deep in thought.

"Do you want to talk about it?" I asked gently.

"What's to talk about?" She reached over to pull another cigarette out of the packet. The simple gesture looked somehow angry, so I knew to tread carefully.

"The best thing he ever did in his whole life was to have a heart attack and die when I was seventeen. Unfortunately, by then he'd spent the inheritance my parents left for me."

I was cocooned in the sound of her voice. I didn't want her to stop talking. "Come on. Tell me about it," I said softly.

She tapped the ash absently in the tray as she talked. Over the next hour, she told me the rest of the story. By the time her uncle died, she'd finished high school and had won a partial scholarship to attend university and for the first time in her life, she felt free enough to concentrate on her studies and to her surprise she found that she was good at academics. Over just a few years, she shed the old Shannon, the timid one, the one who was scared of her own shadow, like a pile of skin, and out stepped the new Shannon, harder, wiser and no-one's fool. As she talked, she spun the pendant.

"The pendant's pretty. Is it special?"

Her mouth twitched, almost becoming a smile. "If I could symbolise who I am, who I truly am, I would be a dragonfly." Her eyes drifted up to meet mine. "And I'm not being fanciful," she teased gently, the smile twitching again. "There's a legend that dragonflies symbolise growing and changing your sense of self. In Japan, they're a symbol of new light, joy, happiness, courage and strength. Some people believe dragonflies symbolise emotional instability in early years of life but bring clarity that comes with maturity. They represent growth from a past that holds back your progression. A new beginning."

She glanced down at the pendant, lost in thought as she twisted it. "What else could I be but a dragonfly? I've progressed and moved on." Slowly the smile disappeared. "And I'll never let my past drag me down again."

She told me how she never forgot the feeling of financial desperation and she never forgot what had happened in her childhood. From that bitter experience, she entered law with money from part-time jobs waitressing and stocking shelves at night, loans and a partial scholarship. She passed her exams four years later and entered a law firm on the Gold Coast and four years after that, she had an affair with a partner in the firm which eventually blew up and created a scandal, ending badly. She took a stack of files with her when she left and started out on her own.

I had laughed good-naturedly. "That sounds so inspiring. Rags to riches. How did you meet Joe?"

"At a seminar on defending medical malpractice cases. May I have another drink, please?"

"When do you have to go home?"

"After this last drink."

"Then we'll make it a double."

5

———

I managed to get Joe through the cameramen and photographers waiting predatorily outside the house, their long-snouted cameras clicking madly as I pushed through. The noise was like a buzzing of mosquitoes. Somehow, in that short space of time, they had ferreted out the details of the crime, the name of the victim and the name of her fiancé, namely Joe.

As if I were still a cop, I batted away the usual inane questions like, "Who do you think killed Ms Connor?" "Have the police charged anyone yet?" "What's your connection to this, Detective Curtis?"

I glanced over to where I'd heard the female voice addressing me by name and I saw a pretty blonde by the name of Sonya Martin from the Gold Coast Bulletin, a reporter I'd seen a hundred times before, when I was on the force. She was pushing her way through the crowd holding a microphone in front of her, with a hopeful look on her face. Somewhere behind her a camera flashed and I blinked rapidly at the bright spots appearing in my eyes.

I did a good job deflecting all the questions as I strategically placed myself between the camera flashes and Joe while I pulled him towards my car. I have learned from experience that one of the best weapons against the media is silence. When she saw her opportunity

51

disappearing, Sonya muttered something under her breath and by the expression on her face, she wasn't wishing me a good day. As we sped off, the cameras were still madly clicking at us through the back tinted windows like alien lights.

The rain had eased a little and was only lightly sprinkling on the windscreen as we drove through the dark night. Joe sat quietly in the car, staring out the window, and I didn't push him to tell me what had happened. His face was green from the dashboard light as we drove through the suburbs to my house.

The street outside my house was dark, quiet and wet. I helped him inside and sat him on the couch, draped my raincoat, still wet with the pockets bulging, over a chair and turned on a lamp behind his head. It bathed his trembling body in a narrow cone of light as I went into the kitchen to get him a beer. A mirror hanging on the wall reflected a tired face with sagging eyes over dark circles.

I passed Joe a beer and he tried to speak but I held my hand up, palm facing him. I didn't want to hear anything tonight. It was late, I was tired and tomorrow there would be plenty of time for him to talk. The silence acted as a comforter, blanketing us both.

I let him sit slumped on the couch, nursing his drink, while I changed the sheets and the pillow cases on my bed. Then I laid out a fresh towel, a new toothbrush and a pair of my old pyjamas in case he wanted to get out of his clothes. On top of my chest of drawers, I placed the gym bag and before leaving the room, I turned on the bedside lamp.

With the bedroom taken care of, I stood in the doorway and watched Joe finish his beer before I went to the fridge and got another one for him, plus one for myself. I pulled a dining chair close to the couch, though not too close, just enough to be inside the cone of light, and sat down. I waited until he couldn't help himself from talking and this time I let him.

"I don't know what I'm going to do." His voice was sharp, the words rushing out of his mouth. Joe had never been one with any self doubt and I knew he found it difficult feeling so confused.

He looked down at his hands in his lap. "I loved her so much. She was everything to me. What am I going to do, Jack? I don't understand any of this."

I leant forward. "What don't you understand, Joe?"

He looked up at me as puzzlement turned to horror. "I know what you're thinking. But I didn't kill her. I couldn't. You're wrong."

"That's certainly how it looks, Joe."

"I don't care how it looks. I didn't do it."

He stared at me for a long moment, his face straining for sincerity except all I could see was fear flowing out of his eyes.

I leaned back. "You need a lawyer, Joe."

"I'll get one. I've heard Karen Sawyer at Barclay & Davidson is good. I'll get her to defend me."

"She'll cost."

"I don't care. Money's not a problem."

I was surprised. Joe had left Sarah and left his job and in doing so, had left all his money and income behind.

"No?"

"No!" He stated as he shook his head. "I don't understand. Who did this to me?"

I shook my head and stared at him for a second before answering. "Who did this to *you*?"

"Who did this?"

"You tell me, Joe."

"I don't know."

"So tell me what you *do* know."

"I got home late. Shannon was already in bed. I said hello and tried to kiss her, but she just rolled over and pulled the sheet up over her. I filled the spa and climbed in and put the headphones of my portable disc player on, turned on the jets and lay back listening to the music. It was loud and the jets were on and I don't know if I fell asleep for a while but for some reason, I jerked awake. I took off the headphones and turned off the music, got out and dried off. I walked back into the bedroom to get dressed and that's when I found her."

I tried not to react too strongly. "What were you listening to?"

"A jazz CD."

"What happened then?"

"I panicked. I looked around and saw the gun on the floor."

"Have you seen the gun before?"

"Of course. It's mine."

"Yours? What the hell are you doing with a gun?"

"You think it was easy what I did, leaving my wife and everything for Shannon? Sarah went nuts, and so did her father. Her father, Christ, he's a scary bastard, as you well know. There were threats. You have no idea what I went through for Shannon. I was scared. So I bought a gun. And before you ask, yes, I've got a licence for it. I keep it in the pantry in the kitchen. I've never used it. I've never even taken it to the shooting range. But when I found her dead, there it was, on the floor. I picked it up and smelt the gunpowder. I thought the guy who did it might still be in the house, so I ran around looking for him. I threw open the front door but there was nobody there. I ran back to the bedroom and saw her again dead on the floor and I just fell apart. I ran to the phone beside the mattress and called you."

"Why me?"

He hesitated. "I don't know. It was the first thing I thought of. Shannon had mentioned something."

"Shannon?"

"A couple of days ago she asked me a strange question. Who would I call if I were in serious trouble? I said I had no idea and that I hadn't really thought about it. She asked what about you, and I said, yeah, I suppose. Jack would be good to call."

"Why not the police first? Or an ambulance?"

"She was dead. What good was an ambulance going to do? I didn't know what to do so I called you. I knew I could count on you and you'd understand."

I stared at him in silence as shadows danced around the room.

"You're all I have left, Jack."

If I was all Joe had left, he was totally bereft.

"Okay," I said. "I don't want to hear anymore. Let's just go to bed and get some rest. Tomorrow we'll call Karen Sawyer and together we'll all figure out how much to tell the police. I set you up in my room with clean sheets and towels."

"I'll sleep on the couch, Jack."

"No. You need sleep. I'll stay out here."

"Jack, how much trouble am I in?"

"More than you can imagine, Joe."

"It's hard to believe it could be worse than I imagine." He paused. "Shannon's gone. And I didn't do anything."

"They found her murdered on your bed, Joe, and from what I can see there was no forced entry. They'll check fingerprints but my guess is they'll only discover yours. By now, they've found the money in the drawer, so they'll rule out robbery. And then they'll dig into your life and find a motive. Have you been fighting lately, Joe?"

"No!" Adamant. "We were in love."

"No trouble in the relationship?"

He looked to his left, the way all liars do, then shook his head no.

"What aren't you saying, Joe?" I stared at him, my face a mask, heat prickling the back of my neck as I fought the urge to get up and hit him across the head.

"Do you think they're too stupid to look for a motive." My voice was thick with sarcasm. "There's always a motive between a man and a woman. Jealousy, passion, anger. It doesn't take much to convince a jury that one lover killed the other. Tell me the truth. How were you and Shannon really?"

"Fine."

I cocked a disbelieving eyebrow. "Was there anyone else?"

"No. I gave up everything for her. We had been planning a future together just the other night. We were going to Fiji for a couple of weeks. Why would I mess it up and screw around with anyone else? I loved her. We were engaged. Everything was great."

I stared harder at him and he stared back.

What probably had happened to Joe wasn't love at first sight. It was probably lust. Shannon had that effect on men. Her mouth, the way it twitched instead of smiling. The intense blueness of her eyes. The way she flicked her hair and tilted her head sideways as she listened and smiled that strange sad smile. But lust had turned into love for Joe. Lust will make a fool of any man, but it is only love that will ruin him. Was it a false projection of all his hopes on the one person who was ill equipped to make those hopes and aspirations come true? That was my bet.

Whenever we look in our lover's eyes, we see a reflection of the person we hope to become and that, I believed, was what Joe fell in love with. The reflection in her eyes was different from the reflection in his mirror every morning. His mirror showed a man trapped by the dreary burdens of a certain kind of success, but Shannon showed him all the freedom of which his soul pined. Shannon had been more than a lover, more than a woman. She was a way out. He despised his job at Simmons, Ryan and Holzman. Only his desire to make partner outweighed his hatred for the place. And he was tired of his wife and her ridiculous, frivolous ways.

Most of us have moments when nothing seems right, and we are desperate for a saviour. Some suck it up and soldier on, some take up writing or painting, some of us take up golf, and some make drastic changes to their lives. But the truly lost amongst us often see their saviour in someone else, someone like Shannon Connor. When Joe gazed into Shannon's eyes, he did not see a woman with her own desperate needs and motivations, a woman with impenetrable barriers forged in a past that haunted her right through to her death. Instead he saw the reflection of a man suddenly free of the shackles he'd made himself.

But what did Shannon see when she looked into Joe's eyes? Her soul mate? Her future? A terrible mistake? I'll take door number three please, Bob.

But then, was I any different from Joe? Had I been projecting my hopes and aspirations upon that slim, beautiful body? I couldn't know then that the answers would come after me with a vengeance and the answers would haunt me to this day.

Joe's eyes had been travelling over my face, waiting me to reply, as I thought about Shannon and me.

All I could think of to say was, "Great."

"Yes, it was. And then *this* happened. It's a nightmare."

"Well, Joe, I'm sorry to have to say this but it's only the beginning. Let's get some sleep."

He put his hands to his face. "What the hell am I going to say to them tomorrow?"

"You'll either tell them the truth or you'll say nothing until you get a lawyer. Those are your only options."

I helped him off the couch and took him to my bedroom and watched him settle down. I closed the bedroom door behind me and began walking to the lounge room when I heard Sherlock push himself through the cat door into the kitchen. I found him standing just inside, motionless.

Sherlock is a refugee from my local RSPCA. I rescued him after my resignation from the police force thinking that having an animal around would somehow break the silence. A dog needed attention but a cat...now that was different.

Like a kitten from central casting he seemed relaxed and friendly, even laid back. It was only after bringing him home that I found out it was a ruse. It turned out that Sherlock was prone to dipping his paw into glasses of beer and knocking them over, his meow sounds like he's being put through a mincer and he prefers drinking from dripping taps in the bathroom, even the toilet bowl, rather than his dish. He also has a radar for muddy puddles. Weeks ago, I'd happily have done him in if I wasn't sure he'd haunt me with his other eight lives.

"Well," I said. "Welcome home." I knew he'd heard voices in the house and had opted to stay outside until he felt it was safe. He's like me, not particularly social, which draws me to him even more.

He stared at me with his luminous green eyes for maybe twenty seconds then crept further into the room, sniffing the air as he went.

"How about dinner? You could have chicken."

I took out the leftovers of my dinner, cut up part of the chicken thigh and put it down beside him.

"What do you think?"

I could see him catch the scent. His eyes widened and his nose twitched, and he took a couple of steps towards me. I stroked his back, but he didn't purr. He gave a low growl, a sound I'd never heard him make before.

"I know, mate. I feel a little disrupted too."

He ate a few pieces of chicken, then high-tailed it out of the kitchen through the cat door.

I returned to the lounge room and waited a while and when I didn't hear any sounds from Joe, I went to my raincoat, still hanging over the chair.

I took out the mobile phone, the licence and the key and placed them in a kitchen drawer. Then with a tea towel, I lifted the gun out of the pocket. It felt heavy and solid. I wiped the trigger guard where my fingers had touched it when I picked it up off the step, and I dropped it into a plastic bag I found in the bottom drawer before putting it on the coffee table.

Using the remote, I turned the television on softly in the background before walking into the kitchen to get myself a beer from the fridge. The digital display on my microwave said 01:53 and I could feel a tightness in my joints and the muscles at the back of my neck. It was a pain that I liked because it reminded me that I was still alive and kicking.

I was popping the top off the can when a late-night news program started and a newsreader, who looked as fresh as she had at the six o'clock news, began reading the news highlights.

The country was lumbering towards election day, she said, lifting her eyes up from notes resting on the desk. There have been claims, counterclaims and promises. The nation's debt was huge, she stated a figure that was difficult to comprehend, and cuts were expected. Painful cuts, she stressed as her eyes bored into mine, as well as an increase in taxes.

The search for the missing girl, Jessica Harding, was still dragging on, she continued. While neighbours had stopped pounding the pavements with flyers, police were asking if anyone had any new information. The studio flicked to numbingly similar footage from three weeks ago and showed cops leaning over car hoods and shining flashlights over maps of the neighbourhood. The little girl's photo filled the screen and the number of Crime Watch flashed below the photo for a few moments before they cut back to the studio. The newsreader fondled her notes and followed the footage with the same sharp, maudlin commentary, the same studied sadness and head-shaking before she said, *And now back to our regularly scheduled program...*

The television station said nothing about Joe and the murder.

I switched the television off and put the remote down on the coffee table next to the photo of Sally and me. I picked it up and the memories flooded in. We'd spent the day walking through the Queens Domaine with the sound of seagulls shrieking in our ears as the wind whipped her hair around her face. Government House had been almost invisible that day and the Tasman Bridge was shrouded in mist - yet again. In the distance near the antique markets of Salamanca Bay, shoebox-shaped brick houses more than a hundred years old lined the narrow streets opposite the harbour. Beneath the snow-caped mountains in the distance, breakers pounded the walls of the harbour like distant thunder and the ocean was the colour of dull steel because of the dense fog.

Sally asked someone walking by to take a photo and they'd gladly agreed. In the photo, I had my arm resting gently on Sally's shoulder and she had her arm wrapped around my waist as we both smiled and snuggled together, as much against the cold as any emotion we were feeling at the time. Someone had a radio on and Frank Sinatra was singing *'Fly Me to the Moon'*. Now, every time I hear that song, I always think of that day and the smile always returns. On that day, it was as though there was no life before *us*. No love, no partners and no past before the day we met. Yeah, I know.

I'd always said that Sally would go far, and she did. As far from me as she could. I remember Sally's words when I applied for a promotion to Sergeant in Hobart. She said, *'If you get that job, you'll be impossible to live with.'* I even remember laughing at the time. I got the job and as Sally can guess, I wasn't laughing much these days.

Being a cop, I knew things and saw things that most people don't.

There's a subtle sixth sense that most experienced investigators have developed over their careers. It's sometimes a scent or a feeling that permeates the crime scene. I have always taken advantage of these thoughts and impressions. Because of my training, it wasn't only kids I watched, it's the people who watch the kids. I used to find myself subconsciously scanning people when the three of us went out and it was a rare day I didn't see someone suspicious. I'd point him out to Jasmine and say, *'Watch out for men who do what he's doing.'* Sally would get upset and say I was scaring our child, but Jasmine would watch anyway. He'd pretend to read a paper but over the top he'd be watching the kids. I told Sally I was educating Jasmine by training her in vigilance. Sally said I went too far, as always, but it wasn't her that got called out in the middle of the night to a crime scene to view the corpse of a young girl.

We turned into the sort of couple that pecks away at each other, disguising insults for jokes, rolling our eyes and 'playfully' scraping in front of our friends, using the banter like some kind of conversational phlegm you can wipe away later. You drink a little too much and try a little too hard, but in the end, you go home to a cold bed, thinking *this is fine.* Before you know it, your whole life is a long line of *fines.*

Eventually she'd had enough, and she moved to Surfers Paradise to start a new life. My world emptied and I became a ghost, moving noiselessly through my days. Eventually it was my work that brought me back to the world, which was kind of funny since it was my work that had driven Sally away in the first place.

One year later I followed her and one year later again, I was no longer a policeman and I was having an affair with my best friend's fiancée.

I put the photo back on the table and swung my feet onto the couch with my head on the armrest and the gun in my lap. Just one doorway away, Joe lay asleep in my bed.

I threw my arm across my forehead and shut my eyes, as if trying to blot out the visions of Shannon as I'd last seen her, just a matter of days ago. She had been where Joe was sleeping now and I could see her, standing at the mirror with her shirt open, telling me how she was going to leave Joe. I could see her press her lips together to set the lipstick and I could see her turn to look at me and smile. That dazzling, sincere smile.

At that time, I would have given up anything for her and I remember telling her I loved her. Maybe it was warped and wrong and misjudged. Maybe like Joe's love for her, it was doomed to fall apart. Even though she avoided the word with me, I believe in my naïveté that she did.

Right now, I had to figure out what I was going to do. Because, you see, I had listened very carefully to everything Joe had to say about Shannon and her murder, and at the end, I knew beyond a reasonable doubt that my dear old friend Joe was lying.

6

Whenever I looked at Shannon, I had the feeling of inevitability. In my previous experience with women, once you've been with someone for a while, her beauty is often the first thing you overlook. But for me, every time I glanced at Shannon, I felt a shudder through my chest cavity from the sweet pain of looking at her.

"Why don't you end it with Joe," I asked.

"I couldn't do that." She was surprised I'd even asked. She said she was committed to Joe so there was no other option. But still, she called me and she picked a place to meet me.

"I am so tired," she said. "Do you ever get tired?"

"I'm too frightened to be tired," I replied.

"Frightened of what?"

"That the best is behind me."

"Sometimes I have this urge to just start over," she said. "Be something new."

"Don't just talk about it. Do it. Joe did it, so can you."

"But I already have. This is it."

"You thought you'd change your life by starting up with Joe?"

"No. Joe is something else."

"And me?" I asked.

"You are an indulgence. Something I like but is not good for me, like a cigarette or a drink."

"Hazardous to your health."

"Exactly."

What she saw in me, I can only guess. What I saw in her, besides the beauty, was the sadness that reached into my heart like a claw. And so I played with fire and called her. I would tell the receptionist that it was Jack Curtis to talk to Ms Connor about the Gibson matter. That was our code, the Gibson matter, in honour of her silver-screen hero. By then, it was usually me who called so I was surprised one day when the message on my machine said to call her about the Gibson matter. When I phoned, she spoke to me in a whisper.

"Can I meet you for lunch?"

"Of course," I said.

"When can you meet me?"

"Now if you want. Where do you want to meet?"

"Pick a place, Jack. Any place."

She was waiting for me when I walked in, all of the tables crowded with businessmen talking loudly and stuffing themselves with food. She was leaning back with a cigarette half way to her lips with a fraction of an inch or so to go before it joined the ten or so in the ashtray.

"What do you feel like eating?" I asked as I sat.

"Nothing," she said. The words had sounded abrupt and I was instantly alert. My first thought was she'd finally broken off with Joe.

"Are you okay? Has something happened?"

"What are we going to do, Jack?" Her voice was far from happy.

"Have lunch?"

"Is that all?"

I hesitated, my heart beating a little faster. "I've been following your lead."

"I'm a lousy dancer."

"Did something happen between you and Joe?"

"Yes. Something happened."

The waitress came to our table and said, "Are you ready?"

Shannon smiled. "Are you ready, Jack?"

I hesitated again, not sure where this was going. "I don't know."

Shannon spoke to the waitress but looked at me. "Can you give us another moment?" The waitress rolled her eyes before turning on her heel and walked away.

"I'm not hungry," she stated. "Are you?"

"Not anymore."

"Then let's leave."

Outside the air was damp but we walked in silence for a few moments, neither of us saying a word.

"Do you want a drink?" I suggested. "I have some beers at home if you'd like."

"Yes. Let's do that."

"Is it something to do with work? This thing with you and Joe?"

"Aren't you sick of talking?" The look of tragedy in her eyes stopped me and so we walked in silence towards my car and my home.

It was a mess, like it always is. Worse than that, it always feels empty. Foreign. The place I called home felt stale and lonely. Functional is a good word but so is characterless. It actually looks like the 'before' photos in a magazine spread.

I left her standing in the lounge room while I gathered up clothes and towels and dumped them in the basket in the bathroom. She stood motionless as I worked, her handbag still over her shoulder. When it was almost presentable, I stopped and looked at her standing still and the sadness was still there, pouring out of her. I could see it like a dark cloud above her head. She looked at me and her eyes were moist and the blueness poured out of them.

I get my sensitive side from my mother. I can laugh, joke, support and praise, but I can't deal with tearful women. I was helpless to stop myself from going to her and wrapping my arms around her.

She felt thin in my arms, just skin and bones. She smelt of flowers and cigarette smoke and I told her it was all right even though I didn't know what it was that was troubling her and I suspected it would all turn out badly. I touched my lips to the top of her head. A brotherly kiss. Then a brotherly kiss to her temple. Then one to the ridge beneath her eye, and I tasted salt from a tear.

I pulled away and she lifted her face to me, looking directly at me. Unless she was a great actress, she'd been through something that had hurt her and worn her down. The hard, brittle surface she always wore had chipped away. She looked vulnerable, as if there was another softer person struggling to emerge. Her eyes were wet and her nose was red, her mouth quivering. She was the picture of desolation and I couldn't help myself. I didn't want to. Something had happened between her and Joe and that was enough for me. I kissed her gently and our lips barely touched. It was the gentlest touch, no mashing, no gnashing, no moisture, just a saving touch and I felt emptiness flowing and growing, hers, mine, hers, mine.

I wanted it to be slow but there was suddenly a hunger in the room. A need. It had an entity of its own that felt like nothing I'd ever felt before. It was brutal and violent and before I knew it, it had taken over. I had wanted it to be slow but what I wanted no longer mattered.

When it was over, we lay back covered in sweat and in shocked silence.

"That was insane," I whispered.

"It always is."

"You felt it too?" My chest was pressed to her back and my hips pressed to her thighs. She didn't want to talk and I didn't understand what had just happened. I held her tightly and felt the sadness.

"What did you want to tell me?" I asked.

"It was nothing important."

"Tell me."

"It is nothing that affects you. Nothing you should worry about."

I didn't say anything. I just held her tightly and waited.

"It was last night," she said eventually. "Joe. We were together in the spa. There were candles and rose petals."

"I really don't want to hear the details."

"He thought it was romantic. The candles, like something out of a commercial."

"Really, I don't want to hear."

"He asked me to marry him as soon as his divorce comes through."

She said nothing more and the silence swelled.

Eventually I asked, "And what did you say?"

"I said yes. What else *could* I say."

7

I snapped out of my sleep, the darkness of the room materialising around me. The wall clock in the kitchen glowed luminously. 4.10.

The best way to solve a crime is to let your subconscious work. It's rule Number One for a policeman. It allows information banging around in my head to order and clarify itself. Tonight was different. Tonight the information and my emotions would not settle.

The last time I saw Shannon, after we had shared my bed and she was looking into the mirror, fixing her makeup and putting on her lipstick in that shocking red she preferred, she told me she was going to end it with Joe.

She had been tense for days ever since she had come back from a business trip. She'd been angry and more lost than usual but that day, she made love to me and she had seemed happier than I had ever seen her before. She was a woman who seemed to be in perpetual trouble and it was probably that which drew me to her in the first place. I had been urging her to take control of her life and that things are not preordained. I told her life is full of choices, not obligations. She had come right over to the bed and sat down and told me how happy she was and that she would arrange for us to be together.

I had wanted to help and if taking her away from Joe was helping, then so be it. Some days, I saw a pain in her that I felt compelled to soothe but that day she seemed less in trouble than before. That day, there was one of the rarest things from her, an ironical smile. Maybe it was based on my perception of her needs and maybe they were misjudged. Maybe it was doomed to eventually fall apart too but I can still feel her hand over mine, her knees touching mine and the thump of her heart against mine.

There may have been a pain in my heart, but my mind was something else entirely.

I took a deep breath and stood, taking hold of the gun as best I could since it was still in its plastic bag. It was time and I was ready.

Joe had lied when he said everything had been great between him and Shannon, and if Joe was lying about that one crucial point, wasn't it likely that he was lying about everything else? And if he was lying about everything, then Joe had definitely killed her.

She had told him she was leaving him and he had reacted like a man about to lose his saviour, like a man driven to the edge, with nothing to lose. Joe's decision had been made and so was mine. I had once made my living determining lies and truths that allowed desperate people to escape the justice of their unjust act. But over the dead body of the woman I believed I loved, I had made a decision that no lie would allow the killer of Shannon Connor to escape the hard consequences of their act. Whatever the price that had to be paid for my actions later. Joe was asleep in my bed, in the sheets I had changed just so he wouldn't recognise Shannon's perfume on the pillow. He was asleep in my bed, but he would not be for long.

I took a step and then another towards the bedroom.

I held the gun, still in the bag, and stepped toward the doorway. I had questions to ask my old friend and the sight of the gun in my hand would compel his confession.

I moved closer to the bed but in the light from the street, the strange lump in the middle didn't look right.

Without taking my eyes off the bed, I fumbled for the light switch. A harsh yellow light flooded the room and then I could see what had happened.

The drawers had been ransacked, the gym bag was missing and the lying bastard was gone.

8

———

The bedroom window was closed. I shoved it open and scanned the street that was still wet even though the rain had stopped. Nothing. It would have been a struggle to get out with the spindly branches of a melaleuca so close to the house and you would have needed to be built like a breadstick, which Joe wasn't. The desperate jump through the tree was not Joe's way although until tonight, I would have said that murder was not Joe's way either.

I did a quick search of the room, opening the closet door, checking the bathroom, then the toilet. No Joe.

How had he done it without me knowing? And then I remembered closing my eyes as I lay on the couch.

I ran back into the lounge room and saw the slightly open door. Damn it! I had let him slip away while I was asleep and dreaming on the couch. He'd slid right past me and now he was on the loose, hightailing it to freedom.

I put on my raincoat again and stuffed the plastic bag with the gun inside into my pocket, grabbed my car keys and bolted out after him. The night was nearly over and I could see the darkness receding in the light of dawn. I must have slept longer than I thought. I must have been dead asleep.

I sat in my car for a second or two and considered the possibilities of where he could have gone. The sorry fact was he could have gone anywhere. Then I realised that wasn't true. He couldn't go back to his wife or go to his old law offices. His parents were dead and all his friends had sided with Sarah. His options were severely limited.

I went over every possibility and then it suddenly occurred to me. There was an old truth I learned as a cop that criminals always return to the scene of the crime and I was sure that was where Joe was headed. Arsonists are often in the crowds surrounding the blaze they have set and I had often sat watching videotapes of funerals of the murdered dead to see if I could spot a killer paying his final disrespects. Without a doubt, I knew he was heading back to Shannon's house. His passport and cash were there, and he was going to need them. Both the lover and the murderer were created in that house, on that mattress on the floor, and he was going back to retrieve what he could. And so was I.

I drove as fast as I dared with a gun in my pocket and I wondered if Joe knew that I had it when he skulked out of my house. Probably not. He hadn't turned on the lights and he had stayed as far from me as possible. Who could have imagined he had developed the honed instincts of a cockroach?

I passed a police car going in the opposite direction and I ducked. I actually ducked. I had once been a cop and now I had been reduced to ducking and skulking around in the middle of the night with a gun in my lap looking for a murderer I had once called my closest friend. It was a strange new feeling and I hate to admit it, but it thrilled me. I felt a trickle of electric current run down the back of my neck making me feel alive and rejuvenated.

I drove through the calm, suburban streets where houses were still asleep in the pre-morning light. Down a short road, left at the stop sign, right at the next, up the hill and to the left again and there it was, dark and solitary.

I scanned the driveway but there was no crime scene tape and in the back of my mind I thought there should have been. The slight filled me with anger because I had a feeling Sam and her new partner were going to screw it up and they were going to let Joe get away with murder through incompetence. It was up to me. All along, I had felt it would be anyway.

I parked across the street and waited, listening to the silence. The lights were off and I began to doubt my instincts. Had he already been to the house, doing whatever he was going to do or was he still inside doing it in the darkness?

I waited. There was no rush. If he hadn't been to the house, he would be soon and if he was inside, he wouldn't be for long. He would do what he felt compelled to do and then he would leave, he would run with the keys to his car in his hand to his car parked in the garage. Both his and Shannon's cars waited in the garage while I waited in the street.

Through the misty rain, I could just make out a man with an umbrella standing over a urinating dog. The rain had made it chilly enough for a jacket and I shivered a little in my lightweight shirt. My blood was singing with the change in temperature and humidity, almost like a change in altitude. Deep inside my chest something stirred the way leaves high up on the trees yank at their branches. Not so long ago, leaves had been burning in bush fires as hot as the sunny side of Mercury and I hoped there wasn't going to be any similarity to my own circumstances.

To clear my head of these thoughts, I opened the window and let the wind blow the salty air through my hair. From a nearby park, the high whistling chirp of crickets rose to a manic drone, overpowering the buzz of mosquitoes and giving me a strange sense of peace.

Then I saw him come out from the back, his shoulders hunched, his black coat making him almost invisible. His head swivelled nervously from side to side as he checked for watchers and he carried a large suitcase in his hand.

I climbed out of the car and stuck my hand in my pocket, gripping the metal through the plastic.

"Joe," I called out, my voice loud in the silence of the night.

He spun around, startled, before setting his shoulders and heading towards the garage.

"Joe," I called out again, this time louder. "Where the hell do you think you're going?"

"Don't try to stop me, Jack. I'm getting the hell out of here."

By now he had reached the garage door and I had reached him. As he fumbled with the remote, I pulled at his arm.

He looked at me with unfathomable fear.

"They're going to send me away for this. You told me that yourself."

"No, I did not."

"Not in so many words, but yes you did. They're going to arrest me and put me in jail. I'm not going to sit around and let them do it. I didn't do anything."

"And this," I waved at the suitcase, "is going to convince them of that? Don't be a bloody fool. Come back to my house."

His eyes widened. "No way!"

"You can't run, Joe."

He harrumphed. "Just you watch me." He pulled his arm from my grasp and swung the suitcase firmly at me while I raised my arm in defence. The suitcase hit me squarely on the shoulder and I fell back onto my butt with the gun digging into my hip.

The garage door opened and I heard the door of his car open, then close again, and the lock click on. He had locked himself in the car and started the engine.

I put my hand in my pocket and tightened the grip on the gun just as a white car screeched to a halt beside me. It missed me by inches and blocked Joe inside the garage.

Joe slammed on his horn but the white car didn't move. From the car, Sam jumped out with her gun aimed directly at Joe. Cavanaugh calmly exited from the other side and ambled over to him, then bent over to peer in the window. He gestured for Joe to turn off the engine and open the door. As he waited for Joe to comply, two more cruisers appeared on the street, their lights flashing red and blue.

I rose from the ground, my hand still in my raincoat pocket, as Cavanaugh held his hand up and motioned me away. All I could do was step back and let them take over.

Joe did nothing until finally, he electronically unlocked his car and Cavanaugh opened the door before leaning inside.

"Going somewhere, Mr Banner?" he said conversationally.

Joe tried to say something but Cavanaugh swung the door open and said, "Get out of the car, please."

Joe began to speak again, but Cavanaugh repeated, "Get out of the car please, sir! Now!"

Joe slowly climbed out, looking at me beseechingly for a moment before Sam holstered her gun and spun him around, pushing him face first onto the car and beginning to cuff his hands behind him.

"Hands on the car!" she said. When the cuffs were in place, she began to read him his rights. "You are under arrest for the murder of Shannon Connor."

"I'm a lawyer," Joe shouted, terror in his eyes.

"Good," said Cavanaugh, reaching into the car to retrieve the suitcase, his nose twitching at the ashtray stuffed to overflowing with cigarette butts. "That means there won't be any misunderstandings."

"What are you doing here?" I asked as I walked over.

"A search prior to arrest," he said riffling through the suitcase laid out on the driveway.

"Shit, I know *that*," I said angrily. "I meant how did you know he was here?"

He twisted his head to look at me scornfully. "What do you think this is, Mr Curtis? Hollywood? A woman was found shot dead in her bed. All the doors and windows were locked, there was no evidence of a break-in and no evidence of a robbery. You think I'd let the only other person in the house walk away without a tail on him?" His eyes dropped to the case again. "I had someone follow you both from the moment you left here. We saw him sneak out of your house, grab a cab and take it here, where I have been waiting, hoping, all night just in case he would do exactly what he did."

I glanced over at Sam then back at him. "Well, aren't you the clever pair?"

"Clothes," he said as he continued his search of the suitcase. "Toothbrush, a prescription for..." he held the bottle away from his face and squinted at the label, "Viagra." He smiled widely at me, teeth gleaming in the glow from the streetlights. "Must have been anticipating some fun." He looked back down at the suitcase. "An envelope full of cash." He flicked through the notes. "Lots of it. Oh, and look, how sweet. His passport." He glanced over at me. "It's what I expected to find. I have the preliminary report from the medical examiner. Miss Connor was beaten before she was killed. Her left eye was bruised."

I fought to keep my emotions under control, biting the inside of my cheek when I heard about the bruise. I stood stone-still as Cavanaugh kept searching the suitcase and then, disappointed, started on the car. He checked the glove box, the back seat and then the trunk. As he did, he called out to Sam. "Pat him down!"

She'd already anticipated the order. "Only a wallet," she called back.

"What are you missing?" I managed to get out.

"You were a detective. What do you think I'm looking for? The gun. We still haven't found it. I figure that will be the final nail in your friend's coffin."

He was good at this intimidation thing and I felt sick to my stomach that he'd notice the bulge in my pocket. I kept my face neutral as I turned away and walked over to Joe now sitting in the back seat of a police car. His mouth was tight and his fists were clenched behind his back. He looked at me angrily.

"I didn't do it," he said through clenched teeth. "Jack, I swear I didn't do it."

"Don't talk," I said firmly.

"I loved her. How could I have killed her? I swear I didn't."

"What did I just tell you? Don't say anything, especially when you're sitting in a damn police car." I glared at him for a second before continuing. "And don't talk to the cop processing you either. And for heaven's sake don't talk to whoever they happen to stick you in the cell with. Nobody. Do you understand?"

"Will they let me out today?"

"Did you just hear what I said?"

"Yes. I understand. I *am* a lawyer, you know. Will they let me out today?"

"Joe, you were running away. You had thousands of dollars in your suitcase as well as your passport. They are going to charge you with murder and no judge in his right mind is going to grant you bail after this. You'll be in jail until your trial."

"I am so cooked."

"Yes, you are." It was out of my hands now. "I'll see you at the arraignment."

I waited while a policeman shut the door and another one climbed into the car behind the wheel. With the lights still flashing, they drove Joe away into the dying night. I suppressed a smile and headed over to Cavanaugh who was continuing to search the car.

When he stood up, I began to talk. "I am not at liberty to tell you how I got this, but I believe I'm obligated to turn it over to you as it may be material to your investigation."

I pulled my hand out of my pocket and offered the gun to Cavanaugh. The detective's eyes popped open.

"Is that...?"

"You will have to do a test to identify it."

He blinked a few times. "Yes. Of course."

He took the bag with the gun and hefted it in his hand. Something suddenly went out of me, something ugly and hard.

He looked at me and said, "I'm sorry if I seemed rude back there."

The words took me by surprise. I searched his face to see if there was a 'but' to follow but he stood silently with both hands clutching the bag like a prize.

"Are you apologising to me, detective?" I could only manage a half-hearted smile.

"I want you to know that I should not have been rude. It has been noted that you went after him when you discovered he sneaked out of your house. It has also been noted that you tried to stop him from running and he knocked you down with his suitcase. It has now been noted that you turned over what might prove to be the murder weapon. The law says you have to turn it over but still, nine times out of ten, it would have been buried. All of that has been noted, and I am sorry if I was rude back there."

His words hung in the air and against my better judgement I mellowed a little.

I nodded. "Thank you."

He nodded back and without saying another word, headed off to show his shiny new prize to Sam.

I stayed at the scene until all the police cars had left and until the dawn had fully broken. In the silence, I thought about what had happened that night, what I had lost, and what I had just done. I felt a weary sadness turn to determination. I was glad the gun was gone but it didn't mean it was over and that I was through with it all.

Now I had to find someone to defend Joe when I knew he was guilty. No matter how many times it had happened before, I always asked lawyers the same question, '*How can you defend someone you know did it?*'

No one can give me an adequate answer except to say it's his or her job. Now I would turn it over to some unlucky lawyer with all the evidence of guilt built up already. I had made a decision that night and I would follow it through. I had discovered the truth in my house when Joe had lied so shamelessly to me and later, on this street, when he whacked me with his suitcase as he was about to escape from justice.

The next part, his indictment, would be a snap.

The rain was beginning to get heavier again so I turned my thoughts away from Joe, put the collar up on my raincoat and made my way back to my car. By this time, the rain was blowing at 45-degree angle and soaking my pants.

The traffic was non-existent as I made my way across the road and jumped into my car dripping water onto the leather seat. I was looking forward to a few hours sleep before the arraignment tomorrow. Today.

9

———

Joe was marched from the lockup through the halls of the courthouse in front of two guards with his hands handcuffed in front of him. The area outside was swamped with lawyers talking on phones and hard-faced police officers watching a queue of worried-looking people waiting their turn in court. Every face twisted towards Joe as he turned left off the hallway into the courtroom.

I could barely stand to look at Joe as he sat next to me at the defence table still in his clothes from the night before, stinking and rumpled. His face looked puffy and his hands trembled. His eyes were red and the fear that overwhelmed him showed in every line of his face as he began to understand the consequences of his single moment of uncontrollable rage. I wanted to strangle him myself so instead, I looked around the courtroom, at the bailiff, at the guards, at the empty seats, at Sam and Cavanaugh sitting in the front row behind the prosecution table. Cavanaugh was leaning back with his arms folded over his chest watching me. Sam was sitting quietly beside him looking down at her hands. In the last row of seats, Sonya Martin, the journalist I'd seen last night at Joe's house, watched me with unblinking eyes.

It felt good to be sitting in the courtroom with its heavy wooden benches and red carpeting because it felt like a harsh place that exuded justice. The kind of justice I was hoping to find.

An hour before, Joe had introduced me to his lawyer, Karen Sawyer, an up and coming newcomer to Barclay & Davidson.

Joe waved his hand in my direction. "This is Jack Curtis, Karen. He's going to help us find out how all this happened."

Karen looked at me like I was King Kong and she was Fay Wray and a bunch of natives in grass tutus were going to tie her down and let me have my wicked way with her. As a policeman, it was a look I'd seen before and I've always hoped it's wasn't my looks that terrified them.

"Hello, Karen." I smiled my best Dudley Do-right smile, the one with the twinkle. "I promise not to hurt you."

I listened to her coaching Joe through the procedure so I could stew blissfully in my own emotions.

"This is just a formality, Joe," she said quietly. "We'll waive the reading of the indictment, plead you not guilty, and get started building your defence."

Joe told her that I had been a good detective and would do the foot work for her and in return Joe had told me that Karen was sharp, faithful and trustworthy. Of course, this meant that I couldn't trust her, with all that had happened between Shannon and me and what I had decided the night before. The good thing was that she would be my canary in the mineshaft, singing every new bit of evidence to me that she would find. I could stay close to the investigation and know everything that happened in the courtroom and I could also keep her in the dark about what I had decided to do about it.

"What about bail?" Joe asked. "I've got to get out of here."

"We'll try to get you out but it's a murder charge and you were trying to run. The judge will grant either no bail or an absurdly high one. How much can you afford?"

"I don't know. There's some money in a joint account, and there's Shannon's life insurance policy. And there's the house. All together, it's worth a million or two."

"Whose house is it you're talking about?" I asked.

"Mine. Sarah's and mine. Our house."

I leant forward across the table and looked at him hard. "That's not your house anymore, Joe. You left Sarah with it when you left her for Shannon."

As soon as I said it, Joe knew what I meant.

"Forget about Shannon's life insurance policy too, Joe," Karen said. "We can't touch that. You're accused of killing her, so no insurance company is going to pay out until the jury acquits you. If anything, the policy goes to prove motive. You killed her for the money, they'll say."

Joe's shocked eyes moved from Karen to me and then back again to Karen. Like it was the first time he'd heard something like this. Like he wasn't a lawyer who should have known this from the outset.

"Would Sarah agree to put the house up for bail?" Karen asked.

This time, I turned to Karen, amazed. "Seriously? Would you?"

Her eyes roamed my face before she turned and spoke to Joe. "You mentioned an account. What kind of account?"

"A joint brokerage account. In both our names."

I turned back suddenly to him and stared. Before his arrest, his features could have been classed as handsome. Now his mouth jerked and twitched, leaving his face looking disfigured.

"How much is in the account?" I asked.

He shrugged. "I don't know exactly. Depending on the market, maybe half a million." He glanced from me to Karen. "There may not be quite that much in the account now. Shannon had to take some of the money out for expenses. I'm not sure how much is left."

"Where the hell did you get half a million dollars from, Joe?" I asked.

"Shannon had a big case before we got together. A medical malpractice suit. The settlement was huge."

"If it was Shannon's money, why is your name on the account?" I asked bluntly.

"Because we were in love. We were going to be married, so we put all our money together. I added some, too. Part of it was mine."

I stared at him hard, my eyes suddenly angry, before I turned away in disgust.

Karen stared at me, a little confused at my reaction, then turned back to Joe. "You won't be able to touch that money either if it was in both names. Same reasoning as before. Do you know where the account is?"

"Westpac," Joe said. "But I let her keep track of everything. I don't even know the account number."

Karen sighed. "That's okay. We'll find out." She reached into her briefcase and pulled out a sheet of paper. "You'll have to sign this power of attorney. It will allow me to access information about your financial accounts. I won't be able to withdraw funds, but it might help to convince a judge to set a lower bail."

I watched Joe out of the corner of my eye as he scanned the document. I watched as he signed and handed it back to Karen.

"And you said you both had insurance?" Karen asked.

"Life insurance policies. I already had a policy and she took out a policy on herself and named me beneficiary."

"Where are the policies?"

"I don't know. Shannon had them."

"Okay," Karen said, disappointment clear in her tone. "We'll find them too. After this arraignment, they're going to take you back to lockup so we won't be able to talk right away. But we'll set up something soon. What I need to know is if you have any idea who could have done this. Any leads we ought to look into."

I turned to look at Joe and found he was looking at me as if he were pleading for answers. I had none, at least none that he would like to hear.

"I don't know," he whined. "Everyone liked her. Why would anyone want to hurt her?"

"Was there anything unusual or out of the ordinary in the past few weeks or months?"

"No. Nothing. There were some calls at home, you know, calls I answered where the caller hung up. That sort of thing. Maybe something was going on. Maybe there was someone else I didn't know about."

I stood abruptly and walked out of the room so Joe wouldn't see the look of disbelief on my face or hear the snort that came unbidden from my throat. It was all too much to take. Joe was professing his innocence, casting about for non-existent suspects and he'd come up with the thing about a caller who kept hanging up whenever he answered.

Near the entrance to the courtroom, a tall man with a briefcase was talking to Cavanaugh and Sam and I assumed he was the prosecutor. As I got closer, I realised he wasn't talking, he was arguing. Sam was keeping her voice low, but her disgust was evident. Cavanaugh looked away, his mouth set with disappointment, like a kid on Christmas morning who finds his present is a jigsaw puzzle and not a puppy. Sam saw me approaching and stopped talking and gestured to the prosecutor. He turned around.

"You're Jack Curtis?" he asked.

"That's right," I said.

He smiled. "I saw your picture in the papers this morning."

"They didn't get my good side," I quipped.

"Well, you *were* facing the camera," mumbled Sam.

Cavanaugh bowed his head slowly and his shoulders shook with stifled laughter.

I looked from one to the other. "Now is that nice?" I asked. "Here I am trying to be pleasant and forge a good relationship and you return with insults."

"That wasn't an insult," Sam said showing off her straight white teeth in a growing smile. "If I were insulting you, I would have started with your tie."

I raised my eyebrows and looked down at the tie my daughter had given me on the last Christmas we'd shared in Hobart. It was all colour and no design and it looked like someone had thrown up on my shirt. "What's wrong with my tie?"

"Please. It's as if you and Cavanaugh go to the same St Vinnies store."

"And here I was just about to compliment Detective Cavanaugh on *his* neckwear."

"If I may interrupt this chatty little get-together," said the prosecutor, "I'd like to introduce myself. My name is Brad Jefferson and I'm going to be the one who prosecutes your friend."

I smiled at him. He smiled back.

"I think you might like to know that I am going to oppose bail."

"I expected as much."

"This thing about the suitcase and passport sealed it. The evidence against your friend is overwhelming and a lot of people, including the detectives in charge of this case, agree with me. We don't like the fact that she was hit before she was shot. And in case you weren't aware, the only fingerprints we could lift from the gun that you handed over belonged to Mr Banner."

"He picked it up." I liked the sound of my righteous indignation. Juries do too. Usually.

He glanced over my shoulder towards Joe and Karen who were talking quietly head to head outside the courtroom. "I'm going to talk to you because you were once a very good detective."

I inclined my head and accepted the compliment.

"We haven't finished with the investigation, Mr Curtis. Not by a long shot. But this appears to me to be a crime of passion. Your friend and Ms Connor were arguing, there was a scuffle and Mr Banner couldn't control himself. He hit his fiancée and then he shot her. It's a common enough story, and it's sad. Truly it is. Because of the situation I just outlined, it appears like nothing more than manslaughter. Something in the ten to fifteen-year range. I'm willing to accept a plea of manslaughter. Your friend could be out with good behaviour in eight to ten years." He looked at Sam and Cavanaugh. "These good people here do not agree with me."

I could only stare at him. "That's very generous of you." And it was. Shockingly and upsettingly so. I didn't like it one little bit and I didn't like where this was going.

"But you should know," he continued as if I hadn't even spoken, "that if our investigation continues, there is no telling what we might uncover." He glanced at Sam and Cavanaugh again. "The detectives are not happy with the offer and they are going to continue searching until they find more of a motive."

He looked hard at me. "You don't want them to find it, believe me. If they dig up a motive beyond the heat of the moment, I'm going to have no choice but to yank back this offer and go for murder. I know it's a lot for Mr Banner to think about and he doesn't have to decide today, but you should tell him not to wait too long."

"I'll pass the message on to Joe and his attorney."

"I'm telling you this because you're a smart man and you seem to be his only friend. Talk it over."

10

———————

As Brad Jefferson had stated, he opposed Joe's bail, stating he was a flight risk, and the judge had agreed with him. After the arraignment, Joe had his hands handcuffed behind him and he was led away to the lockup to await trial.

Afterwards, Karen and I climbed down the steps from the courtroom after the arraignment and in my present mood, I couldn't help noticing that flowers were blooming in the garden beds and birds were atwitter. It was as if the rain from the night before had washed away the remnants of summer and autumn was suddenly swooping down on us. And yet, as I stood standing on the grey concrete steps, a group of reporters hovering menacingly by the door like a flock of vultures, it felt like I was standing in the murky gloom with shadows and secrets all around me. I wanted to get away, but Sam and Cavanaugh stepped in our way.

"Do you have a minute, Mr Curtis?" Cavanaugh asked. He wasn't smiling anymore, a bad sign I figured, but then neither was Sam. "Do you mind if we look at your hands?"

"My hands?"

"If you don't mind."

I looked askance at Karen and she nodded.

I held out my hands and Cavanaugh took one each in his own and carefully examined the knuckles before letting them drop. I wasn't sure why he'd thought to check my hands, but I was sure he'd let me know pretty soon.

"Thanks," he said. He looked at Karen. "You should know that Detective Neil and I both opposed the offer made. Is your client going to accept it?"

Karen smiled. "He says he didn't do it and he pled not guilty in court.'"

"I know, but is he going to accept the offer?"

"He rejected it outright."

"That means the investigation is still moving forward," Cavanaugh said.

"That's correct," said Karen.

He looked at me. "Then I need to ask you a question, Mr Curtis, about the night of the killing because something confuses me."

I could feel the eyes of the vultures watching me, listening to every word. I glanced in their direction and turned my back on them before answering, lowering my voice to make it more difficult for them to hear the conversation. I wasn't sure what the questions would be, but I knew they would be something I didn't want splashed all over the front page of the Gold Coast Bulletin.

"Go ahead," I said.

"You said that Mr Banner called you at your home and then you came right over."

"That's correct."

"Except we took a look at the phone logs from Mr Banner's line just before court and we found that your call to 000 showed up as expected. And there were other calls to you from earlier dates, again as expected. But there was no call registered to you on the night of the killing."

"Really?"

"Why would that be so?"

"The phone company made a mistake?"

He harrumphed. "Are you saying that the computers of the phone company made a mistake? Do you honestly think that's true?"

It was the first time he had looked me straight in the eye and I noticed one wandered slightly. The effect was a little disconcerting. His scrutiny was unsettling, like a snake watching his prey before the attack, and it made me realise I needed to be careful about everything I said.

"Does Mr Banner have a mobile phone?" he asked.

"I would assume so. There would be records."

"I suppose there would be. You didn't happen to see a mobile phone as well when you were in the bedroom?"

"No sir."

He was clearly unhappy with my response.

"Has anything else occurred to you about the night, Mr Curtis?"

"Occurred," I drawled, as if hearing a new word. I gave a long sweeping eye movement as I searched for an answer. "Nope. Nothing comes to mind."

He sighed deeply. "Thank you for your help, Mr Curtis."

"Call me Jack, Detective Cavanaugh."

Cavanagh blinked up at the sun, a deep line creasing his well-tanned forehead. He shook his head slowly. "No, I don't think I will."

The words threw me a little. I'd been seeing him in a different light since the apology, almost as a contemporary, so this change of demeanour hit me by surprise. But I knew what he was thinking. He thought I was concealing evidence and in doing so I was aiding and abetting my good friend Joe. In actual fact, I *was* concealing evidence but for a different reason. I was protecting myself.

I felt a twinge of regret, knowing he'd stepped away from the growing respect he'd had for me. You start your career with moral clarity then gradually you begin to feel disillusioned because the people you are supposed to protect and serve treat you like shit. You begin to believe there are some who aren't even in the same gene pool and wouldn't even make a good bar of soap. You think of them as morally diseased and would happily export the whole criminal population to uninhabited areas of the earth and start over again.

He thought I'd stepped over that line and maybe he was right.

"You think you're so smart." The words were said softly but underneath, I could hear the scorn in his voice. "In fact, you're very transparent."

I tried not to show any emotion even though my stomach was fluttering at the 'transparent' gibe. I didn't even blink.

"I've checked your file."

Sam's head spun to face him, her eyes wide and her mouth slightly open with shock.

He looked me up and down and his lip curled. "You were always a failure waiting to happen," he continued. "And now you're looking for a cause to bring yourself back into the limelight."

I eased air into my lungs through my clenched teeth. I was a failure, but I wasn't a pushover.

I shook my head. "It must be exhausting to be this narcissistic." I turned to Sam. "I'm nowhere near as narcissistic as this, am I?"

Karen's feet shuffled beside me and the air crackled with tension.

Sam scowled at Cavanaugh, making the skin above her eyebrows pucker. He chewed his bottom lip, looking chastised, as she spoke.

"You know, Jack, when we asked you about Ms Connor, you described her as sweet. We've been running the usual enquiries and I have to tell you, we've been talking to a lot of people who knew her and they all seemed to have a lot to say. But not one of them used the word 'sweet' when talking about her."

"Maybe I didn't know her all that well after all." I let that sink in before asking, "What was the thing with the hands?" I asked Sam. For some reason, I put my hands in my trouser pockets.

"Last night, one of the Forensic team was heading into the house to redo a few things. Someone, and we're assuming it was a man, rushed out dressed in black and knocked her over. She grabbed his leg and he turned and beat her pretty badly."

I felt the hair on the back of my neck rise. I couldn't believe what

Sam had just said. "And you thought to check *my* hands, Sam?" I felt my back teeth lock together.

Her face reddened and she exchanged a tight look with Cavanaugh. "Just doing my job. Purely routine, Jack."

I have never been quick to anger but once I get there, I hang on like a bulldog. I don't throw my fists. I do the opposite. I go quiet. The silence dragged on for easily five seconds before I replied.

"Call me Mr Curtis, Detective Neil."

Sam's eyes widened a little. "She's still in the hospital, you know."

"I'm sad to hear that." I glanced down at the concrete steps. "Good thing I didn't fall and scrape my knuckles on these steps then, isn't it?" I said to Cavanaugh, ignoring Sam.

He nodded. "Yes, it is."

"Probably just a burglar who knew the place was empty."

"Probably," Cavanaugh said. "Just like the phone company computer probably made a mistake."

People were walking around us as we stood on the stairs. "One more question, detectives," I said. "Are you ready to release Shannon Connor's body?"

"We rushed the autopsy through in light of circumstances. Her body can be released at any time." He straightened his back and looked at me for a long moment, as if he was about to say something else. But whatever he had planned to say seemed to go out of his eyes.

"There are no next of kin that we could find. Does Mr Banner plan to bury Ms Connor?"

"She was his fiancée," I shrugged matter-of-factly. "Since Mr Banner is not available to make the arrangements," I let that hang in the air for a moment, "I will make them on his behalf."

Cavanaugh considered my reply while Sam scuffed a shoe on the concrete steps.

I looked from one to the other, neither of them saying anything. "Is there something else you want to say to me?" I asked.

"I think we've all said enough," Karen interrupted. "We're leaving. If there is anything else, just call my office."

"Have a nice day," I smiled.

Sam and Cavanaugh marched past us, Cavanaugh bumping me heavily on the shoulder in the process, apparently not pleased, not pleased at all.

Karen looked at me. "What the hell was that all about?"

"How would I know, Karen?"

11

———

"I have something for you," I smiled at Shannon.

It was the last afternoon we'd spent together, and for weeks I'd been trying to find a way to stay in touch with her, even when I knew Joe was close by.

The toughest acting job in the world is behaving normally in the presence of a friend whose fiancé you're sleeping with. Most people think they can handle it, but you're always on the alert that sooner or later someone will pick up on the intimacy. There's always the hitch in breathing, an altered voice and of course, there's the eyes. Reality lives in the eyes and the voice. I had to consciously try to keep the situation from exploding by avoiding eye contact and keeping my voice from going a pitch higher when talking to or about her. What I needed was a way to stay close to her when she wasn't with me. It sounds needy, I know, but you have to consider the extenuating circumstances.

"Diamonds?" she asked playfully.

"Better."

"What could be better than diamonds?"

"What about me?"

"You? You won't look half as pretty hanging from my ears."

Shannon in her normal life was an unemotional, sardonic bundle of habits that act as sword and shield to protect her inner sadness. She was both desirable and detached, which of course made her more desirable. It was impossible to ever get a straight answer from her. She always deflected the line to something less threatening or asked a question of her own that put you on the defensive. She was, after all, a lawyer.

"I want to give you a phone," I told her.

Her eyebrows hitched high on her forehead. "I already have a phone and I'd rather have diamonds."

"But it's really cute and it's red to match your lipstick."

"Red?"

"That's right. No one else has the number. It's just a phone for you and me to call each other."

"Our own private hot line?"

"That's right. And my number will be number one on the speed dial."

"For now." And she laughed.

12

———

The phone Sam and Cavanaugh were looking for was the red one I'd placed in my pocket on the night of her murder. It was my phone. That's why I'd taken it and why I didn't want it found anywhere near that house. *My* phone, now sitting in *my* kitchen, registered in *my* name, with the bills and records going to *my* house.

As soon as I got home from the courthouse, I rang Telstra and asked them to print up a record of calls made for the past two days and email it to me. The lady on the phone was most agreeable and said she'd do it straight away. While I waited, I fired up my laptop and made a cup of coffee.

When the email from Telstra arrived, I stared at the last call. It was registered at 11.02 the night of Shannon's death, made to my number. It had been Joe, using the speed dial, asking for my help.

Why had he used the mobile phone instead of his landline to make the call? How much did Joe actually know?

I sat down hard on the chair and tried to think it through. It made no sense. Was he so shocked by his murderous act that he had picked up the first phone he saw, the bright red mobile phone, left on the floor by the side of the bed by Shannon, and dial my number? It

93

would settle Cavanaugh's concerns and all I had to do was print the email off and give it to him.

Except I couldn't do that. Because then I'd have to explain why a phone registered in *my* name with the bills going to *my* house, was in *that* house on the night of the murder. And then I'd be a suspect who could be used by any competent defence attorney to raise doubt, maybe even reasonable doubt. Wasn't it *I* who was having a deceitful relationship with the deceased? Wasn't it *I* who had possession of the gun until I dropped it in Cavanaugh's hand? Wasn't it *I* who lied about everything so that I could blame poor innocent Joe Banner? How ironic that *I* might be Joe's route to freedom. What I held in my hand was reasonable doubt as to Joe's guilt, except I knew I didn't do it, and I knew Joe did, and so I had to be sure that no one, no one, would ever be able to see this record. I'd have to burn it then delete the message so nothing remained.

I walked into the kitchen and opened a drawer to find a box of matches. I lit the match and a breath of wind from somewhere blew it out. I moved over to the kitchen sink and lit another one, placing the flame at the document's corner. The blue light caught and began to curl the piece of paper.

That's when I noticed something else.

I tried to blow out the flame, but it grew and began to devour the page. I dropped it to the tiles and stamped on it to put out the flame. The kitchen smelled of smoke as I picked up the blackened document but most of the sheet was gone and I could barely read the printing. But I hadn't had a chance to delete the message on my computer.

I almost ran to the computer to check the email. And there it was. A call made on the phone to a strange number. A call made barely an hour after I'd given the phone to Shannon.

I stared at the number for a few long moments before dialling it.

A male voice answered the phone, one I didn't recognise.

"Hello?"

"May I ask who this is please?" I asked.

There was a hesitation before the voice said, "Shouldn't that be my question?"

I hung up without saying anything else and stared at the mobile again for a long time.

What game had Shannon been playing.

13

———

It has always been my observation that the rich like to separate themselves into the haves and the have-mores. Sanctuary Cove is classed as very exclusive, favoured by the well to do, overlooking water and populated by what is commonly called 'new money'. It's prime real estate close enough to the Strip and Marina Mirage and just far enough away from the fast food places, surf shops and trashy souvenir shops at Surfers Paradise. They have an insular approach to living where they believe the chaos of other parts of town could not touch them.

The assessment of personal real estate can be classified according to a few yardsticks. The size and location of the property is always given first priority. The longer the driveways, the more points scored. Beyond that, more factors are reflecting pools, topiary and excessive outdoor lightning.

Real estate material refers to this area as a "sparkling jewel in a parklike setting" and the views are always described as 'breathtaking', 'stunning', or 'spectacular'. Words like 'serenity' and 'tranquillity' abound. Every noun has an adjective attached to it to give the proper tone and substance. The 'lush, well manicured' lots are large and the 'elegant, spacious' homes are set well away from the roads and 'dotted with palms amid tropical gardens.' Lots of 'dotteds' and 'amids'.

When Joe had married Sarah, the house she chose was the Heathcliff model complete with cathedral ceilings, the oversize lounge room and the guest quarters overlooking the spacious gardens and sparkling pool. How could the future be anything but lush? But as Sarah talked of all her redecorating ideas, Joe had put on weight and smoked and drank more.

"Hello, Jack," said the former Mrs Joe Banner at her front door.

She was wearing a flowing dress in summer-appropriate white, edged with gold and matching sandals. From memory, she was the sort to lose the whites in autumn and go to beige and then go to black in winter.

"Mind if I talk to you for a while, Sarah?"

"Of course. I always have time for an old friend."

I thought she was being sarcastic. When Joe left Sarah for Shannon, their friends were forced to make a choice, Sarah or Joe. Sarah being the more sympathetic figure seemed to end up with everyone. I had known Joe for a long time and even though I thought what he had done was shabby, I ended up on his side of the aisle almost against my will. I hadn't seen her since the separation so when Sarah called me an 'old friend', I thought she was making a joke. But she surprised me by standing back and letting me into the formal entry with its French décor where I'm sure people spoke in a hushed tone.

The house was a museum except for the DO NOT TOUCH signs. Even without them, you knew not to touch. The place was immaculate. The floors and the furniture shone and no dust would be allowed to settle. Everywhere I looked was polished wood. Oak doors, skirting boards, architraves and window frames. In contrast, the furniture was white. White three-seater fabric lounge with off-white satin embroidery, two single shite wing-backed chairs. It was like a challenge. Nobody better spill here, or dribble, or drop. White was like a statement that life can be clean if everyone just maintains discipline and pays attention.

Of course, Sarah was beautiful too. A small woman with white-blonde hair pulled back tightly against the whitest skin I'd ever seen. In the muted light, I could see how blue veins criss-crossed her white skin on the back of her hands. She had high cheekbones, a generous mouth and a nose I'd decided long ago had come courtesy of a plastic surgeon's wish book. She observed me through eyes a shade deeper in colour than the sky on a hot summer's day.

Her flowing silk dress swished as she led the way through an open kitchen into the sunroom probably only used by family and friends. As she directed me to a chair, she stepped close enough for me to know that she'd been drinking gin with not much tonic and her breasts were not original architecture either.

There we were, two lemonades on coasters carefully placed on the coffee table chatting like, well, old friends.

When I first met Sarah years ago, I found myself just looking at her. That's what people say when they can't afford to buy something. *"Just looking, thanks."* Something about being in the presence of a beautiful woman puts a man at an immediate disadvantage. It doesn't matter how tough you are or how confident you feel, when a woman who looks like this is in your presence, she has the upper hand every time.

Almost of their own volition, my hands brushed the creases of my suit ineffectually.

"I saw you on TV Jack, as you left the courtroom," she began. "The camera likes you."

I smiled. "Such is the burden of startling good looks and a winning personality."

She laughed at that and curled her legs beneath her on the couch. It reminded me of better times when Sarah and Joe were the happy couple and I was the troubled single guy. Sarah was beautiful, although a little flighty and spoilt by her rich family, but she made a nice contrast to the serious and humourless Joe.

Her smile subsided and she asked, "How is he?"

"Not too good."

"I didn't think so. Joe has always pretended to be the tough guy, but he is anything but and he is certainly not the prison sort."

"Which brings me to why I'm here. Joe could use some financial help with the bail and fees."

"What does he expect *me* to do?" She made a face like she had just eaten something that had gone off. "I don't wish anyone dead, but I won't mourn Shannon Connor. Somehow, she turned Joe against himself and that's a crime. You know I was suing her?"

"You were suing Shannon?"

"Alienation of affection I think the legal term is but basically I was suing her for stealing my husband from me. There have been successful suits in the States so I thought why not here in Australia. I heard one woman won a million dollars over there."

"Sounds like Lotto."

"I was suing that bitch for every penny she had."

"And what good would that have done? It wouldn't have brought Joe back."

"Apart from the money? Well, I suppose it would have cheered me up a little to take something from her that she cared about just like she took Joe from me."

"Joe had something to do with that."

"She bewitched him, Jack. You met her. It wasn't love. Love is based on some sort of understanding of the other. And doesn't it have to be reciprocated in some way? That woman was incapable of love."

"Reciprocated or not, the emotion feels just the same."

"Yes. That's just it." She brought her legs down off the couch and leant forward earnestly, showing me a good portion of her new cleavage. "It feels the same, but it isn't. One is real, an emotion that forms the basis for everything meaningful. The other is delusion that is no different from a teenage crush on a rock star or a stalker obsessed with his prey. Whatever those emotions are, they are not love. Joe was obsessed with her and having seen her once, I can understand the attraction. But it wasn't love. Whatever trouble he is in now is because of that obsession. He thought she was feeling what he was feeling when she was incapable of returning anything."

"How do you know what she was feeling Sarah?"

A *tsk* escaped from her perfect lips. "So defensive, Jack. I know how she met my husband and why, and I've had a run-in with her on my own. After the complaint was filed in my father's office, she called me. Out of the blue. And what she said to me, Jack." She shook her head in feigned disbelief. "I'm no prude and I've heard some things that would shame a sailor. Still, I have never heard such language coming from the mouth of a woman like I heard coming from hers. When she hung up, I was too startled to be angry. What I felt was pity for Joe."

"What did she say?"

"I'm not going to tell you word for word, I don't use that kind of language. But the gist of it was that if I wanted him back so badly, I could have him. And then she warned me that with the taste of her still in his teeth, there was no way in hell he was coming back to me. I'll give her that, at least she knew where her power lay."

"So you hated her."

"Wouldn't you? She was like a force of nature, a raging storm. You felt sorry for anyone in its path."

I winced. It was easy enough to dismiss Sarah's words as those of a woman scorned but I remember when Joe left his first wife for her. Sarah herself had been a presence not easily dismissed.

"Sarah, Joe is in a tight spot. He doesn't have enough assets to pay a retainer for a lawyer."

"I thought there was money from her."

"There is some and we're in the process of tracking it down and trying to get an actual figure. From what Joe told his lawyer, there was an account in both their names but he's not sure how much is left."

"Are you saying there could be no money?" She looked a little taken back.

"We haven't tracked it all down yet so we don't know the exact figure."

The exact figure didn't matter because she started laughing as if some great practical joke had been played for her benefit. "Well, you don't have to tell me where the money went. I can guess all right." Her laughter continued. "So much for my lawsuit and so much for Peter Hobson."

"Who?"

"Forget it. Nothing." She kept laughing until she noticed me sitting glumly. "Well if there's no money, how does he expect to pay the lawyer?"

"I don't know."

"What about you? Are you getting paid?"

"No."

"The loyalty of an old friend?"

"Something like that."

"I wonder if Joe knows how lucky he is to have you."

"The point is, Sarah, Joe wants to know if you will help him out." I felt stupid even asking but I had to make it look as if I was doing everything to help my dear old friend get through this harrowing time in his life. Even though I wanted him to pay for what he'd done. Even though I ached to just sit back and let justice take its toll. The satisfaction of seeing him hauled away to prison was a dangling carrot in front of me but the pleasure would come soon enough. In the meantime, Joe had pleaded with me to come and see her and here I was.

"Yes."

"What?" I sat up straight and blinked a few times. I was stunned.

"I said yes. The mortgage is pretty high and I don't know how much equity there is but part of it is his so I will do whatever I can."

"Do you realise that he might have killed her?"

"If he did, she deserved it."

I blinked a few more times. "You still love him after all he's done to you?"

"Love is not a faucet, Jack. You don't just turn it off."

"Do you ever wonder if he's worthy of it?"

"Every day. But sometimes in the middle of our lives, you don't realise that your dreams have come true. It's only when the dream disappears that you know. I want it all back the way it was before we ever heard of Shannon Connor. I want my husband back and I want my life back. I want it the way it was before."

"It can never be that way again, Sarah. It will be different no matter what you do."

"Thank you for your advice, Jack, but it will be better. She's dead, isn't she? That's a very good start."

I hesitated for just a second, but I knew I had to ask the question.

"On the night that Shannon was killed," I said, "where were you around ten o'clock?"

"That's funny, Jack. The police asked me the exact same question."

"They've been here?"

"Two detectives. An Italian looking woman and a man who did most of the talking, a Detective Cavanaugh, I think it was. The woman spent the whole time pacing the room and snooping in every corner. I'll give you the same answer I gave them. I was at home. Alone."

"I'd like to ask one more question. What made you think Shannon Connor had enough money to sue?"

She smiled enigmatically. "I guess I just supposed wrong."

14

———

"Come on Joe. If it wasn't you, who do you think killed her?" It was only day two and Karen was already sounding exasperated.

"I don't know," he whimpered.

"You have to have some idea. She's dead and you're on trial for her murder. You knew her life better than anyone else. You have to have some theory."

We were in one of the client-lawyer rooms at the Southport Watch house. The room itself was slate grey, walls of besser blocks with a metal table and a steel door and it had that lovely prison smell of urine, fear, sweat and ammonia. We had already been informed that he would be transferred to Arthur Gorrie Prison in Brisbane in the afternoon while he awaited his trial so we needed to get every piece of information from Joe that we could.

Joe looked distraught. His hands shook slightly even as he held them on the tabletop. His eyes were bleary and redlined and there was a tic that jerked his left eyelid developing. There was also a blue-black bruise on his right cheekbone that glowed against his grey pallor. Funny, because Shannon's corpse had the same kind of welt.

I crossed my arms over my chest and leaned against the wall in the corner of the room and let Karen handle the questioning. This was something she had to do. She had to inform Joe of what was happening to him while she dug around for information. But he continued to maintain his innocence as I continued to lean against the wall, watching the lies spill out of his mouth.

"The only answer," Joe said, "is that someone came in while I was in the spa. I didn't hear him because of the headphones. That had to be what happened."

"But who, Joe? Who hated Shannon that much to take such a risk?" Karen leant forward and asked earnestly.

"I don't know." His eyes dropped to his hands, clenching and unclenching nervously on the table.

"Okay then. Why?"

"I don't know that either. They were all mad at *me*, not Shannon."

"Who was mad at you?"

"Sarah was upset when I left, and so was her father." He looked up at me. "You know what Matthew Simmons is like." His head spun back to Karen. "I used to work in his firm and he never let me forget from day why he'd given me the job in the first place. When I left, he told me to stay away from him or he'd shove something down my throat."

"Can you blame him?" I asked from the corner.

Joe shot me a look of annoyance. "There was also an investigator who did some work for the firm, an ugly weasel named Fitzroy. Frank Fitzroy. He's got a bad reputation and I never understood why the firm used him. There was a time when he tried to buddy up with me for some reason. I blew him off because frankly, he gave me the creeps. And then, after I gave up everything for Shannon, I started running into Fitzroy in strange places."

"Where?" I asked.

"Outside my new office. In a bar. Once I was in the toilets of a restaurant and the son of a bitch came out of nowhere. He stood beside me and gave me this weird smile."

"Frank Fitzroy gave you a weird smile?" I asked sceptically.

"Yeah."

"Did he threaten you?" Karen asked.

"Not directly. But he did mention some files I had taken with me when I left. I told him to stay away from me and he laughed. Once when I was walking up to Shannon on the street, I saw her talking to some man and as I got closer, I realised it was Fitzroy. When he spotted me, he gave me a strange look and walked away. Shannon never told me what he said."

"Do you think he threatened her?"

"That's what I assumed. Maybe it was *him* making the calls and hanging up. Maybe *he* killed her."

"Frank Fitzroy killed her?" My eyebrows raised disbelievingly.

"Yeah. Maybe it was him."

He was sitting on the edge of his seat, spine as straight as a pencil, staring into my face.

I snorted. "Really, Joe?"

I wasn't going to make it easy for him. The seconds ticked by as I stared into his face, a slow flush rising from his neck to cover his cheeks. His eyes dropped guiltily to his clenched hands, clearly hiding his embarrassment. Five years I'd known Joe. In that time, I been drunk with him, listened to him bewailing about a job that was stifling him, supported him during a messy divorce, even stood by him when he threw all that away to move in with Shannon. Now he could barely look at me.

"Did you lock the front door before you went to the bedroom?" Karen asked, glancing at me warningly.

"I usually did." His eyes lifted again at Karen's question. "We're still pretty close to Surfers where we live. Lived."

"And that night?"

"I think so."

"The windows were locked when the police came. Was the door unlocked? After you climbed out of the spa, you saw her on the mattress, you picked up the gun, you searched the house. Then you called Jack and went outside to wait for him. Is that correct?"

"Yes."

"When you went outside, did you need to unlock the door?"

"I don't know," he muttered, shaking his head.

"Think, Joe."

"I don't remember unlocking it. I just opened it. It must have been unlocked." He opened his eyes wide as if he had just discovered a wonderful secret. "The killer somehow unlocked it and left it unlocked. That's it. That's the proof."

I stared at him from my corner, my back ramrod straight, and Karen stared at him from the table. Neither of us said a word or moved a muscle. I couldn't believe what I was hearing. Here was a man who'd been a lawyer for all of his working life coming up with such ridiculous statements of proof, I wondered how he'd managed to function in the legal world. Maybe Matthew Simmons was right to bury him in corporate business. Even then he must have been out of his depth.

"And the evidence for that is…?" Karen asked softly.

His gaze shifted crazily around the room and then as if her question had been a pin inserted in him, he deflated.

I pushed myself off the wall and walked over to the desk until I stood over him. "Tell us again about your relationship with Shannon."

"Did you have sex with her that night?" Karen asked.

"No."

"The night before?"

"I'm not sure. We had an active sex life."

"Is that why you took Viagra?" I asked.

In my peripheral vision, I saw Karen's head spin towards me, but I kept my eyes zeroed in on Joe. This had been my first warning. I'd have to be more careful with my questions in the future.

"Why is that important?" Joe asked, not realising my slip.

"Were you and Shannon fighting? Did you have many fights?"

"Sure. Everyone does. We did too. She was fiery when we were fighting and then we'd make up."

"Did you ever hit her, Joe?"

"No."

"What about that night?"

"No! Stop it! What are you saying?"

"There was a bruise on her cheek."

"Maybe the killer...." He looked from Karen to me. "Why would I hit her?"

"Out of anger." I said.

"No."

"Because she was sleeping with someone else," I persisted.

Joe stared at me, horrified. "You're wrong!"

"Am I?" I asked.

I stood over him for a moment longer, ignoring Karen's annoyed look, and then I turned and strolled back to my corner.

Joe's head was shaking as if he were struggling to take in all in. It was a treat to watch him work. He was good. Academy award winning good. He was sliding dramatically through the emotions and giving us a good idea of what a man learning for the first time that his dead fiancée had been cheating on him was like. Then he glanced up at Karen, making sure his emotions had been duly noted and admired, before saying, "He did it."

"Who did it?"

"The guy she was sleeping with. You asked me who did it and I'm telling you. *He* did it. I have no doubt in my mind. She was living with me and he didn't like it. He must have known how to get in or maybe she gave him a key. Maybe she showed him where the gun was. He did it, damn it. We have to find him. He's a murderer."

The guy she was sleeping with. Me. Only I knew I didn't kill her. This new theory was a smoke screen meant to divert attention away from him to someone else and I stared at him in disgust from the corner even as I thought the theory through. It wasn't bad and it had promise. Joe had once been a trial lawyer early on in his career and had always shown promise. Now he had come up with a damn clever strategy. It was just what I did *not* need. His accusations were dangerous, and I wanted Karen to disregard them.

"It's a theory," I said, "but there's no evidence to support it."

"Then find the evidence. Find the bastard."

"Without proof, it's a loser."

Karen was frowning at me. "I don't know," she said. "It sounds pretty good to me."

There was a different feeling creeping up my insides now. Like cold fingers trailing along my ribs. I needed to keep Karen focused on Joe, not on Joe's new story of a fictitious lover.

"If you make this proposed lover the issue," I said slowly, "you just throw Joe's motive in the jury's face over and over again. Every time you mention a lover, Joe's reason to kill her becomes even more evident. Joe was angry. Then, the prosecutor will put every effort into finding him. And if he does find him, and he has an alibi, then you might as well tick the guilty box on the verdict form."

Karen nodded and turned back to Joe. "Have you thought about the offer, Joe?"

"Some. Well, a lot."

"Don't lose your nerve, Joe," I said firmly.

"I can't spend life in jail," he whined. "It's only been a couple of days in the watch house and I'm a mess."

"Don't lose your nerve," I repeated, feeling Karen's gaze on my back.

"Okay, Jack."

"We're solid. Right? A team."

His eyes were fixed on mine. "Okay. I'm sticking with you."

I knew Joe was guilty but there was some slippery, indefinable *thing* lurking in my subconscious. Something I couldn't put a finger on. I found myself simply nodding back at him.

Karen cleared her throat. "That's something we need to talk about. My firm is asking for the retainer. We need to examine your resources."

"Then let's get moving."

"We found your account at Westpac." Karen reached into her briefcase and took out the statement. "It was registered in both your names and I want you to have a look and maybe explain some things to us."

"Fine," he said holding out his hand.

I pushed myself off the wall and walked forward, putting my hand out to Karen to stop her passing the statement to Joe.

"Before you look," I said, "tell us again why you and Shannon had a joint account."

"We were committed to each other. That's what you do when you're going to spend the rest of your life with someone. She had some money from a case and I had some money. We pooled it together."

"What case, Joe?"

"I don't know, some medical malpractice case."

"When did it settle?"

"Last year."

"Do you know the name?"

"No."

"The defence attorney? What was *his* name? He'll know the victim's name."

"I don't know it."

"Didn't you discuss it with her at all?"

"Sure."

"But you don't know the name of the opposing counsel and you don't know the name of the victim?"

"I don't remember."

I looked at him disbelievingly as Karen's eyes flicked between Joe and me.

"Okay," I continued. "How much was in the account?"

"Maybe half a million."

"Who had access to it?"

"Mainly Shannon. I let her deal with it all. Haven't we already gone over this?"

"Didn't you say that you fought with Shannon over the usual things?" Karen asked. "The most usual thing for couples is money. Is that what you fought about?"

"No. Maybe. I don't remember."

We let the silence draw out for a while as he thought. Neither Karen nor I wanted to fill the gap.

"Okay," he muttered. "Yes, once. Maybe a couple of times. There was some money missing and I called up the bank. I wanted to make a payment to Sarah without Shannon knowing. I was surprised at the amount they said was available. It was less than I thought it should be. About half. I asked Shannon about it and she told me it was none of my business, that she was taking care of it and that some investments hadn't worked out."

"Did anyone hear you fighting?"

"No. I don't think so."

"Was it at home?"

"Maybe a restaurant, I don't know. I decided after that to take some cash out of the account, just to be safe."

"The cash you had in your suitcase?"

"That's right. Can I see the statement now?"

"Do you know a man named Peter Hobson, Joe?" I asked.

He stopped, making a show of searching through his memory. "I don't think so."

I waited a few beats. "What about Shannon?"

"No. I never heard her talk of him. I would have remembered. The name doesn't ring a bell." He paused before asking. "Where did you hear it?"

I smiled. "Your wife."

Karen was leaning forward, listening intently to the conversation.

"Well, as usual, I have no idea what *she* is talking about," he harrumphed. "Don't take anything she says too seriously."

I raised my eyebrows. "She's willing to put up the house for you," I stated.

He shrugged as if it was expected. "Can I see the financial statements now?"

I stood there for a moment longer then nodded to Karen, who handed it over. I watched carefully as he read through the document, watched him screw his face up, watched his eyes shift from uncertainty to fear.

"Where's the money? There's nothing here." His voice dropped from confident to shocked to scared, to something desperate. An animal whose only exit had been sealed up. There was nothing deliberate there. This was real and desolate and terrifying. His whole body shook and his voice was bleak. "Where's my money? Where's it gone?"

Joe was still shaking his head as the guard led him away. Karen and I sat quietly together for a moment.

"Things grew a little heated in there," she said.

"It's going to get a lot more heated if he takes the stand. It's time he got an idea of what it's going to be like."

"I had a dog once," she said. "A Pomeranian I called Fi Fi. I had begged my mother to buy me a dog for so long that she finally gave in to me. But she insisted that he didn't come inside the house whenever he wasn't being walked on his leash. He was to stay in the garage and have the run of it, not the house. Fi Fi hated it and cried incessantly, whined and yapped and snapped at all of us whenever he was let out. He had an eye condition common to the breed, so his eyes were surrounded in a red crust that only made his whining sound worse. Then one day, my mother picked me up from school and told me that Fi Fi had been killed by a car."

"That's tough."

"No, it was a relief. I had grown to hate that dog and his desperate whining. It made me feel guilty every time I looked at his red gummy eyes."

"What made you think of the dog?"

She smiled at me. "I think Joe should take the plea."

"It's his choice."

"Seriously, it's a good offer. He should take it. His lover theory isn't bad but there's something not quite right about the money."

"I know."

"He's hiding something. He's not telling us the whole truth."

"I know."

"And when they find out, and they will, it's going to jump up and bite him in the ass."

I didn't say anything, but I knew she was right. It was going to bite him and I had to find out what it was. And the first place to start was Peter Hobson.

"Funny thing about that dog," said Karen. "It wasn't until I was already at university that I began to wonder. If Fi Fi was locked in the garage alone all the time, how did a car manage to drive in and kill him?"

15

It was a beautiful day to plan a funeral. Brisk overnight winds from the Pacific had temporarily cleared the smoke from the sky sending handfuls of dry leaves fluttering down onto the grass. Even the view of Tamborine Mountain was clear this morning as the mercury hovered in the high-twenties. Cirrus clouds scudded across the upper reaches of the sky along with the vapour trails of high-flying jets. To my right, a stretch of silver rooves glinted under the sun and to my left the smell of thick sauces, garlic and freshly back bread wafted over in the light breeze. You couldn't hate the city on a day like this.

The inside of Mary Immaculate Church on Edmond Rice Drive was magnificent. Twin balconies draped with red tapestries extended all the way from the choir to the altar area. The pulpit was hand-carved from teak wood and had been constructed high above the laity with no microphones to project the priest's voice to his congregation. The stations-of-the-cross depicting Christ's passage through Jerusalem to his death made the viewer swallow in both reverence and trepidation.

Inside, the air carried a coolness that only comes from high ceilings, marble and stone. A large wooden crucifix bearing a gold figure of Christ dominated the wall behind the altar underneath an elaborate stained-glass window and I knew that whenever sunlight struck them, the effect inside the church would be stunning, leaving pools of red, green and blues on every surface. Incense and candle wax hung heavily in the air as well as the sad smell of wilting flowers. Mottled dust spun in the shafts of light that slanted through the windows and disappeared into the middle rows of pews.

The doors of the church were open and several people were in the front pews, all of them old, their rosary beads wrapped around their hands. A homeless man slept in a back pew, curled in a foetal position, with a bottle of port hanging out precariously from his coat pocket. I walked over and retrieved it before it fell, tightened the cap and placed it on the floor within arms reach of the sleeping man.

"May I help you?"

I spun around and found a priest smiling at me. He was grey-haired and tall with a long thin nose and his forearms were sun-freckled. His hands were tucked inside the sleeves of his black cassock and the roman collar around his neck fairly shone. "My name is Father Aspinall."

"I'd like to arrange a funeral, father" I said.

The smile saddened instantly and a small frown appeared. I could hear the wind blowing outside and when I looked, the leaves from a nearby maple swirled around the front steps.

The truth was I had no idea what religion Shannon had been but I wanted her to have a decent burial even though I didn't believe in a Catholic God or even the Christian one. My mother was a guilt-ridden Catholic, but I never had a thought for religion once I left home at eighteen, since the age of reason. I always smile and nod so as to avoid a philosophical argument that would benefit no one. There have been times when I would have given anything for faith in God, for the belief that divine justice exists somewhere in the universe. The comfort of belief in an afterlife is obvious in a hospital waiting room or a chemo ward. Faith is something you have, or you don't have, or pretend you do, in the hope of gaining some last-minute dispensation before going to hell.

I understand the appeal of gilded cherubs and plaster saints, of gargoyles and Old Testament angels, of gem-set golden crucifixes and anything that might give an aura of majesty and grandeur. It's a firm promise of an afterlife that is better than the present one, a paradise even.

For me, I have no faith in a just God, or any god at all, when I seen the amount of suffering he allows in this world. Small children murdered and buried on a lonely mountainside, other children dying of disease and starvation, terrorism in the name of religion, wars and numerous other events too numerous to mention have left me with the feeling that belief in God is an eccentricity.

My father once knew read a quote from a book to me that said there are no atheists in foxholes. He laughed at the time and said "It's a lie. In fact, just the opposite is true. When you're in a foxhole, when you're face-to-face with death, that's when you know for sure there's no God. It's why you fight to survive, to draw one more breath. It's why you call out to any entity because you don't want to die. Because you know in your heart of hearts that there is no hereafter. No paradise. No God. Just nothingness." It's one of the reasons I stopped praying a long time ago: that and my impotence to bring some people to justice. Afterward, the world went on and any contact between God and myself was severed.

"The woman's name is Shannon Connor and it will be a quiet affair, father," I said. "She has no family or friends so it will be just a small service at the cemetery."

I had the suspicion that with the absence of mourners it would be a quick and impersonal service and it left me with a feeling of intense sadness that a person so physically beautiful as Shannon should be resigned to such a featureless finale.

I exhaled and felt his hand touch my arm gently in compassion.

"I'm sorry for your loss, Mr...?"

I dug around in my wallet and took out an old business card. He wouldn't be able to reach me on the landline number and the card said 'Detective', but the mobile number was still correct. I took out a pen from an inside pocket of my jacket and wrote Mary's number at the morgue on the back.

"Jack Curtis." I handed him the card. "It's not Detective anymore but you can always reach me on my mobile. Shannon's body is in the morgue at the moment, but I understand it's ready for release." I pointed to the card. "That's the number for the Medical Examiner, Mary O'Brien, at the morgue. She can give you all the details. Please call me and let me know when the service will be held." A little belatedly, I said, "Thank you, father."

He looked down at the card in his hand then looked up at me, a strange smile on his face. "If this woman had no family and friends, then who are you, my son?"

He waited for an answer, but I didn't give him one. I put my sunglasses on and said good bye, then walked out.

I had been wondering the same thing myself.

16

————————

"Do you love Joe?"

Shannon's mouth twitched. "No."

"How can you marry him if you don't love him?"

"The last thing I want to be again is in love," she said. It was a shocking statement that stopped me short.

"Everyone wants to be in love, Shannon."

"Then everyone is wrong."

"You were in love once?"

"Yes."

"And it ended badly?"

"Hiroshima."

"Who was it?"

"The wrong man."

"Maybe all you need is the right man."

"Shut up Jack."

Before she left me, dressed and ready to go back to Joe, she said, "I'm sleeping with one man," her voice a monotone, "engaged to another and emotionally trapped by a third. But I'll tell you this, everything about me is moulded by a love so fearsome it has seared my soul. Don't waste your time trying to understand it because you

117

never will. It still baffles me. But it is something I don't ever want to happen again. Only the insane want to be struck by lightning twice. In the end, you're no different from Joe. You want love while having no idea what love really is. You say love but you think something else. You think love is desire, friendship, comfort and someone to cuddle while you watch videos. That's all fine but don't think such watered-down muck is love. I sleep with you and maybe I like you better than Joe and maybe if I was free I'd choose you to watch videos with and pick up my towels. But don't delude yourself that this is love, Jack. It's not, thank God. If you knew what love is and what it can do to you, you wouldn't want it either. In love there is no choice, no freedom, no dignity, no happiness. Nothing. It eats away at you and it destroys you. Who in their right mind would want that? I'd rather die than go through that again. I'd sooner you shot me through the heart."

17

Traffic was light as I drove back to Karen's office from the church. I stopped at a stoplight at the corner of Hope Island Road and the M1, raised my shoulders up and down, rotating them stiffly, and tapped my fingers impatiently on the steering wheel. It was still autumn but the asphalt glittered in the sun and it looked hot enough to fry an egg on the bitumen. Pretty soon the humidity would be so high, the moist air would feel like you were breathing water, pushing people to the beaches or into backyard pools to escape the heat.

In this weather, the hospitals are full of people suffering from heatstroke, sunburn and God knows how many victims of testosterone-induced fights exacerbated by the heat. What amazes me is that for as far as the eye can see, there never seems to be any orange-peel bums squeezed into their miniscule bikinis. There might not be much good in this world but show me anyone who has a bad thing to say about bikinis and I'll show you a lunatic.

With the car window opened, the effect was like sitting in a fan-forced oven with no hint of the freshness after the night of rain anymore. I could feel sweat trickling down my back leaving an itching trail in its wake. As I sat at the lights, cars, trucks and buses stretched ahead as far as I could see, moving forward when the traffic lights changed, then coming to a halt again while more traffic flowed across the intersection. A shadow flitted across my windscreen and I heard the rhythmic 'whup-whup-whup' of the rotor blades from a helicopter as it sped across the sky on its way to Seaworld on the Spit.

The light turned green and I stepped on the gas.

As I walked in the office, Karen looked up from the small mountain of paperwork on her desk.

"I was wondering when you'd come back." Her eyes roamed my face. "You look like shit. Are you okay?"

"I'm fine. Just tying off loose ends. Arranging a funeral, if you must know."

As I sat down, my phone buzzed and I looked down to see there had been five missed calls. All from an unknown number. It was more calls than I'd had in the past two months and I had no idea who they could be from.

"So what do you think?" she asked as I was scrolling through my phone checking for messages.

"About what?" I asked distractedly.

"Did Joe kill Shannon?"

I gave her a dark look. "That's not my job or yours," I snapped at her like a boxer about to launch into the first round. "Your job is to defend him and not let us look like a couple of amateurs." The truth was I didn't want anyone defending him.

"Whoa there." She held up her hands as if to ward off an attack. "I'm on your team remember."

"Just what are you getting at, Karen?"

She leaned forward and stared at me as if she had on a pair of X-ray glasses. "I don't know, Jack. What *am* I getting at?"

I shrugged nonchalantly despite the knots in my stomach. I had to be careful of annoying my canary in the mineshaft. I didn't want her to stop singing like Pavarotti just because I was having a bad morning. If she suspected something, someone else might, too. I had to get a grip.

"I'm sorry if I was short," I said as placatingly as I could. "I've been on edge about this case. Joe's a friend and I'm feeling pressure because of it. Maybe I'm not handling it well. You want to know if I think Joe did it? Well, I think his story about the headphones in the spa and hearing nothing is unbelievable."

"Maybe the gun was silenced."

"My guess is it wasn't. And anyway, the biggest problem is that nobody else seems to have a motive."

"What about the wife? Shannon stole her husband. What better motive for murder than that?"

"She was angry, sure. And she was suing Shannon."

She sat back in her chair, stunned. "Really?"

"According to her, she was. But that works against her doing it, doesn't it? I don't think you kill someone you're suing. You already have an outlet for your anger and once the victim is dead, it makes it hard to collect the money. You don't kill a cash cow."

I leaned back in my chair and stared at the ceiling, watching the light play across it from the ocean.

"Frankly, I don't know anyone who might have been involved enough to want her dead." I looked back at Karen. "Except Joe. And he doesn't have much of a motive, either."

I let the words linger in the air for a few seconds. "It's the weakest part of the prosecutor's case. The why. Why would he be so angry to shoot her through the heart? And as long as they don't have an answer to that question, Joe has a fighting chance."

I pulled at the collar of my shirt. The coolness of the air-conditioning had begun to dry the back of my shirt. "That's why you advised him to reject the government's offer. There is means and opportunity, sure, but you also need a motive."

"Interesting, because the coroner's report came in while you were out." She waved a document that was in her hand. "Bullet through the heart, like we already knew, and bruising on her cheek, like we knew, and one more thing."

I raised an eyebrow and waited.

"They found traces of semen in her."

I shrugged. "No surprise. She was sleeping with Joe."

"Yes, except that they did preliminary tests on the sample pending DNA typing. It turns out the semen came from someone with blood type A."

My heart skipped a few beats. "And?"

"This is where it all starts looking strange. Joe is blood type B."

I bathed my face in shock surprise.

"That's right, Jack. She *was* cheating on him. There *was* another man."

I stared at her, letting her go with it.

"He can deny knowing it all he wants, but no one is going to believe him. Shannon was cheating on him and there is the motive on a silver platter."

She was right. There was the case against my friend, strengthened right before my eyes, based ironically on my own blood antigens. I stared at her as Joe took a giant leap towards a life sentence and the whole time I was fighting the urge to smile.

18

Peter Hobson.

The name meant nothing to me at the time but Sarah had mentioned it offhandedly and then Joe had made an obvious show of knowing nothing about it. It was too much for me to leave alone.

I kept running the name Peter Hobson through my memory and I still came up with nothing.

Karen had said it for me: something wasn't right about the money. Why did Shannon, who was startlingly unromantic about love, allow her money to be put into a joint account? And where had it gone? Something that could cause a lot of harm to Joe's case was not right here and I was going to make it my number one priority to find out what it was. I didn't know what it was but I knew the name for sure now. Peter Hobson.

Had it been personal or business? Family or friend? Lawyer or client? The possibilities were endless. But I did know that he was important enough for Joe and Sarah to hide the truth, therefore important enough for me to find. There is always a trail, always a betrayal of some sort or other. To say you had a secret meant you knew something that someone else cared about. And I cared too. I decided to call Sarah.

"Sarah, I have a question."

"How's Joe?"

"About the same."

"Did you tell him I'd help? What did he say?"

"He shrugged."

"He's distraught. Give him time."

"I'd like to." *Thirty to life*, I thought. "You mentioned the name Peter Hobson."

"Did I?"

"Yes. Last time we spoke. Who is he?"

"I don't know. Maybe you were mistaken."

"No, I'm not, Sarah. Who is he? If I'm going to help Joe, I need to know everything. I need to know about Peter Hobson."

"No, Jack. You don't." And then she hung up on me.

I stared at the phone for a few seconds before I ended the call on my end as well. Something wasn't adding up. Who the hell was Peter Hobson? And why would Sarah lie?

Just then my phone rang again. I glanced down and saw *No caller ID* on the screen.

"Hello?" I asked tentatively.

"Jack." A female voice answered. "At last. I've been trying to get you all day."

"Mary? Mary O'Brien? Is that you? How did you get this number?"

"Forget that, Jack. I've been trying to let you know you've got a journalist on your tail."

My heart sank. "A pretty blonde?"

"That's right."

"What's she doing talking to you?"

"Digging around your past, it seems." I heard a clatter of something in the background.

"You didn't..."

"Of course I bloody didn't. What do you take me for? But I thought you should know. I told her off and used a few words from my profane teenager vocabulary. I was suspended a couple of times for having a sassy mouth so it was good to know I can still pull them out when needed and still have the desired effect."

"How'd she take it?"

"A little taken back but it will only slow her down temporarily. You're on her radar."

"I appreciate the call, Mary. I'll keep an eye open."

"Don't be a stranger, Jack."

"I won't." I told her. "Thanks."

I knew the pretty blonde was Sonya Martin from the Gold Coast Bulletin. She would have seen Mary and me talking at the crime scene on the night of the murder and like all reporters, she was after an exclusive. That's what I was hoping anyway. Mary's statement that she was digging around my past only made me break out in a cold sweat.

I didn't need to be distracted at the moment. I looked around the office, searching for a phone book. Behind a deserted secretary's desk, I spotted a white pages and a yellow pages and grabbed the white one. I sat down at the desk and flicked through the book to the H's.

There were three P. Hobson's on the coast. Eight in Brisbane. I would have to call them all and ask if they knew a Shannon Connor or Joseph Banner. If that didn't work, I'd have to expand my calls to interstate. It would take days but I wasn't going to stop now until I had an answer. And I *would* find an answer. I had no doubt because Joe thought his secret was safe without realising that they never are. Secrets fill voids, invades sleep, crushes joy and presses down on the soul, waiting to be found.

I would check all records and follow the slime trail. I would turn over all the rocks, one by one, until there it would lay, a fat juicy worm by the name of Peter Hobson.

19

I was going through the whole sleep deprivation thing all over again. At night in my bed, I would feel myself slipping into sleep and then something would happen and I would find myself wide-awake, staring at the ceiling as I had done just a few months ago.

In desperation, I'd pick up a book thinking it would put me to sleep. Each night after hours of tossing and turning, I'd read for more hours. Then in the mornings, more exhausted than I was the night before, I would wash the sleep from my eyes and step out into the blow-dryer-hot morning and head back to Karen's office via a coffee shop on the way. There I would sit and spread my paper across the table and usually eat eggs and bacon, drink coffee, read the comics and do the crosswords.

In Karen's part of Surfers, parking was almost impossible which probably meant that the businesses were doing well and the food in the coffee shops was good. I drove slowly up Nerang Street, past the shops in the town centre, past forest green benches, praying for someone to pull out of a park and amazingly, ahead of me, one did. I pulled in, locked the car and walked the fifty meters to a coffee shop with a lot of vacant tables and chairs on the sidewalk. It wasn't the usual kind of place I'd normally eat at, but it was only a block from the Karen's office and I was getting hungry.

There weren't too many customers at this hour but my guess was the place would be jammed inside of an hour. As I walked to a table, I glanced over to the pastries section. Danish. I have come to believe there is no food more depressing than a Danish. It's a pastry that looks stale upon arrival.

A lanky dark-haired waitress came over to serve me and told me at this time of day, I had a choice of either the 'special' breakfast or brunch menu. Without looking at the menu in her hand, I told her I'd have the breakfast option. What arrived was a large, round, brown pancake with sunflower seeds. While I stared at the pancake, I asked for coffee and syrup.

The syrup was almost transparent, so I smelled it gingerly. It didn't smell too bad. I poured it on my pancake, took a bite, then motioned for the waitress.

"What sort of pancake is this?" I asked.

"Wheat germ, sunflower seeds and soy meal," she said.

"Wheat germ and soy meal?" I asked. "Have you ever eaten one of these?"

"Yes," she said with a smile.

"And you like it?"

"Hell, no," she leant down and whispered, looking around to see if anyone had heard her. "I can't stand anything I serve here except the honey and carob shakes, and even they're not too good."

"Why do you stay?" I asked.

"Meals are free and I'm taking a pound off a week just being here. I get to meet a lot of healthy guys, too."

"Can I have the menu again please?" She pulled it out from under her arm and dropped it on the table. "Back in sec."

I pushed the plate aside and glanced back through the menu. I make a habit of avoiding healthy foods whose names I can't pronounce. Quinoa, for one. I called the waitress back and ordered what I should have ordered at the beginning. Bacon, fried eggs sunny side up, with a side order of chunky chips. It was still pretty quiet so the meal was down in front of me before I knew it and I realised I was starving. I dug in straight away and only picked up my paper after I was halfway through the meal. I opened it up and sat back contentedly with my coffee, ready to start my crossword puzzle.

There I was, safe within my exhaustion, struggling to form a word, when a man in a brown suit sat down opposite me at my table.

"What's good to eat in this place?" he said. He spoke slowly, his voice low and throaty as if his larynx had been damaged. His build, droopy brown suit, tragic tie the colour of pesto and once white wash-n-wear shirt suggested a lightweight bouncer gone to seed.

I leant back from my paper, surprised, and said, "About what you'd expect."

"What've you got there? Eggs?"

I looked down at my plate, the yolks spread like thick yellow paint over the plate and then looked past him at all the empty tables he had ignored when he sat down at my table.

"Yep," I said, as I turned back to my paper. "Eggs."

Unless it's absolutely crowded, no one sits down at someone's table, and maybe not even then. People like to sit and read and eat in their own private world, alone. I turned slightly, turning my shoulder to him and concentrated on the paper.

"I used to love bangers and eggs," said the stranger, ignoring my body language, "toast sopping with butter soaking up the yellow. But then my cholesterol shot higher than Kosciusko." He smiled at me, showing off crooked white teeth, with a large gap between the two front ones. His face was soft and round and his ears stuck out like handles. His nose was a blob and there were scars from stitches on his jawline. He was so ugly, I found myself staring.

"Hey, darlin'," he waved to the waitress. "A bowl of cornflakes here. And skim milk." He turned back to me. "Cornflakes. That's what I'm reduced to. It's a sorry sight when a man my age who has teeth like these is forced to eat cornflakes with skim milk. Right? I started eating raw garlic for a while but people stopped talking to me so now I take pills. They say garlic works wonders on the body. Next week, they'll say something else."

"Excuse me?" I asked stupidly.

"Next week. Wouldn't it be something if for once they tell us the things that actually taste good are good for us?"

I ignored him and continued with the puzzle.

"Zealot."

"What?"

"Zealot." He reached over and pointed. "The word you're stuck on."

"Do you mind?"

"Not at all. The next one is 'brandish'. I used to do them puzzles every day. It's a talent I got for taking things that are all mixed up and putting it in an order that makes sense. That's how I got into my new line of work."

"All I want to do is to finish my paper."

"Yeah. I notice a lot of guys come into places like this to be left alone. Never understood it myself. I used to be a used car salesman. When I was in the business, no one wanted to be assaulted by a salesman right off. They wanted to browse on their own. But I figure, why come into a sales office if you don't want to be sold something? You let them browse too long, next thing you know they'll browse their way over to the Toyota place across the road." He looked up at the waitress who stood at his elbow with a small box of cornflakes in a bowl and a jug of milk. "Thanks, darlin'. And more coffee when you can. Hey, you," he said to me, "you want to pass the sugar?"

He took the sugar from me and continued talking as he opened the cornflakes box and emptied them into his bowl. "Funny thing, I could always tell a cop or a lawyer when they came in. When it came down to negotiating a deal, they were like virgins in a sailor's bar. They would have done the research, sure. They'd come in thinking they knew it all, when really they knew nothing."

As he talked, he slopped milk into the bowl, covering the cornflakes, then began shovelling them into his mouth, chewing as he talked. "Because what was important wasn't the crap they thought they knew, it was how much the dealer was paying in the first place, how desperate was the cash-flow situation. Is my slurping bothering you?"

Bits of cornflakes sprayed from his mouth and I tried to ignore them. "Good," he continued before I said anything. "The cornflakes are good with skim milk. You wouldn't think so, but they are. Anyway, where was I? the cops and lawyers would bypass the salesman and sit down with the assistant manager, which is like bypassing the whiting and going straight for the shark. Frigging cops."

By now my face was out of the paper and I was openly staring at the man opposite me. The hairs on the back of my neck prickled. *There's something about you*, I thought. *Something I don't like.*

"You know what they should teach you first in cop school?" he said as the waitress poured more coffee into our cups. "Thanks darlin'. They should teach you that maybe you don't know everything you think you know. They should teach you that if a deal for some reason is too good to be true, then maybe you should jump off your arse and grab it before it disappears. Maybe sometimes you should advise people to take the damn deal before something bad happens, before something awful happens, that will ruin your day. What do you think?"

More slurping, this time the coffee. Everything about him was relaxed except his brain. I felt my own brain stretching, trying to follow what was going on.

"What line of work did you say you were in?" I asked.

"Nowadays?" He dabbed his mouth with a serviette. "I solve problems bigger than those puzzles you're doing." He nodded down at my paper. "If things don't add up, I find sense of it and make them add up in a way that makes everybody wins. Even me."

He broke into a smile like everything was a mystery then he reached into his pocket and pulled out his wallet. He put a ten down on the table and called to the waitress. "Here you go, darlin'. Keep the change."

"Do you have a card?" I asked.

"Nah. Those who need me know where to find me."

"Can I ask a favour?"

"Shoot. Excuse the expression."

"Next time you want to send me a message, just fax me."

He stared at me with his piggy eyes for a long moment, the geniality slowly draining from his face.

"Don't get too smart with me. I just passed on some good advice to you. I'm doing you a favour and giving you some very useful information. Forget your snooping around about this Peter Hobson. He's not important. What *is* important is that you do the right thing. Take the deal because it's good. It ends everything and keeps everybody happy."

"Who sent you?"

"See, there you go, Jack. You think you know everything like these lawyers, just like you think you knew all about her. But you didn't. You think you understood her but you understood nothing. She was just a fancy watch, all slim-line and sleek on the outside, but inside she had wheels spinning every which way. And you just never knew."

"And you did?"

His head jiggled from side to side. "We understood each other, her and me. We got along. We had things in common and she talked to me."

"About what?"

"You know. About her affairs and such." He wiggled his eyebrows and smiled.

I didn't say anything. I just stared. He smiled broader and leaned so close I was glad he had stopped eating garlic. He was so close his whisper was like a roar.

"I know," he said, as he tapped his head.

"Know what?"

"You know."

"No, I don't know."

"Your little no-no." He wagged his index finger at me and smiled. "I know."

I stood abruptly, as if the secret had propelled itself off my chair. I didn't say anything and I didn't leave. I just stood and listened.

"She told me herself," he said, "but I assure you, Jack, I'm not here to hurt you. I'm here to help you. It's safe with me, your little secret. I don't have a wish to spread it around. But don't be like those lawyers who think they know everything. Tell them to take the deal. It wasn't a picnic getting the prosecutor to go for a plea and don't think we can keep it on the table forever. Forget Peter Hobson and take the deal. Put everything right and no one ends up knowing a thing and we all get to go home happy."

He nodded at me, pushed himself off the seat and turned to the door. He had a strange waddling walk. Then he turned and waddled back.

"You were in the house alone after she was killed, right?"

I said nothing.

"An item is missing. No bigger than a key, if you catch my drift." He wiggled his eyebrows again. "Know what I mean? It wasn't logged in by the detectives and it seems to be no longer in the house."

"How would you know?" I blurted out, my gaze dropping to his hands now in his pockets,

He ignored my question. "You didn't happen to lift the item whilst inside the house, did you now Jack?"

I couldn't answer, and I was too stunned to deny it. I stood there shaking and mute. But it wasn't the type of question that needed an answer. I got the idea this man didn't need any answers from anyone, especially me.

"G'day, Jack." He smiled. "By the way, the name's Fitzroy. Frank Fitzroy."

I watched him push open the door and head down the street.

20

———

I sat back down heavily at the table in a daze. He knew. The bastard Fitzroy knew. I could have bluffed him out with denial after denial but what good would that have done? The truth was there written all over his ugly face. He knew. But how?

Because Shannon told him. Like he said, they had an understanding. Things in common. But Shannon and Fitzroy? What the hell could they possibly have in common? But Fitzroy knew, no doubt about that, and there was no telling what he could do with what he knew.

My mind was in a panic. Had I looked guilty when I stared into his eyes? I stared down into my plate, dried yellow yolk and soggy potatoes covering it. The greasy slop made my stomach turn and I suddenly felt nauseous. There is always a faint tinge of nausea after a heavy meal but this was something else, something far richer and justly deserved.

What the hell did I think I was doing? I had slept with my friend's fiancée, I had taken evidence from the scene of her murder and now I was pretending to help my friend while secretly, I hoped he burned in hell.

In my mind when I played it out, it all sounded very logical, even inevitable, but now I could see the end result as humiliation. Mine. I was a fool, in way over my head, and making mistake after mistake. Just great for an ex-cop.

I closed my eyes to let the nausea fade but it didn't. It twisted inside my stomach until I stood up shakily and made my way past tables to the toilet.

The place was filthy and small, the floor was wet with something I really didn't want to think about and the bin was full and overflowing. It smelled like, well, a toilet. I leaned over the sink and looked at myself in the mirror. My breath was coming out in panicky puffs and my face was shiny and green. What the hell was I going to do? What?

Inside my head, my good angel was saying *'Give it up and let vengeance fade. Back away from it all and hope it all turns out all right. If that doesn't work, own up to the truth.'* My bad angel cut in. *'To hell with that, be a man and brazen it out. Send Joe to jail where he belongs.'* I had to admit I liked the second choice better.

I bent over the sink and rinsed my overheated face and felt the nausea rise and fall again. Fitzroy had said the secret was safe with him and he only wanted to help. But inside, I knew there would be more visits, more threats until the bastard got his way.

As I leant my head against the wall, I saw the solution. Give him what he wanted. Tell Joe to take the plea. Fitzroy wanted it, Karen wanted it, even Joe was turning that way. That was it. The easiest way out and the most obvious. But a plea would hardly avenge Shannon's murder and Fitzroy would still hold the sword of knowledge over my head.

I stared at my red-rimmed eyes in the mirror then reached for a paper towel to wipe my face. I rinsed out my mouth and felt a little better with my emotions now settled. Slowly, I began to calm but I could still see his face.

What the hell was his game? Obviously, money. Wasn't it strange that a case I thought was caused through passion and rage had this underlying theme of money everywhere I looked? The money in the envelope. The money in Joe's suitcase. The funds mysteriously missing from the bank account that Joe and Shannon had fought about. The strange connection to Sarah suing Shannon because she thought she had money and the mentioning of Peter Hobson. Hadn't she then tried to brush it off? I still had no doubt who had pulled the trigger, but Joe's motivation might not be as simple as I had imagined. I remembered the look on his face when he learned that the bank account was empty. Money, money, money. Why should I have been so surprised?

And Fitzroy. What was his relationship with Brad Jefferson? Why did he want Joe to plead? And how did a creep like Fitzroy get an estimable lawyer like Jefferson to offer such a plea in the first place? The answer was clear. He didn't. Someone else did. Frank Frigging Fitzroy had used the first-person plural and my guess is he was not the type to routinely use the royal 'we.'

Joe had said that Fitzroy worked with Matthew Simmons, Sarah's father, at one time. Odds on, that's who he was still working for and Matthew Simmons was the other part of 'we'. Maybe I should storm over and talk to Simmons, see what I could shake up. Except, I knew Matthew Simmons. I'd even met him at Joe and Sarah's wedding. He had nodded at me brusquely and then ignored me like I wasn't worth the effort. He wouldn't shake easily.

Something was eluding me, something basic that explained everything.

I took a deep breath and then another, telling myself that panic is useless. Now with my breakfast down the toilet, I could think clearly and calmly.

Frigging Frank Fitzroy.

Peter Hobson.

Matthew Simmons.

Three names that somehow connected together. How? Or was it more than three? Was Joe in this also?

It came to me in a flash of brilliant insight. It came to me because I was standing in a stinking toilet having just thrown up and realised how low it was possible to go. It came to me because I was treading the same path as Shannon had, and so I could see the footprints of the previous traveller as clearly as I was seeing my own. It came to me and then seemed so obvious that I could barely believe I hadn't seen it before.

Not only did I know how I could find out exactly who Peter Hobson was, but also exactly what he could do for me. He would get Fitzroy off my back and bring Matthew Simmons in line.

If I played this right, Peter Hobson would also convict Joe Banner of first-degree murder as if Hobson had actually seen Joe fire that shot into Shannon's heart.

I was going to head off straight away to the clerk's office in the courthouse and search through past cases that involved a Peter Hobson. Docket sheets were a manner of public property and anyone with time on their hands could walk into the courthouse and request to view the files. Simple as that.

All I needed was to bring his name and his story to the proper authorities so that the ridiculous plea offer would be withdrawn. All I needed was a way to introduce Peter Hobson to Brad Jefferson without seeming to be aware of what I was doing. All I needed was a clever plan that could be done by proxy if needed. A plan so dirty that it would exhibit a complete lack of moral fibre.

I was certainly the right man for the job.

21

———

The parking garage to Simmons, Ryan & Holzman's office was gated and the gate wouldn't open until a gentleman in a blue blazer strolled over and asked my name and who I had come to see. He was polite and discreet as was the bulge in his coat. He kept a close eye on me as he leant in and asked my name and business. Apparently satisfied that I didn't look like a terrorist, he let me in to the garage, giving me directions on where the lift to the foyer was situated. Another guard in a blazer smiled at me in the foyer as metal doors opened with a whoosh. This one would take me to the top floors, he assured me. A third guard just happened to be in the lift and I glanced at his name badge. Ben. Like the guards in the garage and the foyer, he had the corded neck of a man who spends a lot of his time honing confrontational skills. Corded necks are a dead giveaway.

The painful strains of sitar music blending with cascading waterfalls filled the stingy compartment, barely room for the two of us. This mingling of sounds I find as soothing as fingernails on a blackboard. The odour of ripe sweat didn't help either.

"Are you guys from Australia's Funniest Home Videos?" I asked. Not surprisingly, there wasn't a reply.

I could feel the pack working as I walked on the marble floor towards the reception desk of Simmons, Ryan & Holzman. Marble floors are bad for noise suppression. I could hear them all, drafting and faxing, answering phones, trading insults with insults, dealing, hustling, refusing offers, filing interrogations, coaching witnesses, browbeating, snapping pencils, complaining with righteous indignation, filing motions to dismiss, exploding with bursts of calculated anger, hiring jury consultants, settling, settling and more settling. Standing there was like standing close to a hive of drones and feeling the vibrations of their wings beating in crazy disorder towards a common goal – honey. Or in this case - money.

I moved towards the reception desk where a young woman sat listening to someone talking on the phone. As she listened, she picked up a ballpoint pen and began clicking. Impatiently, she put the pen down and began to arrange a row of paper clips on the side of a magnetised holder on her desk. Each one was exactly the same distance apart. I'd dealt with people like her before. She would be a stickler for detail and an avid enforcer of the rules. As I waited, she finished the conversation and put the phone down then looked up at me with a half smile on her face.

"How can I help you?"

"Matthew Simmons, please," I smiled.

"Do you have an appointment, sir?"

"No, I don't."

"Then I'm sorry. Mr Simmons is a very busy man. You will need to make an appointment."

As a policeman, I'd heard the words 'piss off' more times than most, outside of journalists. I am a connoisseur of the phrase and I can detect even the slightest nuance when it's encoded in other words that are usually benign. Sometimes 'piss off' is yelled at you (from a spittle flecked mouth) from someone in eye-bulging fury and sometimes, the message is ambiguously spoken in mellow tones by smiling women who click pens. This woman was trying to smile at me but the unspoken message from the pouty lips was clearly 'piss off'.

"Please get him on the phone."

The smile immediately disappeared and she stared at me in stony silence.

"He'll see me," I stated. "Tell him it's Jack Curtis. Tell him I'm here to talk about his son-in-law."

She sighed heavily and said, "Could you take a seat for just a moment, please?"

She waved a hand vaguely towards a couple of chairs. Her manner suggested that I was making an unreasonable demand on her time.

The chairs were made of soft leather and they moulded comfortably to my body so I was happy to wait for a while. I leant over and shuffled through several outdated issues of magazines that were scattered on top of the table. Home Beautiful. House and Garden. New Idea. Why is it that offices only have women's magazines? Do they think men don't read?

I picked up an issue of House and Garden and for the next few minutes, I flicked through articles on making your own jewellery, the joys of waxing your floor to a mirror shine, growing herbs and easy craft projects meant for Mum as Christmas approaches. That was sufficient time for me to be convinced that there were subjects here I had never dreamed about. To me, it was like life on another planet. All ads showed perfect women with perfect bodies and perfect complexions. All had snowy white teeth. None had hips like fleshy jodhpurs pulling their slacks out of shape. None had cellulite or varicose veins. No droopy breasts either. These perfect women lived in beautiful houses full of state-of-the-art appliances and fluffy dogs but there were never any men to be seen. Were these magazines the castoffs from Sarah? I understand these are purely models we are meant to believe are housewives but from my prospective, they have no connection with my world consisting of death, celibacy and fast food. Probably just as well. What would I do with containers full of tarragon and coriander anyway?

Ten minutes later, Simmons walked out of his office, followed by a burly guy whose nose looked like it had been broken badly at some time in his life. Simmons gave me a look that told me to follow him and the three of us clip-clopped off towards a nearby office. Burly guy opened the door for Simmons then gave me a look as hard as steel as I entered next. Once I was in the room, he shut the door and stood behind Simmons with his hands crossed protectively in front of his crotch.

The office was obviously a conference room. In the middle of the room sat a huge table with a dozen chairs. A bank of windows displayed waves crashing on Surfers Paradise beach while palm trees swayed lazily in the breeze. It was a wonder any work got done in here with a view like that.

Simmons was wearing a black suit, a starched white shirt and a bright red tie. He waved his hand at a chair, inviting me to sit, and then walked around to the other side of the table and sat opposite me. With the sunlight shining behind him like a halo, he seemed taller than his five feet eight inches tall and his tie glowed brilliantly. Almost like an angel. Almost.

"What can I do for you, Mr Curtis?" Simmon's voice was calm as he looked at me with a composed expression. "Please make it quick. I'm very busy."

If there was annoyance there, he wasn't showing it. But I knew there was irritation lurking in there. Image meant a lot to this guy. He was the sort of person who belonged to the class of entitled super-wealthy and deluded themselves into believing they earned their money the old-fashioned way ... with hard work.

"I'd like to have a word with you about..."

"Have we met before?" he interrupted. His head tilted to the side and his eyes squinted as they searched my face.

I nodded slowly. "At Joe and Sarah's wedding."

Disgust twisted his hard features as if something was stuck in his throat. "You're Banner's friend. The detective."

I nodded but I didn't correct him. I wanted him to believe I had some weight behind me in the investigation.

"I'm here to ask you why you are so anxious for Joe to plead to a lesser charge."

His eyes flashed anger and he had a lawyer's way of turning every declarative statement into a barroom brawl. "Don't be damned ridiculous."

"This morning, a man by the name of Frank Fitzroy," I left out the adjective that had become his middle name for me, "invaded my breakfast at a coffee shop."

His tongue moved around inside his cheek like he was trying to dislodge something out of his teeth. "Fitzroy? Frank Fitzroy, you say? Never heard of him."

I raised an eyebrow. "Really? In our conversation, Fitzroy wanted me to convince Joe and his lawyer to accept the plea. In fact, he wanted it so badly he turned the request into a threat. I assumed he was speaking on your behalf since Joe told me he did work for your firm. If he wasn't speaking for you, then the detective investigating the murder will want to speak to him about his interest in this case. I thought I'd check with you first before I head on over to the police station. They'll be more than happy to listen to me."

I stared calmly at him and he stared fiercely back with his blue obsidian eyes. He reminded me of Richard Gere. He was a well-built but shortish man with little blue eyes burning as bright as his tie. His hair had silver threads running through it, giving him a distinguished look that women love. I remembered then that his wife was unusually large and that the two of them were a mismatched comic-looking couple, but no one ever laughed.

"Mr Fitzroy," he said finally, "is occasionally contracted by this firm to provide investigative service. He may have taken it upon himself to voice my concerns about the effects of a lengthy murder trial on my daughter."

"He threatened me, Mr Simmons."

"Very unfortunate."

"I don't like to be threatened."

"Things happen all the time to us that we don't like. To be honest, I don't want to see that bastard Joe Banner's face staring back at me from the newspapers for the next six to twelve months. I don't want them talking about my daughter and I don't want her to be forced to testify. The tragedies of my family should stay out of the tabloids. I want this over with. Is that clear enough for you?"

"Your concern for your family is touching."

He shrugged. "So you're touched. Will that be all? I have a client waiting for me in my office."

"Give him a Home Beautiful to read. Or the newspaper. Tell him there's a great crossword in it and to do it while he waits. Give him a clue to help him out. The answer for thirteen across is zealot. But enough of this chitchat. I have more questions for you."

"You may have questions but I have no answers. You can send Banner's lawyer over here in the future if there are any questions. Good day, Mr Curtis. We are through."

He started the long walk around the table to the door.

"Would you like to be subpoenaed, Mr Simmons? Because Joe's lawyer has one in her briefcase right now."

"I'll quash it."

"Quash away. We'll quash right back. Karen Sawyer was a quash champion in university. And then, when you're under oath, maybe she'll start asking about the promises you made to Brad Jefferson's future aspirations in exchange for a quick plea."

He stopped dead. "There were no promises."

"Call them what you want. The only way an opportunist person like Jefferson backs away from a high-profile murder trial is if the payoff is higher than all his appearances in the six o'clock news."

"Brad Jefferson is a young man with sterling qualities who would be an asset in any role."

"Yes, and he'd have a nice jump-start, too. But that's not what's going on, is it? Why are you trying to end this case before it starts?"

"I told you. My family..."

"Try again."

"My daughter..."

"Sorry. Wrong answer again. Unless your daughter's name is Peter Hobson."

Simmons head jerked in his starched collar as he inhaled sharply.

He turned his head towards Mr Muscle standing behind him, still protecting his crotch with both hands.

"You may leave us, Michael."

Michael's eyes flashed towards Simmons uncertainly before they turned uncertainly back to me.

"Sir?"

Simmons pressed his lips together tightly. "I'm fine, Michael. Thank you. Close the door behind you, please."

On his way to the door, Michael glared at me but said nothing. In the silence, Simmons took hold of the closest chair and sat down unsteadily. *That* was the reaction I was looking for.

"I don't know what you're talking about." His voice had lost its iron edge.

"I can understand why you wanted it kept a secret."

I'd already done my homework. I'd already been to the courthouse and found the file and public documents I needed.

"Peter Hobson was connected to MIA Insurance. They're your oldest and largest client. Their money bought you this building and decorated it for you. It keeps you well fed and well dressed. You could have told them what happened from the start but you kept it from them, kept it your dirty little secret. If they find out now, it will irrevocably destroy the relationship you have with them. They'll leave and tell others and the scandal will ruin you. Who would trust you after that? I certainly wouldn't. It would be over for Simmons, Ryan & Holzman. Except with Centrelink."

"Don't be ridiculous," he almost whispered.

"I can tell by the look on your face I'm right. What I don't understand is how you expected it to remain a secret. It wasn't hidden, really. All it took was a visit to the clerk's office, a review of the case files, the discovery of a medical malpractice action entitled *Peter Hobson v Dr Hugh Oliver*. The whole story is there. I found it after Fitzroy left me this morning, after our little breakfast. I'd like to thank him for that." I gave him my best smile. My Hugh Grant. "Representing the plaintiff was Shannon Connor. Representing the defendant doctor and insurance company was Joseph Banner. Oh, and not only was Joe's name listed, your name is at the top of the list of lawyers and you were the billing lawyer. It was on that case that he met Shannon Connor, wasn't it? It was during that lengthy litigation that he dined her, romanced her and seduced her. And after the settlement, after the three million dollars was handed over from the insurance company to Peter Hobson, a man entering hospital for routine surgery and leaving in a coma, Joe ditched your daughter and your firm, to move in with Shannon Connor. Living on her share of the award, her half a million dollars."

"It was a solid case," said Simmons. "And the settlement was fair. For three million dollars, MIA escaped exposure that could have crippled them."

"Maybe, but I don't think so. There was some piece of evidence that Joe hid until the settlement was signed and the money paid, and he and Shannon had the money safely in the bank. Otherwise he would have just dropped the case once the relationship started. Shannon would have insisted on it. Why allow a tinge of impropriety to hazard a settlement?" My index finger pointed towards the ceiling and my face registered surprise, like an idea had just come to me. "Unless it was the only way to get the half a million dollars in the first place."

I smiled at him. "I had wondered why Shannon's huge fee was placed in a joint account and now I know. Because they both earned it. And you knew about it. You knew and you kept it a secret. That's why you want the plea accepted. That's why you sent Fitzroy to threaten me."

This last part about the hidden evidence was guesswork, but it was a guess that made sense and by Matthew Simmons reaction, a sort of nervous head bouncing, I was sure that my guess was spot on.

"You have no proof."

I did a little shrug then said, "I don't need proof. It won't be too hard to find out what it was that Joe hid, now that I know what to look for. And wouldn't MIA be as interested as hell in seeing the result for themselves?"

He turned pale, then lost so much colour I thought he was going to collapse on the floor in front of me. Then suddenly, he composed himself as if a switch had been turned on. He took off his spectacles and cleaned the lenses with his bright red tie.

"That would destroy this firm's reputation," he said calmly. "I can't allow that to happen."

"Ah. So it's *not* the family you're concerned about after all."

"We all have our priorities. What do you want?"

And there you have it. The negotiations had begun. I was impressed with Simmons' performance after having taken the shot, then recovered, and now was ready to take control of the situation again. Good for me.

"We both have an interest in this," I lied. "If this becomes public, it will look bad for Joe. His lawyer could turn it around and paint Shannon Connor as the schemer behind it all, reduce natural sympathy for the victim, but it still complicates things as far as motive is concerned. And of course, to you it would be devastating. I believe it is within our best interests to work together and keep it quiet."

He blinked and nodded slowly. "But what do *you* want?"

"I want Frank Fitzroy off my back."

"Agreed. I'll tell him."

I gave him my look. The one that stresses I'm not messing around. "I mean it. I don't want to see him again or talking to anyone about this case in any way. Maybe he should take a vacation until this is all cleared up."

"I'm sure that can be arranged."

"One word," I warned with an index finger held up, "and I'll leak out the information and everyone will know that not only did Joe do it, but you knew about it too."

"You've made yourself clear."

"I also assume that there are documents to show what Joe did. A file?"

"Maybe there is."

"I don't want anyone to control that information but me. I want that file and all copies of it. We can't afford this to slip out."

"That may prove difficult. If there is a file, I certainly don't have it."

I hesitated for a second. "Are you kidding me?"

"Do I look like I'm kidding, Mr Curtis?"

"That must keep you awake at night."

"Well, my wife snores so I don't get much sleep anyway."

"Any idea where it is?"

"Ask your friend."

I sat for a moment, tapping my chin. "Okay," I said standing up. "You talk to Fitzroy." I turned to face the door and then stopped, turned around again. This was the crucial moment. What I had to say had to seem off-hand and incidental. "By the way, about your daughter's divorce. Don't be too sure about it."

"What do you mean?"

"Your daughter wants him back."

"Of course she doesn't."

I wiggled an eyebrow. "You're wrong. I visited her." I hate to admit it, but I was enjoying myself. He'd paled and I could see his breathing had become shallow by the rise and fall of his shiny tie. "She wants everything the way it was before. Which, I assume, includes Joe getting his job back here with your illustrious firm. She agreed to put up the house for his bail."

"She...what? She can't be serious." His voice softened.

He didn't react like I expected. Instead of exploding in anger, he looked away from me and his forehead creased in thought. "She can't," he said matter-of-factly. "It's not hers to put up."

"Pardon me?"

"I co-signed the mortgage. She can't do a thing unless I agree and I won't put up a cent to get that bastard out of jail. Not one cent." He turned quickly and stared at me. "That's not part of the deal, is it?"

I made it sound like I'd think about it for a moment or so before smiling to myself. "No. Better not to tip our hand. If you agreed to bail him out it would seem suspicious."

He shook his head. "How could she be such a fool?" His voice now was pensive and his gaze went back on the window.

I said something to end the meeting but he didn't respond. He just kept staring, so I left without saying another word.

22

———————

K aren, crisp looking in a white shirt, dark-wash jeans and bright blue heels, stared at me. "If this leaks out, it would devastate Joe's defence. He wants us to pursue the lover as the killer. That's fine. In a lover's triangle, it's easy enough to point the finger at the missing member."

"So to speak," I said.

I wanted to ask, *Isn't this what a guilty person – nervous and conniving – would say?* Exactly the same thing. On the other hand, and it was a big hand, even O.J. Simpson had sounded sincere as he vowed to find his wife's killer.

"But money trumps love," she continued. "If they can show monetary motive for Joe's anger, like being cheated out of money stolen together, we're dead in the water."

"I know," I said. I was feeling very proud of myself.

"And if Brad Jefferson finds out, he'll withdraw the plea offer in a heartbeat."

"I know that, too."

"Then maybe we should accept before it disappears."

I did a so-so thing with my head. "Maybe we should talk to Joe first. We need to hear his side of this."

She nodded slowly as she searched my face. "Of course we should talk to Joe first. What I'm saying is we can't afford to wait too long." Her eyes locked on mine. "What aren't you telling me Jack?"

I held my hands wide. "You know everything I know."

She shook her head slowly. "No. There's something, Jack. Something you know that I don't. What is it? I can't defend him if there's a white elephant in the room that I can't see."

I avoided her gaze. "Joe and Shannon had the money, didn't they?"

"Yes," she said slowly.

"And Shannon transferred it out of their joint account, didn't she?"

"Again, yes."

I shrugged. "Well maybe Joe knew about it and he reacted badly. Maybe it's Joe who's hiding something."

"Then I'll repeat myself," she said. "We can't afford to wait too long."

She stared at me but I refused to stare back.

"I've been wondering why you don't push Joe to accept the plea. At first, I thought it was because you liked being back in the newspapers and the news. Then I thought you just wanted to keep this alive so you could bury yourself in detecting work again. But I never thought it was because you believed Joe is innocent. Do you, Jack?"

"What?"

"Do you believe he's innocent?"

I turned to face her. "I told you before, it doesn't matter."

"Yes, it does."

"Okay. How would you feel if you learned that Joe was absolutely guilty? We have his fingerprints on the gun, the improbability of his story and the lack of evidence of a break-in. Add it all up and doesn't the total equals guilty? How would you feel about defending him then?"

"I would feel lousy about it."

"But you'd still defend him to the best of your abilities?"

"Yes. That's my job."

"I'm talking about what you *think* about the job."

"Sometimes it's rotten."

"There you go."

"Do you believe he did it?"

"I'm saying I'm in a tough situation but I'm doing the best I can."

"You usually do."

"Thank you."

"But sometimes you do it for the wrong reasons."

I didn't ask her what she meant so I ignored the statement. She scratched her neck and tilted her head as if she was trying to find the missing piece to explain everything. She didn't have it, I knew, and she wouldn't get it if I had anything to say about it. What Shannon and I shared was a secret and even if Frigging Fitzroy knew, that would be where it ended. I had seen to that.

"You look terrible," she said softly.

"Thank you."

"Are you okay?" she persisted.

I looked across the table at her and I knew there was more to her than a pretty face and a great figure. She had no sharp edges and she never seemed rattled. And she was smart.

When I didn't reply she said, "You have bags under your eyes Qantas would make you check in."

"I like to read at night."

"Must be good reading."

"A classic."

It was time for me to bring her on side. It was time for Joe to confess, if only to his friend who was helping to investigate the case and his lawyer. Nothing admissible in court but enough to get Karen to work *with* me rather than *against* me. I needed to get the truth out of him, and I knew how to squeeze it out.

Peter Hobson.

23

Hindsight is a wonderful thing. Six months before the nightmare began, I walked into Billy's Beach House to see Joe sitting at the bar on a stool nursing what I knew was a Jack Daniels on ice in one hand and a cigarette in the other. It was a Sunday night and the band was playing to a packed crowd. The sound of laughter filled the bar and as I sat down on a stool next to him and he gave me an enigmatic look, something you'd expect from Al Pacino.

That was the first sign I missed.

"You look beat," I said, ordering a Jack of my own.

"I am. I told the management committee on Friday I need some help but they just said to make my people work harder." He shook his head. "Look at me. It's a bloody Sunday and I've been at work all day."

"Why don't you just leave your father-in-law's firm? You know you could get a job anywhere you want."

He'd laughed a little. "Nah. Getting too old to start over again. In any case, I'm twelve months away from getting a promotion to partnership. The pay increase will help with Sarah and her passion for redecorating the house. Leaving now would only be going backwards."

A year ago, Joe would have turned the heads of a lot of women. Of late, I noticed he'd aged ten years and looked fifty instead of forty. He was drinking and smoking more and I noticed the suit he was wearing was looking tight. It must have cost him over three thousand dollars but there was a trail of cigarette ash down the front of his shirt and tie.

He squinted at me through the cigarette smoke. "You think I'm crazy, don't you?" he said.

I shook my head. "I didn't say that."

"Your silence is deafening."

"It has its advantages, you know," he continued. "When Sarah is happy, life is pretty good for me." He shrugged. "I had an itch and I scratched it. I come here because she won't let me smoke in the house. She says it leaves a smell over everything, including her. Says it will kill me one day." He gave a quick bark that doubled as a laugh. "Be glad for the rest."

He was looking at me over the top of his glass. His words had been slurred but the waiter still deposited another Jack Daniels in front of him. He spun the glass around making little watermarks on the top of the bar before drinking it down in one gulp.

"You disillusioned with Sarah?" I asked.

"Is that what it looks like? Nah. I knew what she was like when we got married. She's tidying me up and I'm an old dog learning new tricks."

"Just don't slip up and pee on my leg."

"Jack," he said in a mock reprimand. "You're my friend. Would I do that?"

He took a sip of his drink and somewhere in the back of my mind, I had the thought that there was something else going on. That was the second sign. He was still the same old Joe, but there was something else going on that I couldn't put my finger on. A contemplative look about him as if the wheels were grinding away in his head.

"You sure you're okay?"

He glanced up for a second then went back to swirling his drink.

"You ever wonder about fate, Jack? What it has in store for you? Where you're headed?"

"All the time. It doesn't help to ponder too much on it though. The definition of fate is the development of events outside of a person's control. It determines what will happen no matter what you do. Like in the movie Sliding Doors. It doesn't matter what you do, the result will always be the same."

"Kind of a meant to be, you're saying?"

"That's my take on it."

He nodded, lost in thought. Eventually he said, "Like meeting someone for the first time and thinking, *"This is it."*

That was the third sign.

I nodded thoughtfully as I watched him.

"I guess that's how it was with you and Sarah. Right?"

He gave a small smile that didn't quite reach his eyes.

"Something like that."

He stood up a little shakily at that point and with a slap on my back, he said, "That's me for the night, Jack. I'd better get home to the little woman. She'll be waiting up for me."

24

———

It was like banging your head against a brick wall.

Joe denied all knowledge of Peter Hobson. He denied knowing the specifics of the case where Shannon won her big fee. He explained that the only reason the money was in a joint account was that they were in love and that's what lovers do. They shared their lives. Joe said he wasn't really upset that the money was missing because the majority had been Shannon's anyway. He again claimed he hadn't killed her, that he loved her and couldn't have hurt her for the world.

Karen and I listened and then she brought out the docket sheet for Peter Hobson that I'd copied from the clerk's office. She placed it in front of Joe and he looked down at it, then up at us, then back down at the paper. His grey face turned greyer and the twitch on lips was grotesque.

"Who else knows about this?" he asked.

"Just us and your father-in-law," I said.

"Oh, God." He put his head in his hands. "I didn't kill her. I swear."

I sighed. "You can't tell us that and expect us to believe you when you lie about everything else. We don't have anything left here, Joe. We have to know everything. From the beginning."

He stared down at the docket sheet and closed his eyes. "I need a cigarette."

I've been a non-smoker for six months or more but I always keep a *dare-you* pack in my pocket just for the reassurance of knowing that I can if I really have to. I reached into the pocket and took out the pack of cigarettes and a bic lighter and tossed it across the table at Joe.

Karen and I waited in silence while he lit up and breathed the smoke deeply into his lungs. His eyes remained closed for a long time and then they finally opened.

"I made a decision and it turned out bad."

I nodded. "Leaving Sarah for another woman," I stated.

"No," he said. "Before Shannon. The decision to be a lawyer."

"Oh, for God's sake, Joe...." I began with exasperation.

"Hear me out here, Jack. I worked harder than most just to get average grades at university and when I got a job, I put my head down and put in the long hours. I got married and things didn't change. I had to work harder at the marriage than at my job. Then one day, I met Sarah and I left my wife. I figured it had happened, the change. I was someone shiny and new. And in no time, I had a fantastic income with my new father-in-law, a big house, parties and the good life. The goddamned good life. I'm not complaining here or trying to make out I'm the victim. None of this was done to me. I chose it. But even so, something was wrong. I suppose after four years I was still uncomfortable in a suit and tie. I hated my job, hated the work and hated the firm."

He sighed deeply and tapped the ash into an empty Styrofoam coffee cup on the table.

"It all began in a hospitable room. There had been a bad result to a simple surgery. The doctor had notified the insurance company and they had notified Simmons, Ryan and Holzman. In my briefcase was a contract that I was to have the wife sign, a contract that would guarantee the patient's medical care in exchange for an agreement to waiver any claims for future pain and suffering. Hey, bad things happen sometimes and it's nobody's fault. That was our motto at Simmons, Ryan and Holzman. For a while, I sat with the patient in his room. He had intravenous lines running out of his arms, a catheter and a respirator tube down his throat. That man was Peter Hobson."

Joe took a drag of his cigarette before he continued. "He had once been a handsome man. Played tennis and raised a family and worked hard. I looked at him lying lifeless in the bed and in a way I envied him. For him, it was over. That was how far I had fallen – I envied a man in a coma. Then Mrs Hobson walked into the room."

His voice was monotone as he stared down at the table telling his story. "She was a nice lady, sweet and scared. She was worried about her future and her family's and her ability to care for her husband. They had no hospital insurance and I commiserated. In my job, I had become good at commiserating. I was dressed in black and I must have seemed like an undertaker, but I told her I was there to help. In any way I could. I asked her if she was happy with the room, the nursing and the care given to her husband. Anything we can do to help, I said. You shouldn't worry about the hospital bills. I would personally make sure all bills were paid. We wanted to take care of her. I asked her how things were at home. How she was coping. Anything I could do to help, I kept repeating. Anything. I was on her side."

He looked up and gave me a sardonic smile "It was all going so well that I had the brief out and at the crucial moment when Mrs Hobson was about to sign of her own free will with no coercion on my part and the deal would have been closed, a voice from the doorway called out, *'Stop!'* When I turned, I saw a pair of crimson lips set in a pale face. They were smirking at me and I couldn't turn away. I stood and stared. Of course, there was the body too, small and frail even in the suit she wore but it was those red lips, that vivid colour that startled me."

His lips twisted at the memory. "I remember stammering that this was a private meeting and she replied, *'Not anymore.'* The lips widened showing perfect teeth and the pink tip of her tongue. She was sticking her tongue out at me." He smiled sadly at the memory.

"She said that Mrs Hobson's daughter had asked her to come and that she was a lawyer. I tried to get rid of her but at the mention of her daughter, Mrs Hobson put down the pen. It was over. I put the paper back in my briefcase and snapped it shut before turning to Mrs Hobson and saying that I hoped everything turned out well for her and her family. As I walked to the door, the woman lawyer said to my back, *'I'll be in touch.'* I remember hesitating and fought the urge to turn around and see her once more. Instead, I continued out the door and what I was seeing as I walked down the corridor wasn't my failure, but a pair of crimson lips and the tip of her pink tongue. She had said she would be in touch and I was hoping she would be."

A memory surfaced of Shannon mouthing the words, *'Call me'* and I knew just like me Joe had been hooked from the start.

"She did and that was how it all started."

I glanced at Karen to see if she was as impatient as I was to get on with the story. Karen was sitting back relaxed, her eyes never leaving Joe's.

I let Joe continue.

"She made all the calls, at least at the start. She asked me questions about the case and details about the settlement even before she filed. And then there were the other calls, not strictly necessary calls that ended on a light and flirty note."

He reached over and poured himself a glass of water from a jug sitting in the middle of the table. Karen and I waited in silence as he took a gulp then continued. "I began thinking of her at odd moments, her lips, her laughter, her tongue, her cheekbones. In the grey of my life, she was the colour. Her calls became the highlight of my day. Then we began to meet for lunch and that went on to us meeting for drinks after work. It all happened so slowly."

As I listened, I shifted uneasily.

"She filed her lawsuit on behalf of Peter Hobson and his family and I responded. In addition to our business calls, we left each other more personal messages about the Gibson case, named for her favourite movie star. That was our code...the Gibson case. Almost every day, we met somewhere and drank martinis and avoided talking about what we were both doing there. We sat close while we drank and we shared cigarettes while our knees bumped under the table. We never talked about anything personal, but we talked."

I was listening to his story with growing horror and when he stopped, I almost had to shake myself back into the world. The room was exactly the same as before. Dull grey and lit by fluorescent lights humming on the ceiling. The barred windows were still there but my universe had shifted.

Listening to Joe tell his story was for me like falling headfirst into a chasm. I had expected the story to be self-pitying and it was, but I had also expected it to lead to Joe admitting his crime. What I saw instead was the damage and scheming of another person.

It was the bumping of the knees that did it for me. He was at a bar like I had been, not sure what he was doing, not sure what to say or why he was even there at all. Betrayal would have been there like the smoke from her cigarette, swirling all around them. Did she mean the knees to touch? Or was it an accident? I supposed, in reality, the accidental touching was orchestrated and not so inadvertent.

And then there was the 'Gibson case'. The secret message that meant she wanted to see Joe. *My* secret message when she wanted to see *me*. All of a sudden, it was clear to me. She had been following a script, for some unknown reason of her own devising, because there was nothing that I had that she could possibly want. She had wanted to win the Hobson case and Joe had helped her, but *me*? Why was *I* worth using? The questions came crashing down around me, along with a realisation: I'd been duped. A voice inside my head said *Sucker*.

When you think about it clearly, hearing voices is certainly no foolproof test of insanity. Everyone's got a voice going on inside his head every waking moment of every day. A voice says, *Time to get up*. A voice tells you *don't forget to brush your teeth* or *what about the dark suit today?* A voice guides you through the catalogue of ordinaries that weave the tapestry that we call life. Everyone has it, this voice. Everyone.

But this voice was different. This one was barely recognisable, buzzing away in the dark recesses of my mind, mocking and insistent. *Sucker.*

I shook myself mentally and tried to listen to the rest of Joe's story while this relentless voice in my head kept up a steady taunting chatter. Something dark, twisted, impenetrable.

"Every day, I found her lovelier," he continued. "Every day I found the sadness that enveloped her more intoxicating. I couldn't help myself. I came home later and later every evening and for the first time since beginning law, I began to dream again in colour not black and white. And then one evening after work, in the middle of a conversation about something meaningless, she asked me, *'What are we going to do?'*"

My eyes flew up at the mention of those words. I remembered Shannon saying those exact same ones to me. The jeering voice in my head laughed louder. *Sucker.*

"I knew what she meant," Joe continued without noticing my reaction, "but I didn't want to answer, so I said, *'Have another drink?'*

'I don't want another drink,' she said to me. I asked, *'What do you want?'*

'I want to pretend we are simply two lawyers on opposite sides of a case.'

Nothing had passed between us at this stage so I said to her, *'But that's all we are.'*

'Go home to your wife who you have never cheated on.'

In my mind, I was seeing Sarah sitting up in bed reading when I walked in. *'She'll be waiting up for me,'* I said absently to Shannon.

She downed the last of her drink. *'Then go home and make love to her.'*

'I'll be thinking of you when I do,' I blurted out, not wanting to lose her before I'd even had a chance to win her.

She stood up and said, *'How satisfying for me'* before leaving the bar. I wanted to chase her but I didn't. I went home and got into bed next to Sarah. She, of course, was waiting up for me. That night, I dreamed again in black and white."

Out of the corner of my eye, I saw Karen's eyes drop to the table. Joe had her hooked with his sentimental story. I knew better.

"After a few days, I truly believed Shannon had gone from my life. Then she called out of the blue and left the Gibson message and when I met her for lunch, there was no lunch. It was like champagne and abandonment, laughter and teeth-clattering sex."

I had no wish to hear the gory details of Joe's lovemaking with Shannon and it must have shown on my face.

"Don't make a face, Jack, don't be such a prude. It was amazing like some force running through us. It was like she couldn't get enough. Hence the Viagra. Instead of embracing an earth-shattering freedom, I fell into the patterns of simple adultery. I left Gibson messages for her, snuck out for long lunches and I led a double life. It was easier that way. I didn't have to tell Sarah and I kept my job at her father's firm. My love for Shannon hadn't actually transformed my life, it had complicated it."

I grunted but he ignored it. "Still there was the future. Always the future, she used to say. As soon as we had some money, as soon as the Hobson case was over, we could live off her share of the settlement. Without any more words, we understood that we would make the move and settle in together once she had the money. Then the file came onto my desk."

This was what I'd been waiting for. The Peter Hobson story. I leant forward and listened.

"In the beginning of the case, I'd made routine enquiries and received routine answers. Hobson had lived in Western Australia for a time, so I contacted an old employer for his records and used those to track down possible hospitals where he may have been treated. From those hospitals, I requested medical records on treatments he'd had. That was all before the thing with Shannon began and changed everything. And then, one day a parcel came from Western Australia and I opened it. It was Peter Hobson's medical file with a copy of my request inside. He'd had pains in his head and a scan had been taken. They found an aneurysm about ready to burst. There was nothing that could be done. The advice given was to leave it alone and pray."

Karen picked up her pen and pulled a notepad in front of her, ready to take notes. I sat silently, watching Joe's face. Having been a policeman means I see things most people are unaware of. It's what I once did and I don't mind saying, I was damn good at it.

"So now, I had a pre-existing medical condition that he had not disclosed to his doctor and that had caused his serious injury, not the actual surgery. Before I showed the file to anyone, I took it to Shannon. She didn't seem terribly surprised but she took off her glasses and said, *'I suppose moving in together will have to wait.'*"

He looked over the table at me. "She didn't push me, Jack. She didn't so much as suggest it. I could feel the weakness in myself but she didn't push me. It was my idea not to tell anyone, to bury the file and to continue moving the case towards a settlement. My idea. My choice. It wasn't even a hard choice. In my mind, I was already free after having broken every rule in the book so why should one more transgression make any difference."

As he talked, he stubbed the cigarette butt out in the ashtray and reached for another one, tapping the end on the table before reaching for the lighter. "I handed her the file. She said she would destroy it and then she kissed me and whatever dread I felt, washed away. When I hugged her, I held on so tight because I wanted us to be as close as two could possibly be. I suppose deep inside, I had hoped Shannon would tell me to give up the file, to give it to the insurance company and start our lives clean. A foolish hope, I know now."

He paused to light the cigarette, inhaling deeply and blowing the smoke through his nose. "When she didn't say a word and then gave me the kiss, the hope bled out of me and I saw with utter clarity what lay ahead: disillusionment, bitterness, devastation, separation. I saw it all and there was nothing I could do about it." His eyes squinted at me through the smoke. "Because I loved her, Jack, and I had no option in life but her. I was ready to lose everything for a hope I now know was false. I was ruined by my own hand but still I had no choice. What does a gambler do when his luck dies and he loses everything? He doubles the wager and bets his life."

He was turning the lighter absently, end on end, as he talked. "It was never the same after that. I convinced MIA to settle and once the papers were signed and the cheque cleared, I separated myself from Sarah and the firm. Sarah took it quite badly and my father-in-law turned cold with rage. He suspected something about the Hobson case, enough to send Fitzroy after me looking for any files I might have. The one he wanted, I had already given to Shannon."

He looked up at me. "That's when you and I met at Gilhooleys. To cover for the stolen money, I started my own practice and for a while, things forged ahead. But even before I moved in with her, she had changed and become mysterious. I still loved her but she had changed. I introduced her to you even before the move and to a few of my other friends, but something was wrong. We stopped making love and she came up with excuses every night. She would take pills to sleep and drift off into near coma. It drove me crazy, her denying me and slipping away like that. Once when she was drugged, I forced myself on her and she whispered in a girlish voice, begging me not to hurt her again. I hated myself and never did it again, but that didn't stop the wanting."

I knew she'd been dreaming of her Uncle Bob and I gritted my teeth in anger at Joe's coarseness. "She began coming home late, half drunk as I had come home half drunk when I first began to see her. I sensed she was seeing someone else. One night, I set the scene with a hundred candles around the tub. I filled it and tossed rose petals onto the surface and waited. She looked at the scene strangely when she came home as if disgusted with the romantic display. She even sneered at the corniness but then undressed as if she were going to an execution. I fell to my knee and asked her to marry me. She told me she would, in a sad, stone-faced yes."

I remembered Shannon standing motionless in the lounge room while I gathered up clothes and towels and dumped them in the basket in the bathroom. The sadness flowed out of her. I could see it like a dark cloud above her head. She looked at me and her eyes were moist and the blueness poured out of them. We'd made love and as my chest pressed against her back in the tangle of bed sheets, she told me Joe had proposed and she had accepted.

"But nothing changed. We still didn't make love and she still took her pills to sleep. She was distant, distracted and there was a day or two when she disappeared for the whole day and I couldn't contact her. I grew certain she was seeing someone else and it drove me crazy. Our relationship had turned into a nightmare even before I found that most of the money was gone."

Deep inside, I felt happy that things had gone wrong for Joe. Thoughts of them together felt like a knife twisting in my chest, even though I knew she had only been using me. Joe mistook the look of disgust on my face for disgust at her behaviour.

"I know, Jack. I won't tell you blow for blow how I found out, how I confronted her, how she reacted and how I reacted back. There were bitter arguments, threats, tears and more fighting. It wasn't the money I was upset about, it was *her*. I was losing *her*. But she never told me what she had done with it, what she had spent it on."

Karen's pen made a scratching noise as she scribbled madly in her notebook.

"I threatened to call the police about the theft and in response; she said she would turn over the Hobson file to them. *'You destroyed it,'* I said. *'Did I?'* she replied. Her eyes narrowed when she said it and she grew as cold as ice. Frightening cold, really. It was like she was another person, somebody hard and damaged and capable of horrible things. But still I loved her Jack. I think it was the vision of myself that I was afraid to lose. The daring, wild, brave man."

His mouth twisted and I had a feeling he was about to cry.

"Then, a week before her murder, she disappeared for two days. When she came back she was loving again and it was as amazing as it had once been. She asked me to take her on a holiday and I said I'd give her anything she wanted. Anything that kept me from facing my failures was reason to offer her the world."

As Joe gulped water from his glass, the clock on the wall ticked loudly. We'd been in the room for an hour so far and we hadn't touched on the night of the murder as yet.

"Then one night, she came home late - very late - and acted strangely when she saw me. She had been drinking again, back with the other man again I guessed, or someone new. That night, she went back to her pills and the next night, she was waiting for me."

At last.

"She was lying on the mattress, smoking and staring at me. *'There's no kind way to say this,'* she said, *'so I won't try. It's over. You need to make arrangements to move out.'* I cried and begged and threatened to kill her then I threatened to kill myself. I asked her if there was someone else and she said there was. That's when I hit her."

I had to steel myself not to reach over and grab him by the shirt and hit him. Instead, I sat quietly and fisted my hands in my lap.

"I leaned over and smacked her face with the back of my hand and something snapped inside me. She just lay there and took it with a hard smile on her face. I think at that moment, I saw the folly of everything I had done. With that smile still on her face, she told me to put out the light. Without saying another word, I did. I turned off the light and went into the bathroom and filled the tub with scalding water as if I needed to be cleansed. I put a Louis Armstrong disc in the walkman, rolled a joint and slipped into the tub. I turned on the jets and thought about what the hell I was going to do. I closed my eyes and thought about what my future was going to be like without Shannon, without my career, my family, my job and without money."

His chest shuddered as he took a breath. "Maybe it was the joint, maybe it was that I hadn't slept the night before, but I felt strangely peaceful and tired, and with the headphones on and the heat of the water, I fell asleep. When I woke, it was into a nightmare of blood."

25

I glanced at Karen, then at Joe.

"You didn't kill her," I said softly to Joe, as a statement not as a question.

I could have sworn the voice coming out of my mouth wasn't mine. It sounded coarse and weak. And then the question was, so who did?

"No. I've told you that already, Jack. I didn't kill her."

Karen was staring at Joe and I could read nothing in her expression.

"Why not?" she asked Joe. "She took your money, took another lover, left you without your family, your career, without a cent or a future. She used you like she used everyone. Why *didn't* you kill her?"

Joe looked at her strangely. "Because I loved her."

"But what stopped you?" Karen asked softly.

He didn't answer straight away but his face twisted in puzzlement. I expected him to come up with something soulful, like the answer of a beauty pageant. *I didn't kill her because I believe love can make the world a far better place and we should love our fellow humans not use violence.*

What he said was, "Because it never occurred to me."

It didn't occur to him? In this violence-saturated age of ours, how could it *not* occur to him?

But he had come up with the perfect answer because it rang true. Isn't that what keeps us on the razor's edge of the straight and narrow more often than not? With that answer, the last vestige of doubt was erased. I now believed him. I believed his whole story. I had been wrong from the very start. Dead wrong. I had been wrong enough to leap at false assumptions and to consign a friend to a life in jail. I had tried to railroad a friend and to sacrifice means to an end and all along I had been flat-out wrong.

So here I was in a world that was different from the one I had woken up in. I had relentlessly sabotaged him from almost the very moment of the crime, now what was I to do? Save him or save myself? Whatever it was, I had to do it quickly before all the wheels were in motion.

"I have to tell you this, Joe," I said, trying not to let my emotions show, "the evidence against you is overwhelming. Your gun, your fingerprints, your attempted flight, the bruise, which you'll have to admit in your testimony. They don't know yet about the missing money but if they do, that will be worse. That'll be the final nail in the coffin. I don't believe you did it, but it might be the time to consider their offer."

Joe looked at me amazed. "But you said to fight it!"

"Yes, but that was before I knew about Peter Hobson. You might win the murder case but then you'll be up against fraud on the Hobson case. You'll still end up in jail. Brad Jefferson offered you eight to ten years. Maybe Karen can shave a bit more off and maybe she can make sure it covers the Hobson case, too. It's not great but you'll be out before you're fifty with a chance to start over."

"But I didn't do it!" he whined.

"I know, Joe. But you *did* cheat the insurance company and if you go to trial and lose, and with this Hobson thing hanging over you, it's very likely you will. Then they can keep you in jail for the rest of your life."

"But what about the other man?"

"We can argue he did it," I said, "and Karen most definitely will. But it's also a valid reason for you to kill her. Jealousy, rage, that sort of thing. It's a dangerous game and at the end, eight years is better than the end of your life."

Joe turned to Karen. "What do you think?"

"I think it's a generous offer," Karen said quickly. "From what we know, your father-in-law set it up to avoid a trial, bad publicity and any mention of Peter Hobson. I think it makes sense to consider it."

"Can I think about it?"

"No," I said. "There's no time. Every second is dangerous if Jefferson finds out about the Hobson case. Let Karen have the authority to make the deal."

"I don't know."

"Now, Joe. Yes or no. What do you say?"

"God help me, Jack."

"You've read the Old Testament, Joe. God can be pretty ruthless when he wants to be. I think He's going to sit this one out."

26

—————

Brad Jefferson's receptionist made us wait in the waiting area after telling us he was still in a meeting. I had called from the jail and even though I told her it was important and urgent and that it was the Joe Banner murder case, she repeated that he was unavailable at the moment.

So now, here we were, Karen and I, looking at the receptionist with an 'end of a long day' forced smile on her face while we sat and waited. I tapped my foot, looked at my watch and drummed my fingers. There's a lot to be said about flashing a badge and demanding to be seen immediately but that option was no longer available to me.

I picked up a magazine that was a month old and flicked to the crossword puzzle as I pulled a pen out of my pocket.

The clue read *showy, colourful* and I tapped my pen on my teeth wondering where Fitzroy was when you needed him.

"Gaudy," said Karen, looking over my shoulder.

"Enough about my damn tie," I said, even as I filled in the blank spaces.

The door opened and a man with a briefcase stepped out, making his way to the lifts. As the door shut behind him, I jumped to my feet.

"Could you tell Mr Jefferson that we are here, please?" I said to the receptionist.

"He knows."

"Could you tell him again?"

She smiled benignly at me. "He knows. He said to ask you to wait."

The door opened again and my heart sank sickeningly. Matthew Simmons wore a pained expression on his face but Brad Jefferson, standing behind him, was smiling broadly. My heart did a somersault.

As they turned and shook hands, Karen leaned over and said, "I don't trust or like Matthew Simmons. He reminds of the crook in *Oliver*."

Simmons turned, then pulled up short when he saw me.

"I'm surprised to see you here, Mr Simmons," I said getting to my feet.

As Karen reached for her bag and briefcase, I saw something in his stern, dark eyes. Just a flutter like a snake's tongue slashing the air. I looked at him and he stared at me and the thing in those eyes grew brighter and glowed until he turned away.

"Priorities," he muttered as he brushed past me.

I was too stunned to say anything as I watched him go. I had a bad feeling in the pit of my stomach.

"I'm ready for you now." Jefferson almost sang the words.

Karen and I exchanged a nervous look as we followed Jefferson through the door into his office. He sat down at his desk and waved to the two empty chairs, indicating we should sit. The desk was cluttered with paperwork but I noticed all of the documents were face down. Through the bank of windows, I could see a weak sun in the sky. At right angles to the window, there was a trophy wall behind the desk, with a law degree in a gilt frame and several photographs of Jefferson with politicians. There were framed newspaper headlines reporting guilty verdicts in several different cases and on his desk was a photograph of a blonde woman smiling at the camera.

Leaning silently against the filing cabinets were Sam and

Cavanaugh. Sam was keeping her face intentionally blank, but Cavanaugh couldn't conceal a smirk.

This was not good.

"How's it going, Jack? Ready to rumble, Karen?" Jefferson was smiling. It *really* wasn't good.

"That's what we're here for, Brad," Karen said, all sugar and honey.

He grinned wider.

"We met with our client today," Karen said, "and we discussed the plea once again. Although he still professes his innocence, he has asked me to inform you that he will accept the plea."

"Yes. I'm sorry about that."

"Pardon?" she asked.

"As I said at the time, when I made that plea it was subject to us finding a motive other than passion."

"And we have received no notice that you have discovered such information," Karen bantered.

"I faxed your office half an hour ago."

"Half an hour ago?" I almost yelped. "We were in your bloody waiting room half an hour ago."

"Were you?" he smiled at me. "Anyway, here's the fax that was sent." He pushed it across the table.

Without looking at it, I stated, "We don't need to look at it. We're accepting the offer."

"You can't anymore."

"We already have."

"Sorry. The offer has been withdrawn," he tapped the sheet of paper, "as the fax states."

I stared at him and he smiled back at me.

In the uncomfortable silence, I heard Sam's shoes shuffle.

"What did you find?" Karen asked.

He leaned back in his chair and webbed his hands behind his head as he rocked from side to side.

"I found Peter Hobson."

Karen's face betrayed her shock. I tried to mirror the expression, but it was a weak attempt. The moment I saw Matthew Simmons come out of the room, I knew. It was all my fault. By talking to Simmons, I had, in fact, accidentally set the whole thing up.

"Mr Simmons will be added to our witness list," Jefferson said. "He's an interesting man with an interesting story."

"This will ruin his practice," I stated unnecessarily.

"Yes, it probably will, but he feels compelled to tell the truth, the whole truth and nothing but the truth. As you know, at one point, he wanted to avoid publicity." He kept rocking, "but now it seems he wants to see Mr Banner suffer the full extent of justice. He would prefer to lose his business than to allow a murderer to move back in with his daughter."

I closed my eyes and fought back the nausea. This was my doing. I had been the one to tell Simmons about his daughter's intentions and by doing so I had destroyed Joe's chances.

"He didn't do it," I repeated.

Jefferson took his hands away from his head and began gathering the papers on his desk together. "And Karen has every chance to prove that. What we have now is a simple case of fraud where two people fell out over money. Detective Cavanaugh has checked out the finances."

Unwillingly, my eyes glanced over at Cavanaugh. Sam was looking down at her feet but the smile on Cavanaugh's face went from ear to ear.

"Were you aware of the withdrawals?" Jefferson asked me, sitting forward.

"Yes," I said.

"Where'd the money go?"

Karen spoke up. "I can only say that my client knew that the money had gone and he had no problem with it."

Jefferson snorted. "Sure. What's half a million between friends?"

He was shuffling papers around on his desk and I knew he wanted us out.

"We believe we know what actually happened now," Jefferson said. "They stole the money. She transferred it out of the joint account without telling him. In a rage over the money and her dalliance with another, he killed her. It happens all the time. Too frequently actually. And we'll tell the story well."

"It's not the truth," I said.

"It's as close as we need to be. The stakes have been raised, Karen. Our offer is off the table."

Karen and Jefferson argued but I wasn't listening anymore. A girl was dead and she had left me with a mystery to solve. Who the hell killed her? To save Joe and enact my vengeance, I needed to find both a motive and the murderer and I believed just then that I had the key to the solution.

Damned right I had the key.

27

We had gone straight back to Karen's building and she let me use a small office off the reception area to make my calls, no questions asked. I used the phone I had given to Shannon so that I could keep the records off Karen's landline, and geared myself up for a new role. I tried to think of a new voice that would sound right. Everything depended on the right voice. And if you're going to lie, make it one you're going to remember.

I was Tom. Tom Jones with the spreading rear, the receding hair with a comb-over and the rumpled suit. My career had stalled, my wife had gained thirty pounds, my daughter had just had her tongue pierced and my car smelled like a dead cat. My weight was high, my blood was pressure up and I drank too much. What I needed was a tone of jocularity covering an ocean of despair. The jocularity I could fake, the despair I didn't need to.

I dialled the number for Westpac at Southport and went through the process of Press 1 for this and 2 for that and eventually, I was given the option of speaking to an operator. I accepted.

"Good afternoon, Westpac Southport Branch. Hayley speaking."

"Hello, Hayley. It's Tom Jones here. How are you doing today?"

"Fine thanks. Tom, was it?"

"That's right. Tom Jones. From Pacific Fair branch. Didn't I meet you at the Christmas party? Hayley, was it?"

"Yes. Hayley Cummings. I was there, all right. I met a few new people there but I can't put a face to your name."

"Remember that dance?"

"You're the bald guy?"

I sighed sadly. "I like to think I'm follicly challenged, not bald."

I heard a soft laugh. "How are you doing, Tom?"

"Great, except for these damn computers. I've got a detective here asking about an account of ours but with the computers down, I can't do a thing. She said her office was near your branch, so I thought you might be able to help."

"Sure. What was the name?"

"Connor. Shannon Connor. Address in Ashmore."

"Here it is. Account number 241 6755." I scribbled the number down quickly. "She opened the account a few months ago."

"Great. What's the balance?"

"Two hundred and thirty-four dollars."

"Any recent activity?"

There was a moment of silence before she spoke. "Oh yes. A large transfer a month ago for four hundred and fifty thousand."

"That's some transfer. Where to?"

"The computer doesn't say." There was a long pause. When she eventually spoke, she sounded dubious, like I should have known that already. "You'll have to check with Head Office in Brisbane for that information."

"I was hoping not to have to do that. You know what it's like in the big smoke, everyone who calls them has to wait until they feel like helping us locals."

"How true."

"Did she have a safety deposit box, too?"

There was another pause. "No, nothing registered in her name."

"Okay. Thanks for all your help, Hayley. Save the next dance for me, will you?"

She giggled. "See you next Christmas."

28

———

I stared at the small key sitting on the desk in front of me.

This had to be the key to Shannon's safe deposit box, the hiding place of her secrets. A man in black had searched the house after the murder, apparently looking for this same key, if I could trust Frigging Fitzroy. He had told me that he wanted it, wanted it badly. I had taken it on a whim but now I had a great need to know what was inside that box.

Armed with Hayley's name, I decided to try another branch of Westpac for information. I took a few deep breaths and flexed my shoulders, getting myself ready. I dialled the number for Westpac Robina and went through the same process of choosing options. Eventually, a female voice came over the phone.

"Westpac, Robina. How can I help you?"

"Hi, this is Pacific Fair Branch. Who am I speaking to please?"

"Bethany Golding."

"Hi, Bethany. This is Tom. Tom Jones. Hayley Cummings from Southport branch suggested I give you a call."

"Hayley?"

"Yeah. She said if I needed any help, you were always a great help."

"Hayley? Oh, Hayley."

"Yes. Look, I have something she said you might be able to help me with. I've been getting some questions from the police about an account number 241 6755, which was opened here by a Shannon Connor a couple of months ago. Seems she went and got herself murdered. You should see the mess of forms they want us to fill out. It's going to take me a week."

"I can just imagine. First thing, let's get rid of all bloody policemen in the world. Right?"

I chuckled. "Amen to that, Bethany. They've been asking me whether there was a safety deposit box in her name. We've got nothing here but I understand that she could have opened one at your branch since she lived close by in Ashmore. Could you check for me, please?"

"Of course. Wait a second, I'll check."

I heard keys clicking on the other end of the phone and then, "Nope. Nothing here. Sorry."

"No, that's good. It makes it easier for me. I appreciate your help, Bethany. By the way, I have to check out some other things. You know anyone who can help me with some information on large transfers?"

"Corinne Prince at Broadbeach."

"She know her stuff?"

"She's the best. Tell her Bethany sent you."

"Do you have a direct line for Transfers? You know what it's like with the regular lines."

After a few seconds of silence, she rattled off a number and I scribbled it down.

"Thanks Bethany. You've been great. By the way, did I meet you at the Christmas party?"

"You may have. I was with my husband."

"Why is it, Bethany, that all the good ones are taken?"

29

Along with the key, I had taken Shannon's expired driver's licence from the desk in the bedroom and I pulled it out of my pocket. It was the only picture I had of her. Guilt-ridden lovers don't take photos.

I looked hard at the tiny picture, but it was like looking at a stranger. In person, her face was always moving between the beginnings of a smile or a frown, her eyes widening or contracting, her face always alive with emotion of some sort. But all the aliveness was missing from the picture. She looked plain with her hair pulled back in a ponytail, her large black-rimmed glasses hiding the sharp edges of her face. It was hard to imagine that they were the same person except the statistics were there, birth date, sex, height and name. Still the *real* Shannon was missing.

I closed my eyes and tried to picture her as I'd last seen her. The image was blurry. I had thought I knew her and we had been intimate but at this moment, I just couldn't see her in my mind. I could feel, oh yes, I could feel, but it was confusion that reigned supreme.

From the moment of her death, I had been learning more and more about her. Sam had said that the words 'nice' and 'sweet' had not been mentioned by anyone she'd interviewed. Sarah had told me of her conversation with Shannon where she'd uttered the crudest things. I had always thought Shannon was hard, but *that* hard? And then there was Fitzroy who said he knew her better than anyone and I suspected he was telling the truth. The final twist was Joe's own story, which showed how she had used Joe for her own purpose and then, for some unknown reason that I couldn't fathom, had used me. It was as if whatever I had thought I knew about her was gone. I closed my eyes again and tried once more to picture her and failed.

To some people, their life stories are lies. How could they be the heroes of their lives if they told the truth? They shade an incident here, invent something there, leave out a telling detail and change everything. Is there anything less reliable than a memoir? Hermann Goering was only following orders. Richard Nixon did absolutely nothing wrong. Life stories are our greatest works of fiction and so I had learnt to take Shannon's life story with a grain of salt.

I could probably fill in the gaps, all right. Her childhood was less than idyllic, but was anyone's? And I could imagine that the affair with the partner of her first law firm was more torrid and painful and had ended with more difficulty than she had let on. So, with every-thing that I had learnt about her, I had no trouble believing that her life story was more fiction than truth, considering that she herself had once told me not to trust anything she said. Now that she was dead and the reality of her death was my new reality, I very much wanted to know the truth that she had never wanted me to know.

Who *was* Shannon Connor?

It was time to go behind the lies.

30

"Transfers."

"Hi. I'd like to talk to Corinne Prince, please."

"Just a moment."

Music played some piped version of an Abba song. A minute later, I was ready to hang up and call again just to be rid of the music when a voice came over the phone.

"Corinne Prince."

"Corinne. It's Tom Jones here from Pacific Fair branch here. Bethany Golding said if I had some questions, I should ring you. Said you were the only one on the Gold Coast who knew what the hell was going on at Westpac."

"I try, Tom. I try. What can I do for you?"

"Well, here's my problem. It's 4:00 and before I can leave today, I have a ream of paperwork sent to me from the Legal Department. You ever have anything to do with that lot?"

"I try not to."

"I hear you, Corinne. Anyway, there's this account they've been asking questions about. Shannon Connor. Ever heard of her?"

"Nope."

"Girl shot through the heart in Ashmore?"

"Oh yeah. The boyfriend did it, didn't he? Wasn't he married to someone else and he shacked up with her and then killed her?"

"That's what they say."

"Sounds like half the guys I date."

I chuckled. "Not you, Corinne."

"You don't want to know Tom. Seriously. Anyway, what do you need?"

"Apparently, she transferred some money out of her account on February 18th. Account number 241 6755. Legal wants to know where the funds went."

"Hold on a sec. Account number 241....... Yep. Here it is. Went to a bank in Sydney. George Street branch. Commonwealth Bank. Account number 316735811."

"This is so great, Corinne."

"Don't let Legal get to you, Tom."

"I won't Corinne. Enjoy your night."

I sat back and took a deep breath. I was a little surprised at how easy it had been. A few phone calls, a tired voice, a little flirting, and the information had appeared, almost magically. There was just one step left and that was to call the Commonwealth Bank.

I glanced at my watch. 4:25. If I called now, there were two very different possibilities. Option one was they'd cut me off instantly, telling me to call back tomorrow. But if I was lucky, whoever answered would be in a hurry to just give me the information and finish for the day.

My silent prayer was for option 2.

Five minutes later, Directory Assistance had given me the number for the Commonwealth Bank in Sydney and I was listening to the dial tone with my fingers crossed.

"Commonwealth Bank. Heath Boswell speaking."

A voice that sounded as if its owner was right out of tenth grade spoke to me over the phone. I pushed back an image of a kid in a school tie and blazer sitting on a cushion so he could see over the top of the desk and had to stop myself from saying *'Does your mother know you're not at school?'*

"Could I have Customer Service, please?"

"I can help you, sir."

"Hi, Heath. My name is Tom Jones from Westpac Bank on the Gold Coast in Queensland. Sorry for the lateness of the day but I have a client here who also has an account at your branch. She transferred some money to your bank on ...sorry Heath, just a second ... what date was that?" My little act was to let Heath think I was asking Shannon for the information. I waited a few seconds, then came back on the line. "February 18th. She wants to know if everything went through okay. The account is under the name of Shannon Connor and the account number is 316735811."

"February 18th, you say?"

"That's correct."

"Let me see."

As the clicking sounds filtered through the phone line, I asked, "What's the weather like down there right now, Heath?"

"Cool, sir. No warm sea breeze like you must be enjoying, right now." The clicking noises stopped and he said, "Okay, here it is. We received the transfer on the same day. Everything looks fine."

"Do you have a balance on that account please, Heath?"

"Yes, sir. $950,000."

I tried not to stutter when I spoke. "Heath, the amount of the transfer was for $450,000. Is that correct?"

"That is correct, sir. There was already a balance of $500,000 in the account when the money went in. The total amount now is $950,000."

I cleared my throat. "Good, that matches with her calculations. One last thing. She wants to know if the fee on her safety deposit box is overdue. She doesn't want to miss a payment."

"No, it's fine. The fee is paid up to the end of this month."

"That's great. Thank you, Heath."

"Sir? Please give Ms Connor my regards. I remember her. I opened her account myself."

"I'll send along my regards, Heath. And thanks again."

I hung up and stared again at the photo of the stranger in the driver's licence. Then I stepped out of the small office and took the lift downstairs and walked across the road to the chemist. From the rack of reading glasses, I found one that matched the photo somewhat and went back to Karen's office. She looked up when I walked in and asked, "How'd you go?"

"Do me a favour, will you? Pull your hair back and tie it with a rubber band."

She sat back in her seat and blinked. "Why?"

"Just do it."

She looked long and hard at me like I'd gone over the edge but opened her top drawer and took out a rubber band. Her hair fell to her shoulders so after she raked it back with her fingers a few times, and twisted the band around it, she was able to make a small ponytail out of it.

"Okay," I said. "Now put these on."

When the glasses were on, I stared at the photo and back at Karen a few times. It wasn't perfect by any means. The eye colour didn't match and I knew Karen was slightly taller but there was a definite resemblance.

I nodded, satisfied. "How are you feeling, Karen? Tired?"

"Not particularly."

"Worn out?"

She hesitated, not knowing where this was going. "No."

"Funny. So am I. You know what we should do? We should get out of here. Not just the office but the Gold Coast. Aren't you sick of looking at the ocean?"

"Jack, what the hell are you talking about? I have a trial to prepare for. Are you insane?"

"Actually, no. Clear your day tomorrow, my friend, because you and I are taking a trip to Sydney. Expect to be away from the office for the whole day."

31

———

It was nearing 5pm by the time I finished explaining to Karen what I'd done and filling her in on everything I planned for us to do tomorrow. As I sat down in my car, my stomach rumbled and I realised I'd missed lunch. I opted for a drink and something to eat at a place called Billy's Beach House a couple of streets away from Caville Avenue overlooking the ocean on the main stretch of Surfers Paradise.

As I drove, I opened the window and a warm breeze scented with sea salt wafted in. The gentle breeze was blowing smoothly over the water putting white caps on the waves lapping onto the sand that kept the ocean from rushing onto the street. The relentless approach and retreat was soothing and it's one of the things I love most about the Gold Coast. I love the pounding at the shoreline while sea birds walk on the packed sand and I love watching the dark clouds roll in over the mountains in the distance. I'm never as happy as when I am close to ocean water. Not that I go *in* the water where there is all manner of stinging, biting, tentacled things, but I like to *look* at the water.

Miraculously, I found a park three spots down from the front door and walked into the bar and a blessed burst of air-conditioning.

A two-piece band by the name of 'Geek' was playing on a small platform and a group of teenagers were playing pool and swaying in time with the music while they sang along with the band. The music was good and several girls were surreptitiously eyeing off the dark-haired singer/drummer and the blonde guitarist doing back-up vocals. Out back, I knew there was an area they tactfully called a beer garden but in actual fact it was just a concrete backyard designated as the 'smoking area' containing the bins, a solitary wooden table and two bench seats overlooking a dark alleyway. The last time I was at Billy's had been with Joe in November last year.

I ordered a beer and a plate of nachos, but my mind was on booking the flights to Sydney when I got home. I walked over to a booth in a dark corner to think through the plan and waited for my food.

I took a gulp of beer just as Sonya Martin slid into the seat beside me with a glass of wine in her hand.

"Mary O'Brien likes you," she said as she slid a coaster under her glass. She folded her arms on the table and smiled at me.

"Are you stalking me?" I asked.

Hey," she smiled. "It's beer o'clock." She jerked her head towards the bank. "I'm just here enjoying the music."

"Let's get something straight before you waste any more of your time. I won't be talking to you about the case."

"Okay. What about the Tamborine Mountain case?"

I inhaled slowly and took a gulp of beer in the uneasy silence between us.

"I've spoken to Stephen's sister and she's happy to talk to me," she said, her eyes intent on me. "But I'd like to get a few words from you as well. You know. Let the public hear both sides of the story."

"There is no 'both sides'. Stephen was taken and murdered by a traumatised woman who is now in an institution for the criminally insane. End of story."

"Hardly, Jack. He was, what, her fifth victim? How did she manage to kill so many children without being detected? That was long before Stephen arrived on the scene."

I spun my beer on the table, breathing deeply to calm myself. "You obviously have no idea of the circumstances."

She was watching me intently and pulling her phone out of her pocket. "So tell me the circumstances. May I record this?"

"No, you may NOT record this because I'm not talking."

Memories of Stephen's abduction in January have never left my mind. They are always there, lurking on the edge of my mind. I will always see his sister sitting on the edge of her seat watching me with haunted eyes as she told me he was missing. They had stared at me, dark and wide, and just watching her anguish almost broke my heart. As she talked, I watched tiny tremors ripple the skin of her arms when she ran her hand desperately through her hair. Bleeding inside.

The realisation of where the killer may have taken Stephen hit me like a bolt of lightning. It could only have been to Tamborine Mountain, where the other bodies had been buried. I drove frantically through the Surfers Paradise streets with Sam lurching in the car beside me, hanging on to the armrest. Behind us were two squad cars as backup.

We arrived, tyres screaming and stones rising like a cloud around the car, at the excavation site as the sky was darkening.

I grabbed a torch from Sam and ran, slipping uncertainly on the loose, uneven ground of the rainforest. As I ran, I heard her stumbling behind me. I had my gun out, pushing through a turnstile of branches that threatened to tear my shirt as my torch wavered uncertainly before me.

The site came into view and I dropped to a crouch, my gun in one hand and the torch in the other, while I leant against a tree for support.

There was nothing but silence in the canopy of trees. Absolutely nothing. And nobody.

I've heard people say that silence can be deafening and it's true. I spun around expecting to see ... *someone.*

I remember whispering to Sam that the site hadn't been touched. Why I whispered the words, I don't know. But they sounded reverent in the stillness. As though I was sitting in the front row of a church waiting for the service to begin.

Sam had stopped, panting, and was looking at me, a strange look in her eyes. Something akin to doubt and uncertainty. I was shaking my head, saying over and over, *"He has to be here, Sam. He has to be."* My head kept turning from side to side, searching the scrub.

As we stood looking around, we could hear the sound of thrashing coming from the direction of our car. *Backup* I'd thought.

They stopped a few feet from us, and I heard someone say, *"What are we here for? A séance?"*

Sam held up her hands to them and told them it was a false alarm and I heard a mumbled *"What?"*. I think someone even snickered before Sam told them to head on back to the station. I was aware that everyone was looking at me and that I didn't feel like myself. I felt crazed and unhinged.

They all turned to walk back to their cars talking quietly to each other, leaves and bark crunching under their feet. Gradually the sounds became less and less and I was left standing in the darkness listening to the cicadas humming and the mosquitoes buzzing in the background.

That's when I realised my mistake. It wasn't to the excavation site the killer would take him. It was where the body of the last child was buried. Southport Cemetery. Twenty-five kilometres away.

We'd raced back through the same streets we'd just driven but because of my mistake, we were too late. I remember digging in the soft soil next to the last victim, my lungs burning as I wiped the rain away from my face, and I remember a surge of anger flowing through me when I dragged Stephen's dead body out of the soft earth. I should have known this was where the killer was headed. Instead, I'd told Sam to drive to the excavation point on a wild goose chase and because of that error, the young boy with his whole life ahead of him was lying dead in the rain.

How could I tell this story to Sonya Martin? How could I tell her a gargoyle called guilt was riding my shoulders, head back, laughing and showing sharp teeth. A small taunting demon of guilt, whispering things that could have been done and weren't. I knew the gargoyle. We weren't friends, but I knew him well. The think about kicking open a door to the past is that sometimes what's behind it comes out. You can try to run, but no matter how fast you do, you're dragging your demons behind you.

She sat staring at me in the silence, twisting her glass on the tabletop, as memories raced through my mind.

"So you don't have any real answers?" she asked. "Nothing to share with the public?"

I had always known that I would be lost without my job and my badge and my mission. But in the moment I left the force, I knew that I was just as lost with it as well. In fact, I was lost *because* of it. The very thing I thought I needed most was the thing that drew the shroud around me.

"The public know all the details. What you're actually asking is why did I let this happen?"

She shrugged. "You were lead detective, weren't you?"

I sighed. I knew my face was burning and that she was baiting me. Still, I couldn't stop.

"Yes, I was lead detective. And something like this, well, you never forget. I'm not saying I was to blame," I said quickly, glancing at the phone sitting on the table. She hadn't turned on the recorder so my heart stop pounding in my chest. "But you'd have to be a callous bastard not to be affected."

I saw my nachos arrive at the bar. She was sitting back now in her seat, her eyes still watching me with an intensity that made me feel like squirming. I looked around the bar to see if we were attracting attention and luckily, we hadn't. But I wasn't going to stick around eating my nachos until we did. I sculled the rest of my beer just as they arrived at the table.

"Put them in a takeaway box please," I said to the waiter. His eyes did a quick glance between Sonya and me and then he spun around, heading back to the bar.

"Why did you resign, Jack?"

"The records of the case are public knowledge. Check them out and leave me alone."

"But why did you resign?" she persisted.

How could I tell her I felt something cleave inside and tear away that day? How could I tell her it was like a bad dream that I couldn't wake up from? How could I tell her I can never forgive myself for that error of judgement? I had always known that I would be lost without my job and my badge and my mission. But in the moment I left the force, I knew that I was just as lost with it as well. In fact, I was lost *because* of it. The very thing I thought I needed most was the thing that drew the shroud around me.

"If you come near me again, I'm prepared to put in a stalking charge, if that's what it takes."

I slammed the beer glass down on the table and stood up. My face was burning as I grabbed the nachos from the bar. I could feel her eyes boring into my back as I stormed out the front door.

32

The rain was coming down in sheets again and it matched my mood exactly. Thankfully, the traffic at this time of night was light going in my direction. I glanced at the constant traffic still heading south from Brisbane towards the Gold Coast and I tried to calm myself. I was angry at being baited by the reporter, but I was angrier at myself for reacting.

Music they called 'rap' was playing on the radio. I turned it off, angry enough already, and listened absently to the *slup-slup* of my windshield wipers, taking deep breaths.

I followed the signs to the M1 until twelve kilometres later, I had calmed and was heading north towards the turnoff to my house. I eased over to the outside lane in no hurry to get home to Sherlock and the malevolent look I knew I could expect for having left him outside in the rain.

Suddenly, I became aware of another sound: a low-pitched roar, rising in volume, coming from behind. I glanced into rear-view mirror to see a double set of headlights like luminous eyes glaring at me from a distance and coming closer. Behind the lights was a dark shape like some prehistoric monster bearing down on me.

I was in the far left-hand lane with nowhere else to go except for the emergency stopping lane, so I kept glancing in the mirror in surprise as the car continued coming towards me with no intention of slowing down or moving over to the next lane. Even as I watched, it came up to barely inches behind me and kept at an even pace with me. My first thought was Sonya Martin but just as quickly, I disregarded the thought. This wasn't a woman's way. This was testosterone.

"What the hell?" I said as I stared open-mouthed at the car while trying to keep my eyes on the road. It was a 110km zone and I was only going 90 kms because of the rain so I wound the window down, letting the driving rain wash over me, and waved my hand around uselessly in the air trying to indicate that he should go around.

When he made no indication of moving, I waved my hand again and yelled, "Go around, you bloody idiot! GO!"

As if in reply, he accelerated and rammed the back of my car, hard, jerking me forward in my seat. I swallowed against my painfully dry throat and felt the adrenaline wash through my blood like toxic fuel and I could feel panic begin to set in. I was in a lot of trouble here.

One of the things I've learnt regarding panic is that it inspires gross errors of judgement. Events take place in a blur in which the instinct for survival – winged flight, in this case – overrules all else. Suddenly you find yourself on the extreme side of crisis in worse shape than you were to start with.

I sometimes think that death is the only significant experience I've not had – ecstasy, misery, illness, pain, success, love, a degree of wealth and then the loss of it. I thought I'd seen it all but when it came down to it, I slowly came to a sense of reality and my first reaction was irritation. This was quickly replaced by terror. I was drenched in sweat but at least I was still on the road.

I took a shaky breath to calm my pulse and began to access the situation and damage. The seat belt had saved me from any injury to my body but by now, I was furious. For an instant, I thought of pulling over to the safety zone on my left and letting him pass me while I wrote down his registration number ready to report the incident to the police.

Then I changed my mind. All I needed on this quiet highway at 8:30 at night was to pull over and let this maniac have me where he obviously wanted me with no other motorists in sight. And who would believe me if I reported it anyway?

I can just hear the traffic police now.

Someone was following you and rammed you, sir?

Were there any witnesses, sir?

Have you been drinking, sir?

May I see your licence, please?

You're Jack Curtis?

THE Jack Curtis?

The same Sergeant Jack Curtis who went loopy and quit his job three months ago after a case he was on went haywire?

That IS you? Come with me please, sir.

As I was running the conversation through in my mind, the driver rammed my car again. I skidded wildly over the road barely missing the guardrail on my left-hand side. As I tried to breathe, I jerked the wheel to bring the car back onto the road and it fishtailed for a few seconds. My heart did a few somersaults up and down my chest and finally settled in my throat.

My mind was racing. I needed to stay calm and stay ahead of the game, but blood was rushing through my body making me feel giddy. My heart was beating so hard I could swear I could see it thumping through my shirt. The pressure in my chest felt like someone was pushing against my ribcage.

I sucked in air and tried to stay calm as I glanced in the rear vision mirror. I could see my wheels throwing a fan of water behind me, drenching his windscreen so that he could no longer see the road. Or me. Not a thought I wanted to think about at this moment.

While I knew that whoever this guy was had serious intentions to affect my health, in the back of my mind something else floated to the surface. *He's playing with me.* If he meant any serious injury, he would have run me off the road by now and totalled the car and me into the bargain. I'd be dead in a ditch by the side of the road. Instead, he was staying close to my bumper – dangerously close, yes – but not close enough to run me off the road. What the hell was he doing?

Joe's words came back to me in a flash. *I'm being followed.* Was that it? Had Joe stumbled onto something that was meant to stay buried? Had someone seen me with Joe and decided to give me a warning as well? How far was that warning going to go?

The only option I could think of was to try and make a hurried exit before he had time to realise what I was doing.

Up ahead, I saw Exit 57 in front of me. I'd have to gauge my timing exactly. I pressed my foot to the accelerator and the car sprang forward like it had been shot out of a rubber band. The speedometer went from 90, to 100 and then to 110 in seconds but the car following me stayed right on my bumper. Every few seconds, I felt another nudge from behind, but I kept up my pace. His headlights shone glaringly into my rear-vision mirror and I reached up and turned the mirror upwards to keep the glare out of my eyes.

The exit sign loomed ahead but I didn't reduce my speed. I had no wish to give the driver any indication of what I was about to do.

At the very last moment, as the exit and the safety grids began to pass me, I jerked the wheel to the left and felt my car bounce as it ran over the meridian strip. My head bumped the ceiling and I fought for control, but I managed to stay on the road.

To my right, I saw the driver's brake lights flash red, shimmering in the rain as his car skidded but continued along the M1. My plan had worked. He hadn't enough warning to turn left with me and now he was swerving all over the road, not able to control his own car, and not able to stop for fear of having an accident himself. I tapped my own brakes slowly and this saved me from running into another guardrail ahead of me that led to the overpass over the highway.

I made a right hand turn to take the overpass, then stopped in the middle of the road and watched as the driver had no option but to continue northbound along the highway. The next exit was the

Coomera exit three kms ahead and if he took that and U-turned back onto the highway to me, I'd be long gone.

His car moved over to the right-hand lane and sped away into the teaming rain leaving me to wonder what the hell I had gotten myself into.

33

———————

Lights were on the length of my street and as I neared my own house and my heart jumped into my throat once again. The lights of my house were on in the lounge room. I'd left the house early this morning and at that time, I had definitely not turned any lights on. Some people turn them on when they go out knowing they'll be coming home to darkness. Not me. I'm too cheap to do that. I'd rather feel my way in the darkness to a light switch than spend the extra money on electricity. Which is why my heart was pounding in my chest again barely ten minutes after the episode on the freeway.

I drove around the block a couple of times noting the cars parked in the streets and the people moving around on the street. Nothing suspicious.

I parked several houses down from my own, noting as I drove past that my front door was ajar. As quietly as I could, I opened the boot of my car and took out my tyre iron, then I skulked hunched over to my open front door. I had my tyre iron in my hand, but I wished I had the gun I'd handed back when I'd resigned from the force or even the one that I'd given back to Cavanaugh. Breathing heavily, I stopped at the front door, my back pressed against the wall, and listened holding my tyre iron in front of me like an actor from an Anne Rice movie waving a cross in front of a vampire.

There was no noise coming from the inside, but that didn't mean there was no one there. They could have seen my car pull up and were hiding inside waiting to finish the job that the guy on the freeway had started. Or they could have gone and I was standing outside like an idiot with my back pressed against the wall waiting for the sun to come up.

I took a deep breath, shoulders bunched, and toed the door open a bit more, then waited to see if the movement made any impact from the inside. Nothing. Just serene silence. The voice of experience was telling me that silence is rife with bad possibilities. It was the kind of clogged silence that promises malignant surprise. I nudged the gap another couple of inches and stuck my head around peering inside, tyre iron at the ready, and saw why there was no noise coming from inside.

The house was already trashed. Paper from my desk was torn and scattered around like confetti. I could see the drawers in the kitchen had been emptied onto the floor and all the rubbish that I seem to accumulate in the bottom drawer lay strewn around the room. A coffee cup that I hadn't washed up that morning had been swept off the bench and lay smashed on the floor amongst the remnants of cold brown liquid. Whoever it was had gone mad looking for something that wasn't there. And I knew what that something was. The key.

A thought suddenly crossed my mind. The guy on the freeway had probably been the same guy to trash my house. To have turned the lights on meant that it had to have been dark when he broke in. He must have followed me from Karen's office to Billy's Beach House, then come here knowing I wouldn't be home for a while. Obviously, he hadn't found what he was looking for. He must have been angry enough to make his way back to the bar and follow me along the freeway.

Frank Fitzroy.

Still jittery, I stepped through the door and walked into the kitchen, leaving the tyre iron on the bench. With fury still crackling through me, I managed to calm myself enough to put the drawers back in and gather up what hadn't been damaged and put it all back in the drawers.

I grabbed a broom and swept up the mess, putting everything into a white bin liner, then took out a roll of paper towels from under the sink to soak up the coffee dregs on the floor. Glancing over my shoulder, alert for any movement, I walked outside and sloshed my way through puddles to put it all in the wheelie-bin around the corner of the house.

Back inside, I took a beer out of the fridge and tried to calm myself. Somewhere in the night, canned laughter from someone's television broke the silence. In the distance, the surf roared and thunder rumbled many miles into the east.

I was just taking a swig of the beer when I heard a noise behind me. I grabbed the tyre iron from the bench and spun around just as Sherlock squeezed in through the cat door.

"Where the hell have you been?" I asked him.

He walked across the floor and sat by his bowl, a soft *prrrr* sounding in his chest. I half-smiled and my breathing returned to normal.

"What is it you actually do around here anyway?"

Another *prrrr* sounded, apologetic this time I'd like to think, as I opened the fridge and pulled out the only edible looking thing in the fridge. Half a can of sardines sitting next to last night's left- over pizza. I emptied what was left of the can onto his plate and put it down hopefully in front of him.

He took one stiff at it then turned and scratched the floor, like he'd just used the litter, before lifting his tail in the air and exiting back to the garden without a backwards glance.

I glanced up at the clock. It was nearing nine o'clock. I finished the beer and made the bookings on a Qantas flight the next day for Karen and me. The earliest flight I could get us on was 11.00am. This meant that I could look forward to a lunch of two miniscule prepacked sandwiches and a pack of peanuts with, at most, six peanuts in it.

I left a message on Karen's phone telling her what time I'd pick her up in the morning then I switched off the lights and locked the front door, rattling it hard on its frame to make sure it was indeed secure.

Tomorrow was the day I was going to be the friend Joe thought I was.

34

Ah, Sydney. Neon, the crush of crowds, long-legged girls in boots and short skirts, artificial light, artificial air, announcements, lines, queues, doors hissing open and shut, videos, luggage flying, shops, signs, restaurants, uniforms, chrome, chrome and more chrome.

And that was only the airport.

We jumped into a taxi and went straight to the George Street Branch of the Commonwealth. While we sat in the taxi, I filled her in on the events of the night before and she listened with mouth and eyes wide open.

"Who the hell would do all that?" Her eyes suddenly squinted. "Are you hiding something, Jack?" she asked, just as we were about to walk inside the bank. I was saved from lying to her when my phone rang with its usual Storm Trooper theme music from Star Wars. Kind of appropriate, if you ask me. I held up my hand to Karen and answered it. I listened to the voice at the other end of the line, said thank you, then hung up, taking a deep breath.

"You okay?" Karen asked.

I took my sunglasses off and put them back in their case slowly to give myself time to collect myself. A warm southerly wind was blowing down George Street stirring up papers and rubbish left lying in the gutters.

"That was the priest performing the service for Shannon."

Karen waited for me to continue. I turned and looked at her. "Apparently, it's tomorrow afternoon."

"You already organised a service?" she asked.

I nodded and shrugged. "What are friends for?"

"They won't let Joe attend, you know," she said softly, watching me closely.

"I don't think anyone will be attending. I would have been the only one."

Karen's eyes were sharp as they searched my face.

I mentally shook myself. Right now, we had work to do. Grieving would have to wait.

I nudged Karen and began to walk inside the bank. "Come on. Let's get on with this."

We saw two chairs in a waiting area and headed towards them. It was close to 1pm and the staff were filtering in and out, on their way to or back from their lunch hour. A tall man of about twenty-five with cropped hair dressed in a pristine business suit walked towards the security door separating the office from the foyer. He waved and called out that he'd be back in an hour and a tiny voice from beyond called back "Okay Heath."

A few seconds later he walked right past us and stepped outside onto George Street.

I nodded to Karen who stood up and went to the ladies room. A minute later, she came out with her hair tied back in a ponytail and the glasses in place.

"How do I look?"

"Great. Let's hope no one's reported Shannon's death yet."

We sat at a desk and waited as a tired-looking woman with a badge stating, *'My name is Connie Riordan'* retrieved the card for the safety deposit box. So far so good. She hadn't blinked when Karen gave Shannon's name and the box number stamped on the key. While we waited, Karen fingered the key nervously trying to hide her edginess.

"Here it is, Ms Connor. Now all I need is your identification. Then you can sign the card and have a look at the contents in a private room."

Karen reached into her bag and made a show of rummaging around for her purse, searching through its contents. Eventually, she pulled out the driver's licence and handed it to the woman.

Connie Riordan started down at the card and then up at Karen's face, then back down again.

"I see your licence has expired," she stated.

Karen leant forward, staring down at the card. "Oh my, has it?"

"Yes, a year ago."

"I haven't driven a car for ages. I actually sold it when I moved to the Gold Coast. My home and work are so close together, I haven't needed one. I just haven't noticed. I'll take care of that when I get home."

There was a pause while Connie did some more looking.

"It says here your eyes are green. They don't look green to me."

Karen blushed. "There're actually closer to hazel. They're brown in some lights and green in others. I like to think they're green."

The woman studied the ID card again and then back to Karen's face.

"And," Karen smiled girlishly, "in some lights, I can even pass for a size eight."

Both ladies laughed at that, sharing a little secret piece of vanity between themselves. Karen was comfortable playacting, but she was giving away too much information and seemed to have an answer for everything when answers weren't really required. If it had been me, I'd have acted as if none of it was her damn business. But I had to admit, *'they're brown in some lights and green in others'* was good.

"Just sign here, Ms Connor," Connie said, handing the card back to Karen with a tired smile. There was a series of lines on the card with Shannon's signatures duly dated. Without hesitation, Karen signed. She had been practicing the signature the whole trip down in the plane, writing out the name based on the signature on the licence: Shannon Connor, Shannon Connor, Shannon Connor. It wasn't a perfect match, but the flourishers were the same and it was close enough and after the little bonding session between the two women, Connie barely glanced at the card.

"Will your friend be coming with you?" she asked looking in my direction.

"You mean Josef?" Karen smiled benignly. "Sure, why not?"

"Follow me," she said.

I threw her a *'what the hell are you doing?'* look before following the woman through a door that was a foot thick. The walls were lined with boxes, all of them with two key locks on each. She placed a key in one of the locks of Box 124 and Karen placed her key in the other. They both turned at the same time and the metal box slid out of its opening. She handed the long box to Karen and led us to a small room to our left with two chairs and a narrow shelf attached to the wall. When the door closed behind us, Karen placed the box on the shelf and we both sat in front of it and stared at it.

"That went well," she said.

"Josef?" I asked.

She smiled. "It just came out."

"I don't even look like a Josef. I always thought that when I went gigolo, my name would be something like Antonio."

"I wasn't thinking gigolo. I was thinking more like a chauffeur."

I snorted my disapproval. "Just open the damned box before Heath comes back from lunch."

She slid the box over to me and I hesitated. It wasn't as if I thought I was violating Shannon's privacy. Some investigator would eventually cotton on that it existed and get a court order and scour it for clues. I reasoned that the initial scourer might as well be me.

What made me hesitate was the fact that I used to think I knew all I needed to know about Shannon. I used to think I knew the basics and maybe I knew her heart. But I didn't think that anymore and that's what made me hesitate. I was afraid of what I'd find out when I looked inside that box.

Karen put her hand on my arm. "Let's do it, Jack."

We both slipped on a pair of rubber gloves and I took hold of the box. Slowly the top came off and there it was. Shannon's life. What lay inside were the clues to the whole brutal world and I would just as soon have stayed away from it. It was a world that told me more than I ever wanted to know about her past and the reason for her sadness and her death.

35

The photos were faded with age. They were heart-wrenching because I knew how the story turned out. What I didn't know was why.

The first one was of a tiny girl, maybe three or four years old, sitting on a blanket under a tree, her hands holding a teddy bear while a pretty, dark-haired woman sat beside her looking down adoringly. I passed the photo to Karen and flicked to the next one.

A frail, young girl of about twelve stood in a shapeless shift behind a rickety fence, frowning into the camera lens. I could see Shannon's face clearly, the cheekbones not yet pronounced, the eyebrows not yet arched, the lips not yet the rich red they would become, the hair not yet the colour of coal. But it was definitely her sad, heart-breaking face with its haunted look. My heart lurched a little.

The next one was of a young man in a suit. Smiling, self-assured, off to start his new job and I assumed it was Shannon's father. From what Shannon had told me, her father had been a lawyer and had died in a car crash along with her mother when she was eight. I shuffled through the photos and the next was the picture of Shannon aged about eight holding the hand of a man, not her father, but a tall man with a straggly beard. Not a man to be messed with by the looks of him. His angry blue eyes glared at the camera from his emancipated face while Shannon stood with her eyes wide open and vulnerable as her mouth formed a scared 'O'. Looking at her helpless expression, I couldn't imagine her playing with dolls, smiling with gaps in her teeth or thinking life was terrific.

I didn't put them down. I fingered the photos obsessively, as Karen watched me. It was a strange sensation, pawing through Shannon's memories. The trails to her past. I went from photo to photo trying to make sense, trying to divine a story.

When I'd seen them all a few times, I passed them all to Karen. There was a small mewling sound, what you expect from a kitten in distress, and I glanced at Karen. Her eyes were glistening with emotion as she looked through the photos.

Then I picked up the first letter.

S.

I am in heaven! I am floating in the air and I never want to come down. I know I have pulled you into my world of trouble but I am soaring with the joy of it. I feel like I am young again, riding a wave and all I can think about is you. How did this wondrous thing happen to me, I ask? I am overcome with something so powerful that it starts me shaking to think I could lose it. There was a switch and I don't know how it was turned on or why but suddenly everything changed and my world was lit up with a light that I didn't know existed.

I don't know the words to tell you what it felt like to hold you in my arms and to trust someone so completely. I told you about my life and there was no disgust or hate. You just listened. You were the friend I needed. Maybe it was as you said, that we were feeling things we didn't understand and ended up doing things we never expected.

Whatever it is, I am ready to face what comes next. I can't wait to go to sleep tonight so I can wake up tomorrow and see your face again and cover you in kisses and then do it all again the day after and the day after that, again and again.

M.

Whoever had written this, it wasn't Joe. It was signed *M* not *J* for Joe as I would have expected. I put the letter down and picked up the next one.

S.

I know you are mad at me and you deserve to be angry. I have nothing to say except I'm sorry. I'm so very sorry. For a time, it was like the only place I felt free was with you and now there is no place left for me. My lawyer tells me that I am not to see you again and that you would already have received his letter and compensation. Compensation. I hate that word because there is no compensation for what I have done to you. It all keeps getting worse and worse but in my mind's eye, you are there as I last remember you, smiling and loving.

I don't want you to think that this is easy for me, and even as I say that I feel shame. What I did to you, I will have to live with every day of my life and there's nothing to be done about it.

I know you will think me a coward but I hope in time you will forgive me.
M.

The next envelope contained a birth certificate dated three and a half years ago, August 4th, 2014. Baby girl, 2kgs 30 grams. Mother - Shannon Mary Connor, Father - unknown. Baby's name - Rose Shannon Connor. The certificate had been folded and opened many times and the seams were showing wear.

Had I ever really believed I knew this woman? I stared at the certificate for a long time. Another secret not shared with either Joe or me. What had happened to the child? Where was she now?

I unfolded the next document and found the insurance policy

naming Joe as beneficiary, the one he said he knew about but had no idea of its whereabouts.

A manilla folder lay underneath the letters and photographs. I put the rest aside and opened the file. Inside was the missing Hobson file. I glanced over at Karen and waved the file at her.

36

I slept in late the next morning and took two paracetamols, then a third one with a glass of Jack Daniels. I was going to need all the help I could get if I was going to get through the day of the funeral in one piece.

In the morning, I moved around the house like a sleepwalker in a fog until I eventually looked at the clock. I was going to be late.

In fifteen minutes, I'd washed my face, yanked on a white shirt and dark suit, combed my hair and was on the road.

By the time I arrived at the cemetery, the hearse had already appeared, long, sleek and dark, and was resting quietly and empty to the side. Father Aspinall stood over the open grave, head down in prayer. He was wearing an ankle-length cassock, a stole draped around his neck not quite hiding his clerical collar. He must have been sweltering in the heat. I took my hat off to him.

As expected, I was the only mourner present. There would be no outpouring of emotion here today.

Not far away a couple of vultures from The Courier Mail stood in the blazing heat, like sun worshippers. A female TV news reporter with an umbrella over her head, shielding herself from the nuclear heat, saw me approach but turned back to her cameraman pointing the lens of his camera at her. The red light glowed, meaning they were recording, and I heard the words *'police won't comment at this time'* muttered.

The coffin had already been lowered down into the ground and the sight of it, perfectly still and cold in the dug earth, made me queasy all of a sudden. The last time I'd been here, it was Stephen's face I'd seen, his eyes open and staring accusingly at me. I swallowed painfully. My head hurt and I could taste toothpaste on top of the Jack Daniels as a trickle of sweat ran down my back.

People talk about dignity in death. I'm not so sure I believe them. There was certainly no dignity in Shannon's death and I'm not so sure my own mother's death had any dignity. They talk about battling cancer and it's nuanced more like a fight. But with her, it wasn't a win or lose thing. She didn't fight it. She simply gave up. Her eldest son had died horrifically in a foreign land, her husband died shortly afterwards, and she felt more or less alone, despite my close presence. Cancer took her so fast that I didn't have time to tell her that I loved her. That she had been a terrific mother, that I had enjoyed my child-hood or that I forgave her for loving my older brother more than me. And that I didn't blame her. After all, everyone adored Adam. Even me.

I moved forward and stood on the opposite side of the grave from Father Aspinall. The starkness of the gravesite reminded me painfully that I had forgotten to order flowers. He raised his head and nodded, with no sign of a reprimand for being late or the lack of floral decoration, then returned to his prayer book, muttering, "Ashes to ashes. Dust to dust."

He closed his prayer book softly then crouched down to grab a handful of dirt from the soft earth at his feet. He tossed it over the edge and it landed with a hollow thunk onto the lid of the coffin sitting serenely at the bottom of the pit. I had to look away.

When I looked back, his eyes were watching me. He dropped his eyes to the coffin then back again to me, and with the slightest of nods, he silently encouraged me to do the same.

It was the moment when I almost slipped up. Instead, I inhaled deeply and squared my shoulders, shakily bending down and repeating his actions. I heard a series of clicks from behind me and I had to steel myself from turning around and saying something vile to the vultures.

In seconds, the service was over, Father Aspinall and the reporters had gone, and I was alone.

Just me and my breathing.

37

———

Days stretched into weeks, hot and empty. Whenever Karen and I saw Joe, he looked more haggard and tired. Dark pouches had formed under his eyes and the whites were laced with fine red lines. Since his arrest, he had lost the weight that I had been urging him to lose and he was beginning to look gaunt.

While we waited, I worked from home, restless, full of buzzing energy that had no outlet except for my scribblings for Karen concerning the trial. The casualness of it turned into an intensity, almost feverishness, and thoughts came fluently as I jotted down questions I thought needed answering and trails I thought we needed to follow up. We needed a copy of the prosecutor's witness list and we needed to make one of our own, scant as it was going to be.

It was a plan of action and with the activity I was happy for the first time in months. Maybe Joe had been right about the private detective licence. I needed an income and sleuthing was all I knew. I made a note on my calendar to follow it up after the trial was finished.

I thought about the trial every waking moment. And every sleeping moment. When I wasn't scribbling, I would grab a beer and sit on my veranda where I spent most of my time just sitting, watching people and thinking. In the mornings, I would check my mailbox, a habit I wished I could break. The only mail I get is depressing. Bills and catalogues for the happy housewife to browse, reminding me I was alone. Even the mail has given up on me. How bleak is that? Every time I wheeled my almost empty green trash bin to the curb, Thursday mornings, I think about how this chore is so much a part of my hollow life. Mid mornings, I carried my coffee to the front porch and sat looking across the street to the back of the local school. I watched small boys in their blue ties and matching pants and the small girls in their blue pinnies shrieking during endless supplies of frenetic energy. As I listened to the laughter, I wondered what it would feel like to be whole again.

I remembered the skies of Hobart, bright with a light that only comes from brilliant stars. When I was young, we used to brag that Hobart had the most Irish Pubs outside of Dublin. My father and elder brother used to participate in a marathon pub-crawl on St. Patrick's Day to raise money for local charities. Two beers and two shots of Whisky per bar and then they'd move onto the next bar. The idea was to see which man could remain standing long enough to make the circuit that started in Battery Point at Irish Murphy, continued through a couple of small pubs on the way to Bridie O'Reilly, and then finally, after a couple more on the way to the 'Hope & Anchor', they eventually ended back at the start. My father was a hell of a drinker as were most of the Irish men who signed up for the pub-crawl but in all the years that my father participated, no one ever made it back to Irish Murphy.

Hobart is no Surfers Paradise. Surfers is bright, but it comes from streetlights, bars, shops and skyscrapers. I used to joke that it was the absence of stars that made people lose their bearings and morals in life. Now I know better. Some of us can find our way with a single light while others lose their way when the sky is as bright as a neon sign. We all learn to adjust and, given time, we use stars that reside inside us rather than the stars in the sky or constellations.

Unwanted memories of Shannon constantly ran though my head. Pictures we'd found in the safety deposit box of a small child, scared and abandoned to the care of her abusive uncle. And that's when Jazz jumped back into my mind.

It had been six months since I'd last seen her, and as disastrous as it had been at the time, it was high time I saw her again. Since that last time, Sally had moved in with a guy she had been seeing. I made a quick phone call to Sally, asking permission to see Jazz, and when she grudgingly agreed, I headed off to the address she gave me.

Sally's street was empty but the driveways were full of station wagons and 4-wheel drives. Most of the houses were the classic split-level mode of the 1970 housing boom. A few had additions. Others had extensive renovations circa 1980 involving the too-white, too-smooth stucco look. The look had aged as well as the powder blue suit I'd worn to my wedding.

The address was a block of units spread over four separate buildings shaped like the letter H. Melaleucas and gardenias bordered each side of the buildings and each unit had its own patio at ground level. These units would be the sort to have their living areas downstairs and the bedrooms and bathrooms upstairs.

The unit number was 28 and as I walked around looking for it, I could hear music and voices and the rhythmic splashing of someone doing laps in a nearby pool. Somewhere a dog barked. The smell of barbecuing meat filled the air. It seemed like a pleasant place to live and I felt the first pangs of envy.

I found the door and knocked. Someone had built a little sidewalk out of stepping-stones that ran around the side of the place and on each side of the portico, a hanging basket of something green swayed gently. A curtain was drawn across the front window but I could see shadows moving inside. It was a nice, well-kept place. Not well off, but not down and out either. But who knows? Maybe the inside looked like Uncle Scrooge's money bin and the walls were lined with cash.

Within seconds, the front door opened and Sally stood looking up at me. She stared at me the way she always did when she was looking for an explanation. It used to infuriate me, but I can't say I blamed her right now.

She looked drawn with dark rings circling her eyes and I thought she looked tired. But what else I could see was that the pain was still there. Pain and anger. Her arms were folded over her chest in the same old defensive pose I remembered well. Her face had always been a mirror to every emotion she felt but tonight, her face was flat and revealed nothing. She had often accused me of wearing a mask and I had tried to explain to her it wasn't a mask, it was tightly held control that kept me from falling apart during cases that I couldn't talk to her about.

My mind flashed back to when Sally and I were 'us'. I saw Sally reading on the lounge with her legs tucked under her. The big baggy sweaters she always wore. The way her index finger paused over a page, prepared to turn. The way she looked up and smiled when she realised I was staring. The past came at me so hard, I nearly fell backwards.

I've often thought if only I'd chosen another career. If only I'd taken her away on an overseas holiday. Perhaps to Ireland, the home of my father's family. Maybe Rome, the city of art and culture. Or Paris and Venice, the cities of love. A lot of 'if onlys'. Instead, because of my job, we made do with drinking cheap wine in the moonlight at King Neptune's in Hobart and holidaying at the convict settlement in Port Arthur.

The worst thing about my job was what it did to the ones I loved. No matter how hard you try to protect them, you only end up alienating them. Over the space of the last ten years of our marriage, I saw the subtle changes. But whether I was too stupid or too busy, they never registered as a danger and apathy is always the result. It's easier to lose yourself in work than to cope with reality. Love takes time, effort and work and given human nature, are any of us capable of change? It's easy to see the faults of others but not so easy to see your own.

Long ago, I realised I had been to blame for our break-up. I couldn't blame my job – lots of cops still managed to juggle work and home. I hadn't been able to, and here I was staring at my ex-wife who stared back at me with open hostility. In my own defence, I had to say that I am part of an organisation that was 'us' and then there was 'them'. It promoted an isolation that Sally couldn't understand and eventually couldn't live with.

Someone once said: to go forward, you have to look back. I guess he meant before you can move on with your life, you have to see the mistakes you've already made. Not to state the obvious, but I was a little hesitant about looking back: I might not like what I saw.

"You'll have to give us more notice in future when you want to see Jazz." Sally said with her arms still crossed under her breasts. "You can't just call and expect us to drop everything just because you want to come over. We have lives too, you know."

Same old Sally. Straight for the jugular. Hiding her feelings from me wasn't something she suffered from.

I felt embarrassed and nodded. I only nodded because I didn't know what to say. I noticed that she'd dyed her hair a deep auburn these days. For as long as I could remember, it had been brown with gold highlights. Her hair was shorter too, making her face look rounder than it was. I would have suggested something more upswept but then again, she hadn't asked my opinion.

"Have you spoken to Jazz? Does she want to see me?" I asked.

She didn't say anything for a moment, just stared at me until a faint smile touched the corners of her mouth.

"She'll talk to you all right, but don't expect it to be nice. She's at this rotten age when everything is everyone else's fault. So, she's a handful at the moment."

"How's she going at school?" I asked.

She harrumphed. "Average until the beginning of this year. Her last report said, *'needs a change of attitude'. 'Non-communicative'. 'Non-compliance with the teachers'.* She gets mostly C's and her basic mood is sullen. We try to talk to her but we get no response. Just basic teenage garbage. I hope to hell you can make a difference."

She stepped back and disappeared inside, leaving me standing on the front patio like a salesman not welcome inside.

The front door opened up into an entrance about two metres square where a staircase to the left led to the bedrooms upstairs. To the right tucked around a wall, I could hear the news on television and from the front door I could see the kitchen and hear the soft rumble of a man's voice. Against the wall to the kitchen, a leather lounge rested and would have the best view of the television. A CD player and a million CDs were in a wall unit standing on the other wall. In front of the lounge was a coffee table of some dark wood that matched the wall unit. I vaguely wondered if the lounge was indeed leather or mock leather like mine. Mine had looked good in the showroom but it made embarrassing farting noises if you moved on it the wrong way.

What I did notice was the walls weren't lined with cash, but I hadn't seen the bedrooms. One shouldn't jump to conclusions.

One minute later, Jazz stood at the door in front of me.

Her hair was shoulder length now, not the bob she used to have, but it was the same golden brown. And she'd grown three inches.

She was wearing snug denim shorts and a tank top. When young girls flaunt, the result is often comical, but she seemed totally at ease advertising her body. Smooth, tan arms and long, tanned legs were showcased by the minimal clothing and toenails displayed blood red polish.

She had my colouring, her mother's bone structure but had changed enough in recent years to bear no resemblance to either of us. Her cheekbones were high, her full lips glossed pink and her eyes heavy lined. Her nose was dusted with freckles she had tried to obliterate with lots of make-up that made her look beige.

"What do you want?" she asked. Her eyes shone with anger and small spots of red glowed through the make-up on her cheeks. I remembered when she was little and about to throw a tantrum, those small red spots would always appear just before the onslaught.

"Hello, Jasmine. I just came over to see you." I offered a smile, but it wasn't returned. "I'd like to come over more from time to time. Maybe I can take you out to dinner sometimes or to a movie? Maybe we could just hang out wherever you want to."

"Christ! My name's Jazz! And I'm twelve years old! I don't *hang out*."

Gone was the little girl running through the kitchen at an age when kids are always in a hurry, rushing from one interest to the next. Gone was the little girl with eyes full of innocence and fun.

A memory of her popped into my mind. The sun directly behind her so that the curls around her face were orangey red, a halo of fire, her features softened even more because of the light shadow. Her eyes crinkled at the corners as she smiled up at me. Ice cream dribbling down the front of her dress.

Sally was right. It wasn't going to be easy.

"I don't know the terms you kids use these days. What I'm trying to say is I just want to keep in touch more often."

She huffed derisively and shook her head like she couldn't believe how stupid I was. "Like what? Make a new start? Get to know me and then I'll open up my heart and tell you all my deep dark secrets? Is that what you mean?" She huffed again. Tossed her hair. "You ended our family two years ago and now you want a new start?" She was still shaking her head in disbelief.

"Life is all beginnings and endings, Jazz. Nothing stays the same. Parting, losing the people and things we love the most, well," I shrugged, "that's life."

"Shit. I know that! It's *you* thinking you can just walk back into my life. *That's* the problem."

I decided to let the swearing go, after all she had a point. I *was* just turning up and trying to walk back into her life. But I felt the need to defend myself.

"*I* didn't leave, Jazz. Your mother took you from *me*. Remember?" We were going over old ground again and memories of my last disastrous visit popped into my head.

"That was two *years* ago. How many times have you even seen me in that time? How many times did you even *ring* me?"

"I had a job that included working nights a lot of the time. I wasn't always home when it was convenient to ring." Even to my own ears, it sounded weak.

"That's a pathetic excuse." She huffed again. "Mum said even when you were with us, you never bothered to talk to her."

What did I expect? Sally to tell her what a nice guy I was?

She continued to glare at me. She was so close. All I wanted to do was reach out and hold her. I wanted to spend time with her. Get to know her. Now it looked like it wasn't going to happen. If I believed in God, I'd say it was God's way of punishing me for the way I'd treated them. Very Old Testament of me.

"You know what I think?" she said. "I think you liked the *idea* of a family but when it actually came down to doing all the stuff that families do, you were never around. Mum did everything. I hardly ever saw you!"

I looked at this defiant child who was almost a woman and realised that in just a few years, a different sort of problem would raise its head and we would look back on this and wonder which was the worst. I remember myself at twenty-one. So confident. I was a man and could make all my own decisions without anyone's help, thank you very much. Every Friday night at six o'clock after work, my friends and I would be at the pub ordering our first drinks. We'd be pretty much drunk by eight.

That was a long time ago. But you still see the pubs full of kids on Friday and Saturday nights, so I guess some things don't change. The only thing different now is the legal drinking age is eighteen. If Sally thought it was tough now, she was in for a surprise in a few years time and I could only hope that she allowed me into her life enough so that I could help when that time came.

I took a deep breath and said, "I'm not a policeman anymore Jazz but being one is a hard job with unusual hours and you see too much of what's wrong with people."

No matter what I said, I had let work take over my life – our life. I'd been working long hours to try and build my career and even though I could try and justify my actions by saying I was doing it to secure my family's future, the fact remained I had isolated them.

I shifted from one foot to the other and looked at her. "Most times, you don't want to go home and chat about it. I tried to explain that to your mother but she could never understand."

She shook her head, telling me she didn't understand it either.

"Do you think I'm an idiot or something?" Now she really sounded pissed off.

I was getting one of those headaches you get when you know that nothing you say is going to be right. Maybe my blood sugar was just low.

I took a deep breath and then I let it out. I felt tired and when I spoke, my voice was inaudibly soft.

"No. I'm trying to make you understand that my intentions were to make things easier for you and your mother. If I went around it the wrong way, I'm sorry."

We grew silent. Eventually, she asked, "So, what now?"

I was wondering that myself.

"I'd like to get to know you again," I repeated.

She laughed. "And help me get my act together and be a *good* girl. Do better at school. Get better grades. Something like that?"

"How are you going at school?"

She snorted through her nose. "School's a waste of time." She played with her hair as she talked. "Too boring. Too slow. Too full of rules. Don't do this. Don't do that. Even Mum nags me."

"Nags how?"

"Clean my room," she singsonged. "Do my chores." She rocked her head grumpily from side to side as she spoke. "Get ready for school without calling her a bitch. Stop swearing. Go to school, pay attention, build up my grades, don't break curfews, get some decent friends." She rotated her hand as if spooling yarn and rolled her eyes. "On and on and on. Says she's really *worried* about me."

"Maybe she is."

"Mom *likes* to worry." She frowned at me and gave me more of the impatience. "How much longer do I have to stand here and talk to you?"

"You don't have to stand here at all, if that's what you want. I just want you to know that I'd like to get to know you better."

"Well, I don't know about that just yet," she said petulantly.

We held each other's eyes for a long time.

"I DON'T KNOW! ALL RIGHT?" she yelled, then turned around and stomped up the stairs.

Sally came out of the kitchen and walked towards me, glancing up the stairs at the same time.

The small smile had appeared again. "Nice seeing you again, Jack. I told you it wasn't going to be easy." She shrugged. "Hormones."

We both nodded, neither knowing what to say. As if we were a couple of strangers. As if we hadn't been married for thirteen years and as if we didn't share a daughter that I could hear stomping around upstairs.

I nodded some more. "Okay. Well. I'm sorry about the short notice. I'll ring earlier next time."

"Do that," she nodded. Our eyes held for a moment. "I was sorry to hear you left the force, Jack." She glanced down at her feet for a second before lifting them. "I know how much it meant to you."

Little unconnected memories surfaced. The creak of the wooden swing in our yard as I pushed Sally the first night we moved into the house in Hobart. The maple tree dropping its fiery red leaves on the front lawn as four-year-old Jazz scooped them up and threw them above her head, laughing. Then I remembered sitting on the front steps the night Sally left me. Rain fell softly onto the leaves of the Leopard tree with a soft pitter-patter. In the distance, I could hear the sorrowful barking of a dog. A baby crying in the distance. Tyres crunching down the neighbour's driveway.

Sally opened her mouth to say something just as a male voice from inside the house called out, "Sally?" She glanced quickly over her shoulder and the moment was gone.

She turned back with a tight smile and said, "Bye Jack."

She closed the door softly and left me standing on the portico.

That went well, I thought.

38

I t took us almost a month to get to court. On the night before the trial, I did not sleep well. I woke often and when I did sleep, it was permeated by dreams where a shadow stood silently in the darkness watching me.

That morning, my eyes flipped open at exactly six a.m. with the alarm. There was no fluttering of lashes, no gentle blink toward consciousness. The awakening was sudden like a spooky ventrilo-quist-dummy click of the lids. The world was black and then suddenly, it was *Showtime!* My head was throbbing and I fumbled to quieten the shrill noise that was reverberating around the inside of my skull.

The darkness was only just easing away leaving a salmon colour in its wake. I had been floating in that groove between slumber and consciousness where you sometimes stumble and plummet and need to grab the sides of the bed. My therapist would have had a field day with that dream.

As I drank my coffee on the veranda, early morning fog shrouded everything except for patches of topaz sky streaked with pink behind the mist. In Tasmania, fog usually doesn't clear until a couple of hours before sunset with intermittent rain during the day but in the tropics, fog means a clear hot day on the way. I dressed in my best suit despite the itching I knew it would cause in the heat and glanced at the mirror. The face that stared back at me was what Sally had called 'dog-sad'. I looked like someone who had just come out of surgery, still groggy with anaesthesia. The hair could have done with a cut, my eyes looked grainy, lines were etched deeply on either side of the nose and an unhealthy glaze filmed the eyes. Forty-five was too young to look this bad.

I had one of those dull aches behind the eyes when you know you haven't had enough sleep, so I had one more coffee to help clear my head before picking the keys up from the hall table, locking the door behind me and heading off towards Surfers Paradise Court House.

At this time of year, the stretch of the M1 is one of the ugliest pieces of land on the coast. Treeless and flat with a brown stubble interrupted only by power lines and street lights, it looked like all of the goodness had been sucked out of the earth. This morning, there was a slight haze to the north and the west and a thin band of cirrus clouds were forming high over the mountains to my right. Yep, a warm day on the way.

My route to the courthouse took me past residences, then town houses and on to tower blocks shining and glittering in the suffused light that gradually filled the sky, making the water look like liquid fire. Where I lived and these imposing buildings was like two worlds with one simple division – those with money and those with little. The strange part was that they lived side by side.

It wasn't just material worth: a big house, a new car, a boat, a profession. Money bought more than that. It bought control. The judges and the judged. The rulers and the ruled. Those who made fashion and those who followed it. The two understood each other even if they didn't like each other and they understood the inequalities.

The sun had inched high in the sky, pulling shadows shorter and shorter and the morning warmth shimmered off the roads and cars giving an illusion of a silver lining. White gulls floated and circled overhead and girls in minuscule bikinis were already on their way to the beach ready to soak up the autumn sunshine with no regard for the ads on television about slip, slop and slapping.

When I arrived at the courthouse, reporters had converged around the entrance and the buzz was like a humming of flies. Behind the tightly packed paparazzi stood a white van from a television network with an enormous satellite dish perched on top. As I drew closer, it spat out a few more reporters. A cameraman for a Brisbane television station saw me and swung his camera around, knocking a blonde female talent off kilter. She stumbled and shot him a nasty look before running towards me with her microphone held out in front as I walked towards the entrance. In seconds, everyone was talking at me at the same time. The buzz was like a humming of flies.

I muttered *'shit'* louder than I intended as I pushed my way through, walking with my head held high to the courthouse door. A seagull hovered in the breeze and as he floated past, he looked down at me. I glared at him and he banked away quickly from the building. If only reporters were that easy to get rid of.

I heard someone yell ... *'the public have a right to know'* ... and I hesitated for a second and looked in the direction of where I'd heard the voice. Sonya Martin stared back at me in the crowd of hopeful faces. Alerted, everyone held up their microphones in case I had something vital to say. These faces would be the ones that people watched tonight, glued to their televisions, or web sites and Facebook feeds. These people would try to express their sorrow, horror, anger and they would cry for justice and demand action. And then they would move onto the next story tomorrow.

Instead of saying anything, I opted for a scowl while cameras flashed and the red light from the camera crew blinked.

The night before, Karen had sent me an email telling me to head to Courtroom 3. Joe's case was the first case on the list and she wanted me sitting next to her well and truly ahead of time. As I made my way to the courtroom, my mobile pings with a text. It's Karen. *Where are you?* I glanced at my watch and realised I'd only just made it.

Joe and Karen both frowned at me as I sat down next to Karen. I gave Joe what I hope was a reassuring smile before whispering to Karen, "You'll be treated to my handsome face all over the news tonight."

She shushed me, obviously annoyed, as Brad Jefferson shuffled some papers on his desk, ready to stand and give his opening speech. The buzz from spectators quietened as the presiding judge, Judge Everly, banged her gavel for silence.

Jefferson cleared his voice and walked around his desk to the open space in front of the jury.

"It was a rain-swept night." His smooth voice echoed in the court-room. "Kids were asleep, cars were parked in their garages and the houses were dark. Everything was locked up tight. An unlikely night for...."

I nudged Karen hard in the ribs. She blurted out, "Objection, your honour."

In the month preceding the trial, both of us were lost in our own worlds. Karen had work to do and I helped where I could. Mostly, I went home to a quiet house and memories that kept me awake well into the night. Now, I was sitting at the defence table with Joe to my left and Karen to my right as Judge Everly peered over her glasses at me, giving her a schoolmarmish edge.

She glanced at Karen and said, "We're only on the fourth sentence, Councillor. Don't you think it's a bit premature?"

"Mr Jefferson is implying that all the houses were locked up on the night of the murder when he knows full well that there is no evidence that Ms Connor's house was locked at all. He can't prove the possibility that everyone could have strolled into the house at any time for any purpose, whether......."

"Miss Sawyer, that's enough. You'll have your turn to discuss failures of proof. Objection overruled."

"Let me start again," Jefferson said smirking at the jury. "It was a quiet rain-swept night. The kids were asleep, the cars in their garages and the houses were dark. Everything was locked up safe and sound. An unlikely night for ...."

I jabbed Karen again just as she jumped up. "Objection, your honour. He did it again."

"Miss Sawyer, I have already overruled the objection. Mr Jefferson can say what he pleases. Sit down. By the way, who is that gentleman sitting beside you?"

"This is ex-detective Jack Curtis and he is a colleague helping me with the investigation, your honour."

"Please put a leash on him, councillor."

"Yes, your honour."

"An unlikely night," said Jefferson hurriedly, "for a murder."

"Objection," I blurted out.

"Oh *please*," moaned Jefferson, spinning around to face me.

"What now?" asked the judge.

I stood. "Whether or not there was a murder is a legal conclusion for the jury to decide later after receiving all the evidence. An opening is not the time to throw all kinds of legal terms at them at this early stage because it might not be warranted by......."

"Overruled," she said, glaring at me. "Murder is the charge, and so he can use the word if he wants to. Sit down, Mr Curtis. I've had enough of you already and we're only......" she glanced at her watch, "three minutes into the trial." She closed her eyes an infinitesimal second. "Let me make myself clear. I will not put up with you interrupting Mr Jefferson's opening again. I don't want to hear your voice again, even if the building is on fire. Do you understand?"

"Yes, your honour. Thank you."

"And don't thank me when I reprimand you. It puts me in a foul mood, Mr Curtis."

The jury laughed at that one and I smiled back at them. Jefferson glared at me before turning around and beginning again with his back to me, as if anticipating the next interruption but without the same assurance he started with.

I closed my own eyes and listened absently to Jefferson's opening speech. I was still in an unsettled place, confused as to what had really happened that night, uncertain about who had done the murder, certain that Joe *hadn't* done it even though I had done everything in my power at the beginning to screw it up for him. I was keeping facts from Joe and Karen and I was playing a dangerous game.

My life, to this point, had been an unmitigated failure. I had little money, no job and very few friends, one of whom was sitting beside me. My life had somehow veered out of control and was looking pretty dim. Somehow, after all this time, I still had not figured out the rules. But where did I find a rulebook? Others seemed to know because they had fancy cars, fancy houses, a loving spouse, dozens of kids and they knew how to play the game and come out winners. How did *they* get hold of the rulebook while my hands were still empty? During the course of my career, I had spent enough time elbow-deep in the law to learn these rules, and lots of others besides. Inside was the only place where I *did* know the rules but I wasn't there anymore. I was an outsider and I was lost.

To keep within the rules laid out by Judge Everly, I spent the rest of Jefferson's opening speech restraining myself from objecting at his every word. I was halfway to standing many times until I noticed the judge's frown of displeasure and meekly sat back down again, squirming in the chair. I must have been something to behold. I knew this by the expressions of the faces of the jury members as they watched me, even as Jefferson continued.

As openings go, it was good, laying out all the facts that he would eventually prove Joe Banner was guilty with a devastating simplicity.

Motive. Joe and the victim had been involved in a fraud in the Peter Hobson case. Shannon had turned on him by stealing most of the money from their joint account and sleeping with another man. Joe had every reason to be furious, murderously so, and on the night of her murder, Shannon had been hit in the eye before being shot to death.

Opportunity. Joe was the only one we knew to have been in the house with the victim on the night of the murder.

Means. Joe's fingerprints were on his gun which forensics would prove had fired the bullet into Shannon Connor's heart. And then there were other little things. Joe had called *me* before he called 000.

And after the cops came, Joe had tried to run with a suitcase full of money, Viagra and his passport. Jefferson's opening alone should have been enough to clamp the irons on Joe if the jury hadn't been watching my valiant efforts to restrain myself. In fact, it got to the point, where the jury would glance my way after Jefferson said something and I would raise an eyebrow and they would understand to take what had just been said with a dubious look of their own. Have I said I love the courtroom?

When it was Karen's turn, she stood and squeezed Joe's arm.

"This is my client," she began. "Mr Jefferson over there is trying to convict him for something he didn't do. What then is Joe Banner's crime? Mr Jefferson says it is murder but he's wrong. Joe did not kill Shannon Connor. Someone else did. Someone came into the house and walked into the bedroom and shot Shannon Connor while Joe was in the spa with the whirlpools noisily whirling, wearing a set of earphones, listening to a jazz CD blaring in his ears. That is what happened, no matter how strange Mr Jefferson thinks it is. When the police came, they found the spa full, the earphones by the side of the tub with a CD loaded and primed with the sounds of a saxophone. When they checked Joe's hands, there was no evidence that he had fired a gun, because he hadn't. He was listening to the CD and when he came out of the tub, he found Shannon Connor dead. He didn't do it. So, why is he on trial?"

Karen stood behind Joe and put her hand on his shoulder. "His crime was he fell in love."

She walked slowly as she talked, moved toward the jury until standing right before the box.

"Joe had a life we all wish for. A lovely wife, a lovely house, a job that paid well and would pay far better when he made partner in a law firm owned by his father-in-law. And that decision to make Joe Banner a partner would have been made by his father-in-law, Matthew Simmons. Joe had a life we all wish for, but he gave it all up. Why? Mr Jefferson will claim he gave it up for money, but don't you believe it, members of the jury. Whatever Joe Banner did or didn't do, it had nothing to do with money. The evidence will show that Joe was in line to make millions and he gave it up. You will see that it was not money that motivated him. He sacrificed his wonderful life and tossed everything aside.... for love."

She let the sentence hang in the air before continuing. "Shannon Connor was beautiful, smart, sad and enticing. She was a siren calling Joe away from his wonderful life into an unpredictable one, and he couldn't help himself. He abandoned his wife, his job, his career – all for her. For love. You may condemn what he did and he'll have to suffer the consequences but he did it for love and that is not an offence in this country."

Part of my job was to watch the jury for any tell-tale emotions. While Karen paced, I watched.

"Now, you've all heard the name Peter Hobson from Mr Jefferson's opening statement. This man entered the hospital for a simple operation and ended up in a coma. Shannon Connor represented the Hobson family, seeking compensation. Joe Banner represented the insurance company and the doctor, seeking to avoid paying the family for the disastrous result. There is a file showing Mr Hobson had a pre-existing condition which might have won the case for Joe's client, but he buried the file so that the family of Peter Hobson could get some money and so that Shannon Connor, his love, could get some money, too."

A few jury members glanced over towards Joe. His head dropped to his chest and his chin rested on it, a look of contriteness written all over it. He knew this was coming and we'd practiced his reaction over the past weeks.

"It was wrong what he did, and it could be classed as stealing and I am not defending that. I don't think he did it for the money. If he was thinking of money he would have stayed with Matthew Simmons' daughter and become a partner in the firm and then stand in line to inherit Simmons' fortune. He would have ended up with more money than he could ever have spent."

Her shoes sounded like hooves on the wooden floor as she paced in front of the jury. "We can only imagine and suspect the motivation behind Shannon Connor's involvement with Joe Banner. But Joe

Banner buried the file and failed his responsibilities to his clients and the law and stepped over the line. Again, for love. What he did was wrong and a crime and maybe for that he should be tried. But he didn't bury the file for the money and when Mr Jefferson says he later killed his lover for that same money, you will know he is wrong."

She glanced quickly at the prosecutor before turning back to the jury. Their eyes swivelled to him as well then looked back at her when she began talking again. "You have also heard that Shannon Connor had another lover and *that* could be the reason why Mr Banner killed the victim."

She looked hard at the jury. "You'd think Mr Jefferson could make up his mind as to which reason it is that he thinks Joe Banner committed the murder. We have no dispute with the results of the DNA test resulting in the evidence of another lover only that Joe Banner did not have access to these scientific tests to learn the truth in the first place."

She stopped pacing to glance at each member of the jury. "It seems ridiculous, doesn't it? But Mr Jefferson will rely on this to show motive when there is not a shred of evidence that Joe knew of this other lover. Mr Jefferson assumes that Shannon was leaving Joe for another man and that is why he hit her and then killed her. But we all know that they were engaged and planning a future. So, ladies and gentlemen of the jury, who was Shannon Connor leaving my client for?"

She held her arms out, the palms of her hands facing the ceiling. "You could equally assume the opposite of what Mr Jefferson claims, that she was leaving this other lover for Joe and that was why the other man hit her when she told him it was over and then later killed her. The coroner will state that he cannot place the time exactly that the blow occurred to cause the bruise. It happened before the killing, but we don't know for sure how far beforehand. Could it not have been when Shannon told the other lover good-bye? Could it not have been *him* that lost control?"

She let the question hang in the air. "So, ladies and gentlemen, what will you learn about this other lover? Will you learn who he was? No. Will you learn whether or not Shannon had given him a key to her house? No. Whether Shannon had shown him the location of the gun? No. Whether he was murderously angry with Shannon for leaving him? No. Whether he had an alibi for the night of the murder? No. Watch as the trial unfolds and see if *any* of these questions are answered and wonder why not. Ask yourselves about the mysterious patch of wet carpet found by the police at the front door and wonder who it was who had an umbrella and left it there. Ask yourselves about the mysterious man in black who returned on the night after the murder when Joe Banner was already in police custody."

She had them in the palm of her hand. No one seemed to breathe as they watched her pace in front of them. "That is what the evidence will show. The evidence will show that Joe had no motive but that someone else did. The prosecution has brought this to trial without the evidence needed to answer these crucial questions that I have just raised. They have accused Joe Banner of killing Shannon Connor because his is the only name they have come up with and the link between the two of them is undeniable. Love. He loved her. He had given up everything for her. And that is why he is on trial today." She turned to look at Joe then turned back to face the jury.

"And so, what I want you to ask yourselves, is when did love become a
crime?"

39

The jury was let out for the day and we stood as the courtroom emptied. I put my arm around Joe and said a few encouraging words before the bailiff escorted him away to the transport that would eventually take him back to the watch house.

We were gathering up our notes and folders when I sensed someone standing behind me. I turned and saw Brad Jefferson.

"That was pretty good, Jack," he said, "that song and dance routine of yours."

"Thank you, Brad."

"Maybe you should have lowered your voice a little and done a Barry White imitation. I can see you singing, *'When did love become a crime?'*"

I smiled my Tom Cruise smile and he smirked back at me before he turned to Karen.

"I had thought blaming the lover would be your strategy. As good as any, I suppose. But I didn't think you'd sprout it at the opening, Karen, especially when any day he could walk into the courtroom and blow your defence out the door."

"Well, there you go," I said, before Karen could say anything. "Karen and I are just a couple of fools."

"Blaming the lover in the opening might just force his hand. I'm spending all my resources on finding this mysterious missing man. And believe me, we'll find him and get his alibi. By the way," he turned to me, "Detective Cavanaugh has asked if you would consent to allow us to examine your phone logs for that night."

"And once again, I refuse." I said. "I'm working with the defence and that is classed as attorney-client privilege. Besides I don't think the judge will allow you to rummage around in the defence's phone logs after the trial has started."

"Maybe not. But not every defence team is called moments after a murder has been committed. I suppose we'll just have to see." He tossed a black folder onto the desk. "I'll be filing this before I leave the courthouse today. I'll expect the judge to rule on it tomorrow."

Karen and I watched as he turned and left without another word.

I scanned the document. MOTION TO COMPEL THE DISCLOSURE OF CERTAIN TELEPHONE LOGS.

I tossed the document to Karen and said, "You'll have to answer this tonight."

She scanned it and looked up at me. "He's right about the lover, you know."

"Brad? Nah."

"He looked pleased."

"I thought he looked rattled."

"We should have left the lover out of it until the end. Now if he walks in and the DNA matches, and if he has a perfect alibi, we're sunk."

"Trust me, he won't."

"Why not?"

"He has a reason to hide. And if he hasn't come forward yet, he won't in the future."

"He might if he thinks Joe is the killer and Joe might get off if he keeps quiet about his affair."

"He's not that noble."

"How do you know that, Jack?" Her eyes scoured my face as she frowned.

"Trust me."

She stared at the door Jefferson had just walked through and said, "It's as though he already knows who the lover was."

"Wouldn't he have to disclose that to you?" My voice sounded a little shaky even to my own ears.

"Not if it's only a suspicion."

"We had to do it, Karen. To win this jury, we had to make the jury see that the missing lover was the answer to the question of who killed her. If we tried to offer him at the end, it would have looked like nonsense. Now he's right here in the courtroom with us ready to shoulder the blame when the evidence is confusing. He's what the jury will see when the police state that they couldn't find gunpowder on Joe's hands. They'll say that the rain washed it off but the jury will be wondering about the other man. And when the DNA pattern of the semen goes up on the chart, they'll be wondering if they're looking at the DNA of the killer. By the time we get to closing, they will have come up with reasonable doubt."

Karen stared at me, amusement in her eyes. "You make it sound easy."

"Genius always does. Have you decided if Joe is going to testify?"

"He wants to, but I don't think I'll let him. He'd have to say he knew about the other man and that he hit her on the night of the murder. Those two facts alone could end it for us."

"But what about the open door? What about someone else slipping in through the door that night?" I asked.

"That, dear Jack, is why they invented cross examination."

Cross examination, in my opinion, is a witch's brew. It mostly acts as a truth serum, which wasn't our problem at the moment. There were no liars here and no false testimony. The case against Joe was powerfully circumstantial but those circumstances were basically true. It was the nature of those circumstances that we had a quarrel and it meant we had to have a different type of cross. We had to turn the inconceivable into conceivable, the unthinkable into the thinkable and the improbable into possibility.

What Karen had to do was turn phantoms into flesh and blood. I sat her back down at the defence table and told her how to do just that.

40

———

"Mrs Jackson," Karen began. "You told the police that you saw my client, Joseph Banner, sitting outside his house at around eleven o'clock on the night of the killing. Is that correct?"

Mrs Jackson sat on the stand looking prim and proper in her starched blouse, powder blue cardigan and firmly sprayed blue hair tied back in a chignon. She was the neighbour who lived directly across from Shannon's house.

"That's correct," she said, her false teeth clattering as she spoke.

"What was Mr Banner wearing, Mrs Jackson?"

She squirmed. "There were a lot of shadows but it looked like he had nothing on."

"Were the lights on, do you remember?"

"Yes, they were."

"And from where you were standing, you saw a man walk up to Mr Banner and then go inside. Do you see that man in the court room, Mrs Jackson?"

She pointed to me. "That man there."

I resisted the urge to finger wave to the jury.

"Please note that the witness is pointing to Mr Curtis," Karen said to the court reporter before turning back to Mrs Jackson.

"There were shadows that night, you said?" she continued.

"Yes."

"I notice you wear glasses."

"Yes."

"Were you wearing them that night?"

"Yes." Her hand fussed with a gold earring. "I wear them all day until I go to sleep and I put them back on when I get up in the morning."

"When you saw Mr Curtis, was he holding an umbrella?"

"No."

"A bag then that he could have placed on the carpet inside the front door?"

"No."

"How long had you been watching from the window, Mrs Jackson?"

"I resent that remark." She straightened up and pointed her chin at Karen. "I have more things to do than sit and watch out of my window."

"What if somebody had walked up the steps before Mr Curtis with an umbrella or a bag? Would you have noticed? You having more things to do than sit and watch your neighbours, that is?"

She hesitated, glancing at Jefferson who sat as still as a rock in his seat.

"Perhaps," she muttered.

"In fact, an army could have gone in and out and you wouldn't have noticed. Is that correct?"

"I suppose."

Karen pretended to consult her yellow pad, but she was actually allowing Jefferson to understand that she'd won this round.

"Thank you, Mrs Jackson," she smiled sweetly and glanced at the judge. "No more questions, your honour."

Karen sat down beside me and smiled. Like me, she was not above poking holes in airtight cases just to create doubt where none should have existed. But this was not a sham defence. In my heart, I knew Joe was innocent but someone had killed Shannon and I wasn't above widening the boundaries.

41

———

"Officer Barrett, in your report you said you did a quick examination of the house after finding the corpse and you noticed a wet patch of carpet inside the front door."

Karen was pacing in front of the stand as the policeman settled himself into the seat. There wasn't a sound in the courtroom and every member of the jury was watching her closely.

"That is correct."

She stopped pacing and made eye contact. "Was the roof leaking above the wet patch?"

"Not that I noticed."

"So the carpet could have been wet because an umbrella had been placed there."

"Yes, I suppose."

"Was there an umbrella stand there?"

"No."

In the past month, we'd rehearsed this next question and we both knew she'd get the door slammed in her face for asking it. If Jefferson sat still long enough to let her complete it.

"So, it would seem that the front door wasn't the usual place were Mr Banner and Ms Connor would leave..."

Brad Jefferson shot to his feet. "Objection, your honour."

I have never seen a prosecutor leap up like that. A *Perry Mason moment*, the reporters could call it. If any of them remembers Perry Mason.

"Sustained," said the judge.

"But Mr Jefferson gave no reason for his objection, your honour," Karen said.

"I'm sustaining it anyway," repeated the judge.

Karen looked amazed as she turned to the jury. As if – *Can you believe this? Don't we all want it to be fair?*

"But I'm just trying to show that this was not a usual place for a wet umbrella or such."

"Oh, Your honour!" Jefferson yelled.

"Move on, Ms Sawyer." Judge Every glared at Karen.

"O...kaaay," Karen said slowly, eyes flicking to the jury again. Twelve eyes turned to me and I raised a questioning eyebrow, adding to the combustion. Without saying anything else, her words screamed 'reasonable doubt' as they floated in the hushed courtroom.

As if weighing up her words, she took a deep breath. "Okay, then. Is it possible then that if someone came in with a wet umbrella and left it by the door..."

Jefferson was on his feet again. Karen ignored him, talking faster.

"...then he would have taken the wet object with him when he left, unlike Mr Banner who was still inside the house?"

"Your honour! I object in the strongest way! You have already ruled for Ms Sawyer to move on!" Jefferson's voice cracked with derision.

Judge Every sighed. "The question has been rephrased, Mr Jefferson." She glared at Karen. "You may proceed, Ms Sawyer. But the door is closing."

Karen nodded. "Please answer the question, Officer Barrett."

"I suppose anything's possible."

"It certainly is," Karen smiled broadly. "Thank you."

She walked over to our table and took the sheet of paper I held out for her.

"Now, Officer Barrett. You stated that you found a portable CD player with headphones in the bedroom beside the spa. Is that correct?"

"Yes, that's correct."

"And the spa had jets?"

"Yes."

"Did you check to see if they were operable?"

"Yes, I did."

"And were they loud?"

"It was a small bathroom, so yes, I suppose you could say that."

She walked over to the table again, picked up the bag with the headphones inside, then walked back to the stand. She handed the bag to the officer and said, "Are these your initials on the bag?"

He looked closely at the signature. "Yes, they are."

"And those are the headphones you found?"

He looked down at the bag and shrugged. "If the initials are mine, then those are the headphones."

"Can you open the bag please, officer?"

He pulled the tape from across the top of the bag and reached in for the portable CD player.

"On the night of the murder, the disc inside was a jazz selection. Is that correct?" Karen asked.

"Yes, that's right."

"Is it still inside?"

He opened the case and said, "Yes, it is."

"And the digital readout states the track number being played and the volume it is being played at?"

He shut the case and looked at the readout. "Yes, it does."

"Did you make sure it was operable before you put it inside the bag?"

Jefferson was leaning forward, the palms of his hands on the prosecutors table, ready to leap up at the first inadmissible word if needed.

"Yes, I did. I listened a little to it."

"Was it loud?"

"I suppose."

Karen looked at Judge Everly. "May I approach the witness, your honour?"

The Judge gave Karen a sceptical look but nodded.

"Officer Barrett, I'm going to put in fresh batteries and I would like you to tell me whether or not it was this loud when you listened to it on the night of the killing."

Karen put in the new batteries and handed the policeman the headphones. When they were secured on his head, she asked, "Are they comfortable?"

"Yes, ma'am."

Karen reached over and pressed *play*.

"How are the headphones now, Officer?"

"Pardon," he yelled.

Karen reached over and lifted one of the earpieces. "Is the volume the same as the night of the murder?" She left the earpiece fall back onto the policeman's ear and stepped back.

Just then, I picked up a large legal volume on the table and dropped it flat onto the floor. The noise was like a shot in the courtroom and every member of the jury jumped in their seats as I apologised loudly and bent to pick up the volume. Brad Jefferson leaped to his feet, a laser shot of animosity directed at me.

"Objection! Really, your honour!" His face was seriously crimson as he spat the words out. "This is beyond..."

Judge Everly glared at me and was about to start launching onto a reprimand when Officer Barrett took the headphones off and said, "It's hard to tell, but I would state, yes, the volume is the same as it was on that night."

The policeman looked around in surprise and confusion as the courtroom broke into laughter.

"Thank you, Officer," Karen said sweetly. "You've been very helpful."

42

Joe's trial continued with our witch's brew of cross-examination hoping to bring a big enough gap of time for a murderer to walk through. As we methodically worked against everything Brad Jefferson brought out, I began to feel a shift.

A friend of Shannon's testified for the prosecution which was strange because I never knew she had any. Her version of Shannon wasn't very flattering, saying she was materialistic, mysterious and cunning. You can see I use the word 'friend' loosely. As she spoke, I felt something, a distortion that I had begun to see with crime scene officers, neighbours and witnesses. I looked around to see if anyone else saw it too, but no, the feeling was coming only from me.

The friend testified that once when she was in Shannon's office listening to her talk over the speakerphone, she heard a man's voice that she didn't recognise. This friend had already met Joe, and it wasn't him, but no names were used and Shannon didn't tell her who it was. Something about the Gibson matter was all that was said, but she could tell something was going on with them.

Karen was great on cross, making it obvious that from the conversation the woman could have no real idea if the man on the other end of the phone had murderous intent. She stated that Jefferson had brought this witness to court in the effort to defuse the theory of another vicious man who could have killed her but instead, he had proved our theory that there was indeed a mysterious man with a disembodied voice who was able to wreak havoc.

I had been trying so hard to save Joe that I had forgotten that I myself could easily be where Joe was now. That realisation made me sick to the stomach as the testimony came to an end.

Judge Everly looked at her watch, which made everyone else in the courtroom do the same thing. It was nearing 3.00pm.

"I am going to call it a day, ladies and gentlemen," she said. "We will reconvene tomorrow morning at 10.00am." At that, the bailiff said all rise and the judge walked out of the room, robes billowing behind her.

Just then, a note dropped over my shoulder onto the desk and I turned around to look into Sam Neil's dark, brooding eyes.

I want to talk to you.

Six frightening words.

43

We sat and stared at each other like this was our first date and we knew there wouldn't be a second one. Sam glanced down at her coffee from time to time, but she looked uncomfortable being alone with me as if she was cheating on her partner.

Our conversation was the kind that strangers have when they don't know what to say to the other person.

"So, what's up Detective?" I said finally.

She looked hard at me then. "I'm trying to figure out what's going on inside your head."

"You know me," I smiled. "Not much."

"So it would seem. But I keep wondering." She sighed. "Cavanaugh thinks you're hiding something." She tilted her head to the side. "Are you Jack?"

I put my hand over my heart and managed to look hurt. "Moi?"

"Why do you keep fighting our attempts to examine your phone logs?"

"Attorney-client privilege," I stated.

She snorted through her nose. "I know what it's called, Jack. What I want to know is why."

"Privilege is like a muscle. If you don't exercise it from time to time, it becomes weak and ineffectual."

Her eyes were chips of ice, cold and shrewd. "We're still trying to work out how Joe called you after he found his fiancée dead."

I waited a moment and tried to figure out how to play it. "Let's hope you get to the bottom of *that* mystery."

I could see the frustration written all over her face. "I don't have to tell you that this act of yours is ridiculous." She let out a sigh, exasperated and frustrated.

"It's called paralipsis. It's a rhetorical statement by which you add emphasis to a subject by professing to say little or nothing about it."

"Thank you, professor."

She shook her head and took a sip from her coffee cup then set it down heavily on the table. She picked out a packet of sugar jammed with others into a glass jar in front of us and began twisting it between her fingers. When she looked up, I was surprised by the emotion in her eyes. Something was weighing on her mind and she wasn't sure whether to say something or not. For once, I didn't say anything. I sat and waited for her to decide.

"Half of me wonders if it's worthwhile laying into you. Maybe you're too dumb to know how stupid you're being."

I smiled. "I'm hoping you'll listen to the other half then."

She didn't like my answer and I didn't like the fact that she was still asking the question.

She sat staring at the cup for a few seconds before continuing. "Did you find anything of interest in the safe-deposit box?"

My heart skipped a beat. "Safe-deposit box?"

"Shannon's box at the Commonwealth Bank in George Street, Sydney."

"Who exactly are you investigating, Detective?"

"I'm struggling here, Jack. Cavanaugh doesn't like you and he thinks you're smarmy."

My eyes widened. "Smarmy?"

"Smarmy and weak and definitely hiding something. I don't like what you're doing either and frankly, considering your past career,

I'm surprised by your behaviour. I think you're manipulating the case and you'll end up in a screaming heap."

"Does that mean you won't go out with me afterwards?"

She put the sugar down on the table and put her elbows on the table, cupping her chin on her interlocked fingers. "Tell me a story, Jack. Tell me a story about a man who leaves his wife for a scheming woman and finds himself up to his neck is something more terrible than he could ever have imagined. Tell me a story about a man who is out for revenge. A man who will do anything to get even. A man who has motive, means and opportunity."

"Are you writing a book, Sam?"

"Somehow," she continued as if I hadn't said anything, "I have this strange feeling that you're looking desperately for a different outcome here. But the evidence points right to Joe." She did a so-so thing with her shoulders and sat back in the seat. "I have to admit, though, that some of the evidence has been on my mind from the beginning. Like Joe really *did* love her. Like he really *wasn't* in it for the money. Like he doesn't seem the type to end a fight with a bullet. But it's not the doubts about the case I'm struggling with now. It's you that's confusing me."

"And what is it about me that confuses you, Sam? That I would stand by a friend accused of a murder he didn't commit? That I would leave no stone unturned to prove his innocence? Don't insult me, Sam. You know me better than that."

She sighed. "What I'm saying is you are in this deeper than you let on. I think you are in this up to your neck. But I can't quite figure out how. You are in this in ways that give me serious doubt."

"In what way?"

She shook her head. "This isn't about you asking me questions, Jack. I'm the one asking you."

She was letting me know that no matter how involved in the case I was, she was the one pulling the punches.

"Okay," I nodded. "Ask away."

She cocked her head. "Why did you hand over the gun?"

I paused for a moment, wondering what she actually knew and whether I could trust her, even with a little bit of truth.

I spoke slowly. "I thought possessing the gun might further the ends of justice."

"Don't insult my intelligence, Jack. That excuse sounds like bullshit."

I smiled. "It does, doesn't it? That's how good I am. I can even make the truth sound like lies."

She leant forward. "Then believe this too, Jack. All I want is for whoever killed Shannon Connor to go straight to hell."

"Oh Grandma, what big teeth you have." I laughed.

"I'm being serious here, Jack."

"Then look somewhere else, detective, because Joe didn't do it."

"What makes you so sure?"

"Okay, let's go over this. Here's your story. She seduced him for Hobson's money. She set him up for it, met him at a bar, let their knees touch accidentally, and seduced him totally and completely. He fell stupidly in love with her and yes, he lost everything because of her. But I'm telling you his hope for a better future together was real and he would never have killed that hope."

"An obsession couldn't have turned to violence?"

"Not with him and not with her. No matter what happened, he'd always remember the first time their knees touched under the table."

Maybe it was the catch in my voice that betrayed me, because she stared at me for a while in silence.

"And how did that feel exactly, Jack?"

There was nothing else I could say. I'd just cracked my halo and the holy ground I was standing on was burning my feet. I couldn't explain how the knocking of knees felt, the confusion, hope and lust mixed together. Not without betraying myself.

"I'm telling you what I can, Sam. Let's not turn this into a pissing contest."

She sighed. "That's not what this is about. But you sound like you had a connection with her, apart from Joe."

I struggled to keep the anger out of my voice. "Of course there's a connection. She was my friend's fiancé. She was *my* friend. I saw the body on the night of the murder, detective. I saw her on the bed with a bullet through her heart. I've seen more corpses than you and they never fail to stun me with their lifelessness. It's not like you can breathe life back into them or that they're asleep. The sight of her lying on the mattress in a pool of blood is something that haunts me, and I'll never be able to let it go." I took a deep breath to steady myself. "So yes, there's a connection between us."

I could see the hardness soften.

"It wasn't your fault, Jack."

Our eyes locked and I knew full well what the *'it'* was that she was referring to.

In my lap, my fingers curled into fists and my breath quickened.

Most people would have been rewarded with the view of my back as I walked out the door because I still don't want to face the fact that I've screwed up my life in a big way. Sam was different though. She had been my partner for a year and I missed her, and that life, every day of my existing one.

Instead, I took a deep breath and blew air out through my mouth in a loud push.

"If I'd been doing my job the way I should have been, Stephen would still be with his family today, happy and alive."

There were a few seconds of ticking silence before Sam replied softly, her eyes boring into mine, dark and clouded with sorrow.

"You did everything you could. Deep down you know that." Her head was nodding as she spoke, almost like she was talking to a child trying to convince me that what she was saying was true.

"What happened wasn't your fault," she repeated, stressing each word.

I felt something cleave inside and tear away. I sometimes hope I will eventually feel settled about the things I've done, the choices I've made. But then I wonder if I'll always look back and think about all the things I could have done. I had such high hopes when I joined the force and now I look back on my life and all I feel is exhaustion and bitterness. They have lodged themselves deep in my bone marrow.

When I was little, my mother used to read nursery rhymes to my brother and me. One of the ones I hated the most was Humpty Dumpty. It's a very scary poem. Humpty falls over the edge and breaks into a lot of pieces and no one knows how to put him back together again. Not all the king's horses or all the king's men. No one. Nobody wants to think there's anything in the world that could fall apart as badly as that. Right now, I was Humpty Dumpty. I felt broken beyond repair. And when you begin to feel yourself going over the edge, all you can do is hang on to your mind tightly.

Sam's voice brought me back from my misery.

"You're something else, you know." She was looking at me with soft eyes and I felt my heart twinge. "You're not like the rest of them. You're not hard and uncaring. You feel things far beyond what the others feel. You won't admit it but inside, you're tender. And that's what makes you special."

I could feel tears burning behind my eyes. I needed to change the tone of the conversation.

"You're right, as always." My voice came out a little tight, but I was pretty happy that I hadn't blubbered in front of her. "I don't think I get enough credit for the fact that I do this unmedicated."

Instead of the expected laugh, Sam looked ravaged.

"Oh, come on!" I laughed. "That was funny!"

She swallowed audibly and glanced down at the remains of the dark liquid in her cup.

"I'll be fine," I whispered. The prettiest of lies versus the ugliest of truths.

She tilted her head to the side. "You look...different somehow," she began.

"More handsome?"

She smiled. "Yes."

"Calmer?"

She nodded.

"I know. And all my tea towels are lined up neatly in the kitchen. Can we move on now?"

She nodded and seemed to come to a decision.

"I'm wondering whether I should tell you something."

I sighed heavily. "I'm not up to these games right now, Sam. What is it?" I asked tiredly. My head hurt and I had no time for where I thought this was going.

"Do you remember what Joe was working on before all this happened?"

My eyes narrowed because I couldn't see the connection. I shrugged. "Yes."

"The Jessica Harding case? Right?"

I still didn't know where this was going. "If you're wondering if I've taken the case, the answer is no. I've done my time working for the greater good. I'm staying here on the Dark Side. I'm not about to fit back into your world. I'm here to try to make my own life work."

She stared at me in silence, her eyes glinting as she ran her index finger around the top of the coffee cup.

"Okay. What are you trying to tell me, Sam?"

She seemed to come to a decision. She stopped fidgeting and sat back again.

"I'm telling you that the officer in charge of the Jessica Harding case resigned after two weeks on the case. Grayson was furious because there was no explanation."

When I worked with Sam, her opinion of Inspector Grayson differed from mine. While Grayson and I were forever at each other's throats, she tried to make me see that his job couldn't be easy. He had to cope with budgets and bureaucrats. Somehow Grayson sensed an ally in Sam and always gave her a little leeway where I got none.

"Why are you telling me this?"

"After only one week into the case, he was seen with a woman in the station on several occasions and someone overheard Jessica's name being mentioned on at least one of those occasions. A dark-haired woman, thin, piercing blue eyes and bright red lipstick. Ring a bell?"

My heart did a double flip, but I kept quiet.

Sam never missed anything which is why she was the best partner I'd ever had. I could depend on her and she knew she could depend on me. Together our solve rate had been higher than any other partnership in Surfers Paradise Station. We knew each other's mannerisms and moods and nothing escaped our attention.

Sam continued, her eyes intense as she watched me. "Whenever she was noticed, she turned her back so as not to be seen." She smiled now. "But of course, she was noticed. She was definitely noticed. How could she *not* be? Someone who looked like her?" Sam snorted. "And don't you think it was strange that the detective assigned to the case resigned so suddenly when it hadn't even been solved? The case that he'd put so much time and effort into?"

"Why should it be strange? People resign all the time for lots of reasons." I gave her what I like to think was my *knowing* smile. "My advice is to check the file and see if something doesn't ring true."

She smirked. "I tried. The file is missing."

Now she had my full attention. "You're sure?"

"Absolutely. No one can locate it anywhere." She pointed an index finger at me, warningly. "This is *not* to get to the press or anywhere else. Am I clear on that?"

"Is this what I think it is? You want *me* to check this out? It's a four-month-old case that the police haven't been able to solve but you want *me* to look into it? Is that what you're actually saying?"

"Maybe it's just a coincidence" she shrugged. "But maybe it's not. I would think you'd want to cross all your t's and dot all your i's."

"What makes you think Joe had anything to do with this?"

"Maybe he didn't. But Shannon Connor was his fiancé and they were both helping the parents look for Jessica. Maybe she was just trying to find out more information for the family but that doesn't explain the secrecy and it doesn't explain the missing file or the fact that this police officer resigned very soon after her visits. You know better than anyone else, Jack. You resign at the *end* of a case not *during*. It's a matter of closure."

I sighed then reached into my pocket and pulled out a pad and pen. "All right. What's the detective's name and address?" I asked.

"The name of the officer is Mark Bartlett and the last known address was 3 North Street, Labrador. But that was three years ago."

I knew Mark Bartlett. I'd worked with him a couple of times and I'd liked him. I had no idea if this meant anything to Joe's case. I looked at my watch. 4.00pm. I still had a good hour and a half before it started to get dark.

"Okay Sam. I'll go and see him."

"You just remember what I told you that first night," she warned. "You come to me with anything, *anything*, that you find out. You be nice to me and I'll be nice to you. It's a little game *you* taught *me*. Remember?"

I crossed my heart. "I promise I'll call you, Sam, and I'll play nice."

She breathed in sharply or was it just a snort? I couldn't tell. Then she picked up her jacket and took out a $10 note and tossed it onto the table before turning away and walking out.

I tapped my pen on the table thinking how I was going to proceed. I couldn't just turn up at his door, especially if he didn't live at the North Street address. Sam said the address was three years old, but most police officers know that if you change addresses, you let the department know before you even tell your mother. It's more than just routine. It's mandatory. He'd left the force four months ago, but my bet was that if he hadn't changed the address before he left, he was still living there.

I called directory assistance and sure enough, they found a listing for a Mark Bartlett on North Street. I stared hard at the number they gave me, trying to remember where I'd last seen it. Then I remembered.

I picked up the red mobile phone and located the first call that Shannon had made on it. It was the same number.

I called the number and the same male voice answered after three rings.

"Hello?"

"Is Mark there?" I asked.

"This is Mark."

I hung up. In my career, I found that if people know you're coming, they often find reasons to leave before you get there. Harry Callaghan would just turn up unannounced. So was I.

44

The air was damp with the breezes coming off the ocean as I drove along Marine Parade on my way to North Road. I could see patches of darkening blue sky where the cloud cover was breaking up. I opened the window and the smell of seaweed and salt filled the car. I breathed in deeply, going over in my mind what I was going to say.

I parked outside the house and sat looking at the front door. Briefly, I closed my eyes trying to conjure up the smell and feel of the Shannon I'd loved. I wanted to keep this Shannon in my mind and hold her there because in my heart, I knew everything was going to change after my visit with Mark Bartlett. The Shannon I believed I knew would disappear and a cold, calculating woman with an agenda I couldn't begin to understand would replace her. I wanted to remember that person one last time before stepping out of the car and walking up the cracked pathway that led to the front door.

I took a deep breath and got out of the car, locked it with my remote before adjusting my belt and tightening the knot in my tie, the same one my daughter had given me for Christmas.

The gusting wind whipped at me and flattened my shirt against my body and my pants against my legs. Out on the Broadwater, I could barely make out the shadow of Stradbroke Island. In the distance, a foghorn sounded, and I knew it was the Southport ferry on its way to Stradbroke. To get to there, you have to pass through a collection of other small, forgotten islands that grip the sea in hard tufts of mangroves, sand, wiry trees and rock formations. This ferry was the only way to reach the island, apart from a private boat. The ocean roared and I noticed that the sea had lashed the beach in recent days. It was strewn with shells and driftwood, mollusc skeletons and some dead fish half eaten by scavengers. Trash had blown down from the streets as well as cans and sodden paper.

In the silence, I could hear the muffled sounds of country music. Just as I was about to knock on the door, the screen door opened with a protesting squeak and a man appeared in the doorway.

"Who the hell are you?" Then he stopped and stared disbelievingly at me. "Jack Curtis?" His eyes roamed my face before asking, "What the hell are you doing here?"

The tired face said early fifties, but I knew that Mark Bartlett was ten years younger. His watery blue eyes were dull and his pallor seemed more pronounced because of the red blotches on his face. His dark hair was thinning but the same couldn't be said about the unruly ruffle of his eyebrows. His skin tone said 'indoors': chalky white. Beside him, I looked positively ruddy. Even from three feet away, I could smell the odour of sweat, stale beer and bad breath. It took every ounce of willpower not to step backwards.

I decided to get straight to the point. "I'd like to talk to you about Jessica Manning's disappearance four months ago."

At the name 'Jessica Manning', the tired eyes widened.

His eyes glanced over my shoulder towards my car then back at me. "What are *you* doing looking into it? You're not a cop anymore, last time I heard."

"No, I'm not. Jessica's parents hired a couple of lawyers to help them find her and they have asked me to help them as well." Not exactly a lie but certainly not the whole truth.

He hesitated and looked behind him.

"A bad time, Mark?" I asked.

He nodded slowly. "Yeah, it is."

"Then I won't keep you long." The screen door banged behind me as I walked past him into the house.

Think of fresh air and sunshine and then imagine the exact opposite. That was the room I walked into. The curtains were pulled tightly closed across the windows and the room felt dingy and dank with the lack of sunshine. Dust particles rose from the carpet and circulated in the air with every step I took. The walls were dun-coloured and a plastic-looking chest of drawers, probably from Ikea, sat under the window. At one end of the room was a tiny eating area, a cheap radio and the remains of lunch sitting on the counter. From outside the window, I could smell garbage in the dumpsters and the peculiar smell of feral cats.

He sank down into a recliner and picked up an opened can of beer resting on a side table. He held it up to me, asking if I wanted one, and I shook my head. He motioned for me to sit down in another chair.

"You were the detective in charge of Jessica Manning's case?" I asked as I made myself as comfortable as I could on the wooden chair.

There was a slight hesitation before he answered. "That would be me."

"You resigned a week or so into the case?"

"Again, yes."

"Were there any suspects? Leads?"

He looked at me for a long time with a hard gaze. "Who did you say you were working for? The lawyer?" He laughed, a short abrupt noise that came out like a grunt. "Would that be Joseph Banner, by any chance?"

"That's right."

His eyes remained on mine. "He'll go broke paying someone to look into this."

"He's not paying me at all."

"And you think that's somehow going to change anything with me?" He smiled softly and shook his head.

"I can only hope."

He shook his head as he put his beer on the table. "Hope is nothing."

"Hope is everything."

I watched his face for a reaction. For a moment he seemed not to have heard me. When he spoke, his voice sounded dry, like dead leaves rustling in the breeze.

"I have a daughter, you know. She lives with her mother now. They left two years ago." He stared out the window, his mind somewhere else. "She went missing for a day once. Not even that, really. From four o'clock in the afternoon until ten o'clock that night, but she was only five at the time. And I'll tell you, you have no idea how long six hours can be until your child is missing."

He rubbed his eyes with the heels of a hand and blew a rush of air out of his mouth at the memory. "My wife went out back to take some things off the line and Carey got on her bike to ride around the block. We never let her do that by herself and it really pissed Carey off. Even at that age, she was a handful. But that's all it took. Five minutes and she was gone. We found her in a ditch near the park. She'd fallen off the bike, broken both ankles and had a concussion and passed out from the pain."

I wanted to speak, to try to communicate the empathy I felt but in the face of grief, words have no power.

He noticed the look on my face and held up his hand. "She's fine now. The ankles hurt like hell for months and she was scared for a while but that was the beginning of the end for my wife and me. She blamed me because I was sitting in a pub drinking by myself when it happened. If I'd been home where I should have been, it would never have happened. Angela was looking everywhere, tearing her hair out and I walked in at 9 o'clock, drunk. I looked at Angela and she looked back at me and both of us, without even saying a word, knew that whether we found Carey or not, we were finished. Any happiness we may have had was over. Everything good and hopeful, everything we lived for, really, was gone."

He stood up and walked over to a sideboard, picking up a photo.

He looked at it for a while then walked back and handed it to me.

"This is Angela and Carey," he said.

Angela had a fresh, young face and clear healthy skin with a halo of auburn hair. Pretty. The kind of happy, innocent pretty that starts inside and works its way to the outside. She was wearing a pair of jeans with a white cotton shirt that looked good on her but not expensive. She looked the sort to shop for bargains and found them. Over her shoulder, she had the strap of a large bag the size of my car and she sat almost primly with her knees and ankles together, her hands clutching the purse. The little girl beside her was about four or five, full of blonde curls and toothy smiles.

"They're beautiful," I stated. And they were.

"Yeah." He took a deep breath and walked back to his chair. "I guess what I'm saying is, no one can survive the loss of a child." His eyes raked mine. "No one."

My skin crawled. "What's your story, Mark?" I asked to break the silence that had started to swell between us.

Something rippled deep in the dark eyes, like the flick of a fish tail. He rubbed his face with his hands then he smiled. He was stockier and shorter than me, maybe five eight or so and he had a head of tight, curly, greying dark hair, olive skin and slim delicate hands. One cheek bore a small scar and he tapped it with his index finger.

"I always start with this. People usually ask me about it sooner or later. I got this case a couple of years ago, you know? Worst one I've ever been involved in when I lived in Adelaide. This guy was killing women in ways you can only imagine except in nightmares. Took me more than a year to find out who it was. But I did. Shot him five times after he got one shot off at me." He tapped his cheek. "Nearly got me but I moved my head at the last minute." He stared out the window at the rolling waves on the beach. "Saw my life flash before me and decided right then and there it was time to start thinking about leaving the force." He turned and smiled at me as he rubbed the stubble on his cheek. "Like you, I never found the right time until just recently."

"I'm going to say another name to you. And I want the truth." I leaned forward in the chair. "Shannon Connor."

He paled visibly and his eyes widened.

"Now I'll tell you what *I* know," my voice dropped almost to a whisper. "I know that you are aware Shannon Connor is dead. I also know that one day before her murder, after you'd resigned from the Jessica Harding case and then the police force, she called you here from her mobile." I watched his eyes burning into mine. "What I don't know is why."

The silence dragged on. He breathed heavily but said nothing.

"I also know the file is missing," I said softly.

He swallowed and for a full minute, the only sound was the hum of the refrigerator in the kitchen.

"Tell me what you know, Mark," I repeated.

He stood up suddenly. "Let's go outside."

I followed him and we stood in silence for a bit, the sea undulating in the distance, pockets of it dark silver and velvety. By now, the streets were sprinkled with rain and the clouds were beginning to gather again more threateningly on the horizon. I could hear the intermittent moaning of the foghorn on the ocean and from somewhere in the harbour, the sound of laughter drifted over to us.

There is a small population of 'live-aboards' in the harbour – people who actually use their boats as a primary residence. The idea was mildly appealing to me but with the size of the boat I could afford, the reality was I'd be showering and using the toilet in the marina and that put an end to that notion.

For something to say and looking up at the sky, I said, "Looks like it's going to be another big one tonight." The sky was dark, as dark as the foam churning against the sand.

He began as if I hadn't spoken at all. "I slept with that file while I was on the case. I knew it inside out. Then one day, barely a week into the case, in walks this woman that looked like an angel. A dark angel."

I said nothing but I knew who he was talking about. What I didn't know is why Shannon was involved in the case way back then when Jessica had only just gone missing.

"It started out just with a couple of lunches and a few drinks after work. She used to call me at work and when I wasn't there, she'd leave a secret message for me to call her back. The Gibson case, she'd say. Call me regarding the Gibson case."

It's strange how my heart once burned for Shannon and now it suddenly turned to ice. The blinkers were finally off and I saw her for what she really was. There was indeed a primordial evil that had blown through her and caused a swath of destruction wherever she went.

I read somewhere recently that weeds are just unloved flowers growing in the wrong place. It's never valued where it grows and according to some, they can be beautiful and resilient and they tend to dominate. One of the most beautiful and toxic is Belladonna, literally translated to 'beautiful woman' in Italian. If asked what word I would use to describe Shannon best, I couldn't think of a better word.

"She had a thing for the actor. Ever since *Braveheart*." He smiled sadly as he continued. His gaze was fixed on the watery red sunset barely showing behind the thin trunk of trees that had turned dark in the growing darkness. "Anyway, it got so that I couldn't think straight. She was always on my mind. And then I found out."

I shook my head and frowned. "Found out what, Mark?"

He didn't say anything for a moment, just stood there with his shoulders hunched as if waiting for the weight of the world to drop down on him. "About Jessica Harding," he said eventually.

I shook my head. "You've lost me. You were already working on the case. What are you talking about?"

"I found out who took Jessica Harding."

The air pulsed around us as I stared at him dumb-founded, almost not breathing. I had this feeling that what he was going to tell me would tilt my own world.

He nodded. "That's right. Shannon."

I blinked a few times. I know I did. "*Shannon* took Jessica? Are you mad?"

"I thought I was." His eyes scanned my shocked face. "Then I found out why and it all fell into place."

I waited.

"Jessica Harding was adopted at birth. Shannon was her birth mother."

In my heart, I knew he was telling the truth. I had seen the birth certificate myself. I just hadn't put two and two together. But, then again, who would have?

"But *she* took Jessica?" I stuttered. "*Shannon* took her?" I was repeating myself because it was so ... crazy. "After three years? She actually *stole* her?" I felt my stomach turn and my head begin to swim.

"She wanted her back." He was staring out past the breakers. "She told me she had been forced to give Jessica up but that she was going to change all that. She had money put aside." He glanced at me, "almost a million, she said." He turned and looked back at the ocean. "She had saved the money that had been given to her as a payoff when she fell pregnant and she'd saved some more since then."

He straightened his back and squared his shoulders as if he was trying to smooth out a pain between his shoulder blades.

"I was to keep Jessica safe with me until Shannon came back to us and then the three of us would go away together." He shook his head sadly. "For only a couple of days, at the most, she said."

The silence between us was deafening. What could I say?

"That was never going to happen," I eventually said.

He turned to me confused, as if he had been trying to explain that one and one equals three and I just didn't get it. He made a little blowing thing with his mouth and leant forward with his elbows on the railing, his hands clenched tightly.

"You think I'm crazy." I heard the anguish in his voice.

There are sudden rips in your life, deep knife wounds that slash through your flesh. One moment you have a life and the next moment, it is shredded into another. It comes apart like it's simply unravelling. A loose thread pulled. A seam gives way. The change is slow at first, but when it starts, there is no turning back.

Believe me, I know.

"No, not crazy, Mark. Never that." I cleared my throat. "But over the past two months, I've learnt a few things about Shannon Connor that no one knew. She had plans that didn't include you, Joe or any other man."

He was nodding and shaking his head at the same time and his eyes glistened. "Yeah. Yeah."

I had to ask one more question. "Where's Jessica been for these past four months, Mark?"

In the silence, it felt cold and damp as darkness closed in around us. Not fifty feet away, cars and trucks thundered on the roads and hundreds of people sat huddled in the heat of their cars heading home to their families. Not one knew that Mark and I were discussing the life of a little three-year-old girl taken from the warmth of her loving home and who was just another pawn in Shannon's private game.

"Safe," Mark said. Then added, "Safe and well."

"She has to go back to her parents. You know that."

He nodded slowly. "I know. What I don't know is how to do it without ending up with life in prison."

I could see the questions and doubts in his eyes and I felt wired into his mind somehow. I could almost read his thoughts. In times like this, everyone wants to know: Why me? How could this happen to *me*?

I knew he was asking those questions because I was asking the same ones myself.

I said my goodbyes, saying I'd call him after Joe's case was finished and he nodded when I repeated that he had to find a way to return Jessica.

When I walked back to my car, Frank Fitzroy was leaning on my bonnet, legs crossed inside khaki pants and wearing a tweed jacket that I quite liked, despite my feelings towards him.

"I'll buy you a drink," he said. "I've got a story you might want to hear. In fact, I *know* you will.

45

"This bloke sets up a meeting, wants me to spy on his wife. Oldest story in the book but this one has a twist."

The pub was busy, which I liked. There was lots of noise which meant no one could overhead our conversation. I was being paranoid, but a lot happened in the past few days and if I've learnt anything from my years as a cop, it's that you can't be too careful.

We were seated in a quiet corner, out of the way, and in front of each of us was a beer.

"He's a fancy dresser," Frank said. "You now what I mean? Silk hanky out of his suit jacket, a diamond pinky ring and his fingernails all manicured. I hated him on sight. And you know what? He didn't show the slightest bit of nervousness. Normally, a guy thinks another guy is doing his wife and he's all jumpy and angry. Not this guy. He's arrogant and it didn't feel right, even to me. There was something else going on." He gave me a little Groucho Marx eyebrow wiggle before continuing. "I've always said, never believe the client, believe the money, so I took the retainer and set about tailing the wife."

Frank took a sip of his beer, then continued. "She woulda been pretty once, you could tell, which is what you'd have to be if you're going to be married to a handsome rich guy and live in a house overlooking a golf course and a pool with a view to the ocean. Young and pretty are baseline qualities if you wanted to even fill out the application form. But she's older now and the thing that happens to women as they get older, y'know, that thickening thing around the waist, happened to her just as you'd expect. But you see, with her it mattered. I could see the vulnerability."

Something in the way he spoke gave me a little inside to Frank. A glimpse of a sensitive side. Had I been too quick to judge him?

"Anyway," he settled back a little in the chair, "I watched her lumber around the tennis court, have lunch with the girls, manicures, shop. Boring shit. Then one day, it's lawn day and in comes this guy with cut-off jeans to mow the acres of grass they call a backyard. This guy's not wearing a shirt and he's what women would call frigging gorgeous. An Adonis. Now I ain't that way inclined, but I can appreciate what I ain't got and I could tell the girls would go for him. Dark complexion, Elvis lips, a perfect nose and a whole bunch of abs. A damn rock star is what he looked like. The next thing I know, he's talking to the missus and she's bringing him a glass of water while sweat drips of his tits. While he drinks, his pecs twitch and she almost reaches out to touch his shoulder, but stops when he steps back." He grinned at me. "Oldest trick in the book, eh? Get them hot for you then pull back." He chuckled a bit and took another sip of the beer.

"Anyway, the lawn boy leaves but at three o'clock, he comes back in a clunker and starts searching around like he lost something. She comes out to help him and they search around together for a while. And when he finds it, the shirt he planted there that morning by the way, he doesn't put it on like you'd expect. He tosses it over his shoulder and waits like he's waiting for an invitation. And she gives it. The next thing, I've got a roll of film, jobs done, fee earned."

He leaned forward. "But you know what, Jack? Something doesn't feel right, and I don't like it. So I stopped following the lady and began to follow the lawn boy. I met him in a bar, a funny bar, if you know what I mean, and I bought him a beer. Then I bought him another one and he thinks I'm an old poof interested in that athletic body of his and I can tell he's interested, too. As long as I'm paying, that is. I go out back with him into an alley behind the bar. It's dark and rubbers are everywhere." He chuckled. "Lawn boy puts his hand on my hip and smiles his gorgeous smile. I lifted my elbow and broke his nose. So much for perfect," he snickered. "Now he's on the ground with blood leaking through his fingers. I leaned over and told him to tell me everything and he spills the beans. Everything. It was the husband who put him up to it, he says. The husband who paid him to do this trick with his wife while I was there with the camera taking pictures."

He crossed his legs under the table. "I figured the guy wanted a divorce on *his* terms." He spun the glass around on the table, making little wet circles. "He was hoping that the wife will give up everything so as none of this gets out to the tennis club girls."

As he talked, his eyes flicked around the room, never resting in one place. "So then, I went back to the missus and showed her the photos and she broke down, begged me not to give them to her husband. I told her how I had no choice, that I was paid for them in advance and I've got my ethics to consider. Then I tell her about the lawn boy and how her husband paid him and how she ought to have herself checked out at a clinic because of what lawn boy does in his spare time. She started crying and asking me what she was going to do. So I told her and she spotted me another retainer. Now, I'm back on the road, following the husband this time. Isn't this a great job? I love it."

He chuckled some more as he sipped his beer. "You really should consider it, Jack. You and me, we'd be great together."

I had to admit it, Frank was good. So far, he had two retainers for the same case, and he hadn't finished his story yet.

A plate of buffalo wings we'd ordered earlier arrived at the table and Frank put his drink down to grab one. "Thanks darlin'," he said to the waitress. He spun an index finger in a circle above the drinks. "And another round when you're ready." He turned to me. "Dig in, Jack. Remember I told you garlic works wonders on the body?" He stared at me with his piggy eyes for a second. "Looks like you could use some. You're looking a little pasty around the gills."

I put up my hand to say I was good, but he pointed insistently to the plate as he reached for one. I was anxious for the rest of the story, so to move it along, I took one as well.

"Anyway," he mumbled as bits of chicken dribbled from his mouth. "It turns out the husband's a lawyer. Big surprise eh? Drives a Merc and lunches at the Versace with political heavies, including your old boss Grayson. Then I find out he spends stray afternoons with some young piece from his law firm." He wiggled his eyebrows and smiled. "It's harder getting photos from a hotel compared to a private home but with the right equipment including a bit of cash for the hotel staff, it ain't long before I get a roll of stuff from that son of a bitch with his arse hanging out in bed with this doll."

He reached over for a napkin. "You with me, Jack?" he asked as he wiped sauce from his face. "Not boring you?"

"Come on, Frank. Finish the story."

"Okay, okay." He mumbled his thanks as the waitress deposited the drinks in front of us and he awarded her with a gappy smile. I noticed her eyes widen a little before she turned and walked away. Frank took another bite of his wing and continued.

"As you can see, both parties are on equal terms now, and I'm feeling pretty good about things. But why stop there? I figure I'll start following the bird from the husband's law firm now. Gorgeous too, I have to say." He swallowed noisily then began eating again. I turned away as the sauce dripped off his chin onto the table.

"I was curious to find out what pitch to make and how to make it," he continued. "I read her as a spoiled brat, never wanting for anything, a yuppie lifestyle and not minding that she'd grabbed some other woman's husband if it helps her climb up the corporate ladder. You know what I mean?" His eyebrows rose in question. "Anyway, I figure a little pressure and she'd be willing to pay me anything to go away. It all seems pretty obvious, right?"

His head jiggled from side to side. "Except this girl isn't obvious. One night, I followed her to a dive in Surfers where she meets up with some shady types. Next night, I follow her and she has dinner in some seafood joint alongside the Nerang River with some scum-bucket with about three teeth to his name. After that, I followed her to a lesbo bar. That's a switch eh? But I can't go in without getting noticed so I waited outside. An hour later, she's on the street with some dyke in a black leather jacket and they're kissing. Not like cousins, you understand? I sat in my car and watched from across the street and then she opens her eyes while she's kissing and stares straight at me. Then she's off, alone, heading away from me."

He picked up a fresh napkin and wiped his fingers, throwing it on the table before continuing. "I got out of my car and followed through the back streets and I saw her go down an alley. I had no idea where she was going but I was curious, right? Who the hell is she? I kept making turns and getting glimpses of her just turning a bend. Then I make this last turn and the next thing I know I'm on the ground with a knee in my crotch and a knife at my throat. The dyke was staring down at me with a look that lets me know she'd do it with the greatest of pleasure. And behind her, calmly leaning against the wall, fag in hand, stands the girl."

"*What do you want,* she asks."

"*A word,* I says."

"*Go ahead,* she says."

"*Let me up first,*" I says.

"*No.*" And the dyke presses the knife a little harder to my throat.

"*Fine,*" I says. And then I tell her about the husband coming into my office, about the missus and the lawn boy, about the pictures of the two of them. I told them the whole story because when you're in a situation like that, you don't hold anything back. And you know what she did? She laughed."

He shook his head and smiled at me, as if we were sharing a great joke. "And then she says giggling, *"Is that all? I hope you caught my good side."*

"*From what I could tell, that's all you got*", I says.

"The dyke looked down at me and said, *"Don't make me puke."* Can you believe that, Jack? Me?" He chuckled.

"Then she says, *"All right, Tiffany. Let him up."* The dyke lets me up and I look at her in her leather jacket with her shoulders bulging and the short, spiked hair, Doc Martens, and all I could say was, *"Tiffany? You got to be kidding me."* The dyke snarls but the girl laughs."

He shook his head and tittered lightly. It was a strange sound coming from a face that looked like a mad Frankenstein had put it together.

"The next thing I know the girl and I are in the lesbo bar knocking back martinis, swapping cigs and laughing like we're old buddies. I asked her if she wanted to marry this lawyer and she said, *"Oh please!"* I asked her why and she gave me this smile and looked around. Then she writes a name on a napkin and tells me before I meet with either the husband or the wife I ought to find out what I can about it. For her. The only thing is she wants no one to know it was her who set me on the name. And right there and then, she writes me a retainer. My third one." He put his hands wide in a 'ta da' fashion.

"So I look up the name and then I knock on the door. Some old lady answers and she invites me in, pours me a cup of tea and puts out a plate of biscuits. Nice old lady she was, too. Skin like tissue paper with blue veins pulsing in her neck. Never had children she said, but she was married for forty years to Ernie. I heard a lot about Ernie, how he fought in the war and through no fault of his own contracted a disease transmitted by a mosquito that left him sterile. So now, I'm thinking that if Ernie has convinced her that the clap is transmitted by mosquito, what else could she be convinced of? I asked her about her estate and she said it's all taken care of. She's going to leave it all to the church and this nice lawyer comes by every day and tells her how the market moved that day." He settled back in his chair and it groaned a little with the shift in weight.

"It would be nice except there's no money left in the trust account, is there?" He was shaking his head like he couldn't believe how low some people could sink. "The nice lawyer took it all, except he's not nice and he's not young. What he is, is the frigging husband who hired me in the first place." He wiggled his eyebrows. "So now I go back to the girl and tell her what I found, and she's not the least bit surprised. And then, listen to this, she tells me to give it to the wife, the name and the story, to let the wife do with it whatever she wants. I tell her she's crazy like she could do so much more with this piece of information, but she just tells me to shut up and do what I've been told. Well, that's what she's paying me for, right? So, I give the pictures of the husband and the girl to the wife. And with those pictures I give the name, address and the story of the old lady."

The waitress appeared at the table and began taking the plates away. "Would you like another drink, gentlemen?"

"Nah, darlin'. Just finishing up."

I'd been silent for the whole story because I didn't want to alter Frank's chain of thought. I had a feeling the end of the story would change the whole case and we were close to the finish line.

As if he read my mind, he continued. "Now, I don't know what happened for sure, but it must have been something big because in the end, the husband and the wife stayed married after all. In fact, they went on a long holiday to Europe and my sources say the wife had herself a terrific shopping spree. And funny thing, I ran into the missus a little while after she got back, and she'd lost some weight and was looking svelte. So svelte, I'd have done her myself except now, she's a happily married woman, isn't she?" He snickered.

"And the girl? Listen to this. The wife insists that the girl leaves the husband's firm. But the girl doesn't want to go. No way! Then she found out she was pregnant. The husband, now desperate, gives the girl a bunch of cases, some profitable ones, too. And some money, half a million to remember him by, if she just leaves. And she does. Starts her own practice, turns those cases into cash. We became partners of sorts, the girl and I. Six months later, she had the baby and gave it up for adoption. A kid didn't sit well in her plans, so she got rid of it. Just like that." He clicked his fingers.

"I stayed on with her and did her investigations, working on the sly mostly, and helped her fees roll in. And she was something. Too smart for the likes of me."

I jumped into the rabbit hole and said "Shannon."

"Hell of a girl and I miss her," he nodded. "Know who the lawyer was?"

I had an idea but I said, "No."

"Matthew Simmons."

Everything was falling into place. I knew he'd had an affair at one stage with someone in his office. Everyone knew. I even remembered some things Shannon said to me.

'The last thing I want to be again is in love,'

'Everyone wants to be in love.'

'Everyone is wrong.'

'You were once in love?'

'Yes.'

'And it ended badly?'

'Hiroshima.'

'Who was it?'

'The wrong man.'

An affair that she had referred to as Hiroshima.

'Everything about me is moulded by a love so fearsome it has seared my soul. Don't waste your time trying to understand it because you never will. It still baffles me. But it is something I don't ever want to happen again. Only the insane want to be struck by lightning twice.'

And then there was Joe.

She'd said, *'In the end, you're no different from Joe. You want love while having no idea what it really is. You say love but you think something else. You think love is desire, friendship, comfort and someone to cuddle while you watch videos. If you knew what love is and what it can do, you wouldn't want it either. In love there is no choice, no freedom, no dignity, no happiness. Nothing. It eats away at you. Who in their right mind would want that?'*

I was trying to get my head around this. Something was buzzing loudly in my head.

Joe worked for Simmons and was married to Sarah, Simmons' daughter. Shannon had an affair with both Simmons and Joe, both of whom had a connection to Sarah – one the father the other the husband. Odds were that Shannon knew who Joe was the minute he walked into Peter Hobson's room. Had she played him purely for the money or was it some agenda to get even with Simmons for getting her pregnant and then tossing her away?

Fitzroy gave me a half smile. "What you don't find at home, you look for elsewhere. And generally, you find it in the worst places possible. I'm not saying she was evil. Girl I knew was hard as nails and twice as sharp. But not evil. There was a softness in the middle and there was so much need in her. When something's soft and needy like that, it doesn't take much of a trick to turn it around to suit your own needs."

"You think she was manipulated?"

"Don't know. But money has a way, don't it? When Simmons wasn't getting what he needed at home, he went looking for it. He found himself a girl that had nothing in her but pain and hurt. You could almost tell just by looking at her. And that might have been the attraction at the beginning." He shrugged. "Who knows? In any case, Simmons wanted nothing to do with her after she told him about the baby. Said to her face that it probably wasn't even his. That got to her. Nearly drove her mad. She swore black and blue that she'd get even with him some day, and you know what? I believed her because she had this fire in her eyes and when you see something that intense, you know that no matter what, they'll make it happen. I guess that's where Joe comes into the story. She took Joe away from Simmons' daughter and stole a whole lot of cash from him when the Hobson case came along."

"Your level of enlightenment is dazzling."

"Well, thank you," he nodded.

"What did you do before this, Frank?"

"This and that."

He nodded to himself and I let the silence linger until he was ready.

"Back in the old days, I helped a few bad guys get back in touch with nature, if you know what I mean. Not anymore. I have other means of income now. I have to keep my retirement plans moving along. And this is more rewarding." His crooked teeth flashed at me.

"I thought at one stage you might have killed her," I said.

"I know you did. I could see it in your eyes. But I figured I owed the girl something, which is why I came on to you so hard over my cornflakes. But after watching you for the past couple of months, I got a different idea of you."

"What?"

"This is what I think." He leaned forward, lowering his voice. "I thought at first you didn't take the deal because it was too good to be true. You thought the bastard did it and you were standing by and making sure your friend paid for what he did. That was what your meeting with Simmons was all about, wasn't it? Setting him up to tell the cops about Hobson."

I stared at him and he stared back.

"You don't think he did it anymore, do you?" Fitzroy asked.

"Nope."

"What changed your mind?"

I picked up my beer and stared at it before taking the last gulp. "Shannon changed my mind. I finally learnt the truth about her and Joe. She was in control from the start when Joe walked into the hospital room to the very last, on the night of her death when she told him it was over. Total control. Joe never had a chance."

"I've got to agree with you on that one."

"But if she was in so much control, how could she let this happen? How did she miscalculate?"

"Your friend Joe may have fooled her like he fooled you. He's a harder piece of work than he lets on. He left his wife at the drop of a skirt and stole half a million dollars in the process. That bastard is capable of anything. I think you were right from the start. It was your friend who did it."

I shook my head. "No. It was someone else."

"Optimism," he grinned. "Tsk. Tsk. And after all you've seen." He downed his own drink and stood up. "Well, I'm off."

He put out his hand to shake mine but before I let it go, I turned it over and checked the knuckles. Rough and hairy. And ugly. But no remains of scrapes or bruises. Still holding on, I asked, "How did you know the key was missing from her house?"

He smiled. "It would be a violation of my ethical duties if I were to disclose the name of my client."

"It's nice to see you concerned about your ethical duties."

"At least one of us is."

"Was it Simmons?"

"Now, Jack. You know I treat the information I have with respect."

"Did you break into my house looking for it? And while we're at it, were you the one who tried to run me off the road?"

He shook his head with mild reproof. He looked around the bar. "You should watch yourself a little more in public. People will be thinking we're a couple of raving poofs having a lover's spat. Calm down and have another drink. Think about what I told you." He smiled. "I'll be seeing you."

And then he walked out.

46

———————

"Do you think that bastard actually killed her?" Joe asked.

By the time I'd finished with Fitzroy, it was eight o'clock and the three of us - Joe, Karen and I - were now sitting in the grey conference room at the watch house. We'd been told we had an hour of visiting time left with Joe so as concisely as I could, I told them both the whole story from the meeting with Mark Bartlett to the story that Fitzroy had told me.

I stoically withstood the tirade from Karen, being as it was totally justified. She was the lawyer, I was the investigator. We were supposed to be working together on Joe's case and all the time I was off on my own, doing things without even letting her know. It made her wonder, she said, what the hell was going on.

I explained to her that part of my routine as a detective had been to observe and calculate. I watched everyone. I looked for nuances, inflections and subtle changes in behaviour patterns. While things are fresh in my mind, I like to jump from one interview to the next rather than lose my momentum and stop to report my findings.

Some cops run around making a lot of noise without keeping to a fixed schedule. Some, like me, note everything and never give up until the crime is solved. You hope for things like a chance remark, an ex-spouse with a grudge but you always expect dead ends. As Mel Brooks once said, *'Hope for the best. Expect the worst.'* What you know is that you've done this all before and you have the determination to pull it off. What I also know is that you have to keep going while the window of opportunity is wide open. I could have lied to Karen and squirmed like a worm but when you're dead wrong you don't make excuses.

I let her blow off her steam and get it out of her system and then I said, "There's still a lot of unanswered questions."

By now, Karen was staring angrily at the floor.

"What are we going to do about it?" Joe asked.

"I have an idea but if it doesn't work, it will blow up in our faces."

I leaned forward and clasped my hands on the table as I outlined what I would have to do, what we hoped Jefferson would do and what Karen would then have to do, all beginning with putting Simmons on the stand.

Karen looked up at me, still angry despite the lecture she'd given me only minutes before.

"You're right. It's risky."

"I know you don't trust or like Simmons, but this could work out for us," I said trying to make it look like it was her idea.

"I don't like Simmons?" she asked.

"That's what you said to me when we saw him coming out of Jefferson's office the day he pulled the offer back. You said he reminded you of Fagan."

"From *Oliver*?"

I nodded.

"Wasn't I the perceptive little thing?"

"The point is, the trial's gone pretty good so far for us. The jury already thinks there is a possibility that someone else might have entered the house that night. What bothers me is *how* did they get in if the door was locked? And if they had a key, where the hell did they get it and who gave it to them? How did they know where the gun was? We've created a suspect in the other lover and I think we've created a hole in the prosecutor's defence for both opportunity and motive." I looked hard at Joe. "But we have one big problem with all of that."

I stood and walked over to the window that looked out over another brick wall. "Joe," I turned around and looked at him. "Sam and Cavanaugh want to know about the phone call you made on the night of the murder."

Joe stared at me for a moment. "Oh," he said.

"They have questions about that call that hasn't been resolved by your own phone logs."

"Oh, I see."

"I haven't asked you yet but I have to now. Why hasn't the phone call you made to me shown up on your phone records?"

I already knew the answer, but I wanted to hear Joe say it.

"I was flustered...I couldn't remember your number."

"So what did you do?"

"I used Shannon's phone. The red one."

"Why her phone?"

He sat in silence.

"Joe?"

He turned his head slowly towards me and his gaze was steady. I could see it in his eyes. *'Should I continue the lie or should I just come right out with it'.* Eventually, he took a deep breath.

"Because I knew your number was on the speed dial."

I didn't say anything. Neither did Karen. She just sat there looking from Joe, to me, and back to Joe again.

Outside I knew it was a beautiful summer's night, the kind that reminds you of the coming winter and the kind Shannon had told me to beware of. *Bad things happen on beautiful days.* It had been a beautiful day but there was a deep chill in that grey room.

"Did you think I wouldn't check it out, Jack?" Joe asked with a coldness in his voice as he looked hard at me. "I gave myself over to her completely. I sacrificed everything for her. My wife, my job, my very soul and she repaid me by sleeping with someone else. You didn't think I wouldn't do whatever it took to learn who that bastard was? So, I spied on her and followed her."

His mouth stretched into a slow sardonic smile. "Yes, Jack. I followed her. And then the phone appeared and when she was in the shower, I checked out the numbers on the speed dial and guess what I found? Your number was the first one. I think by then she wanted me to know about the two of you, which is why she didn't hide the phone. I think she was using you to tell me it was over and the money was all hers now. You were her little get-away-from-Joe boy, the perfect excuse. But by the time I found out, I wasn't even angry at you. I felt sorry for you instead. Sorry you'd fallen into her web like I had. Because you were going to be the next one to get shafted."

A gargoyle called guilt was riding my shoulders, head back, laughing and showing sharp teeth. A small taunting demon of guilt, whispering things that could have been done and weren't. I knew the gargoyle. We weren't friends, but I knew him well.

"Joe..." I began.

"So who would I call when I found her dead? Who could I trust? Only you, Jack. And in my panic, I knew where to find your number. That's why I used her phone."

Without even looking in a mirror, I knew I looked like a man who was ashamed by his infidelities. Only the other night, I had watched an old Leno show from 1995, featuring a stuttering, stammering Hugh Grant, apologising to the nation for sleeping with a prostitute. He squirmed throughout the whole interview. *'I think you know in life what's a good thing and what's a bad thing. I did a bad thing ... and there you have it.'* God, he was good. He looked nervous, sheepish and so sorry, you just wanted to take his hand and say, *'It's alright. Don't beat yourself up about it. It's not that big a deal'.* Which was the affect I was going for. I watched that show so many times, I was in danger of borrowing a British accent. I would be the ultimate apologiser.

"Joe, I'm sorry...."

He interrupted and snorted. "No, you're bloody not."

"Then why did you keep me on here," I glanced over at Karen, "working with Karen on your case?"

"First, I was desperate. Then I thought it through. There's not a lot else you can do in here but think. I analysed it and came up with a strategy. The strategy I came up with was one that made the most sense. I blamed the other lover. That's why I kept suggesting it. But I couldn't have the other lover just walk into the courtroom and take himself out of the case by providing an alibi for himself," he smiled sardonically, "like being at home when I called. I needed to make sure *that* never happened and as far as I could see, there was only one way."

I nodded slowly. "Keep me working with Karen on your case."

"Exactly."

Most of my life, I've done a good job of staying away from macho histrionics. I could handle myself in a violent confrontation and that had always been enough for me because I was just as certain that there were always people meaner and tougher and faster than I was. And they were only too happy to prove it. So many guys I'd known from childhood had died or been jailed because they needed to show the world how mean they were. But lately I was tired of the pathetic depravities of the whole damn human species and tired of the sort of people who needed to prove they were smarter than everyone else.

I calmed myself before I spoke. "You're a son of a bitch, Joe."

My voice came out deceptively calm although inside my stomach was churning with anger. I'd been used. Not only used but when he'd called me on the night of her murder, he'd deliberately implicated me in her murder.

He snorted. "Aren't we both?" He was shaking his head. "You think you're so smart. You're like a bloody dog running around with your nose on the ground, sniffling through bushes and piles of shit until you find what you think you're looking for. Then you step back and let the hunters shoot it dead. Why couldn't you just let things stay as they were?"

It wasn't the analogy I would have chosen, but it wasn't entirely false either no matter what I wanted to think. He was right. Shannon had played us both for fools in her scheme and I wasn't about to let it go.

Karen sighed heavily, her hands up in the air in surrender. "Okay, boys. I never heard any of this. What are we going to do now?"

"Shannon used us both," I began. "When I first saw her on the mattress, I was devastated. Whatever she did, she didn't deserve to die, especially like that. I think we need to do something about Simmons."

Joe turned to Karen. "I'm with Jack. We need to put Simmons on the stand." He took a hard look at Karen. "Do you think you can pull this off?"

Gone was the snivelling, nervous guy worried about his life being in ruins. The Joe I knew from the past was back and he meant business. It must have been a relief for him to shed the pathetic persona and return to the real Joe.

"I can certainly try," she nodded.

"You'd better do a hell of a lot better than try."

Karen's face turned red. "Okay Joe, but if you want me to represent you to the best of my ability, make sure you give me ALL the information, not just parts of it. Am I clear on that?"

Joe had the grace to look suitably abashed.

She stood up and straightened her blouse. "Now if you will excuse me, I have a couple of things to do in preparation for Simmons taking the stand tomorrow morning."

47

I was half an hour early the next morning, but I hadn't beaten the courtroom hopefuls waiting in single file on the concrete steps outside the courthouse in the sun. The line started at the double doors and continued down the ten or so concrete steps and spread around the corner. Some were smart enough to bring shade-providing umbrellas. A hum from the line grew in intensity as I powered up the steps past them, jaw set and frowning, while many held mobile phones taking pictures.

There are always retired sixty-somethings who want to feel alive and part of life. Then there are detective wannabees, the CSI fans, who think that after binge-watching the shows, they know about crime scenes and forensics. Then there are the reporters and media.

A puff of cool air hit my face as I detective-walked through the heavy front door, revolving out of the morning sunshine and into the dusty gloom of the dark-panelled courthouse, clutching my paper cup full of bitter deli coffee.

Driving there, morning radio stations were full of speculation. *If Joseph Banner didn't do it, who did? The poor defence attorney is clutching at straws. If there's a mistrial, clearly the State will bring charges again and it will start all over again,* one commentator sneered.

So far, we'd been lucky with the trial. Jefferson was still trying to make it seem a simple case of murder and I was still complicating things with the theory of an unnamed, undiscovered, vicious lover. Outside the courtroom, we kept our interchanges civil but inside the courtroom, the judge refereed with a certain fairness, which kept the jury attentive. The prosecutor was confident. We were hopeful.

Sarah Banner was in the courtroom every day, sitting behind the man who had fled from her to another lover. I would like to have seen a little more spite, maybe even anger, but instead she sat quietly with concern on her face. I supposed it was always useful to have the loyal wife supporting you, but it looked slightly off kilter to me. Karen and I hadn't asked her to sit there like an ornament for the defence and I wasn't even sure it was helpful. But there she sat and from time to time, Joe would turn around and they would whisper quietly to each other.

When Karen called Sarah's father to the stand, she sat with a face like stone knowing that her father would try to bury the man who had married her and then deserted her for another woman. I knew this would make Joe look bad, but I had a few questions that needed to be answered.

"Are we ready to proceed?" Judge Everly asked.

Karen stood. "Yes, your honour. But my client has requested me to ask your permission that Mr Curtis do the cross on Mr Simmons."

She frowned as she looked at me, then she looked at Joe. "This is your request, Mr Banner?"

"Yes, your honour."

She hesitated but looked at the court reporter and said, "This is highly irregular, but this court has ruled that if Mr Banner is willing to put his life in the hands of someone such as Mr Curtis who has no trial experience, then who are we to object?"

I stood. "Thank you, your honour."

Her eyes sent daggers across the room. "Do not thank me, Mr Curtis."

"Yes, your honour. I mean no, your honour. Tha... Yes, ma'am." The jury sniggered.

She eyed me over the top of her glasses. "You may proceed, Mr Jefferson."

"We call to the stand, Matthew Simmons, your honour."

The doors in the rear of the courtroom swung open and a cool breeze came in with Simmons. He was dressed in a deep blue Armani suit, a pristine white shirt and a sombre black and blue striped tie. He had walked past Joe and Sarah without a glance and as he settled himself in the chair, he watched me with the blank stare of a natural-born cheat. His upper lip curled back in a twist of a smile. I, in turn, smiled back at him like we were old friends.

"Mr Simmons." Jefferson stood and walked slowly over to the witness stand. "Please state your occupation."

"I am a lawyer."

"And where do you work?"

"My firm is Simmons, Ryan and Holtzman."

Jefferson asked Simmons all the necessary questions regarding Joe and Sarah, the Hobson case and his decision to testify against Joe despite the possibility of losing his practice. Then it was my turn.

"How much did you make last year?" I began.

"Oh, for goodness sake your honour!" Brad Jefferson jumped to his feet. "Objection! For a start – relevance?"

"It will become clear in time that this is very relevant, your honour," I said.

Judge Everly hesitated. "Overruled. But be very careful with this, Mr Curtis."

"Yes, ma'am." I turned back to Matthew Simmons. "Please answer the question."

A ghost of a frown crossed Simmons face, but he recovered quickly. He slid around the seat for a second before replying, fixing me with a hostile stare. His chin was set in a challenging thrust. A dry, obstructed rasp, something like a grating scrape of sandpaper, rose from his throat.

The number was staggering, and the point was made. Joe had been in line for a huge amount of money if he had stuck it out with his wife and his job as partner in a law firm that offered this amount as a yearly salary to its partners. Joe had been a fool for leaving, yes, a fool for love. But a fool for money?

I went straight for the jugular.

"Did you know the victim, Shannon Connor?"

He studied the floor. Apart from the small sigh he emitted, there was silence. It was me who broke it. "Please answer the question, Mr Simmons."

He looked up at me. "She once worked in my firm."

"How long ago was that, Mr Simmons?"

A scowl crossed his face. "It's a big firm and I am a busy man, Mr Curtis. You probably already have the answer to that question."

"I'd like to hear it from you, sir."

He looked at the judge and then at Jefferson. When he could see there was to be no help, he said, "About four years ago. February, I believe."

"Why did she leave?"

Jefferson stood up. "Objection, your honour. We have been patient with this line of questioning, but we see no relevance in something that happened four years ago."

"Mr Curtis?" asked the judge.

"The relevance is coming, your honour. It shows a connection to the victim and I have proof that there is still a connection."

The judge sighed. "Please proceed. You may answer the question, Mr Simmons."

He leaned forward, squared his hands on the railing and in a voice as thick as tar, said, "I object strongly to this line of questioning."

"That is not up to you to decide, sir." I looked up to the judge then back at him. "You have been advised to answer the question."

Simmons looked at Joe pityingly. A twinkle came into his eyes but when he looked at me, it vanished suddenly, the way a social smile will evaporate.

"We had a brief affair." He straightened his back and squared his shoulders. "She was trying to extort money from me and I was advised by my own lawyer to pay her off. Which I did. It all ended rather badly with a lot of ill-feeling on her part."

Through the small speech, Judge Everly stared at me, giving me a look that said to tread carefully.

"I'd like to show you some letters that we have uncovered."

Jefferson jumped up again. "Your honour. We have had no such letters shown to us. These have not been disclosed to us." His face had gone a deep red as if a stroke was seconds away.

"Mr Jefferson, Mr Curtis, Miss Sawyer. Please approach the bench."

Karen and I both walked over to the bench, our shoes clicking in time on the tiles. Jefferson was hopping behind us.

"Yes, your honour," Karen purred demurely while beside her, I sweated profusely.

The judge sat quietly and stared at both of us.

"I can understand Mr Curtis not being aware of procedures but you? What game is this you're playing?"

Karen spread her hands wide, a look of confusion on her face. "Your honour. I don't know what to say. We sent the appropriate paperwork by fax to Mr Jefferson's office last night when we were made aware of the letters. Is it our fault the efficiency of his office is less than desirable?"

I had visions of Karen and me sitting patiently in Jefferson's office while Jefferson faxed the letter to our office stating that the offer had been rescinded. I looked at Karen and glowed proudly.

Jefferson did another couple of hops. "Oh, please! Last night? Your honour, this is outrageous!"

"If I find out this is not true, Miss Sawyer, we will have the testimony struck from the records. Is that clear?"

"Absolutely, your honour. I have the status report in my file at the desk. Would you like to see it?" Her voice was like silk.

Judge Everly turned to Brad Jefferson. "Perhaps you should contact your office to see if they received the fax, Mr Jefferson?"

"Oh yeah," he said. "I'll do just that! I certainly will." He looked at me, anger clearly visible on his face. "I will *certainly* do that."

I smiled at him and then said to the judge, "May we continue with the questioning, your honour." Butter wouldn't melt in my mouth.

Judge Everly nodded but gave me her look again. Karen and Jefferson returned to their seats and I walked over to the desk and picked up the two letters that had been stored in Shannon's safe-deposit box. As I turned, I saw Sam standing at the back of the court-room, her arms folded and a knowing look on her face. One row in front of her, Sonya Martin sat, an intense look on her face. Then, sitting one row in front of her, I saw Jazz and Sally. Sally nodded slightly while Jazz just gave me a *'what?'* look. It threw me a little, but I was thrilled to see them here. I nodded to Jazz and she scowled back at me.

I walked over to Simmons.

None believe they are evil, not even the evil do. I knew that he would try to deny everything and deny it with a conviction worthy of his profession. When he was trapped, I guessed he would turn ugly and search for someone else to blame for his indiscretion. But once I started, everything would become apparent. More doubt would be presented that here was another person besides the undiscovered lover who had a grudge against the victim, another reason to want her out of the way. If I did this right, Joe could very well be acquitted and Simmons would be under suspicion of Shannon's murder. That was the upside and that's what I was focused on.

Of course, there was a downside. If I failed, Joe's defence could look like he was trying to foist blame on to his ex-father in law who had tried to be rid of a scheming woman out for any money she could get.

What bothered me was that after reading through the letters, the insurance policy and listening to all the evidence so far in the trial, something still didn't seem right. Something seemed out of order. Something was not as I thought it should be and it was right in front of my face. But whatever it was, I couldn't put my finger on it.

"Your honour, I would like these letters to be labelled Defence Exhibits 10 and 11." I waved them at the judge who nodded in return.

"Now, Mr Simmons, please take a look at these letters. Actually, would you mind reading them out to the court?"

He took the letters from my outstretched arms and I turned my back on his evil stare while I let him peruse the letters before reading them aloud.

He read them out, one at a time, stumbling slightly. *'I don't want you to think that this is easy for me, and even as I say that I feel shame. What I did to you, I will have to live with every day and there's nothing to be done. I know you will think me a coward but I hope in time you will forgive me.'*

When he'd finished reading, he passed the letters back to me silently.

"Tell me if you have ever seen them before, Mr Simmons."

"No," he said quietly.

"They were both addressed to 'S' and signed 'M'."

"I noticed that."

"S could stand for Shannon and M could stand for Matthew. Don't you agree?"

"I have never seen these letters before." His voice had lost its gruffness and as I looked at the jury, I knew they had noticed as well.

I spun around. "You don't recognise the writing, Mr Simmons? Are you sure? Please have another look."

"Your honour," Jefferson said. "My witness has already stated that he has never seen these letters before."

"Move on, Mr Curtis," the judge said firmly.

I nodded. "Okay. You've never seen them before, Mr Simmons. Is that correct?"

"OH, YOUR HONOUR," Jefferson yelled, almost hopping on his feet.

"I said move on, Mr Curtis." The judge stared hard at me. I had to be careful. A mistrial is the last thing I wanted.

"Sorry, your honour."

I walked over to Karen and whispered. "How am I doing?"

"Terrific," she whispered back. "You have him sweating up there. Stick the knife in."

I nodded, stood up straight, and turned around.

"All right, Mr Simmons. We also have here the birth certificate of a child born three and a half years ago naming the mother as Shannon Mary Connor and stating that the father is unknown." I handed it to him. "Three and a half years ago, Mr Simmons. Not long after you finished your affair with Ms Connor. Actually, I believe you mentioned that she left in February four years ago?"

He stared silently at me.

"And if you look at the birth certificate," I leant over and pointed to the date, "it states here that the baby was born in August of the same year Ms Connor left your firm." I did a little playact of counting on my fingers. "That would make it...six months later."

I spread my hands wide and did a little 'ta da' with them like I was David Copperfield producing a rabbit out of a hat. While I was talking, Karen gave Jefferson a copy of the birth certificate and the letters with a smile.

Jefferson stood again, this time not so confidently.

"Your honour? This birth certificate," he glared at Karen then looked back at the judge, "apparently states that the father is unknown. This in itself exonerates my witness. I am not sure where this is going, your honour."

"We have another letter here, your honour, Exhibit 2 for the Prosecution, of which Mr Jefferson has so kindly given us a copy." I turned and nodded my thanks to Brad Jefferson sitting quietly down in his seat. I turned back to Simmons.

"It was written by you, Mr Simmons, before the trial had started, when an offer from the prosecution was rescinded, and it states that while Joseph Banner was in your employ, you were aware of his involvement in the Hobson case and his attempt to defraud the insurance company."

I handed the letter to him. "Is that your writing, Mr Simmons?"

Simmons stared at it silently.

I repeated my question. "Do you recognise the writing, sir?"

He sat staring at the letter, not moving, but all the time I watched him like a moth circling a flame, getting closer, closer. And then slowly, he nodded. The pain in his eyes was hard to behold.

"Let the record state," I said, "that the witness nodded yes."

"The record will so reflect," said the judge.

"Is it your writing, Mr Simmons?"

There is always a moment of shock when we catch a glimpse of another's humanity. We don't want to see it but when we do, it never fails to shock us or to change us. And the shock is even greater when in our arrogance we believe that our understanding of things has reached beyond the secrets of the other person's being. Now, seeing Matthew Simmons' soul bared to the courtroom, I received a shock.

He was a cruel man, pitiless and vicious. He had proved that. But as I stood looking at him, I saw another side. He was stupid, too. Just as I had been stupid. Joe *and* me. And Mark Bartlett. This one bit of stupidity had wiped out all the successes in Simmons' life. I saw it all and something changed inside me as I stared at this beaten man wiping away the tears from his face.

"It wasn't dirty like you think. It was love, real and sincere. Fearsome in its intensity. Something more alive than anything else I'd ever felt."

The whole courtroom inhaled sharply, and several members of the jury put their hand over their mouths in shock. I turned and looked at Karen, feeling triumphant, and that's when I noticed Sarah. She looked like the devout wife in a neutral grey skirt and a virtuous white blouse sitting behind a haggard looking Joe, one hand resting on his shoulder. Both were staring silently at Simmons with no emotion. No reaction at all.

In the split second it took to realise that something wasn't right, like a thunderclap I understood. They knew. They already knew about the child.

Memories of sitting in Gilhooleys pub that first night Joe introduced me to Shannon flashed into my mind. When he had asked me to help him find Jessica Harding, a strange undercurrent in his voice had made me hesitate. He had stared down at the drink in his hand and then finally, he had blinked a series of rapid-fire clicks like someone coming out of a trance. Looking back now, I realised he had already known that Jessica was Shannon's child.

"It wasn't my doing. It was hers." Matthew Simmons voice brought me back to the present as I stared from Joe to Sarah.

I shook myself and turned back to Simmons. He was trembling as he spoke.

"She started it. She seduced me. I had no choice in it. Whatever she wanted, she got. She told me she was going to break me if I didn't pay her this enormous amount of money. I had no choice."

There it was. The shift. The shift of blame I was looking for. I looked over at Brad Jefferson and he stared back at me.

I turned my attention back to Simmons. His eyes were glossy with tears and my heart lurched with pity for him. He was right, in a way. Whatever Shannon wanted, she always seemed to get.

"Was Ms Connor in contact with you prior to her death?" I asked softly,

He nodded, then whispered, "Yes."

"Would you tell the court why she did that, Mr. Simmons?"

"She wanted more money. She wanted $20,000 a month put into her bank account."

"Because of the child?"

"Yes," he whispered.

"Where is that child now?"

He continued looking down at his hands as he shook his head. "I have no idea." His voice had been soft and barely audible.

I had one more question.

"Where were you on the night of the murder, Mr Simmons?"

Brad Jefferson jumped up. "Your honour. I have to advise this witness not to answer that question."

Judge Everly looked at me and nodded. "I have to agree with the prosecution on this one, Mr Curtis."

It didn't really matter. The damage had been done. I turned and watched as the eyes of the jury followed Simmons from the time he stood up from the stand to the time he shuffled past his daughter. Sarah sat watching him coldly to the very last second as he passed through the back doors of the courtroom. It's often hard to read a jury, but I could read *those* eyes.

In that instant, Sarah glanced at me and I saw something, a smugness around her mouth, or a flutter, like the final flicker of a snake's tail before it disappears into the bush. Then it was gone. It caught me completely off guard and I turned and frowned at Karen. She had been taking off her glasses and putting them on the table so she had missed the exchange.

I looked back at Sarah, blinking rapidly a few times to try and take in what I'd just seen. She was still sitting stoically behind her husband, touching him lightly on the shoulder but for me, the room had become still, like the lull between songs on a CD. Something with a hundred sticky feet crawled along my spine.

There are moments in every case when everything alters, just like optical illusions. One minute you're viewing one reality and then, with a tilt of your head, everything changes. Nothing was as it appeared a few minutes before.

When I was still in primary school, I had a book of optical illusions. You'd look at say, palm trees on an island. You'd look a little longer and then, whoosh, it appeared to be a school of dolphins jumping in the surf. Sometimes, it took a long time and you'd even start to wonder if there was anything different in there at all. And then, suddenly, the image surfaces again.

The human brain is an amazing organ that no computer can duplicate. It can process zillions of stimuli in a hundredth of a second with a curious mix of chemicals and electrodes. We understand more about the planets and the cosmos than we do about the brain and its workings. And like any tricky compound, we are never sure how it will react to a certain catalyst. That was what was going on now. That and something shifting in my soul. A feeling that if I could look laterally, the answer would suddenly appear.

Sometimes, you have a feeling you're being watched. There's no reason for it, just a sense that someone's attention is focused on you. The feeling is never the same for everyone but when it happens, there's no mistaking it. Sarah's eyes had shifted from Joe and were staring across at me.

Cats, both wild and domestic, watch with unblinking regard, alert for the smallest variation in posture, the tiniest shift of attention. She had that intensity as she held my eyes.

When most people think of a murderer they think of a glassy-eyed lunatic. Someone who looks the part and acts the part. Actually, the typical murderer is something completely different. They look ordinary. The kind of person you wouldn't look twice at. Not a monster sitting stoically behind her husband with her hand resting supportively on his shoulder.

There's a moment in film and television when a particular shot or word signifies that moment when the penny drops. Sometimes, it's something little that goes 'click' and everything seems to fall into place. For real people, it triggers something in your memory and we remember where we left our car keys or the name of that someone or that song we've been wracking our brains to think of. For Harry Callahan, it's usually a darker revelation. It's the instant that signifies the break in a case. Then when comprehension dawns, the camera zooms towards the face of the hero and the music reaches a crescendo as the light of realisation grows in their eyes. You also know when danger is imminent by ominous music underlying the scene that warns sharks are approaching or an alien is near. Real life is not like that. It's dead quiet so you're never really sure when trouble is near.

But I knew. I had this bad feeling in the pit of my stomach like there were ten snakes in there and all of them were fighting to get out.

My mother used to tell me there were no monsters in our world, no real ones. They only existed in the movies. She was wrong. They're all around us and if we give them the opportunity, they'll crawl out from under their rocks. Even as I felt my stomach contract, even as I felt my heart turn to ice, I somehow managed to detach. I felt something in me harden and I felt that old familiar surge of adrenaline rushing through my veins when pieces start to join up. It was like looking through a fog and suddenly coming through into brilliant sunshine.

Karen took that exact moment to look at me. "You look like someone who's just stepped into a puddle deeper than his shoe."

"We have to talk."

48

Brad Jefferson was sitting at the bar where he told me he would be. I walked over and sat down on the stool beside him and told the waiter I'd have a Jack Daniels on ice.

Jefferson turned and frowned at me. "I see Dr Jekyll has returned. You've got a cheek, you know? Reading letters without proper foundation and then using the threat of extrinsic testimony to badger the witness into a sort of confession. The testimony should be stricken and the jury instructed to ignore what they heard. And then, after that little stunt you pulled, you call me and ask me to have a drink with you?"

"Nice to see you too, Jefferson." I took a sip of my drink which had just arrived, but never took my eyes off him. "But I don't think the judge will disallow the evidence, do you?"

"Then we will ask for a mistrial. A mistrial based on the misconduct of the defence and we'll try this all over again."

"You're actually admitting that the testimony has raised doubts as to Joe's guilt in all of this. Isn't justice the prime reason for all this?" I took another sip of my drink.

He laughed sardonically. "Don't give me that crap. All you want is to get Joe off the hook no matter how you do it or who you blame.

What you managed today was to use your practiced skill of deception and trickery to badger an old man into admitting a past indiscretion for which he has already paid a huge price for."

"Thank you," I said. "I think."

"And what about the mysterious lover?" jeered Jefferson.

"A minor detail that was wrong," I turned and faced him, "but honestly, do you think that the jury will convict Joe after what they heard today?"

"The evidence against Joe Banner remains the same," he said as he took a sip of his own drink. "He was the only one in the house. It was his gun, his fingerprints on the gun and there is a strong monetary motive as regards to the insurance policy......."

I interrupted. "And what about the wet patch at the front door that suggests someone coming in with an umbrella and then leaving soon after? And what about this person in black who came back later on, when Joe was in custody I might add, obviously looking for something crucial. How did this person enter through a locked door if not with a key that had been given to him? There was no break-in was there? How did they know where the gun was kept?"

I hesitated before asking the next question. I had to be very careful about what I was saying.

"Who else could have wanted Shannon dead?"

I was staring intently at Jefferson, urging him to concentrate. "Think, Jefferson. Think."

I watched him in silence as thoughts ran across his face. Silence is one of the many tricks in my bag that tends to unsettle people. Silence affects people in different ways. My silence made him feel awkward, as I knew it would. He would be wondering what I knew and how much he could say without giving anything away.

He turned and stared back at me with a frown on his face. "What are you trying to tell me?"

I've always believed that no matter what, I can see through any lie or deception and come up with the truth. And without being egotistical, my instincts have always worked for me. Until I saw Sarah's face.

"I can't tell you anything, Jefferson. But from the very beginning, I have promised to find Shannon's murderer no matter who it was and that is a promise I am going to keep."

He stared at me for a moment, his strange gaze playing across my face. Then he burst into laughter. "Why are you doing this?"

"Because I'm a sweetheart. Because I want justice. And because I want this all to be over with so I can get on with my life, such as it is."

He turned to me. "Are you trying to tell me that you think Banner's *wife* committed the murder?"

"I didn't say that at all."

I was tempted to drop my revelation at his feet, like a golden retriever would do with a dead bird. But I stopped myself in time. Why not wait for the flock of dead birds?

His eyes dropped to the table. I could see them moving rapidly across the surface but seeing nothing. His mind was working so furiously, I could almost hear the gears crunching.

He lifted his eyes and stared at me in silence. "Not in so many words, no." He bit his bottom lip as he watched me sipping my drink. I knew the doubt was there now, the unanswered questions roaming around inside his head, a way out of this fiasco.

"Why don't you call her as a witness for the defence, if that's what you think?" he asked.

"Karen is in the process of doing just that." By tomorrow morning, Sarah's name would be added to the list of witnesses for the defence. "But then," I took a sip of my drink, "there is always cross-examination."

"And you're happy to let me take the glory of solving this case if it turns out she did it?" he asked sceptically with a touch of sarcasm.

"I was never in it for the glory, Jefferson. I have always wanted to know who killed Shannon and bring them to justice. That has always been my prime motive in being involved in this case."

He stared at me a while longer, as if he was wondering whether he could trust me or not. Then he nodded slowly.

49

———————

"**T**hings never turn out the way you think they will."

Those were my last words I spoke to Karen as I left her office the night before. Now, Karen, Joe and I were sitting at the bench as Judge Everly walked into the courtroom. She sat down, arranged her gown behind her, ready for the proceedings to commence.

"Are you ready, Mr Jefferson?" she asked.

"Yes, your honour. The people call Sarah Banner to the stand."

In my peripheral vision I could see Joe's head spin towards me. I kept my eyes fixed on Judge Everly, but I could see the frown cross his forehead. I had known that once Sarah's name was mentioned last night, Jefferson's pride would win out and he would try to beat us by putting Sarah on the stand as his own witness.

"Sarah Banner?" asked Judge Everly. "I don't see Sarah Banner's name on the witness list, Counsellor."

"It's a late addition, judge. We think Mrs Banner may shed some light onto the proceedings."

Judge Everly stared at Karen and me over the top of her glasses. When neither of us said anything, she asked "Any objection, Ms. Sawyer?"

"No, your honour."

She raised her eyebrows, not sure of where this was going, then turned to Brad Jefferson.

"All right, Mr Jefferson. You may proceed."

The doors of the courtroom swung open again and Sarah walked through dressed sombrely in a black dress and a tasteful string of pearls around her neck. She looked the epitome of the demure and long-suffering wife.

Joe continued to look at me quizzically until finally he said, "What's this all about, Jack?"

His face was cleanly shaven and his hair had been combed back. All this was for show. The jury was meant to see his confidence and be assured that he was innocent of anything as foul as murder.

"I'm not sure, Joe," I frowned convincingly. "She's been called as a prosecution witness."

Joe stared at me for a moment longer before turning towards Sarah who was settling herself in the witness stand.

"You are Joseph Banner's wife, is that correct?" Jefferson asked.

"That is correct."

"Have you applied for a divorce from Mr Banner?"

"No."

"Do you plan to?"

"No."

"Why is that, Mrs Banner?"

Her expression suggested she was waiting for the punch line. "I love my husband."

"Even after he left you for another woman? Even though he and Ms Connor stole money from your father's law firm? Even though he is on trial for the murder of that same woman?"

Through this little speech, Judge Everly stared openly at Karen and me, giving us that look of hers that wondered why I wasn't objecting like hell from the first word and why we had allowed this woman to be on the stand in the first place.

"Again.... is there no objection, Ms Sawyer? Mr Curtis?" she asked finally.

The jury stared at me. "No, your honour. But thank you for asking," I replied.

She stared at me a while longer, then shrugged. Jefferson continued.

"You even offered to put up the money for his defence. Is that correct?"

"Yes, it is."

"Why did you do that, Mrs Banner?"

"Because he is my husband and I love him."

"And you'd do anything for him?"

"Yes."

Jefferson turned to the jury and said, "Anything?"

Sarah hesitated.

The judge's stare was aimed right at my skull as she asked for Brad Jefferson, Karen and me to approach the bench.

When we stood before her, she asked, "Ms Sawyer and Mr Curtis, do either of you have any idea at all what you are doing in this trial?"

"Searching for the truth?" I asked.

She blinked then turned to Karen. "And Ms Sawyer, are you happy with this line of enquiry?"

"Yes, your honour," she said quietly. I would have liked her assent to sound more confident but that's the way it goes.

"I have given you opportunities to object at every step in this testimony and you have ignored them. Is there any motion you would like to make now?" she asked, looking at both Karen and me. "This is your last chance."

"No, your honour," we said in unison. Karen looked at me and then turned back to the judge. "Mr Jefferson is doing a fine job as it is," she added.

The judge sat back in her seat. "Then do NOT ask me for leniency when it comes to cross-examination, Mr Curtis. The courtroom is not the place for intimidation or psychological manipulation. We can leave that to the police interrogation room." She looked at me knowingly. "There will be no request for a mistrial if information *not* to your liking is unearthed. You have opened the door for Mr Jefferson and now you must put up with the company that has arrived."

During the early years of my career, I watched a lawyer try to break a man on cross-examination. Everything had been carefully prepared, laying out all the traps building up to a devastating blow. He brought out flashes of anger and showed the jury the inconsistencies of the man's story, but that was all. He had actually murdered the man, proven later by a piece of evidence held by his wife. It taught me a lesson.

Cross-examination is a way to highlight inconsistencies and expose falsehoods and painting a witness as a hapless liar. But it is not the place for crushing blows. There are too many formalities involved and too many rules to follow, as the judge had just warned me.

But there were questions that needed to be asked and if Brad Jefferson did not ask them, then I most certainly would.

Joe stared at me as I sat back down at the defence table. "Jack?" he asked. "What's going on?"

"If Sarah has nothing to hide, Joe, everything will be fine."

"I don't understand how this is going to help me." When I didn't say anything, he turned his attention back to Sarah.

Jefferson continued to ask questions about her finances, her reaction to Joe's leaving her, her future. While he paced before Sarah, occasionally glancing at me to make a point, I flicked through the statements, motions, bank statements and phone logs. Joe was leaning forward, listening intently to the questioning.

Suddenly, I felt a pain between my eyes like someone had punched me. There was sweat on my face that wasn't there an instant ago. I felt it in my hair, on my forearms and behind my knees. The skin on my forearms tingled. That small intuitive part of me that always has suspected the worst had taken possession of my body. In an instant, it all became clear. In a sudden burst of insight, I saw something I had overlooked when looking through the phone logs. The crucial piece of evidence had been there the entire time, right in front of my face.

Jefferson asked Sarah, "Did you have any contact at all with Ms Connor?"

"I rang her once to tell her she was making a mistake taking him away from me and to leave him while she could."

"And what did she say to that?" Brad asked.

"She was very crude."

As the questioning continued, I picked up a red pen and circled the phone numbers that had jumped out at me on Joe's phone logs. Then I circled the dates and times.

I gaped at Sarah's pretty face, sad and incredulous, as she spoke calmly.

I coughed into my hand, trying to get Jefferson's attention somehow.

As he kept up the line of questioning, I began to tap the top of my pen on the phone logs absently. The tapping wasn't loud but it was annoying, as I meant it to be. Karen glanced at the paper in front of me and frowned. Within seconds, the frown disappeared and her eyes grew wide. Then she looked at Joe, still hunched forward listening to Sarah's replies. Her mouth made a small 'o' as she began to realise what I had discovered.

Jefferson paced slowly before me again, and as he did so, I tapped the phone logs with my pen quickly and looked him hard in the eye. He glanced down, seeming to think about his next question and without breaking pace, continued over to his desk and opened a manilla folder resting on the top. He took out a sheet of paper and stood silently looking down at it.

I held my breath, willing him to see what I had seen.

In the silence, I could hear the clock on the wall ticking away the seconds as Jefferson concentrated on the sheets of paper in front of him, scanning through the top one then placing it on the bottom as he scanned the next.

"Mr Jefferson?" asked the judge eventually.

Jefferson continued to scan the sheet of paper.

"Mr Jefferson!" she asked loudly. "What is the holdup?"

He glanced up, nothing showing on his face. "Sorry, your honour. I am just trying to find a way to word the next few questions."

"That is what should have been done during preparation, Mr Jefferson. You are wasting the court's time. Please continue."

"Yes, your honour."

Jefferson walked slowly over to Sarah, still glancing down at the sheets in his hand. "Did you have contact with your husband during the months that he lived with Ms Connor?"

She glanced quickly at Joe. "He rang once or twice to see if I was making the house payments."

"No other time?"

She hesitated. "I don't remember."

"What is your home number, Mrs Banner?"

She seemed taken aback by the question. She turned her head and stared for a moment out the window before she haltingly said the number.

Jefferson handed Sarah the phone logs and said, "I would like the court to record the fact that I am handing Mrs Banner the phone logs for the residence of Joseph Banner and Ms Connor for the month prior to the victim's death."

Judge Everly said, "Let me see them, please." She examined them and then examined my face to see if she could figure out what in the world was happening here. I stared back silently.

"No objections, Mr Curtis?"

"No, your honour."

"Normally, I would find that encouraging." Without breaking eye contact with me, she handed the sheet back to Brad Jefferson. "You may continue," she said.

"Do you see that number listed on the logs?" he asked Sarah.

Joe leaned over. "Jack, do something for God's sake." His eyes flashed with anger.

"Do you have something to hide, Joe?" I asked. I turned and looked at the jury. They were watching both of us intently. I took a few deep breaths. It was now or never. I had set the stage.

As I looked into Joe's eyes, I wanted to stop and take a break, to talk to him. I wanted to hold on to the hope for a little longer before it turned to hard reality. Something had bothered me from the very beginning. Something I couldn't put a finger on. Something just out of reach in my mind that teased me, flicking across my subconscious. Now I knew the doubt had started when I first spoke to Sarah and she'd mentioned suing Shannon. Sarah had assumed that Shannon had a lot of money tucked away and the only one who could have told Sarah that information was Joe.

Even as these thoughts were running through my head, I saw Sarah's hand shake as she took the sheet of paper from Jefferson's outstretched hand. Her eyes glanced down the list and then she looked at Joe. Pleadingly.

"Do you recognise your number amongst the others, Mrs Banner?"

In a voice soft and weary with resignation, she whispered, "Yes."

"How many times was a call made to your number over that month, Mrs Banner?"

"Several times."

"More than five?"

"Yes."

"More then ten?"

"Yes."

"To ask you whether you had made the payments on the house?"

Jefferson smirked and almost did a pirouette in front of the jury.

"He was unhappy," she whispered. "Things weren't working out. She was taking money from him and hiding it, leaving him with nothing."

Joe's head spun to face me. "For Christ's sake, Jack!"

I simply stared at this stranger beside me. I'd spent twelve years as a cop interviewing rapists, murderers and child molesters and none had looked like fiends to me. Some looked harmless. There is no 'killer look'. I couldn't see the truth in his face, but I knew his heart was black.

I turned back to Jefferson. I could feel Joe's eyes boring into the side of my head.

"Are you talking about the money he and Ms Connor stole from your father in the first place?" Jefferson asked.

Her shoulders slumped, then she nodded.

"Money that wasn't his or hers to begin with?"

She nodded again.

"Let the court record that the witness has nodded affirmatively on both questions."

"It has been noted," the judge said.

"Okay, Mrs Banner. I want you to look at the phone logs again for the night of the murder. Was there a call to you that night?"

She swallowed. "Yes."

"At what time?"

Her eyes dropped to the sheet but she would have been unable to see anything. Tears fell freely and ran down her cheeks, drops falling heavily from her chin.

I saw the breath seize in Joe's throat and the blood go out of his cheeks. "You set me up," he growled.

"No, Joe," I turned and faced him. "*You* set *me* up."

I remembered how I'd found Joe sitting naked in the rain on the night of the murder, his whole demeanour one of desolation and despair. Through all the talks we'd had, he had maintained his innocence with amazing cunningness and to top it all off, despite everything, he managed to convince me.

In my mind, I saw the photos of Shannon as a little girl, sad and lonely, and it made my heart ache. I had always seen her as strong, in control, always the master of the situation and I knew that she was by no means innocent in the events that had unfolded. I had imagined that I loved her but what is love when it is based on lies and myth? Can that be love at all?

"Please answer the question, Mrs Banner." Brad Jefferson brought me back to the present.

"8:21pm," she sobbed softly.

"To tell you what, Mrs Banner."

There was a pause, where she seemed to carefully compose her face. Her back straightened and she visibly pulled herself together.

"That he needed my help." She glanced over at Joe. "He realised that she was not the woman he thought she was and he wanted to come home. To *me*."

Her tone throughout the little speech had been monotone. She took a deep shaky breath in the overwhelming silence of the courtroom. Every jury member had leaned forward and was listening intently. I watched their eyes watching Sarah who was watching Joe who was staring at me with hostile anger. Karen's head was bowed as she stared at her hands splayed on the table.

"He said if we wanted our life back the way it had been, I had to help him."

Her voice had started out quiet, composed. But I could sense that was about to end.

"And how could I not help him? He's *in* me! He always *has* been. *He* was the one who made me strong when I was so lonely. *He* was the one who took me away from my father and gave me a life. My father," her face twisted into a snarl, "never had any time for *me*!" Her breath stuttered out of her mouth.

The certainty and the passion in her voice told me everything I needed to know. But I found the fact that Joe had used and manipulated Sarah into killing Shannon hard to comprehend. And that I was to be used as part of his defence. That was by far worse than anything Shannon had done. Joe had played Sarah. Just like he had played Shannon towards the end of her life and just like he played me.

"What happened that night, Mrs Banner?" Jefferson asked quietly.

"He told me we should make it look like a break-in," Sarah sniffled.

Her words unleashed a colossal shit-storm, as if the whole courtroom had gasped at the same time. Sarah continued as if she hadn't heard the intake of breath. As if she didn't want to stop telling the story now that she'd started. I glanced at the reporters in the gallery, one of whom was Sonya Martin. They were poised ready to take notes, their eyes intent on every move Sarah made. Her hands were clasped tightly in her lap and from where I sat; I could see her knuckles had turned white.

"He said there was some cash in the house," she whispered. "A few thousand dollars, and a key to her safety-deposit box in a bank in Sydney. There was an insurance policy there that left everything to Joe. Half a million, he said, and there was also a lot of money in her personal account that was half his anyway as well as her will that left everything to him. I was supposed to take both the money and the key along with any jewellery lying around to make it look right. The only way Joe could claim the money was to make it look like a burglary gone wrong."

She swallowed hard. "It was raining hard and I hate driving at night in the rain but Joe said that was perfect and it had to be tonight or never." As Sarah spoke, I remembered Carl checking for gunshot residue on Joe's hands and asking how long he'd been out in the rain because his hands seem a bit too clean.

"He told me I had to park around the corner and walk to the house because there was a nosy neighbour across the road who did nothing but sit by the window all day and night spying on everyone. He said he would leave the lights off so that it would be too dark for her to see anything and I was to wear black as well, just to make sure. I didn't know how to break in to a house," she looked at the judge pleadingly. "I told him that, but Joe said he'd leave the door open and afterwards, he would take care of the break-in part."

She took a deep breath. "I did what Joe said to do. I parked around the corner and walked to the house in the rain. The wind gusted every now and then and it almost took the umbrella out of my hands at one stage, but I held on. I crept along the wall of the house in the dark and the front door was open, just like Joe said it would be."

The only sound in the courtroom was the quiet hum of the air-conditioner. No one moved. They stared at Sarah and waited patiently as she struggled to pull herself together and told her story.

"It was dark inside. All the lights were off, except for a light down a hallway, which I knew would be the bedroom. Everything was quiet, so I leaned the umbrella softly against the wall by the front door and closed the door softly. I tiptoed down the hallway until I came to the room where the light was on. My heart was pounding so hard, I was sure she could hear it. But still, there was no sound."

She closed her eyes and lowered her head. "I was so scared. But I knew Joe would be there to help me. I stepped into the doorway and that's when I saw her lying on her side on a mattress on the floor. I remember thinking at the time how strange it was for someone who had stolen my husband from me couldn't make the effort to buy a bed for them to sleep in."

She wept softly, tears filling her eyes and overflowing. Brad Jefferson picked up a box of tissues from his desk and walked slowly over to her, putting them on the railing of the witness stand. She nodded her thanks absently and took one. Then she continued.

"Joe was standing in the entrance to the bathroom, a smile on his face," she gulped. "He walked over to the mattress and kicked it with his foot and she jerked awake. When she saw me, she sat up quickly and looked at Joe. That's when she knew something was going to happen."

Sarah was staring out the window again, tears flowing down her cheeks, as if she too were seeing the images in front of her eyes.

"She didn't cry out like I thought she would. It would have been good to see her as upset as she had made me. I would have enjoyed seeing *her* cry for once. But she didn't. She smiled at me instead. That's when I knew it was all going to go wrong. She turned to Joe and said, *'Taking the coward's way out again, Joe?'* Then she smiled at him."

She paused as she wiped the tears from her face.

"He hit her hard across the face then and I heard her head hit the floor when she fell sideways. But still she didn't cry. She sat up again slowly and smiled at him. Joe had this strange look on his face, one I'd never seen before. *'Get the gun from on top of the dresser,'* he told me. I was wearing my black leather gloves like Joe told me to do so I wasn't scared about leaving prints. I walked over to the dresser, keeping my eyes on her, and picked up the gun. *'Now, shoot her in the heart,'* he said to me as he looked at her. All the time he spoke, he had this smile on his face."

She took a few uneven breaths, her chest shuddering. "I didn't know *I* was the one who was going to shoot her, I swear." Tears were running down Sarah's face and I heard the jury shuffling their feet. Judge Everly stared at Sarah over her glasses, the eyeglass chain hanging from her temples. Karen was still staring at her hands. Joe was glaring at me.

The motivation in most crimes is not complex. Usually people steal and cheat because they're greedy or lazy or both. People kill for reasons of money, sex, and power. Even revenge.

It was funny how at the start of the case I had wanted nothing but the cruellest vengeance for the person who killed Shannon Connor. I had done what I could to make sure the law was served but I was surprised to find that I now felt sorry for Sarah. Joe was the one who should be made to suffer. He had set it up, manoeuvred and conned Sarah, and all for one thing. Money.

"I just stared at Joe," Sarah continued. "'*I can't do this'*, I told him. *'I've never killed anything in my life. You never told me it was going to be me!'*"

Sarah was shaking her head as she remembered. "In all the months that Joe had lived and slept with her, I had dreams about killing her. I dreamt that I would walk up to her in the street and she would know who I was. I would tell her she was going to pay for what she had done and she would look terrified and plead for mercy. *I* would have power over *her* while she begged for her life. But now that I had the opportunity, I just couldn't do it. She just sat on the mattress smiling at me and I couldn't do it."

Sarah swallowed hard. "She said, *'Yeah, Sarah'. Make it easy for him'.* She was taunting me and I knew it. Her voice had this whining sound to it and I knew she was imitating *my* voice. Then her voice changed. It turned hard. Cold. *'You do it. And you know what? He'll leave you with it, too. You'll be the one who gets charged because he'll say he knew nothing about it. You came to the house and killed me.'* And then she smiled at Joe again. *'Aren't I right, Joe?'*"

The courtroom was quiet. The clock ticked, the sound reverberating and filtering through the floating dust particles. It almost felt like some strange phenomenon of suspended time.

"Joe was so angry," she continued. "He yelled at me not to listen to her as she just kept smiling and staring at him, almost daring him to pull the trigger. I closed my eyes so I couldn't see her face but before I knew what was happening, I felt Joe's hands over mine. He clamped my hands over the gun and then he pressed my fingers tightly over the trigger. That's when I heard the explosion. I remember clutching my own heart in shock with my other hand because I never knew that the sound of a gunshot could be so loud. When I opened my eyes, she was dead and Joe was staring down at her, the gun still in my hand."

Her sobs filled the courtroom but nobody moved. "I ran." Tears were forming rivulets down her face and the words stammered out. "I..I..ran. I...I...didn't...know...what...to...do." Eventually the sobs subsided and she took control of her voice again. "I grabbed the umbrella and ran to my car. I have no idea where I went from there. It's all a blur. I know I stopped at a quiet spot in Labrador and turned the car engine off for a while. I don't know how long I sat there but it began to sink in what had happened. I had helped to kill someone. Then I went home to wait like I was supposed to. And then, I don't know how long later, I realised I hadn't done what Joe had told me to do. I was supposed to take the key, money and jewellery with me so that it would look like a robbery. I hadn't taken anything. I didn't want to go back there, but I had to. Joe needed me to help him and I wasn't going to let him down. Not again."

Her voice broke. She paused and gulped another breath. "When I got back to the house, I parked around the corner like I had before and made my way back the same way I had before. The lights were off and everything was dark but all I could think of was that key and money. I'd have to get them anyway I could."

She touched her lips with the back of her hand, then continued. "The door was unlocked so I went in and ran to the bedroom. I searched, but everything was missing. The money, the jewellery, the key. Everything. The policemen had taken everything. I was too late. I turned and ran again and as I got to the door, a person in white over-alls, a forensic person I think, was walking in." Sarah dropped her head. "I didn't mean to hurt her. I panicked. I hit her as hard as I could in the face then I shoved her backwards into the garden. She was unconscious but I kept running."

She shook her head. "It's been killing me a little every day what I did but I did it for Joe. I'm sorry for what I did but I had no choice."

Jefferson turned to the jury then turned back to Sarah.

"We all have a choice, Mrs Banner," he said.

50

The jury had taken less than ten minutes to bring back a result of guilty of murder in the first degree for Joe. Sarah was to be held on a charge of accessory to murder.

Frank Fitzroy was waiting for us outside the court room, his ugly face stretched in a smile, wearing the same tweed jacket he'd worn the last time I'd seen him. The scars on his jawline were more prominent than I remembered.

I stood on the steps and looked around me. Somehow, I expected things to be different. I expected something to show the enormity of what had just happened. But people still bustled past, some talking, some eating. Birds still chirped and the heavy rain promised by the weather bureau had not occurred although storm clouds still hovered over the horizon. Life was still continuing despite this hollow feeling in my heart that I knew would never really go away.

In my career, I knew ordinary people sometimes did bad things. A wrong business decision, a romantic adventure in a bar, a rivalry with a neighbour over the placement of a fence, any of these seemingly insignificant moments can initiate a series of events that, like a rusty nail in the sole of the foot, can systemically poison a normal, law-abiding person's life and propel him into a world he only thought existed in the imagination of pulp novelists.

I knew all this. I just didn't understand it.

Fitzroy handed me a newspaper and I read the headlines.

JESSICA HARDING ALIVE

Against all odds, Jessica Harding, the three-year-old who has been missing for four months now, has been found safe and well. She was discovered by a woman who had taken her own daughter to Anzac Park to play. Jessica was alone and after an hour, the concerned parent approached the child and asked where her mother was. The little girl answered that she didn't know, sparking fresh concern.

She has been reunited with her distraught parents and has been given a clean bill of health. Doctors say that she has been well cared for with no signs of abuse or trauma.

The article began to outline the case from when Jessica went missing but my attention was centred on the picture. From the front page, a tiny version of Shannon's face peered back at me. In the photo from the safety deposit box, a tiny girl, maybe four years old, had been sitting on a blanket under a tree, her hands holding a teddy bear and staring at the camera. There was no teddy bear in this photo, but it was those same beautiful haunted eyes staring sadly back at me from the newspaper.

There were moments when I felt a deep connection with Shannon, moments when I believed I had caught a true glimpse of the interiors beneath that beautiful shell. And there were moments, when I thought the solution to Shannon's sadness might just be me. As I stared at the photo, I realised how little I had understood or known her. There had been a deep sadness in her even at this early age and it had been delusion on my part to think that I could have changed everything and made her happy. All I could hope for was that the sadness in this little girl's face did not overpower her life as it had her mother's.

Fitzroy drove Karen down to The Grande Hotel and I joined them after I parked my car. We sat on bar stools on the veranda while we drank beer and ate potato wedges and nachos with our fingers, watching the storm clouds on the horizon roll in and the surf lap softly on the sand. Fitzroy made jokes and smoked while noisy patrons laughed at nearby tables and shooed away a couple of seagulls that were standing nearby. I heard somewhere you weren't supposed to feed the seagulls. They just kept coming back for more. They only have two sections of brain – one larger part in constant search of food and one smaller part that stores information on where food has been scrounged from.

The light on the horizon had gradually faded under the band of storm clouds and the ocean water grew dark. The saltwater would be eye-stinging further out in the ocean. On the esplanade, lights would soon be starting to come on, turning yellow, as businessmen with well-defined hairdos made their way home talking into their mobile phones with one hand and carrying their laptops protectively in the other. In my youth, laptops were a whole other pleasure.

Looking out over the ocean, Wave Break Island was lost as the horizon became black and immense, the water looking like dark blue ink. Nearby a dog barked as he shook water from his coat. Even from this distance, I could see his coat standing straight out from his body like an echidna. While I watched, all sounds seemed louder. Laughter from people, dogs barking, cars shushing past. They all echoed around me, making me feel even lonelier.

You might say I was missing my old life. But for once I could see the truth with a horrible inescapable clarity. Like something sitting in front of you waiting to be noticed for what it is. It was time for me to start a new chapter of my life. So often you're just sitting too close to really see it.

As I drank and pondered, I regarded Frank. He was no longer Frank Frigging Fitzroy. He was now just plain Frank. I had started out hating him. I had been angry at him for warning me to take the plea that Simmons had arranged. I had strongly suspected him of shooting Shannon and I had a sneaking suspicion it was him who almost ran me off the road. But was it Sarah who ransacked my house again looking for the key that Joe wanted so much?

"Frank," I said as I took a sip of wine, "it had to have been Sarah looking for the key at my house, right?"

"Looks like it, mate," he said with a crooked smile.

"So, who tried to run me off the road while I was on my way home that night?"

"What... I should know that?" he asked, one hand placed earnestly over his heart. "You should know better than anyone that some people are just assholes."

"Let me get a pen and write that down," I quipped. "But seriously, Frank. You always seem to be around somewhere. I hope you're not developing Stockholm's Syndrome with me."

He chuckled as he sipped his beer.

"I thought you'd have some idea, ethics considered," I persisted.

"Well, mate, like I said before, I have my ethical duties to consider in my profession. People have to trust me, Jack."

Hatred is probably a strong word for what I had once felt toward Frank, but while I was sitting at that table, drinking Merlot, which was excellent by the way, my emotions softened. He was a creep clearly, but a pleasant little creep, pleasanter with every glass of wine that I drank. And I certainly admired his taste in jackets.

Eventually, the streetlights came on and soon within the circle of those lights, families would be sleeping, kids would be in bed and everything would be ready for the next day. Work, school, friends, family, happy triumphs, sad defeats, hope...always hope. Tomorrow, I would go to Shannon's grave with some red roses, the colour of the lipstick that she loved so much. I will sit and say a few prayers, if I can remember any from my childhood, while the breeze blows the smell of salt in from the ocean. I will watch the ducks paddling around the lily pads in the nearby pond and hope that I was wrong and that there *is* a heaven where she can find happiness.

Frank bought all the drinks that night and at one stage, a waitress bought out a platter of prawns, split and grilled, a wild assortment of antennae and legs sticking helter-skelter from the shells. It looked like some bizarre Klingon meal but we all dived in and ate like it was our last meal.

At some stage, Frank said his good-byes and stood up. He straightened his jacket and left Karen and me to finish the wine, not quite celebrating, but happy nonetheless with the outcome. I watched him walk to his car, unlock it and buckle up before doing a u-turn on Marine Parade, heading back towards Labrador. That's when I noticed the front grill of his car. The bonnet was creased backwards where he'd run up the back of another car. One headlight had been broken and his left front fender would need replacing. I stared dumbfounded as he wound his window down and waved to me with a wide smile.

"That frigging bastard," I whispered as I watched his car disappear around the bend.

As I watched, a dragonfly rose out of the bushes bordering the verandah. For a moment it floated, its iridescence changing in the refraction of light from red to green to back to red again. It fluttered its wings, suspended itself in front of my face, before darting towards the table and settling on the rim of my beer glass, the wings ceasing movement except for the occasional twitch.

I heard an intake of breath from Karen as she watched in awe and I reached out slowly to it, gently urging it on to my index finger. It sat there and glowed, it actually glowed, a deep red and I was mesmerised.

I remembered the words Shannon said to me about dragonflies. Sometimes it seems a lifetime ago and other times, it seems like only yesterday. '*They represent a new beginning,*' she'd said. '*A transition from a sad past to a promising new future.*' It's what I needed more than anything else.

It sat there for ten seconds before it fluttered its wings and darted off again.

Karen and I shared a lovely evening, proof that life is not always sordid. It can be perfect in its simplicity with the company of people who had changed things that had needed to be changed.

Perfect enough to almost make me forget.

Almost.

ALSO BY TRISHA HUGHES

Autobiography

Daughters of Nazareth

Historical Fiction Trilogy

Book 1

Vikings to Virgin - The Hazards of being King

Book 2

Virgin to Victoria - The Queen is Dead.

Long live the Queen.

Book 3

Victoria to Vikings - The Circle of Blood

WHAT'S NEXT

Here's a sneak Peak at Book Two in the Jack Curtis Mysteries.

Chapter 1.

We all make mistakes, there's no doubt about it. And to be honest, my track record of late is pretty grim. But sometimes the worst decisions you make start with good intensions.

She was standing by the side of the road, hair plastered to her head in the pouring rain with her shoulders hunched over to protect her drenched clothes against the drizzle. Over her shoulder was a large black purse she clutched close to her body like it was a lifeline.

She was watching my car with her thumb stuck out as I approached the traffic light close to her and she straightened a little in anticipation, moving forward slightly.

No way I thought. Picking up a male hitchhiker was stupid enough. But a teenage girl? A guy in his mid-forties picks up a girl by the side of the road on a dark rainy night? Well, you can see it. I've done a lot of stupid things in my life but that would be an all-time low for me.

Up ahead, the traffic light changed to amber, then red, and I silently muttered *fuck*. My eyes swivelled involuntarily towards the girl, then back again to the road as I put my foot on the brake. For a second, I considered running the red light but there was too much traffic on the road. Apart from that, it would be just my luck for a red light camera to pick up my registration plate as I sailed past. In the end, I thought *toughen up* and kept my eyes straight ahead as the car slid to a stop.

That's when I heard the tap on the window.

I kept my eyes focused straight ahead at the traffic light, ignoring her and willing the light to change to green.

Sometimes you know something bad is going to happen. You can feel it in the air and in your gut. I put it down to the abundance of bad decisions I've made in my life of late. While my good angel and bad angel squabble over what I should do, I invariably make the wrong choice. Three years ago, when my ex-wife Sally asked me, almost begged me, not to take the promotion to Sergeant because she didn't want to answer the phone one day and hear that I'd been killed on duty, I didn't listen. Sally left me, taking our daughter with her and now I live alone with a cantankerous cat. After a particularly horrific crime involving small children buried on Mount Tamborine, Inspector Grayson advised me to accept counselling. I didn't listen. Instead I ignored him and resigned from the police force without any prospects on the horizon. Not the smartest thing to do, I grant you, but at the time, I wasn't thinking too far ahead. Then to top it off, I had an affair with my best friend's fiancée and it ended badly for everyone. Hiroshima bad. But that's another story entirely. I should have listened to my good angel and stepped away. Again, I didn't listen.

The tap sounded again, this time more urgently.

My eyes involuntarily swung left and I saw her there, bending down with her stringy hair in her eyes, looking at me. Even in the shadows, the scar running down her cheek stood out, red and cordy. I shook my head but she did a little spin with an index finger, indicating for me to wind down the window. As I powered it down a notch, I took a deep sigh and shook my head and said, "Look. I'm sorry. But I can't......"

"Please. I just need a ride home. My car's broken down and I don't have roadside assistance. It's not too far and it's pouring out here." She held up the phone, "and my phone's dead." She shook it like that was going to make it start again. "And I think someone's following me." Her brow furrowed as she pleaded. "Please."

With those last spoken words, everything changed. *I think someone's following me.* Having been a cop, those words meant a lot to me. Some things never leave your life.

If I'd been smart, I'd have taken more notice of the unsettling feeling in my gut, uncurling like a snake. It was telling me that on the snakes and ladder board of life, I was definitely headed towards a snake.

I should have listened to the feeling, but that's my problem, I never listen. Instead, I trust my instincts. I've always believed that no matter what, I can see through any lie or deception and come up with the truth. And without sounding egotistical, my instincts have always worked for me. But up until then, I would never have thought I'd be stupid enough to pick up a teenage girl who was hitchhiking. I'd have to be a total fool, and mostly I believe that's not me. Not totally anyway. It wouldn't be too bright on her part either but right now it's *my* stupidity I'm talking about.

I took a resigned breath, jerked my head and said, "Okay. Get in."

Her eyebrows shot up and her eyes were a big as saucers. "Really?" She sounded like she was surprised that her line had actually worked.

I paused again, allowing myself another second to think about what the hell I was doing. Then I repeated, "Yeah. Okay."

Someone behind me sat on the horn and I glanced up to see the light had turned green. I opened my side window and made a hand gesture to the guy behind me to drive around. As he went past, he gave me a one-finger salute and a snarl.

She pushed her hair out of her eyes and gave me a weak smile. "Thanks."

The door was opened in a heartbeat and she slid in, moving her phone to another hand, throwing her bag at her feet, dripping water on the seat. She turned to me and looked a little shamefaced.

"Sorry about your car."

Her eyes drifted to the oozing cut on my cheek and the collar of my shirt splattered with blood and they widened a little. *Out of the fat and into the fire*, my mother would have laughed but I didn't say that to the girl. She looked like she'd had enough frights for one night. She hesitated, her eyes glued to my face.

"An accident at work," I said and shrugged.

She was a bit older than I thought when I first saw her. She would be maybe around twenty-one, twenty-two at most, and probably good looking on a better day. But right now, she was so wet, rivulets of water were running down her hair and the tailored pants she was wearing looked like someone had driven past and splashed water on her. She looked like a shaggy dog coming out of the ocean. It made me feel a little sorry for her but then I remembered the sticky spot I was putting myself into.

I waited until she came to a decision whether to stay in the car or make a run for it. The guy following her must have scared her senseless because she put her seat belt on and sat back, staring straight ahead.

"Where are you going?" I asked.

"Oh yeah," she said with a laugh. "Just keep going straight on along Marine Parade."

I glanced up and saw the light was still green so I turned my head to the right to see if any cars where coming before putting my foot on the accelerator. While I pulled out into traffic, she dug around in her bag and pulled out a band for her hair. She quickly gathered her hair together at the back and haphazardly made a ponytail. The smooth skin of the scar running down the side of her face took on a light of its own, making it almost glow in the dimness. She settled down, clutching her bag, glancing every now and then at the watch on her left wrist.

Neither of us said anything for a few minutes but she kept

glancing nervously in my side mirror. I glanced in my rear vision mirror and saw a SUV close behind so I slowed down a little to let him pass. He stayed right there on my tail. The girl seemed to be taking a lot of interest in it as well.

"You okay?" I asked as I watched the car in my mirror. "Boyfriend stuff?"

"What?" She saw my attention focused on the mirror and made a soft noise through her nose as she shook her head. "No. That's not it."

Her eyes swivelled again to the side mirror again.

"You seem a bit nervy," I said, watching her shoulders rise and fall in time with her quick breathing.

In the silence, the only sound was the windscreen wipers swishing from side to side.

"Are you okay?"

She nodded her head a little too hard.

"You sure?" I asked as I turned my head sideways to look at her.

She nodded vigorously again without saying a word.

Not a good liar, I thought.

We were still on Marine Parade. On my right, the long slender arm of the Broadwater curved around Marine Parade towards Surfers Paradise and on my left, fast food joints and surf outlets whipped by. Wave Break Island was lost as the horizon became black and immense, the water looking like dark blue ink. The wind was blowing hard and I could see luminescence from the whitecaps out in the bay. The ocean pounded on the small beach and the force of the waves created a plume of spray that marched from right to left. The salt-water would have been eye stinging further out in the ocean.

The lights were bright and cold against the deep shadows of the ocean. Businessmen were scurrying from shop to shop on their way home, trying to protect their well-defined hairdo from the rain, talking into their mobile phones with one hand and carrying their laptops protectively in the other. In my youth, laptops were a whole other pleasure.

We drove on for a minute in silence.

"Are you going to tell me where home is or do I have to guess?" I grinned.

"Oh yeah." she smiled weakly. "Can we just keep going on this road for about two kilometres? I'll let you know where to drop me off."

Her eyes kept glancing in the rear mirror as she clenched and unclenched the handle of her bag nervously in her lap, the leather making a creaking noise.

I took my eyes off the road and glanced at her. The wipers repeated their rhythmic swipes across the glass, but I said nothing for a while.

"Someone told me once," I began quietly, "that when you're afraid of something, what you want more than anything else is for your life to go back the way it was before you found out there was something to be afraid of. You want to build a high wall and keep your old life behind it, safe."

She turned her head to watch me intently, not saying anything. She was barely breathing now at all.

"But nothing ever stays the same and it's not your old life at all. It's your new life with a wall around it." Even to my own ears, I sounded wise. "Sometimes it helps to talk to someone."

She snorted through her nose and shook her head as she turned her attention back to the window.

"You sound like my therapist," she mumbled. "You know nothing."

My eyebrows raised at the mumbled words 'therapist'.

"So tell me," I said softly.

This tactic always worked when I was a cop. The softness of my tone invited confidence and before I knew it, they were opening up like we were old friends. Except this time, it sparked a bitterness that surprised me.

She turned back to me, her face twisted in a sneer.

"I don't want my..." she put two fingers up as quotation marks, "...*old life*...back." She harrumphed scornfully then grew quiet. "What I want is to be allowed to live my new life in peace."

The last words had been whispered and I let them settle in the silence.

"What's your name?" I asked.

She hesitated. "It doesn't matter."

She glanced nervously in the mirror again and I did the same. Something was bothering her about the SUV sitting close behind me. The headlights switched to full beam and I instinctively put my hand up to cover my eyes from the brightness in my mirror.

"What the…?" I said, as I adjusted the mirror.

"Can you pull over and let me out here, please?" She sounded panicked.

"What?"

"Right here," she almost yelped. "This will do. Just here." She pointed through the windscreen. "At the corner."

I knew *where* she was pointing. I just didn't understand *why* she wanted me to pull over all of a sudden. I'd committed myself to driving her home, but I put the blinker on anyway and began to pull over. Before I'd even come to a stop, she was looping her purse over her shoulder like she was planning a quick getaway.

"Hey, if someone's following you, maybe you shouldn't be getting out here. I'll take you all the way home. Okay?"

"Look. Don't worry about it. This has got nothing to do with you."

"Are you in some kind of trouble?"

"Just stop the car, okay?" She was beginning to sound panicked. She had unbuckled her seat belt and grabbed the door handle even though the car was still moving. I didn't think she'd actually open it but she did. Just a bit to make me more nervous.

"SHIT!" I shouted. "Shut the damn door until I stop. Are you out of your mind?"

"I WANT TO GET OUT," she screamed, loud enough to make a couple of heads in the restaurant turn and look our way. Her fear was pretty palpable.

She didn't say anything for a second, then she spoke in a little girl voice. "Please."

I pulled into a park and hit the brakes hard but left the engine running.

"Look," I said. "Like I said. I can take you all the way home. I'll even promise not to talk. You don't have to get out. It's still raining."

She threw open the door and swung her legs out, not listening to me at all.

I leant over and yelled. "Are you sure you're okay?"

"Yeah. I'm sure." She glanced up as the SUV, recognisable now as a Subaru, passed us but slowed down to a stop fifty metres ahead. She raised her purse above her head to block the soft rain and said, "Look, thanks. I saw someone I know inside and they can take me the rest of the way."

She gave me a half-hearted smile then ran back in the direction we'd just come from, glancing once over her shoulder. She gave me a little wave and just like that, she was gone, her feet splashing through the puddles.

I glanced over to the Subaru and tried to see the driver. The window was tinted so heavily I couldn't even make out if it was a male or a female inside.

If I was still a cop, I could have radioed the incident in. I would have be able to see if there were any priors or look up the licence plate number of the owner. I could have seen if the car was stolen or if the owner had any outstanding offences against them. But I couldn't do any of that. I couldn't even see the license plate number.

I glanced back at the restaurant but I couldn't make her out anymore. Here I was, late at night, worrying about a girl I didn't know, who I'd given a lift to only five minutes ago. I knew I should have known better than to get myself into this position but after she mentioned that someone was following her, what could I do? What I should have done was give her my mobile to call someone and ask them to pick her up. But even then, I knew I was only kidding myself. I'd agreed to give her a ride and see that she got home safely and by doing that, I'd made her my responsibility.

I glanced over at the Subaru again but it was hard to see the colour because of the rain. I scanned the inside of the restaurant again. A couple sitting there with two children. A boy and a girl in their late teens by the window and a guy at the counter putting in his order. No girl.

My heart was pounding. I'd lost her. I hadn't wanted her in the first place but now I felt a little panicked that I couldn't see her.

When I looked back towards the Subaru, it had gone. My mind raced as I tried to form a plan. Should I call the police or just forget the whole thing? What the hell would I tell them anyway? Even as I was thinking, I knew it was stupid. The Subaru was gone and so was the girl. And I hadn't even been able to get the licence plate number.

Just this morning, I was sitting in traffic listening to Jimmy Barnes over the radio competing with honking horns and squealing tyres. I was blissfully unaware that in just a few short hours, there would be this.

I took one last look at the restaurant before pulling out of the park and heading home.